FISHING
FOR
AMBER

A Long Story

Ciaran Carson

Granta Books
London

Granta Publications, 2/3 Hanover Yard, London N1 8BE

First published in Great Britain by Granta Books 1999

This edition published by Granta Books 2000

A CIP catalogue record for this book is available from the
British Library.

1 3 5 7 9 10 8 6 4 2

ISBN 1 86207 371 6

Typeset in Perpetua by M Rules

Printed and bound in Great Britain by
Mackays of Chatham plc

In memory of my father
Liam Mac Carráin / William Carson
14 April 1916–24 March 1998

Contents

CONTENTS

ANTIPODES

It was long ago, and long ago it was; and if I'd been there, I wouldn't be here now; if I were here, and then was now, I'd be an old storyteller, whose story might have been improved by time, could he remember it. Three good points about stories: if told, they like to be heard; if heard, they like to be taken in; and if taken in, they like to be told. Three enemies of stories: endless talk, the clack of a mill, the ring of an anvil —

I've often wished I could begin a story in the manner of my father, who liked to use a gambit like the one above to generate his stories told in Irish. As I've translated it, it's lost the riddling equipoise of the original; but when I heard its conjugated rhythms as a child, it summoned up another world through which I could glide easily to sleep before the echoes of the story's close had faded into silence. Then again, he might have begun with a simple

'Once upon a time . . .' and plausibly engrossed you in a narrative, until it dawned on you that the opening preamble was embodied in the recitation. The main action had not yet begun.

Or sometimes, plagued by his children for yet another story, my father would appear to yield, and begin, It was a stormy night in the Bay of Biscay, and the Captain and his sailors were seated around the fire. Suddenly, one of the sailors said, Tell us a story, Captain. And the Captain began, It was a stormy night in the Bay of Biscay, and the Captain and his sailors were seated around the fire. Suddenly, one of the sailors said, Tell us a story, Captain. And the Captain began, It was a stormy night in the Bay of Biscay, and the Captain and his sailors were seated around the fire. Suddenly, one of the sailors said – until we would plead with him to stop this narrative Chinese-box torture, though at what point we might intervene was difficult to gauge, for he might relent, or, indeed, have meant to do so all along; in which case, the Captain of the seventh or the eighth interior would embark on a real story, and we could at last settle down in a warm glow of anticipation, as a true storm careered outside, knocking slates off roofs and lashing rain against the window. In any case, the scenario was not an unattractive one. I would think of the fire on board the boat as a dangerous paradox, until it would occur to me that it was not a hearth fire like our own, and I would visualize a pot-bellied iron stove with a little door opened in it, like a miniature stoke-hole. Down in the bowels of the rusty tramp vessel there were men stripped to the waist, glistening with sweat, while the pistons and tappets worked nineteen to the dozen; the furnace roared; steam hissed from the leaky valves. But then, I thought, what were the

2

Captain and his sailors doing, engrossed in fictional relations when a real adventure was unravelling about them? Perhaps they were all safe on shore, after all, snug in some taverna, drinking Spanish wine and spitting olive pits into the fire.

At any rate, most of my father's Captain stories had to do with water. A typical example was the Submarine Realm series, where children like ourselves would get to meet a Nemo or a mermaid figure. Then there was a stock of quasi-historical Great Flood or Broken Dam stories: one variant of this sub-category, the saga of the building of the Silent Valley Reservoir, deep in the Mourne Mountains, never ceased to entertain and educate. The Story of the Little Dutch Boy was another favourite; for my father, never one to take the direct route, would wander off in search of yet another bit of local colour to inform his narrative – the tourist brochure would be constantly revised. So, for example, he'd describe how coffins were wont to float up from the church crypts of Holland and bob around untidily in the town squares; or explain how their system of building on piles was replicated in the reclaimed clabber of central Belfast. Dutch children would have a great time in the summer, when they'd take off their clogs, put little paper sails on them, and launch opposing navies on the shallow, cloud-reflecting meres. Their cheese industry was a wonderful thing, for the ingenious Netherlanders, in their constant struggle against nature, would ascend to the Moon in argosies of hot-air drifters, there to mine the lunar cheese deposits; in that high atmosphere, even fully laden boats were weightless, so they were anchored to terrestrial winches.

3

Yet the Boy himself was never disconcerted by these fanciful excursions, but kept his finger plugged in the dike. The water would get to be a manacle of ice about his wrist. Then he'd be up to his elbow in it. Then his armpit. He'd be nearly petrified with cold. The red-herring fleet would glide by overhead, deaf to his calls for help. At last, a passing milkmaid, balancing two buckets on a yoke, would take notice of him, and alert the Dike Watch. Whatever time it took to tell the story, he'd still be there at its conclusion. The Little Dutch Boy had the bold iconic status of an Early Christian martyr. I am told there is a statue of him in the town of Spaardam.

My father never set foot in Holland but maintained a constant interest in it. He had a long-time Nederlander pen-friend, Arie Kuipers of Voorburg, with whom he corresponded through the medium of Esperanto, until Arie – Uncle Arie, as we called him – died. They exchanged studio photographs of each other wearing the Green Star, which is the badge of fellows everywhere who seek a common tongue. They never met, at least not face to face. But I can see Uncle Arie's picture in my mind's eye yet, and see the picture postcards he would send. *The Mills of Kinderdijk. Fishermen of Volendam. Pier and Bathing Station, Scheveningen. Keukenhof: a Paradise of Flowers. Marken: Folk Dances on the Ice. Cheese Porters at Alkmaar. Punt traffic in Giethoorn. Dutch Girl. The Ever Present Hazard of the Sea*. We loved the ruled perspectives of the dikes, the regimental multi-coloured stripes of tulip fields. Holland was a wondrous place, a made-up land.

*

Now I think of stone and water: Mourne stone and Mourne water, Mourne granite setts transported by the medium of water to the Lowlands, laid in herringbone designs, or cable-knits, in streets and squares. The Mourne granite men smoked meerschaum pipes from Holland – *Meerschaum* being sea-scum, or petrified foam, so it was believed. They exchanged stone for foam. It is strange to think of the streets of Holland being paved by bits of Irish mountains, whose blue stacks seem to defy gravity, rushed and steeped and angled to the tattered glimpse of sky at their summits. By contrast, Dutch skies are enormous. In Vermeer's *View of Delft*, the early morning sky takes up most of the canvas; below it, the fabric of the town glitters with hints of amethyst and topaz thrown and filtered by the clouds which float above it. The red brick-and-tile work and the blue slates shine like precious minerals. Sudden rain has cleansed the air and left raindrops gleaming in the cracks and crevices of the façades. Scales of light drip from the moored boats. Herring-coloured water reflects the town and the clouds.

After a downpour, the scarps and inclines of the Silent Valley scintillate with water. Waterfalling veins pulse down the mountainsides, with cloudy wisps blown off them. Pebbles of smoky quartz shine rapidly in screes and cascades. Stones chatter and shiver; in the distance, you can almost hear the clink and tinkle of the ancient granite men about their work. Granite for setts, granite for gravestones; granite for dolmens, plinths and mass-rocks. Granite for the ubiquitous *bullauns*, thought to be basin-stones for grinding barley, but now venerated everywhere as holy wells, for the water they contained had many virtues, especially for healing warts. Embedded in overgrown haggards or churchyards, it seemed the *bullauns* had put roots back into the rock from whence they were hewn, and were metamorphosed into conduits for a subterranean realm of water.

So, as children, we believed the mirrored altitude of puddles – huge clouds drifting in them like a fleet of sailing-ships – were portals to Australia, through which we could dive, had we the correct magic formula, to emerge in a water-mirage trembling in an arid desert. In a dream voyage to this nether world, capsized Flying Dutchmen manned by skeleton crews drifted past your slowly falling body. Centuries of flotsam revolved around them: broken spars, intact powder-barrels, ship's decanters, wicker armchairs, wheelbarrows, astrolabes, and bottles of wine disgorged from the breached cellars. Sinking like Icarus, I could almost catch hold of one of those heavy dumpy Dutch lager bottles with their spring-clipped ceramic plugs, which must cost more to produce than their contents, like the Schiphol airport blue Delft souvenir Genever flagons with their windmill landscapes. There are windmill sails entangled in the leaning masts and shrouds, evidence that these galleons once ploughed the Lowlands Low, appearing to glide waterlessly on the dike horizon just above your head.

I wake with a jolt as my KLM flight hits an air-pocket over Amsterdam. I press my nose against the damp triple glazing of the porthole, seeing the landscape tilt by in a flat spiral holding-pattern. It is a sharp cold winter's day, and the bright air magnifies everything. There are many skaters out on the frozen canals: families and social groupings, some more loosely bound than others; those who are obliged to keep within each others' ken; burghers, doctors, ministers; solitary beings performing infinity signs; those who wander in and out like refugees or spies; knots and nodes of influence; wavy phalanxes and columns; conga dancers teetering, some parts of the file collapsing, skidding at a helpless tangent; manually propelled children on tin trays; hockey players; marathon racers pushing the ice behind them with their giant zig-zag treadmill steps; regiments of skated soldiers exercising; ballad-mongers, dudelsackers, gypsy violinists; cabals of revolving lawyers; Casanovas; search parties; and painters at their easels and palettes, depicting all the aforementioned scenes.

Goggle-eyed, the high observer in his aeroplane feels the chill of distance, and looks forward to being a tourist on foot, smoking a cigar in one of the many deep, narrow, brown bars, or examining the extensive cannabis menus of the 'coffee-houses'. Some of these come in mock burgundy-leather folders, like wine-lists, or stamp albums; and, indeed, it is pleasant, after a little smoke, to wander the labyrinth of Amsterdam and happen on a meeting of philatelists in a little square or on a traffic island in an urban tributary. Typically, they will have brought along collapsible card-tables covered in green baize, and folding chairs, so as to create the illusion of a private club. In this companionable haven they peruse and debate each other's specimens, mounted and described on cartridge paper, or exchange their duplicates slotted into coin-screw, peg-fitting binders in best-quality leather-cloth. They're armed with the usual array of philatelic paraphernalia: nickel-plated tweezers with milled spade-ends; perforation

7

gauges engraved in stout transparent plastic; surcharge measurers with their side-screw adjustments; authoritative colour guides, showing the seventy-five colours most useful for stamp description; benzine droppers to accompany the watermark trays; magnifying glasses, watchmakers' eyeglasses, and the pocket microscopes invented by the Dutch. Given this equipment, the philatelist can spot defective clichés, or minute varieties of die, and detect the various grades of paper, whether wove or laid. Many hours are given over to these studies.

One can also pass the time quite happily gazing into the windows of the dope-accessory outlets, wondering what names and functions to assign to articles unfamiliar to the casual smoker, to whom a simple hubble-bubble pipe is the epitome of decadence. But we can leave this interesting area of speculation for another time, as, seeking temporary refuge from the incense of patchouli oil and marijuana, we find ourselves between the cool walls of a little gallery. We are captivated almost immediately by a seventeenth-century studio interior, marvelling at the precision with which the artist has depicted the various attributes of his profession. Here is the wooden mannikin with jointed limbs. The artist's brushes in various stages of use. His palette, with a thumbprint visible on it. The young apprentice grinding pigments. A map of the Netherlands. A sleeping dog. Telescopes and compasses. A vase of variegated tulips. A ship in a bottle. All these are reflected by a tiny convex mirror, in which we discern a dim self-portrait of the artist.

Underneath this study, printed beautifully on a pale buff card, are English words:

As for the art of Painting and the affection of the people to Pictures,
I thincke none other goe beeyond them, having bin in this country
Many excellent Men in that Facullty,
some at present, as Rimbrannt, etts,
All in general striving to adorne their houses,
especially, the outer or streete roome, with costly peeces,
Butchers and Bakers not much inferiour in their shoppes,
which are Fairly set Forth,
yea many tymes blacksmithes, Coblers, etts,
will have some picture or other by their Forge and in their stalle.

Peter Mundy, 1640

So it would appear that the objects arranged in the artist's stall of this still-life are a kind of currency: emblems which negotiate the distance between things, how they might be represented, and whatever value might be assigned to them. They are parables; and the Dutch are fond of proverbs. To fire roses at the swine. To fill the well after the calf has drowned. Why do geese go barefoot? The cupboard invites the dog to go in. To stand gaping at the stork. Not horse-droppings: figs. To weave so fine a web the sun will see through it.

It is a theme expanded on in a book we purchase in the gallery: *Picturing Words: Correspondences in the Painting of the Dutch Golden Age*, by Lucy Juliana Hollander, M.A., Professor of the History of Art, Bryn Mawr College. Back in our small but comfortable hotel, we open its pages at random, and read:

These were some of the implicit captions to their emblematic narratives. Words lay behind the world made visible. Light illuminated open Bibles. It poured through oriels and bays and doorways, down alleyways and stairwells. Sometimes it ends up concentrated in a tin scoop, or a lead crystal decanter, or a pewter basin dented like the moon. Yet the titles simultaneously reveal and hide, since they are never full descriptions of the many fictive things on show and their connections with the private figures that we contemplate. *Astronomer by Candlelight*, *Man Spinning and Woman Scraping Carrots*. *Woman Plucking a Duck*. *Soldier Offering a Young Woman Coins*. *Soldiers beside a Fireplace*. *The Alchemist*. *Woman Eating Porridge*. *Card Players Quarrelling*.

In Pieter de Hooch's *Woman Drinking with Two Men and a Maidservant*, painted around 1658, the woman, standing on the *trompe-l'œil* chessboard floor, has her back turned towards the viewer. She holds an air-bubble-twist stemmed glass not quite filled with a pale amber liquid. Seated at a table by the window – hinged shutters drawn upwards to admit the light – two men gaze at her. One holds a pair of long-stemmed clay pipes as if playing the fiddle with them; the other, red-plumed beaver resting on his knee, appears to beat or hold time with his right hand. The woman, it appears, is singing. Behind, and to the right, a servant brings a brazier of coals. Her eyes are downcast. A map of the seventeen provinces of the Netherlands, tentatively identified as the work of Huyck Allart, active *c*. 1650–75, hangs on the back wall. Above the mantel of the fireplace is a painting of the *Education of the Virgin*, attributed to Ferdinand Bol in the 1804 van Leyden sale catalogue; this painting within the painting has a possible source in an unidentified altarpiece in the Esterházy chapel at Ering, south Bavaria. A pipe broken into mouthpiece, stem and bowl is scattered on the floor beside a crumpled piece of paper: correspondences of past actions we can only guess at. Infra-red photographs have revealed that the figures were painted only after the spatial environment was complete, and there are numerous *pentimenti*, including a bearded man, who has emerged through time as a ghost to the left of the maidservant. (It is interesting that *pentimento*, an underlying image, has a moral connotation, since it derives from Italian *pentire*, to repent; and the artist can absolve himself.) This painting can be seen in the National Gallery, London. Van Meegeren, the renowned or notorious forger, was inspired to fake it. In the original, the low table partly visible in the lower left foreground bears the initials *PDH*, as if carved there with a chisel.

De Hooch's *Woman Drinking with Soldiers* is also signed *PDH* lower left, and dated 1658. In many ways it is a companion piece to that described above. Again, we see the raised overhead shutter, the carefully organized perspectives and dimensions. We are left to judge the implications of the arrested attitudes and gestures of the figures, as if we were the fourth, moral wall. A seated woman in a red dress holds her glass to be filled by a hatless man in black. His black-hatted companion sits smoking at the table. An older woman, hand on her heart, hovers in the background. Is she looking to be paid? Two pictures hang on the back wall: an engraved view of Amsterdam, and a painting of *Christ and the Adulteress*, whose implied text is, *He that is without sin among you, let him first cast a stone at her*. (The same painting within a painting occurs in de Hooch's *The Cardplayers*, where one of the soldiers holds the Ace of spades.) A small dog, emblem of fidelity, sleeps in the foreground. Fido the dog. To his far right, hardly visible at first glance, especially in this reproduction, lies a playing card, the Five of hearts. Is it crumpled, or uncrumpled? Through the open doorway in the back wall we get a telescopic view through a room through another open doorway to another room in which there is a chest on which are placed a jug and a statuette of Mercury, the god known to the Greeks as Hermes, son of Zeus and of the naiad Maia, daughter of Atlas, who bears the world on his shoulders.

Born in the morning upon Mount Cyllene in Arcadia, by midday Hermes had invented the lyre. Getting up from his cradle, he ventured out and found a tortoise. He killed it and scooped out the flesh. Then he found a goat and beheaded it. He put the curved horns of the goat through the front leg-holes of the tortoise-shell, and he made strings of the goat's guts. Immediately he played this apparatus with amazing skill. By evening he was in Pieria, where he stole half a hundred head of cattle from his brother Apollo. This episode may be long or short in the telling, according to one's sources.

Again, as to what happened next, different authorities have differing accounts as to how Apollo was led to suspect the miscreant, and take him to Zeus, their father, to make judgement on the case, but they substantially agree on the outcome. Apollo, ravished by the music Hermes produces from the lyre, proposes an exchange: Hermes can keep the cattle, if he keeps the lyre. And so it was. Apollo thus became god of music. To Hermes, Apollo also resigned the golden staff of fortune, together with the gift of prophecy in its humbler forms.

To this day, in remote districts of Arcadia where time stands still, Hermes is regarded as a fertile god, bestowing bounty on the pastures and increase on the cattle. Nothing pleases him more than to spend time with the cowboys and the shepherds, wearing his flat broad-brimmed hat, sharing their humble bread and rough wine, singing the old songs, when he is not dallying with the nymphs, by whom he has countless offspring, including Pan and Daphnis. God of tradespeople, god of thieves, god of the stock exchange, he escorts and protects heroes in perilous enterprises. Inventor of the alphabet, of figures and astronomy, he is, besides, the god of sleep and dreams. And as he is the guide of the living on their way, so he is also the Psychopompos, conductor of the souls of the dead through the netherworld. The number four is sacred to him. He is the god of mining, and of digging for buried treasure. He is highly esteemed by fishers of amber, and of those who sell water as whiskey. He is the god of roads and all sorts of traffic. He is the father of Autolycus, the king of thieves. At cross-roads his devotees drop white pebbles in his honour, forming, through time, pyramidal cairns of thousands, each pebble representing hope, anxiety, a journey's end. And every serendipitous event, every happy chance, every unexpected find, is known as a Gift of Hermes.

BERENICE

Having read this account of Hermes, I remember how I used to dream recurrently of finding coins – usually, the old king's or young queen's shillings – lying in the gutter, shimmering in the black silt after rain. I see one in the corner of my eye; I stoop, and pick it up; another one appears. One thing leads to another, until pounds of shillings jingle in my pockets. Then, sometimes, I find myself in a dark wood, where the moonlight glimmers in small pools among the glades; or the dream mutates into a Hansel and Gretel scenario, where the white pebbles dropped by the boy to help him find his way back home glitter like newly minted money. In dictionaries of dreams, finding money, providing you do not find too much, is a portent of imminent good luck, or of a successful conclusion to a protracted litigation. But the shilling is also the token given to drunken Irishmen enlisted by a sergeant at the feast-day of a local patron saint.

It is recorded that many of these unfortunate recruits carried pebbles from the holy streams and wells of their home parish in their pockets. These stones were employed as amulets or magic charms, sometimes as gambling tokens. During the Dutch wars they became a currency, for there is not a pebble to be had in the whole of Holland. Especially prized were the Mourne quartz pebbles, and the amber crystals from the Holy Pool on the shores of Lough Neagh, which were known to prevent death by fire or water. Some of the smaller pebbles were used as bullets, but only when the soldier had exhausted his buttons, for the uniform buttons of the time were perfectly fitted to the bore of the standard flintlock. So it was that buttons too became a currency, for the coin of warring realms had been locked away for years, gold and silver columns measured into cartridge-paper tubes, stacks of notes deposited in rat-proof greased leather bursaries in salt-mines, catacombs and sewers underneath the banks of Switzerland, held in hock until the wars were ended, or forever.

Throughout these troubled times the Irish pebble held its own. The legendary miracles effected by the holy wells of Ireland were famous throughout the continent of Europe from the earliest days of the Hibernian missionaries, who brought with them illuminated books full of marvellous events and elaborated words. These explained the world in microscopic detail, down to the tonsured monk drawing water from a well on a clear spring morning after Matins, with birds twittering around his head. It followed that a pebble sprung from such a well would be capable of transferring its properties to other waters. The Irish pebble was a purifying agent also: in times of war, even the holy wells of

France and Germany were fouled by saboteurs, so that the plagues and dysenteries once cured by them became endemic. Dropped into such wells, the Irish pebble was found to be the perfect remedy.

Nevertheless, pilgrims would still resort to waters not cured by the Irish pebble, believing their efficacy would be restored by a more fervent application of the proper rituals associated with them. Where hitherto they had made one circuit of the stations associated with the shrine, they now walked it three times on their knees; where once they had said a Pater, Ave and a Gloria at the focal points marked by worn stones with holes in them, they now said Rosaries; where they had touched the stones, they now kissed them lingeringly, corroding them further with their salt tears.

This excess of zeal was particularly evident in the low-lying marshy country of the Pas-de-Calais, where for centuries the shrine of St Bertin, patron of ships and canvas factors, had been the brightest jewel of the town of Saint-Mommelin. In the year 1598 the rye crop was totally blighted by ergot. A Solemn Novena was initiated; dukes, lords and earls prayed with peasants, sailors, whores and lepers, and the scent of rose of attar mingled with the stink of bandages ingested by live maggots. At the end of nine times nine nights, a silver bucket was let down into the well by the Abbot of Saint-Omer; when it was drawn up, it was found to contain nuggets of amber to the exact number of beads in a rosary. These were the tears that Bertin had shed for the world before he died. As the Abbot told the miraculous drops between his fingers, the reflection of a comet was glimpsed in the depth of the holy pool. To this day, the Amber Rosary of Bertin is venerated on his feast, the fifth of September, and is passed around the congregation to receive the blessings of those generations who have kissed and fondled it before them.

Amber, indeed, was an important commodity in those times, not least for its use in the more superior varnishes employed by map-makers and painters, who wished to keep for our posterity the truth of what they recorded. Hence we now can observe their work pleasantly crinkled and ambered by time.

Varnish – French *vernis*, Portuguese *verniz*, Spanish *berniz* – derives from the amber-coloured hair of Berenice, Queen of Cyrene, sister-wife of Ptolemy Euergetes, King of Egypt. She vowed to sacrifice her crowning glory if he would return home conqueror of Asia. She had it cut with gold shears and she hung it up in the ophisthodomos of the temple of Arsinoë at Zephyrium, but it vanished the first night, or was stolen; and the astronomer Conon of Samos told the king that the winds had wafted it to heaven, where it forms the seven stars near the tail of Leo, called *Coma Berenices*. So, when a hair strays from the stock of an artist's brush to flaw the application of paint or varnish, it is known as a *berenice*.

Hesperides, Barce, Cyrene, Appolonia and Tenchira: these were the great cities of the Pentapolis of Cyrenaica. And Hesperides was renamed Berenice by Ptolemy. This is the city we know as Benghazi. Here Aristippus founded the Cyrenaic school, whose philosophy was clarified by the blue light that wafts in from the ocean, and the white light of the desert. Here were fragrances of musk and ambergris, pervaded by the sound of water whispering the name of Berenice from aqueducts and ornamental fountains. Aristippus said: A man knows that things external to himself exist because they move him; but he can know nothing of their nature. All he can perceive is the way in which he himself is affected by them; how other men react is unknown. The fact that two men give the same name to their experiences is no proof of identity.

To the Cyrenaics, the statement 'a rose by any other name would smell as sweet' was fraught with immense difficulties, and its ramifications were discussed endlessly under the pergolas. Indeed, in their awareness of the individuality of scent, Aristippus and his disciples anticipated the modern analysis first postulated by George Curtis in 1898. He offered sixteen broad categories, as follows: sweet brier scent; moss rose scent, as in the common moss family; Austrian brier scent; musk rose scent; myrrh, as in the Ayrshire family; China rose; damask; Scottish rose scent; violet scent, as in the White Banksian Rose; old cabbage scent, as in the Double Provence; attar scent; hybrid Perpetual tea scent; sweet tea scent; hybrid tea scent as in La France; fruit scent; and the Verdier scent, represented by the Victor Verdier hybrids. Moreover, the inadequacy of 'rose' is evident in the plethora of modern varietal names, of which a small sub-section might represent a grand soirée. The ladies present include Albertine, Diana, Jenny Wren, Maid Marian, Zulu Queen, Violet Carson, Adelaide d'Orléans, Rose of Tralee, Minnehaha, Queen Fabiola, Madam Butterfly, Phyllis Gold, Mistress Quickly, Constance Spry, Dorothy peach, Dolly Varden, Isabel de Ortiz, Lady Curzon, Baby Betsy McCall, Mrs Sam McGredy, Carmen Talon, Queen Nefertiti, Goldilocks,

Ma Perkins, Wendy, Stella, Mexicali Rose, La Follette, Thumbelina, Lucy Cramphorn, Polly Flinders, Miss France, Miss Liberty, Miss Ireland, and Violinista Costa. Among the gentlemen are Marcel Proust, Christian Dior, Hiawatha, Chief Seattle, Uncle Walter, Jiminy Cricket, Rabbie Burns, Robin Hood, Montezuma, Mister Lincoln, Fred Cramphorn, Lord Penzance, Don Juan, Cupid, William III, El Capitan, John Clare, Henry Ford, William Shakespeare, Sir Walter Raleigh, General McArthur, Jude the Obscure, Pinocchio, King Midas, Oberon, and the Seven Dwarfs.

Such nominal elaboration was evident in the great Tulipomania which flourished in Holland from 1632 – the year of the births of the painter Vermeer, the microscopist van Leeuwenhoek, and the lens-grinder Spinoza – until 1636. The tulip – so named, it is said, for a Turkish word signifying 'turban' – had been introduced into western Europe about the middle of the sixteenth century. Before long, it was deemed a proof of bad taste in any man of fortune to be without a collection of tulips. Soon the middle classes of society caught the fever and began to vie with each other in the rarity of these flowers and the outlandish prices paid for them, which were exacerbated by the excessive fragility of the cultivated varieties. As one commentator observed, 'This masterpiece of culture, the more beautiful it turns, grows so much the weaker, so that, with the greatest skill and most careful attention, it can scarcely be transplanted, or even kept alive.'

The mania increased; prices augmented. Farms of land were exchanged for a few bulbs, so that by 1635 it became necessary to sell them by their weight in *perits*, a small weight less than a grain. A tulip of the species Admiral Liefkin, weighing 400 perits, was worth 4,400 florins; an Admiral van der Eyck, weighing 446 perits, was worth 1,260 florins; a Childer of 106 perits sold for 1,615 florins; and, most precious of all, a Semper Augustus, weighing in at 200 perits, was thought to be very cheap at 5,500 florins. A bulb of the black-and-amber Viceroy, also known as Berenice, Amber Whore, Devil's Pantaloons or Wasp, was traded for two lasts of wheat, four lasts of rye, four fat oxen, eight fat swine, four fat sheep, two hogsheads of wine, four tuns of beer, two tuns of butter, one thousand pounds of cheese, a complete bed, a suit of clothes, and a silver drinking-cup.

At that time, a wealthy merchant, who prided himself not a little on his fine tulips, received upon one occasion a very valuable consignment of merchandise from the Levant. Intelligence of its arrival was brought to him by a sailor, who presented himself for that purpose at the counting-house, among bales of goods of every description. The merchant, to reward him for his news, made him a present of a fine red herring for his lunch. The sailor had, it appears, a great partiality for onions, and seeing a bulb very like an onion lying on the counter of this liberal trader, and thinking it, no doubt, very much out of place among silks and velvets, he slyly seized an opportunity and slipped it in his pocket, as a relish for his herring. He got off clear with his prize, and proceeded to the quay to eat his lunch. Hardly was his back turned when the merchant missed his valuable Admiral Tromp, worth 3,000 florins, or some £280 sterling. The whole establishment was instantly in an uproar; search was made everywhere for the precious root, but it was not to be found. Great was the merchant's distress of mind. At last someone thought of the sailor.

The unhappy merchant sprang into the street at the bare suggestion. His alarmed household followed him. The sailor, simple soul! had not thought of concealment. He was found sitting quietly on a pile of ropes, masticating the last morsel of his 'onion'. Little did he dream that he had been eating a lunch whose cost might have regaled a whole ship's crew for a twelve-month; or, as the plundered merchant himself expressed it, 'might have sumptuously feasted the Prince of Orange and the whole court of the Stadtholder'. Antony caused pearls to be dissolved in wine to drink the health of Cleopatra; Sir Thomas Gresham drank a diamond dissolved in wine to the health of Queen Elizabeth, when she opened the Royal Exchange; but the lunch of this opportunistic Dutchman was as splendid as any. He had an advantage, too, over his wasteful predecessors: their gems did not improve the taste or wholesomeness of their wine, while his tulip was quite delicious with his red herring. The most unfortunate part of the business for him was that he remained in prison for some six months on a charge of felony preferred against him by the merchant. All of which goes to show, there's no such thing as a free lunch.

As the tulip frenzy intensified, nobles, citizens, farmers, mechanics, seamen, footmen, lens-grinders, chimney-sweeps and rag-and-bone men dabbled in tulips. People of all grades converted their assets into tulips. The operations of the trade became so extensive and so intricate, that it was found necessary to draw up an elaborate code of practice for the guidance of dealers. Notaries, agents, clerks, scriveners, interpreters and bondsmen were appointed. Studio painters, who hitherto had maintained a steady if modest business, found their still-lifes, landscapes and interiors to be worthless; but many found employment as illustrators of the magnificent catalogues published by the tulip marts. Poets were hired to write eulogies on the conformations and the colours of the various specimens. Indeed, as the tulip breeders were driven to produce further adumbrations of the spectrum, new shades of pigmentation became visible daily, and the wordsmiths pored by candlelight over glossaries and ancient flower-treatises, exploring new ways of describing colour.

The auction houses laid on sumptuous entertainments. Braised tulip leaves, reposing on a bed of wild Sumatran bird's eye rice, drizzled with exotic oils and spices, were served for starters. Turkish turban dumplings stuffed with aubergine and cumin floated in tureens of tulip soup. Tableaux of rare specimens in full bloom were displayed on the dinner tables and sideboards; tulips were embedded in elaborate ice sculptures depicting scenes from the Rise of the Dutch Republic, beneath the vast aquaria of swimming fish and crawling blue-black lobsters. Saltimbancos, jongleurs, tightrope-walkers, posture masters, the dancing Sibyls of Cyrenaica, rope-trick men from Pakistan, and humble clowns performed their silent arabesques.

As the tulip mania staggered towards its inevitable climacteric, fortunes were made and lost. Millions were invested in ancillary speculations: patents and charters were granted for fictive gold mines in the Bahamas, coral fisheries in the Oroonoko, and lead mines in Mayo. Bubble companies were formed to manufacture iron from coal, and spirituous liquors from spring water, or 'for the transmutation of quicksilver into a malleable fine metal'. Paradoxically, the nation which enthusiastically embraced these vast delusions had been a model of good husbandry: a people who, by incessant watchfulness, had kept the soil of their country from the ever-present danger of the sea, who formed rich meadow land where none had been before, and who brought the cultivation of the turnip and potato to a hitherto unknown degree of excellence. Their methods of supplying winter fodder to animals were unparalleled, and they were the first to develop the growing of clover, red and white sainfoin, and lucerne. In addition, Holland was the origin of modern international law and physic. It was the country from which the best mathematical instruments, the best optical instruments, the best nautical instruments could be procured. It discovered the art of cutting and polishing diamonds. It was the centre of the amber trade. In short, there was no branch of learning or skill in which the Dutch did not excel.

The tulip mania occurred in the middle of a protracted and ruinously expensive war. On the 23rd of May, 1618, two Governors of the Holy Roman Empire, together with a minor official, had been seized and hurled through the south-west window of the Green Room of the Bohemian Chancellory. A miracle happened: all three survived the fall, and fled. It was reported by some that the Virgin Mary had wrapped them in her wondrous cloak; others claimed a dung-heap had broken their fall. Whatever the facts of the matter, the Defenestration of Prague was the spark that ignited the Thirty Years' War. The perpetrators of this abrupt deed had hoped to initiate in Bohemia a revolutionary transformation on the pattern of the Netherlands. Shortly afterwards, a comet appeared in the sky from the vicinity of Scorpio, when Jupiter, Mercury and the Moon were under the Earth, but Mars and Saturn were above. Mars Peregrinus, it was observed, had left the eleventh house of the heavens, and was four degrees in front of the tail of Leo, in the vicinity of Coma Berenices. Berenice, it was noted, had been put to death on the orders of her son, Ptolemy Philopater, in 216 BC.

David Herlitzius, the Physikus of Stargard and the court astrologer of Pomerania, immediately composed a treatise on this strange conjunction, prophesying many hostile murderous attacks, false alliances and betrayals; pestilence, monster births, rain and floods, and a consequent rise in the price of fish, and, above all, hate and dissatisfaction among the kings, rebellion, discord and war would inevitably follow. And so it came to pass.

Perhaps the tulip phenomenon is a reaction to these catastrophic events, as the Burgher of Amsterdam withdraws into his ordered rooms to contemplate the transitory beauty of that fragile flower. Even so, from time to time, the glass of his tall windows trembles with the dim noise of the panoply of war: blaring trumpets, fifes and drums, the rolling crack of musket-fire, the thud of shells, a solitary bugle, and the whispering of nodding plumes. With night comes silence. And so to bed, where he sleeps soundly with his good wife, holding a tulip bulb to his heart, dreaming of the riches hidden in its many layers, and the microscopic germ of life at its core.

CLEPSYDRA

On the night that I was married and laid in marriage bed
There came a bold sea-captain and he stood at my bedhead,
Saying, Arise, arise, young married man and come along with me
To the low, low lands of Holland to fight the enemy.

I put my arms around his neck thinking my love to save
But the captain gave the order and he was forced away
Saying, There's many the blithe young married man this night must
    come with me
To the low, low lands of Holland to fight the enemy.

O Holland is a wondrous place, it's a land where grows much grain
'Tis a fine inhabitation for your true love to be in
Where the sugar-cane grows plentiful and tea grows on each tree
But the low, low lands of Holland have parted my love and me . . .

'The Lowlands of Holland', a folk song

I was married to Deirdre Shannon on the 16th of October 1982, in St Comgall's Church in Antrim town. The reception was held at the Cranfield Inn some few miles away, on the shores of Lough Neagh. This is the lake described by the eminent cleric, Giraldus Cambrensis, in his account of Ireland, *Topographia Hibernica*, published in Oxford in 1187, to much critical acclaim.

— This lake, says the Welshman, is twice as broad as it is long, and you could fit the Isle of Man into it. A mighty river called the Bann flows north from it, jumping with all kinds of fish. There's that many fish in it that the locals spend most of their time fixing their nets, for the catches are that big that the nets get burst. I heard tell of a fish that they got there last spring, that looked like a salmon, but it was such a monster that two squads of men couldn't carry it, and they had to cut it up and sell it off in lots all over the province . . .

— They say that the rise of this fantastic lough came about as a result of an accident. Long ago, and that wasn't yesterday, nor the day before, the area now covered by the lake was lived in by this tribe who were a real bad lot. More than any other people on the island of Ireland, they liked nothing better than to be fornicating with animals. And there was this spring well that they always kept covered with a stone lid, for there was an old saying among them, that went:

> Leave the cover off the well,
> The spring within you'll never quell —

— Now it happened one day that one of their women came to

the well to draw water. And she was filling her bucket; and God only knows why, but she'd left her brat in its baby-basket under a tree a good way off, and it started to whinge and bawl. So she left her bucket there, and went over to the imp to calm it down, and clean forgot to put the lid back on. And she was coming back when she met with such a gush of water from the well that the pair of them were knocked off their feet. And within the hour, the whole bad tribe, and their cows, and their sheep, and their pigs, and their goats, were swept off the face of the earth and were never seen again, thank God, and the whole place has been under water ever since. For it looks to me that the Author of the Book of Nature, in his wisdom, judged that a land which had witnessed such abominations against nature was unworthy not only of its first inhabitants, but of any others in the future.

That this story is not far from the truth is evident from the stories of the fishermen, who can clearly see church towers under the waves in calm weather. They frequently point them out to visitors, who are amazed at this phenomenon.

The Book of the Dun Cow, transcribed from older books by Maelmuire Mac Ceilechair, who died in 1106, is now in the Royal Irish Academy in Dublin – or rather, a large fragment of it, for the book has suffered much mutilation. It gives another account of the origin of Lough Neagh, of which this is my version:

Long, long ago – long before our times – there was a king of Munster. Marid Mac Carido, they called him. He had two sons, Ecca and Rib. Now Ecca was a malcontent. Nothing pleased him more than to be kicking against the reins; and he often had the king in a twist over the head of it. He was forever plotting and planning to leave home, to go away and get himself a kingdom of his own in some far-off part of the country. Rib would try to stop him. So he did, and so he did again; but Ecca was determined.

It happened that Ecca's stepmother Eibliu came to him one night, and talked to him about the kingdom he might have. And Ecca did a grievous wrong against his father. So he had to leave. His brother Rib and his stepmother Eibliu went with him. Ten hundred men too, besides women and children. They headed north.

They had travelled for some time, and the druids told the brothers that their futures lay apart. So, when they came to the Pass of the Two Pillars, they went their separate ways.

Rib and his tribe headed west. They travelled till they came to the Plain of the Lone Farm. There a fountain momently was forced from underground, and burst across the land. The whole tribe was drowned, and a great lake was formed. It is called Lough Rib to this day.

Ecca kept north. Slowly they journeyed, till they hit the Boyne Acropolis. No sooner had they stopped, than a long fellow came out of the palace, namely, Angus Mac Indoc of the Boyne Heights. He told them to be off. But they were tired to death of travelling, and pitched their tents on the plain below the citadel. Angus was not amused. He killed all their horses that night.

Next day, he came out again, and said, I killed your horses last night. Be off with you, or I will kill you too.

And Ecca said, How can we go? Without horses we cannot travel.

Then Angus went in, and brought out a gigantic, fully harnessed horse, and they put everything they had on it. They were about to set off, and he said to them —

> *This steed you must keep on the go,*
> *For if you don't, he'll be your woe.*

They set out again, and travelled on, and on the second Sunday of the second month of autumn, they reached the Plain of the Lone Wood, where they intended to abide. They gathered round the great horse to unload their baggage, all of them so busy with their own things that they clean forgot to keep the beast of burden on the move. The moment he stood still, a well sprang up beneath his feet.

Now Ecca, when he saw the well spring up, was worried, for now he remembered the warning. So he told his men to build a house around it, and he built his palace right beside it, to be double safe. He picked a woman to take care of the well, and said to her —

> *There's water for my people,*
> *Water for my kin —*
> *But keep the door locked fast,*
> *When no one's in.*

Now Ecca had two daughters, Ariu and Liban. Ariu was the wife of Curnan the Simple. And Curnan went about among the people, saying that the well would overflow —

Build your boats, and build them fast,
The torrent will be deep and vast;
I see our chief beneath the wave,
And Ariu, whom I cannot save —
But Liban east and west will swim
By lonesome shores and islands dim,
And down in the deep sea cave!

He sang this verse to everyone he met; but no one heeded the words of Curnan the Simple.

One day the woman of the well forgot to lock the door, and then the spell was free to work. Immediately, the well burst out of the house, and flooded the plain, and made a great lake. Ecca and his tribe were drowned, except his daughter Liban, and Conang, and Curnan the Simple. They buried Ariu. Of Conang we know nothing more. Curnan died of grief for Ariu. He was buried in a mound. They call it Curnan's Cairn to this day.

So the Lake of the Lone Wood was formed, which is called Loch n-Ecca — that is, Lough Neagh — in memory of Ecca, son of Marid Mac Carido.

As for Liban, she was swept away like the others; but she was not drowned. She lived for a year in her chamber beneath the lake, together with her lap-dog; and God protected her from the water. But at the end of the year she yearned for other company; and when she saw the salmon sporting all about her, she prayed, and said, O Lord, I wish I were a salmon, that I might swim with all the others through the clear green sea!

And at the words she took the shape of a salmon, except her

face and breast, which kept their human form. Her dog became an otter, and he followed her wherever she went in the sea. So she swam from sea to sea for three hundred years: that is, from the time of Ecca, son of Marid Mac Carido, to the time of Comgall of Bangor.

And she prayed for Comgall and his monks to come and catch her in their nets. Yet many trials did she undergo before it came to pass. One day an angel came and told them where to catch her. They put her in a golden chariot and brought her before Comgall. The saints gave her a choice: either to die immediately she was baptized, and go straight to heaven; or to live on earth as long as she had wandered in the sea, and then to go to heaven after that long age. She chose instant death. Comgall baptized her there and then. Some say he christened her Murgen, that is, 'Sea-born'; others say her name was Murgelt, that is, 'Mermaid'.

She is counted among the holy virgins, and is held in high esteem, as God ordained for her in heaven; and wonders and miracles are performed in her name.

That is the story of Lough Neagh. But others say that Lough Neagh is Loch n-Eacha, that is, Lake of Steeds, because of the water-horses that reside in it, and who crawl out of it at night to prey on sheep and cattle, whose picked bones can be clearly seen by fishermen.

And at the wedding reception at Cranfield, on the shores of Lough Neagh, my father told to the company the story I am about to relate. Recently, I came across it in the Irish original he'd translated into English for the benefit of those who had no Irish.

The story was collected by Douglas Hyde, scholar, cultural activist, and first president of Ireland. The man he got it from was Frank O'Connor, who at that time – 1896 – was an inmate of the Poorhouse in Athlone. O'Connor told Hyde he had got it from a man called Austin Casey from County Sligo. Here is my version.

Long ago there lived a woman near Antrim town. It seemed she had lived there forever. She looked just as she had three score years before. Men looked at her when they were boys, and they looked at her when they were bent and grey with age; but none could say that she had changed.

The lady was rich, but no one knew where her money came from. Another thing about her was that she had this big sign up outside her house, saying there was bed and board for anyone who sought it, providing they had a good story to tell every night; but the story had to be true.

There was a young man that time by the name of Jack the Lad from Randalstown. Jack was great company, and he liked good company himself. Each night, he'd go from house to house, listening to the old folk telling stories, and any tale he'd hear, he'd have it off by heart forever. He'd often heard tell of this lady who lived near Antrim town, and he thought to pay her a visit, but he dared not, without a brand-new story to tell, for he reckoned this lady would have heard his stock of yarns before from others.

Now Jack the Lad was going home late one night, after playing cards and drinking poteen. He came by an old graveyard, and he heard a voice from the graveyard, crying, Fix my tooth, that hasn't been fixed for seven years! Jack, being brave and well on, jumped over the wall. And when he came out of it, he had one story to tell, that no one could have heard before.

Come dawn the next day, he told himself he had a bargain of a story to approach the lady with. He went to Antrim there and then, and from there on it wasn't far to go to reach the lady's house. Night was falling fast. He plucked up his courage and knocked on the door. A doorman appeared. The porter asked him his business. Bed and board, says Jack the Lad. Do you have a story? asked the doorman. I have, says Jack.

With that, the doorman brought him in and made him sit alone in a great room. There was a jug of Spanish wine on the sideboard, and a boiled ham, and bread and butter, and a big red cheese. An hour went by. The doorman appeared and announced that the visitor was now summoned to his lady's presence. Jack followed the doorman to another room which was as bright as day for all the candles that were lit in it. He was gazing around him, when the lady made her entrance. She was a long tall lovely woman. She looked neither young nor old. You would take her for thirty. She wore gold hair and a green silk cloak.

Jack thanked her for the good supper, and said he had come with a story, should she care to listen to it. She said she would like that very much, except for one thing. She pointed to a table in a corner of the room. On the table sat an hourglass, but instead of sand, it was water that was in it. You may tell your story, said the lady, but when the last drip's gone from top to bottom, you must end it. Fair enough, said Jack. The lady reclined herself on a couch. Jack sat down on the big oak chair, and began his story.

*

Noble lady, I was born and bred in Randalstown. One night I left my aged parents' house, and I went to a big Fair Day up the road, and I fell in with great company, and got very merry with them. It was late at night when I was going home. I took a short-cut by the old graveyard, a way I'd never go except I'd drink taken. When I reached the graveyard, I heard this voice coming out of the dark, roaring, Fix my tooth, that wasn't fixed these seven years!

I took pity on the creature whose words these were, for it's a sore thing to have a bad tooth, and since the drink was working in me, I never stopped to think of where I was, or what was speaking to me, but I put my hand into my pocket and I pulled out a horseshoe nail I had about me that was great for tamping tobacco into my pipe, or scraping out the bowl of it, and I said, Come out of there, whoever you are, and I will fix your tooth. I can't come out, said the voice, but come you in here, and give me some light, and have no fear. Begod, and I will, says I, and with that I put my hand on the graveyard wall and vaulted over it. What should I see but a big man with a red cloak on him standing under a hawthorn tree. Come closer, says he, and put your finger in my mouth, and you'll find a bone splinter just behind my wisdom tooth, and take it out, if you're able.

I got scared then, and broke out in a sweat. Better far, I thought, to be on the road home, but it seemed I had no option. I approached him. As he opened his jaws, they seemed so big I thought of being swallowed whole. Each tooth was six inches long at least and as sharp as a razor. I'd rather have stuck my hand into the mouth of a shark than into that terrible mouth . . .

*

The lady raised her hand. Your story's good, she says, and it is not a usual story. Pray don't continue till my friends come in. With that she put a little whistle to her mouth and blew it. In a split second a door opened up in the wall of the great room, a door that Jack had never seen till then, and twelve men walked in with a young woman on the shoulders of each one of them. They were all dressed up in a fine array of gold silks. Every man wore a sword, and every woman held a black knife in her hand. No word was uttered by them, but they all sat down on chairs and looked at Jack the Lad. Tell your story again, says the lady, from the beginning. Jack the Lad began the story again, till he came to the place that the lady had told him to stop, and then he continued –

I plucked up my courage, I put my right hand into his mouth, and I felt the bone splinter behind his wisdom tooth. I pulled out my horseshoe nail, and got the point of it in behind the splinter, but no sooner had I done so than he let out an almighty scream. Every dead person – man, woman and child – in the graveyard arose. I leapt back and looked around me. Such a sight was never seen before. The graveyard was all lit up like broad daylight. I saw the sun and the moon dance overhead. I saw hundreds of dead in their bright shrouds. I thought it was the end of the world, and that the dead had risen for their final Judgement. But then they all started to laugh and clap their hands. Mr Fix-my-tooth stuck his fingers in his mouth, let out a whistle, and in the twinkling of an eye the dead returned to their graves. The sun and the moon vanished, and I found myself standing before Mr Fix-my-tooth again.

You did your job well, said he, for I'd that splinter in my tooth for seven years, but I couldn't get anyone to take it out till you came along. You've earned your reward, but you'll not get it in this life; but I promise that you'll get it after death. You've just seen some of the departed. Come with me now and I'll show you the dwelling-place of sinners.

To tell you the truth, I'd no great urge to see this place, but before I could open my mouth to say so, he stamped his foot three times, and the ground opened up and swallowed us. We travelled down till we came to the shore of a great lake. Instead of water, it was filled with brimstone. I saw thousands there in chains amidst the fire, all screaming in their agony. I was full of pity for them, but I dared not speak.

Then he took me to the shore of another lake, and said, This is Purgatory. I looked down and saw a great host tied to beds of burning coals. They, too, were screaming in agony. He brought me then to a great plain and showed me another host of people. They were crawling around with broken wings, and weeping bitterly. These are the angels who were cast out of Heaven for daring to wrangle with God, he said. Then he took me to the foot of a narrow crooked road, and said, This is the road to Heaven, but no one may walk it until they die, for it is guarded by an angel with a sword of fire.

And now, said he, I've some advice for you: shun all drinking and bad company, or the gates of hell will open for you. You can go home now. I am not permitted to speak further to you until seven years from tonight. Come to the old graveyard that night, bring your horseshoe nail with you, and I will come to you.

Then my eyes were blinded by a fog. I fell asleep, and when I woke I found myself by the old graveyard wall. It was dawn, and the lark was singing high in the sky. The sun was well up when I reached my father's door. My father was beside himself. He gave me an almighty going-over. He bade me go, never to cross his threshold while he lived. I felt sick, sore and tired. When I saw him go out for the day I sneaked into bed and lay there till the next morning. I dared not face my father again, so I got up and left by the back door, and hit the road till I arrived here.

That is my story, but if I could have the honour of your company tomorrow night, I'll tell you another one.

All this while, the water-clock had been dripping away, and when Jack finished his story the last drip fell to the bottom of the bowl, and there was silence. Then one of the twelve men said, We'll all be here tomorrow night. They all got up, a door opened in the wall, and they walked out as they had come, with the young women on their shoulders.

As soon as they had gone, the lady laid a fine table for Jack, with mutton, ham, veal, cheese and bread, and a big jug of wine. Jack ate his fill but didn't touch the wine. Then the doorman appeared and brought Jack to another fine room with a four-poster bed in it. Jack lay down and instantly fell asleep, and didn't wake till the next morning.

When he woke, the doorman brought him his breakfast. Jack didn't see the lady, nor any of the company, though he spent the day wandering the house and its many beautiful rooms. When night fell, he was summoned, and another feast was laid before him. He ate and drank his fill. Then he was brought to the lady's chamber.

Are you ready to tell your tale? she said. I am, said he. She put a little gold trumpet to her mouth and blew it. The wall opened up and the twelve men emerged, dressed as they had been the previous night, with the twelve women on their shoulders. When they were seated the lady said to Jack, You may begin.

But before he could open his mouth, one of the women spoke. Jack couldn't make out a word of it, but the lady snapped out, Control your women, for otherwise, how are we supposed to hear the story? With that the men struck their women with magic wands and turned them into hounds, and told them to lie down. The hounds lay down at the men's feet, and Jack the Lad began his story –

My father peered at his watch. I see, he said, that if I am to go on with this story, we'll be here all night. So if you want to hear the next bit, we can meet here this day month, and I'll tell it to you. Everyone agreed, and we all went up to the bar for more drink. And there was much talk of water-clocks, and sun-dials, and how the digital watch had changed our concept of time.

DELPHINIUM

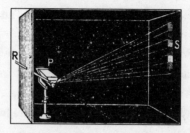

The water-clock referred to in the story just related is the clepsydra, Greek for water-thief: a vessel filled with a certain measure of water, and having a hole in the bottom of a size to ensure the water running away in a definite space of time. The invention of the best kind of water-clock is attributed to Plato. In this, the hours were marked in one of two ways: a dial was placed above the vessel, the hand of which was connected by a wire with a cork floating on top of the water; or the vessel was transparent, and had vertical lines on it, indicating certain typical days in the four seasons or the twelve months. These lines were divided into twelve sections, corresponding to the position which the water was experimentally found to take at each of the twelve hours of night or day on each of these typical days. It must be remembered that the ancients always divided the night and day into twelve equal hours each, which involved a variation in the length of the hours corresponding to the varying length of the day and night: thus, the measure of the hours was temporary. At the winter solstice, even if the sun shone all day there would be, by our modern measure, only 8 hours, 54 minutes of sunlight, leaving a long night of 15 hours, 6 minutes. At the summer solstice the time was exactly reversed. In ancient Rome, at the winter solstice, the first hour of their day (*prima hora*) began at what we would call 7.33 a.m. and lasted until 8.17 a.m., while the twelfth hour (*hora duodecima*) began at 3.42 p.m. and expired at 4.27 p.m., when the longer night hours began. Platonic time was elastic; but one area in which the clepsydra functioned practically, in modern terms, was in the courtroom, where it was used to allot equal times to the lawyers of opposing parties. Time was water.

The elegant Tower of the Winds, also known as the Horologium of Andronicus Cyrrhestes, served at once as the public clock and weather-cock; it still stands in Athens. It is an octagonal tower of marble, with prominent porches, each supported by two simple Corinthian columns, on the north-east and north-west. On the south it has a turret to contain the cistern for the water-clock. The eight sides correspond to the directions from which the eight winds blow. The figures of these are represented in beautiful relief on the frieze, and beneath them on the marble walls are engraved the lines of the sun-dial. The culminating point of the sloping roof was once surmounted by a bronze Triton, placed on a Corinthian capital, so as to revolve and point with his staff to the figure of the wind which was blowing at the time.

Triton is the son of Poseidon, and performs some of his functions. Poseidon is the Greek god of the sea and everything liquid; a younger brother of Zeus, according to Homer; an elder brother, according to Hesiod. At the distribution of the world, the rule over the sea and all its gods and creatures fell to him, as the rule over the sky fell to Zeus, and that over the underworld to Pluto. Poseidon has his dwelling in a golden underwater palace. As Zeus bears the lightning, so Poseidon wields his mighty trident, with which he stirs up the sea, cleaves rocks, and makes fountains and horses spring forth from them. He is the god of springs and wells, especially in Arcadia and Argolis. The horse, the dolphin, and the pine tree are deemed sacred to him. Colossal statues of Poseidon often stood by harbours and on promontories. His wife is Amphitrite, mother of Triton. Her amber hair is confined by a golden net; crab-claws make up her diadem, and her chariot of shells is drawn by a team of dolphins, as Triton blows his twisted conch, now violently, now gently, to raise or calm the billows.

Meerschaum is attributed to Amphitrite, since, like amber, it is found cast up on sea-shores. Others call it sepiolite, supposing it to be derived from the bones of the cuttlefish, reminding us of the sepia ink ejaculated by that wary animal in times of stress, clouding its immediate whereabouts.

This is the meerschaum used for the famous Delft tobacco pipes, whose smoke is cooled by it and imbibed through an amber mouthpiece. Delft, city of reflections multiplied in still canals: one sees there polished blacks, bluish, deep, like mussel shells or glossy tar, and bronze and flowing tones that look like tentacles of seaweed; there are butter yellows, spinach greens and cabbage blues, such as one finds on ancient polychrome faïence. White is never white, but blond like bread crust or ivory, and its colour is so rich that the humblest things evoke an image of precious materials: amber, gold, coral, and all the green gems. One can imagine Venice in the labyrinthine waterways of Delft, or see a Chinese aspect to the narrow channels of its suburbs. Here, the houses, made completely of wood, are painted and gilded from top to bottom. In front of each is a garden of boxwood, cut into the shapes of monkeys, hares and stags; often, these little plots are enclosed by multi-coloured fences, adorned with painted tulips and convolvulus. Drifting on the current like an autumn leaf, our boat eventually returns us to the harbour in the centre.

From the high window of our small but clean hotel, we look across the courtyard to see other windows. Each casement is the frame where a cook sits dreamily gazing down at the red hens scratching at the yellow earth between the tiled walkways, or where a girl combs her floating hair. In other frames, two soldiers play at cards; an ageing man peers at a globe; some of the rooms are empty, and reveal nothing but the light which slants into them. There are many window-boxes planted with tall delphiniums, this flower also known as the larkspur, delphinium from the dolphin features of its nectary, *delphus* being Greek for womb; and Delphi, home of the Oracle, is the navel of the world. The flowers, adumbrated pinks and blues and whites, remind us how the dolphin changes colour when it's taken from its element: Parting day, writes Byron, Dies like the dolphin, whom each

pang imbues / With a new colour as it gasps away, / The last still
loveliest –

We were privileged to see the dolphins in the Delft Aquarium,
as they gambolled in green-roofed pools floored with blue tiles.
Here was a cool escape from the heat of the day, as we imagined
the breakfast room might be in the morning, with the light from
the tall Dutch window illuminating the shiny, ironed linen cloth,
and the silverware, and the platters of various sliced cheeses and
hams, and fat sausages, and the dumpy bread rolls, and the curls
of butter, and the six cold hard-boiled eggs whose whites are
glistening and slippery when you crack their shells and peel them.
Coffee percolates a caffeine high throughout the room.

If you look closely across the canal from the window, you
might be fortunate to see an amber worker bent over his lathe in
one of the many ateliers of Delft, turning and drilling the precious substance, shaping it with files and graving tools, polishing
the end result with pumice, tripoli and rouge. There are beads,
bracelets, cameos and amulets of amber, figurines of wild animals, hair-bands, fancy combs and chessmen. This stuff was
called electron by the Greeks, for it emits a charge of electricity
when rubbed. When burned as incense it gives off a resinous
odour of Poseidon pine. In this glowing medium millions of years
old, insects are found embedded. Much of it comes from the
seam of the Blue Earth under the Baltic, where amber men
prospect for it with nets and tridents after gales when Triton's
horn becomes diminuendo, sometimes in moonlight, or at break
of day. There is a green amber thought to come from primordial
marshes. Of the rare blues and reds we have no account. As for

ambergris, this is French for grey amber, a product of the sperm whale, sometimes found floating on the sea, or hauled by whalers from the stomach of the whale. There were found in this amber-gris, writes Melville, certain hard, round, bony plates, which at first were thought to be sailors' trouser buttons, but it after-wards turned out that they were nothing more than pieces of recalcitrant cuttlefish bones embalmed in that manner. Ambergris, it would appear, is caused by indigestion. The stuff found in the whale's head, called spermaceti for its likeness to congealed semen, may be a migrant form of ambergris: both are made into candles and ointments; but ambergris is better known as a fixative or base for perfumes, especially for those which con-tain the more volatile oils. Ambergris is carried by the Turks to Mecca, as Roman Catholics bear frankincense to Rome.

Sir Thomas Browne, in his 'Urn Burial', mentions that 'in an hydropicall body, ten years buried in the Church-yard, we met with a fat concretion, where the nitre of the Earth, and the salt and lixivious liquor of the body, had coagulated large lumps of fat, into the consistence of the hardest Castile soap'. This substance, adipocere, or grave-wax, must resemble ambergris. And in an urn preserved by Cardinal Farnese were found, besides a great number of gems, 'an Elephant of ambre, and a crystal ball'. If the elephant stands for memory, and the crystal ball for divination, how much more magically effective must be the rare amber balls cited by several authorities; for amber is imbued with magnetism, and preserves things incorruptibly. To view the future, or the past of spirit beings, the clairvoyant sits in a darkened room, with a light source, such as candle power, bouncing off the surface

44

of the ball. Initially, it may appear clear and flat, or merely reflect the available light, but as the psychic gazes into it, the amber or the crystal may become misty or foggy; subsequently, figures may appear, their edges tinged with preternatural radiance. Such light is sometimes witnessed trembling on the stone embrasures or the sills of stained-glass windows; and viewers of the camera obscura, which also produces its best effects in a darkened room, have commented on how the colours of the spectrum were transformed and heightened, glimmering like flowers remembered from a childhood spring excursion, when the dew still lies on them.

The instrument maker, John Cuff, published an anonymous poem on the virtues of the camera obscura:

> *Say, rare machine, who taught thee to design?*
> *And mimick Nature with such skill divine . . .*
> *Exterior objects painting on the scroll*
> *True as the Eye presents 'em to the Soul . . .*

Vermeer, like many other painters, used the camera obscura, and was charged with witchcraft for it, as was van Leeuwenhoek for his use of the microscope.

Similarly, the work of the early Irish scribes and limners, as exemplified by works like the Books of Kells and of Durrow, were seen as nothing short of miraculous. Cambrensis witnessed such a book, which had been made under the auspices of St Brigid. There are innumerable drawings in this book, he says, which a casual reader might take to be mere scrawls. But look closer, with an educated eye, into the secrets of the art-work, and you will see such delicate complexities of vision, so organized and interwoven, so vivid in their rendering of colour, that the more you look, the more you will declare, that this is not the work of men, but of angels.

On the night before the scribe was to begin the book, an angel appeared to him, and showed him a drawing, and said to him, Do you think you can make such a drawing on the first page of the book you are about to begin? Truthfully, the scribe said, No. For such art was beyond the realms of his knowledge, and he could not fathom how its subtlety had been achieved. The angel said, Go tomorrow to your lady, and ask her to pour forth prayers for you, that the Lord might clarify your bodily and mental eyes, and guide your hand to draw correctly. All this was done. And from there on, night after night, the angel came to him, and held before him many other drawings; and the scribe remembered them so well, that it seemed they glowed on the parchment sheet before him, in all their majesty and majuscules of colour, so that all he had to do was follow them. In this manner, with the angel dictating the designs, Brigid praying, and the scribe imitating, the book was composed.

But before inspiration comes the labour. First, the vellum: the skin of a lamb, or a kid, or a calf. Vellum is from Old French *veel*, a calf. The patron saint of artists, Luke the Evangelist, is depicted as a winged calf in the manuscripts. You skin the calf, and you soak the skin in water, then in a vat of lime and water, to wash out some of the fats and soluble proteins. You scrape off the surplus

flesh and fat with a blunt knife. You soak the skin again in lime
and water. You wash it in water. You stretch the skin on a rack
with cords tied to where the calf's feet would have been. You cut
it, and dry it, and rub it with a pumice stone. You dust it with a
goose's wing. The vellum is then ready to be written on, and
made into a book: sometimes, the spine of the calf can be seen
running down the spine of the book. To every cow its calf, as the
judgement has it, and to every book its copy.

Then, the quill. Select the feather from one of the first five
flight feathers of any large bird, such as a goose. Feathers from the
left wing fit the right hand best. Soak the feather until it is soft,
and then harden it in hot sand. Proceed as follows: (1) Having
shortened the plume, strip away the barb, which would otherwise
rest uncomfortably against the knuckles of the index finger. (2)
Cut away the tip of the barrel at an angle. (3) Make a slit in the
top centre of the barrel, by levering the knife blade gently
upwards, releasing pressure as soon as a crack occurs. (4) Slice a
scoop from the underside of the pen, to about half its diameter,
and centred on the slit. (5) Shape the nib on one side of the slit.
(6) Shape the nib on the opposite side, making the two halves
match. (7) If the underside of the nib is too concave, scrape it flat
with a clean scoop, removing as little of the quill as possible. (8)
To 'nib' the pen, rest the underside of the point on a smooth,
hard surface. Thin the tip from the top side by pushing the blade
forward at a shallow angle; then make a vertical cut, either at
right angles to the slit or obliquely. On a very strong feather the
last cut can be repeated to remove a fine sliver, avoiding rough-
ness on the underside of the writing edge.

An array of inks and pigments must be acquired. Indigo from
India, from the red and purple flowers of *Indigofera* in the sweet
pea family. Raw sienna from the earth of Italy; ochre from the
yellow soil of Greece. Green malachite, from carbonate of
copper. Red worm vermilion, brewed from mercury and sulphur. Realgar, 'powder of the cavern', from Arabia, a disulphide
of arsenic. The purple of Cassius, obtained from a solution of
gold by the action of a solution of tin. The fabulously expensive
ultramarine, from lapis lazuli of Persia. The carmine known as
kermes, got from the crushed dried bodies of pregnant female
scale insects of the genus *Kermes*, formerly supposed to be red
berries. Orpiment, the amber-yellow arsenic also known as
King's Yellow, which gives off an odour of garlic when volatized.
The deep blacks, from lamp-black, or pounded burnt fish-bones,
or sheep-bones. Oak-gall black.

We will pass over the unremitting discipline the scribe or
limner undergoes to learn his craft, and proceed to the pages of
the finished book, whose words are wrought with lacertine con-
volutions. There are patterns composed of geometrical
combinations, or developments of straight or curved lines from
the sole elements, namely, spiral and interlacing: from the plain
twist, or guilloche, to the elaborate chain composed of knobs of
torturing intricacy and varied construction, being laid in squares,
oblongs, triangles, hexagons, octagons, et cetera. The phyllo-
morphic ornaments include the single wavy stem with alternate
recurved scrolls terminating in trefoil-shaped leaves, or disgorged
from the open jaws of a nondescript. The zoomorphic elements
abound with peacocks, horses, fishes, dogs, hares, cocks, otters,

cats, rats, lizards, serpents, dragons. In their deliberate unlike-
nesses to living things, they achieve the status of heraldic beasts,
who trumpet forth the gospel of the living word with twisted
bugles. Some are frightful, monstrous forms of animals, whose
limbs twine and copulate into a labyrinth of ornament, where
one can hardly resist the impulse to search for the secret parts of
their bodies, which are concealed in, or evolved into, the parts of
different creatures, who breed microscopic beings in the mansion
of a particle. Think of a piece of tripoli employed by burnishers
of parchments, which contains the chalky skeletons of myriad
animalcules. Or look into a drop of pond water: here are the
animals with ruby-coloured eyes, whose three stomachs are filled
with deep green vegetable matter; or contemplate the bell-flower
beasts, their shapes like champagne flutes or glass tulips wavering
on long contractile stalks; sing the praises of these infusorians,
whose cilia are finer than the lashes of a fairy being's eye, or the
smallest size of camel brush. Smaller again than the monad is the
rotifer, who creates a whirlpool with her eyelid-like appendages,
of which the pupil is her mouth, which swallows up the monads
thereby drawn in; or they maintain the purposes of oars, and
through their aid the animal swims swiftly about. They also serve
the offices of gills. All this is connected to a lobed brain; and the
tail terminates in a three-pronged forceps, by which it is enabled
to attach itself to any spot. They increase themselves by spon-
taneous longitudinal self-division. So it is written.

At times Jokers appear in the margins, two at a time, typically,
one pointing out an error of transcription, the other doubled
over laughing. Disembodied sign-posting hands forewarn the

reader of the opening of a problematic passage. Little spon-
taneous haiku-like poems based on conventional themes appear
about to fall off the edge of the page: the yellow-billed blackbird
sings in the yellow whin bush; my nib is weary with writing;
pleasant is the sun today upon these margins, because it flickers
so. Four Jokers try to pull a capital letter apart. In one line the *m*
of *unum* forms an equestrian monk's tonsure as his horse's hooves
clatter over the last words of the line below, thus overriding the
splendid acrobat letter A's articulation beginning the line below.
The horseback monk cues the reader to continue. In his original
green cloak, now self-destructed because of the unstable pigment, he would have been highly prominent on the folio, even at
a distance of some metres; and thus the monk on the page would
have reminded his audience of the real monk who stood before
them reading the script aloud, his fingers measuring the words.

The Book is a picture of the world. Beyond the small stone
church set in the clearing where the Book resides for now, wild
animals cavort and rumble in the thickets of the forest. Eagles
drift above the canopy in predetermined thermal spirals.
Sometimes nameless stars fall from the heavens, yet they acquire
a story. Subtle auguries are witnessed in the tumbled clouds; the
raindrops trickling down a lichened wall require interpretation.
The track of a cock's feet after he crows is not without meaning.
If the candle flickers, that is a good omen; if the flame leans to
one side, there will be a change of circumstances. The hazel wand
is good for cleidomancy. If the liver torn from the ox is flabby,
then beware the Ides of March.

This year the corn has been blighted, and strange apparitions have appeared to many. The water saints have been busy performing miracles and creating holy wells. There are many methods of production. Some strike the butt end of their crook against the ground. Naile of Inbher Naile cast his into the forest. The shedding of a saint's blood, or tears, is also effective. So is the blow of his horse's hoof, or the horse pissing on the spot. Water poured from the saint's bell produces a sweet everlasting spring. Many saints have been seen walking on the waters, or driving over them. It is known that Colman Mac Luachain was a night and a day under the river Brusna, and the water beasts came and ran races before him to welcome him. The swans at Killarney came at the call of Cainnech, those on Lough Foyle to Comgall. Meanwhile, the fire saints have brought down fire from heaven, or have prolonged daylight beyond reasonable expectation. Rain and snow evaporate around their glowing bodies; the streams in which they bathe produce clouds of steam. Molaisse of Devenish is called the Flaming Blaze; Molaisse of Inishmurray, the Red-plumed. Moling is the Sacred Fire. When they are not creating wonders, the saints retire to their beehive stone cells to pray. Bread and wild garlic is their diet. Time is not important to them. They look forward to the resurrection of the body, and the life of the world to come.

ERGOT

St Antony was born in Coma, Upper Egypt, in 251. When his parents died, he found himself possessed of a considerable estate, and charged with the care of his younger sister. He was not yet twenty. Six months later, he heard a preacher speak in church these words of Jesus to the rich young man: Go, sell what thou hast, and give it to the poor, and thou shalt have treasure in Heaven. Considering these words were spoken to himself, he gave away what land he had, except what he thought necessary for himself and his sister. Soon after, hearing in church these other words of Christ, Be not solicitous for tomorrow, he gave what remained to the poor, and placed his sister in a house of maidens. He then withdrew from the world. He lived on bread and salt and water, and took his rest on a rush mat. Yet Satan harassed him night and day with gross and obscene imaginations; in search of greater solitude, he retired further, to the interior of a ruined necropolis.

Concerning demons, Antony has this to say: There are two kinds of demons: those who are the offspring of women and angels, and those who are fallen angels; though why some of these should be cast down to hell and kept in chains of darkness, while others are left free to roam the earth, is not clear. The bastard demons will attempt to copulate with us, to reproduce their kind. The fallen ones, forever envious of us, who may achieve by grace the transcendental heights from whence they were cast out, will seek to terrorize us, and appear in the most extraordinary forms.

How often have they surrounded me like phalanxes of armed soldiers helmeted like beetles, their claws terminating in the tails of scorpions, and their fanged horses breathing brimstone in my face; how often have their regiments of insect beings seethed into my residence, so that my rush mat crawls across the earth invaded by them? How often have they crawled into my eyes? Or they come to me surrounded by a brilliant light, saying, We come to you, O Antony, to bring you our eternal light; but I have closed my eyes to it, and prayed, and that infernal clamour was extinguished. So if demons disguised as angels show themselves to you, arm yourselves, and your dwelling-places, with the cross, and they will disappear. For otherwise it is difficult to know demonic actions from angelic interventions, for an angel of darkness has the power to remember light and let himself be clothed in it. And their names, like Tutivillus, Asmodeus, Azazel, these too they can transfigure into holy names. Sometimes, they will not manifest their bodies, but will whisper lewd suggestions from the cavities in walls, or keep up all night a drunken revelry of youths or brigands playing with their whores: this is because the soul is disordered with bad thoughts, and despair, and moral turpitude.

It is believed that Antony caused these observations to be dictated in Coptic and written down in the form of epistles; but the papyruses have crumbled into dust. It is only thanks to the authority of Athanasius that these fragments of his thought remain. Antony is the master and the archetype of all anchorites and solitaries. About the year 285, he moved from his ruined tomb to a more remote abode high in the mountains, in which solitude he lived for twenty years in a deserted shepherd's hut, rarely seeing any man, except a follower who brought him dry bread every equinox. Of him he would ask, Who has the right to say to himself, I worked yesterday, today I can rest? Or to measure the time passed so as to waste away the future? The servant always puts the care of his soul above all other things, for if he disregards it for one instant, he will risk the fate of Judas who, that ill-starred night, lost the fruit of all his previous labour. But if we contemplate eternity, we will not cease to labour for it.

Such was the philosophy that caused rich and poor alike to importune him to descend to them. About the year 305 he came down and founded his first monastery at the Fayum. He did not dwell permanently with his disciples, but visited from time to time, crossing the crocodile-infested Arsinoitic canal on his journeys to them. In 311 he appeared in Alexandria to give courage to the martyrs persecuted by the Emperor of Rome. He publicly wore his tunic of white sheepskin, yet took care never to provoke the governor, as some rashly did. Returning to his mountain, he cultivated a small garden. It was there an angel visited him and showed him how to weave mats and baskets. In 355 he came to Alexandria again to confute the heretics of Arian. Even the pagans flocked to see and hear him; he converted many, and wrought miracles. It was in Alexandria that he met the blind catechist Didymus, and exhorted him not to regret the loss of eyes, which were common even to insects, but to regard the treasure of that inner light, by which we see God. It is related that St Antony, hearing his disciples express astonishment at the multitudes who embraced the religious state, told them with tears in his eyes that the time would come when monks would be fond of living in cities and stately buildings, of eating at well-laden tables, and be only distinguished from the persons of the world by their dress; but that still some amongst them would strive for true perfection.

He visited his monks shortly before his death. Knowing that it had become the fashion with many Christians to be embalmed, he exhorted his followers not to indulge this pagan custom with him, but to bury him in the earth in a secret place beside his mountain cell, where none might find his body, saying, In the day of the Resurrection I shall receive it incorruptible at the hand of Christ. He ordered them to give one of his sheepskins to the Bishop Athanasius, and the other to the Bishop Serapim, and to keep his sackcloth for themselves. He died in 365, at the age of one hundred and four. It is reported that he was fit and well until the day he died, that his vision was unimpaired, and that he had a full set of teeth, though they were slightly worn.

About the year 561 his remains are said to have been discovered and translated to Alexandria, thence to Constantinople, and eventually to Vienne, in France. The Bollandists printed an account of many miracles wrought by his intercession, especially those connected with the epidemic of the Wrath of God, the Sacred Fire, the Hell Fire, or St Antony's Fire, which raged in Europe in the eleventh century, about the time of the reputed translation of his relics thither. The disease existed in many forms. In some victims the abdominal viscera were affected and, although much pain was undergone, death was speedy. In others, an uncontrollable twitching of the limbs caused them to dance. New choreographies appeared daily. Swirling chains of dancers accompanied by stricken pipers lurched through the medieval squares in twisting sarabandes and tarantellas, dancing unto death, for they could not stop to sleep, nor eat, nor drink. They were enthralled by wildfire. As more victims joined in, the dancers' phalanx became a massive organism, that seemed possessed of independent motion. It thought in terms of waves and particles, of chemistries of complicated double helix curves, of interlocking swastikas of male and female chromosomes. The music generated by its willing slaves reached pitches hitherto unknown to the human ear, spiralling in baroque hierarchies of death. It seemed possessed of eternal life for, as its monads dropped off one by one, there were plenty more to take their place and join the long pavane.

In another form of the disease, the extremities were affected by dry gangrene. An icy chill developed in the arms and legs, and this was succeeded by a sensation like being tortured by hot irons.

As though consumed internally, the limbs became black, then shrivelled and fell from the body. Some died; many recovered, some with three limbs, some with two, and some with one. Others were left with a head and torso.

All these symptoms were preceded by a range of visions or hallucinations. People would sit for hours, engrossed in the folds of their garments, which seemed as undulating meadows shimmering with colour. Complex narratives could be discerned in the weave, as each thread proclaimed its origin and destiny. Shopkeepers were paralysed by the magnificence of their stock. Angels appeared to many, in trees especially, which responded to the merest zephyr with celestial whispers. Publicans and moneylenders were seen sprawled face-down in the common fields, examining the vast dimensions of the insect universe therein. New Messiahs were born daily.

It was to give succour to the victims of the Holy Fire that the Hospital Brothers of St Antony were founded in Clermont in 1096. Here, until recent years, were displayed a collection of withered and blackened limbs, relics of the afflicted. Here, too, are many images and ikons of St Antony. These are of two broad types. The first shows him being assaulted by demons; the second depicts him carrying a tau cross, a bell and a book, and being accompanied by a pig. Sometimes flames are indicated in both types. It is thought that the cross initially referred to the saint's use of it to banish demons; more latterly, it was associated with the crutch employed by victims of the Fire. Likewise, the pig was originally a semblance of the Devil, but acquired a new significance through the charitable work of the Brothers, which so endeared them to the people that they obtained the privilege of feeding their swine on the acorns and beech mast of the surrounding forests. Each pig had a bell attached to it, as an advertisement of its immunity to prosecution. As for the book, no doubt this refers to the book of nature which compensated the saint for the lack of any other reading matter. Antony is the patron saint of farm stock, butchers, brush-makers, basket-weavers, and epileptics.

It has long been established that St Antony's Fire is caused by eating bread infected with ergot, which is the black sclerotium of *Claviceps purpurea*, a sac-fungus growing within the developing grain of rye plants. It contains numerous alkaloids, many of which are toxic. Lysergic acid diethylamide (LSD) was first synthesized from ergot. Ergotamine, another derivative, is used in treating migraine, high blood pressure, and to facilitate uterine contraction in childbirth. The obstetric virtues of ergot are first mentioned in Loneer's 1582 edition of Rhodion's *Kreutterbuch*; and its fungoid nature was first recognized by Baron Otto von Munchausen in his *Rural Economy*, dated 1764.

Ergot is from Old French *argot*, a cock's spur, for its likeness to the mycelium of the fungus. Argot, the thieves' cant, may be similarly derived, as it forms an offshoot to the mainstream of the language. Picture the roads and the inns thronged with tinkers, tooth-drawers, pedlars, ostlers, carters, porters, horse-gelders and horse-leeches, idiots, apple-squires, broomsmen, bawds, chive-fencers, kinchen-coves, soothsayers and sow-gelders, rogues, rat-catchers, runagates, and proctors of spittlehouses, duffers and Dutch widows, forks, spooks, hackney carryknaves and hurry-whores, lumpers, little snakesmen, screevers, vampers, paper-hangers, Jemmy Jessamies, and waste-butts. Imagine the buzz and tangle of their lingo bullied into being, skimmed across the table like a marked deck, jabbered backwards into pockets, vanished into skive-time nooks and crannies of the labyrinthine premises, adopting foreign chits and chats as comrades, bosom-buddy bugger-lugs who snog the words regurgitated, spittle-fists of dealers, grifters, grafters of the wagging vine, Adamites, and sewer-navigators, roaches up for hire, who mangle lovingly the old material, and pass it off as shiny current coin.

The Autolycus of Shakespeare's *The Winter's Tale* is such a rogue, named after a son of Mercury: Autolycus, the prince of thieves, who carries a magic staff and a purse which conceals his stolen goods, while his cloak confers invisibility upon himself. He is a precursor of the cartoon burglar with his jemmy, swag-bag, stripy shirt, and mask, by which attributes he is known to the audience. The Autolycus of *The Winter's Tale* is a snapper-up of unconsidered trifles, a trafficker in stolen linen − inkles, caddises, cambrics, lawns − *'you would think a smock were a she-angel, he so chants to the sleeve-hand and the work about the square on't.'* He sells trumpery to gullibles at shearing fairs: ribbons, glass, pomanders, brooches, knives, tapes, gloves, shoe-ties, bangles. He is a wise-guy. He is a cut-purse and a ballad-monger:

> *Lawn as white as driven snow,*
> *Cypress black as e'er was crow,*
> *Gloves as sweet as damask roses,*

Masks for faces, and for noses;
Bugle-bracelet, necklace amber,
Perfume for a lady's chamber . . .

The girls crowd around him as he displays the contents of his bundle. They love a ballad in print, for then they are sure they are true. '*Here's one,*' says Autolycus, '*to a very doleful tune, how a usurer's wife was brought to bed of twenty money-bags at a burden, and how she longed to eat adders' heads and toads carbonadoed*' — '*Very true, and but a month old.*' And here's another, '*of a fish that appeared upon the coast on Wednesday the fourscore of April, forty thousand fathom above water, and sung this ballad against the hard hearts of maids. It was thought she was a woman, and was turned into a cold fish for she would not exchange flesh with one that loved her. The ballad is very pitiful, and as true.*'

Autolycus flits in and out of the action, donning or whipping off his false beard, and trying to con everyone he meets. His mercurial role is crucial to the masque-like, romantic improbability of the plot, which Shakespeare, as usual, has stolen from another source, Robert Greene's *Pandosto: The Triumph of Time*. No doubt Greene had his own sources. It is said he died of a surfeit of Rhenish wine and pickled herrings.

The story of *The Winter's Tale* goes more or less like this: Polixenes, king of Bohemia, is visiting his childhood friend, Leontes, king of Sicilia. Leontes begs him stay a while longer, but Polixenes is adamant that he must get home, for you never know what goes on when your back's turned, and he'd love to stay, but business is business. Leontes then asks his wife to put in a few words, and she talks to great effect, reminding Polixenes of the days when he and her king were lads, et cetera, and she charms him into staying, and she takes him by the hand. '*Too hot, too hot*', says the Sicilian king, '*to mingle friendship far is mingling bloods*', and he takes a mad fit of jealousy. One bad thing leads to another. Polixenes, advised by Camillo, a lord at the court, makes good his escape. This only serves to confirm Leontes in his worst imaginings. Hermione has a baby girl, which Leontes takes to be Polixenes' bastard. He has the whole royal household in an awful turmoil. His son falls badly ill. He blames this on the alleged adultery. He orders the baby to be banished. He sends messengers to the oracle at Delphi, asking it to confirm his story. The messengers come back with the oracle's pronouncement: '*Hermione is chaste, Polixenes blameless, Camillo a true subject, Leontes a jealous tyrant, his innocent babe truly begotten, and the king shall live without an heir if that which is lost be not found.*' Lies, says Leontes. A servant appears and tells him his son has just died. Leontes realizes his mistake. Hermione falls down as if dead and is taken away. Meanwhile the baby girl has been found on the coast of Bohemia by a shepherd and his son. They will rear her as their own.

Sixteen years go by. To cut a long story short, Florizel, the prince of Bohemia, falls in love with the beautiful shepherdess. Polixenes won't have her, and disowns his son. But of course the proofs of her real identity are discovered, and everyone is reconciled. Leontes now has only one regret, that Hermione is dead. Act V, Scene 3: Paulina, a lady at his court, has commissioned a statue of the late queen which she proceeds to exhibit to Leontes.

He is amazed at the likeness, except he reckons Hermione was not as wrinkled in life as she now appears. Of course this gives the audience a pretty broad hint that it is indeed Hermione, who wasn't dead at all; but Shakespeare does a great job in spinning out the situation. Leontes and Hermione eventually embrace; Leontes disentangles himself to tie up a few loose ends in the happy ending, and they all *Exeunt*.

This summary, I realize, leaves out most of the play, which is embodied in the language. Even the Old Shepherd's son, the Clown, has a power of words, as he describes, for instance, the wreck of the ship which bore the baby Perdita to the wild coast of land-locked Bohemia, the ship boring the moon with her main-mast, and anon swallowed with yeast and froth, as you'd thrust a cork into a hogshead. Or the gossiping Gentlemen, piecing together the latest reports of the action: '*The oracle is fulfilled . . . Such a deal of wonder is broken out within this hour, that ballad-makers cannot be able to express it . . . How goes it now, sir? . . . Did you see the meeting of the two kings? . . . No . . . Then have you lost a sight which was to be seen, cannot be spoken of.*'

I can easily imagine amber-fishers on that mythic shore, where transformations of identity are common. I'm reminded of the magic origins of Lough Neagh, whose water readily converts wood into stone. Numberless pieces of this fossil-wood are found on or near the shore, and may be seen adorning gardens, rock-eries, and shrubberies in the vicinity. In the Ulster Museum is a large piece of a trunk of a tree, weighing many hundreds of pounds, in which the bark and the fibres are as distinct as in a living tree. Holly is popularly regarded as a kind of wood most readily susceptible to the petrifying action of the water. Sticks of the fossilized wood are used for sharpening scythes and razors, hence the hawkers' call, *Lough Neagh hones, Lough Neagh hones! You put 'em in sticks and you take 'em out stones!* Many of the Lough Neagh fishermen spent so long in the water, trawling and the like, if popular opinion be true, that while remaining upward men, they were downward stone, and had no need to buy hones for their razors; all they had to do was turn up their trousers, and sharpen them on their shins. The Revd Richard Barton, referring to a particular specimen in one of his lectures, says, That it is a whetstone, which, as Mr Anthony Shane, Apothecary, who was born very near the lake, and is now alive, relates, he made by putting a piece of holly in the water of the lake near his father's house, and marking the place so as to distinguish it, he went to Scotland to pursue his studies, and seven years after, he took up a stone instead of holly, the metamorphosis having been made in that time. This account he gave under his handwriting.

But now a month has passed, and we are assembled again at the Cranfield Inn on the shores of the Lough. There is a good fire blazing in the hearth, and the landlord has set up some good whiskey punch, and my father begins the second episode of Jack the Lad's story:

FOXGLOVE

Once upon a time, and it was a long time ago, there was a king in the north of Ireland, who secretly married his swineherd's daughter. She had a son. They called him Peter. The king was ashamed that anyone might find out he had married one of such a low degree, so he put his son away till he grew to be a man, and would have hidden him longer, only for what I'm going to tell you now.

There was a Knight-at-arms who lived close by the king's castle, and a great friendship sprang up between himself and Peter. They often used to go out hunting and fishing together. The Knight taught Peter how to use a sword, and he'd make him little secret gifts of gold and silver, and Peter had a horse, hounds and a hawk, just like the king himself, except the king didn't know it.

One day the king was alone in his chamber, and he started pondering his state, and he said to himself, Wasn't I the great fool not to have married some great lady long ago, and I'd have a proper heir to leave my kingdom to when I am gone. Better late than never, says he, the king of Munster has a good-looking daughter, and I'm sure I'll get her hand in marriage.

Early the next morning the king arose. My chariot! he says, Men-at-arms! And he got together a great retinue, and off he goes at top speed, and he doesn't stop till he comes to the province of Munster, and enters the king's castle there, and he asks for his daughter. It's not for me, says the king of Munster, to give my daughter against her will, but if she wishes it, you can have her, and welcome. So they sent for Medbh – that was her name – and when she came up, her father said, Here's a noble king from Ulster, and he's come a long way asking that he wants to marry you, my daughter, and would you like to marry him?

– I wouldn't have him, says the daughter, if he was the last man in Ireland, and I'll tell you what, I'd rather marry his son.

The king from the north flew into a rage at that, and he swore she was a liar, that he had no son.

– You're a liar yourself, says she, a liar without honour.

– I'll prove with my sword that I'm no liar, says he.

– You will not, says she, and by the sword of Munster, I will make you own up to your lies, before you go back to the swine-herd's daughter.

– I am no coward, says the king, I don't fight women.

– I know you are a coward, says she, and with that she grabbed a sword from the wall, and made a swing at him. He put up his left hand to protect himself, and she took the hand off him. Now, says she, you can go back to your pig-woman, I've got my satisfaction from you.

– I'd rather be with one hand, says he, than be married to a witch!

When the king was going home his men asked how he had lost his hand. Fighting a lion, says he, and I beat the lion.

When he arrived home the people took great pity on him, for losing his hand to the lion. But before long the truth started to come out, and it wasn't pity that they felt then, but they laughed at him behind his back, and they made up this rhyme:

> *There once was a king, and here's the dirt –*
> *He lost his hand while chasing skirt.*

The king was raging when he heard this, but he didn't let on that he knew it was him they had in mind.

One day the king and the nobles went out hunting. When the deer was started out of the wood they all followed, but the nobles got out ahead of the king, for he wasn't the horseman he'd been before he lost his hand. He followed the track of the horses till he came to the edge of a wood. He lost the track then, and he was thinking of going back, when he saw a beautiful woman riding on a snow-white steed. He hailed the lady, and she hailed him back, saying, Don't go any further, for the deer is dead.

– Who killed it? says the king.

– Your own son, says she, the swineherd's daughter's son. Listen to me now, says she, if you want to go on living, conceal your son no longer. I am the daughter of the king of the Golden Isle. I live within the Mountain of the Fay, and if you want to marry me, I'm ready to marry you. If you go to my father I am certain he will give you my hand in marriage.

The king fell in love with the beautiful lady at first sight, and he said he'd go with her, and that he would ask her father for her, but he didn't know where his kingdom might be. Come here, says she, and take my horse's reins, and I'll take yours. With that she spoke some words the king couldn't make out, and in the twinkling of an eye he was flying through the air beside the lady.

When they came to the foot of the mountain, they alighted, and she said some more words. The mountain opened, and she walked in, and he walked in behind her. They had not been long walking when they came to a fine garden where every sort of fruit and flower grew. There was a castle at the far side of the garden. They crossed the garden and entered the castle. The lady knocked on a door, and the door opened, and they both went into a grand room. There was a throne there, and a great grey-bearded man sitting on it. This was the king of the Golden Isle. Father, says she, this is the king of Ulster, and he has come to ask for me in marriage.

— He won't get you, says the father, for he's nothing but a disreputable scoundrel, and if he doesn't go back and make a lawful queen of the swineherd's daughter, I'll have him strung up by his heels on the top of the mountain, for the birds of the air to pick the meat from his bones. Out with you now, and leave the rascal where you found him.

They walked back out of the mountain. The two horses were

still there. They got up on them, flew through the air, and she left him at the edge of the wood where she had found him. They bade each other goodbye, and she said, Do as my father says, or he'll do to you what he said he'd do.

– Now, noble lady and assembled company (said Jack the Lad), all of what had happened to the king was a only a dream. The truth was, the king had thought to take a short-cut through the wood, and he'd run into a big tree, and knocked himself silly. And while he was lying there unconscious, he had this vision. When the hunters returned they found the king standing at the edge of the wood. They asked what had happened to him that he didn't follow them. I think my horse must be blind, says he, for he ran me into a tree and I got an awful batter. Who killed the deer, by the way?

– Peter did, said they, not knowing he was the king's son.

They brought the king home and the doctors were sent for. They told him not to stir out of his bed for seven days, and he'd be all right after that. Now, the king was convinced that he had gone to the Golden Isle with the beautiful lady, but he didn't let on to anyone. When he was better, he sent for the swineherd's daughter and told her he was truly sorry he hadn't given her official recognition until then. He would announce that she was his lawful wife, and they would have a proper wedding. He sent out invitations to the lords and ladies of the province. A great crowd came. When they had all gathered, he called on his son Peter, and said, This is my one and only son, whom I have hidden away till now.

At that time, it was the custom for rhymers and guisers to

68

attend the weddings, and there was a big team of them about that day. There was one joker amongst them, and he came out with this verse:

> *The very best wedding I ever was at –*
> *The one-handed king and the swineherd's brat.*

The king flew into a rage, and he said, Catch hold of that trickster, and bring him here, till I run my sword through him. So they got the trickster, and when they pulled off his disguise, who was it but the Knight-at-arms, the friend of the king's son.

So Peter was in a rage too, and he says to the Knight, I never thought that you would bring dishonour to me, or my parents, on such an occasion. My father may not get satisfaction from you, but I will. Be at the foot of the hill tomorrow morning and we'll see which is the better man. Fair enough, says the Knight, and he called out:

> *Tomorrow morn, you can be sure,*
> *There'll be a mighty spat*
> *When the Knight-of-arms comes up against*
> *The swineherd's daughter's brat!*

Then the king called his men and ordered them to show everyone out of the castle, save his wife and son, and his servants, and to shut the gates.

The king's son was sorrowful that night, alone in his room, thinking about the day that was before him, and the battle with his best friend. His mother and father came to try to talk him out of it, but it was no use; he said he'd prefer death to dishonour.

Next morning he rose early, put on his gear, and went to the foot of the hill. The Knight was there waiting for him. They shook hands. I never thought, said the King's son, that I would ever see us fight.

– Nor did I, but it was you who asked for it. I am known as the Knight-at-arms, and the name means nothing if I do not fight you.

The two unscabbarded their swords and fell to. Then the hack and thrust began. They made heavy weather of the light, and light of heavy weather, and they smoothed the rough and roughed the smooth, and water ran from the rugged rocks with the weight of the war they wrought. Forked lightning from their swords lit up the ground for miles around. Then, as the sun declined in the sky, the king's son said, Time to stop until tomorrow.

– Fair enough, I will be here tomorrow at break of day, says the Knight.

Next morning the two heroes were found at the foot of the hill at dawn. If they had fought hard the day before, the fight this day was seven times as hard. No fight like it had been seen in Ireland since the Fight at the Ford, between Cuchulainn and Ferdia. Just as the sun was going down that second day, the Knight-at-arms dealt the king's son a mortal blow, and he fell dead.

Shortly afterwards, the queen, the swineherd's daughter, was alone in the castle gardens, lamenting the death of her son, when an old woman suddenly appeared at her side.

– You are grieving, says the old woman, tell me the cause of your woe.

70

– I had a fine son, and the Knight-at-arms killed him, says the queen.

– If I got satisfaction from the Knight-at-arms, you'd have no cause for sorrow, says the old lady.

– I will grieve forever, says the queen, but it is a great grief that no one got satisfaction from the Knight.

– Control your grief, says the old lady, for I will get satisfaction from the Knight-at-arms – for you, and for myself. I had a daughter once, and the Knight reneged on his promise to marry her. I have magic powers, but it was not permitted for me to go near the Knight until he killed your son. Now that it has been done, he is in my power, and I'll put him in such a plight, that he'll never draw sword again. This I will do before sunrise tomorrow.

The old woman vanished; and when dusk fell, she took the juice from seven bells of foxglove, known also as the Fairy Thimbles, and she smeared it on her magic wand. She changed her customary shape, and she went to the house of the Knight-at-arms. Now, the Knight was in love with a young noblewoman, whom he hoped to marry. The old woman told him that his love was waiting on the Lough Neagh shore, and that he must come quick, for the noblewoman had words of import to impart to him. Off went the Knight with the old woman; but no sooner had he reached the shore, than she struck him with her holly wand, and he was turned into stone.

The next morning the queen was walking in the garden when the old woman appeared by her side.

– Queen, says the old woman, I have done what I promised.

The Knight will never draw sword again. He is now a heap of stones lying by the Lough shore, and he will never find succour, but must stay there until the woman he loves comes to him, and calls him by his name; but that will never happen till the crack of doom, for she'll never know that it is he who lies there in the form of a stone cairn.

— What can I do for you, for all that you have done for me? says the queen.

— You need do nothing for me, and I will ask nothing from you. I have my own satisfaction for the trick he played on my daughter. That was all I wanted. That is my reward.

With that, she vanished just as suddenly as she had appeared.

The Knight still lies on the Lough shore, a heap of stones from that day to this, and so he'll be forever, unless the one he loves can free him.

Now, my honourable companions, no one else in Ireland has that story but myself. And it wasn't from one person, or two or three, that I got it, but I got it from all over the place, and I put the whole thing together in such a way that it is the truth, the whole truth, and nothing but the truth; and if you'll allow me, I'll have another story for you all tomorrow night. No sooner were these words out of his mouth, than the last drip fell from the water-clock.

That was a good story, said one of the men, as he pulled out his wand and tapped the white greyhound at his feet. She turned into a fine lady again. The rest of the men did the same to their hounds, and they too turned into ladies. The door opened in the wall, the men and women bowed to the lady of the house, and they walked out slowly and majestically, with the women on the men's shoulders, as they had before. The door closed noiselessly behind them. Now that Jack and the lady of the house were left alone, it seemed to him she didn't look herself. A light would flicker in her eyes, then fade away. Three times she opened her mouth to speak, and three times she thought better of it. Eventually, she went out without a word.

The doorman came in. A good supper was spread before Jack, and when he had eaten it, the doorman took him to bed, where he fell sound asleep.

Jack spent the next day as he had spent the day before. He saw none of the fine company, nor the mistress of the house, nor anyone else save the doorman, who maintained a stony silence to anything Jack would ask him about the goings-on. When night came, he was summoned to the big candle-lit chamber, where the lady sat in her chair. She greeted him, and asked if he was ready to begin his story. Jack said he was. She put a little gold trumpet to her mouth and gave it a blast. Instantly, the big door opened in the wall, and the twelve men walked in, with their twelve women on their shoulders. They sat down as they had done the night before, and the lady said, Begin your story. Jack began . . .

Well, said my father, it looks like the story's going to take longer than I thought. Why don't we all meet here again in a month's time, and I can tell you the next episode?

We had all one or two or a few drinks taken when someone

suggested going out for some air. It was a beautiful cold night, unseasonably clear for November. We stood beneath the old cypress tree in Cranfield churchyard and gazed upwards at the stars, trying to make out their figures and to tell their stories, and the legends which preceded them. I thought of foxgloves, constellated by a wooded lane, whispering their plurality of names: Witches' Gloves, Dead Men's Bells, Fairy's Glove, Bloody Fingers, Folk's Glove, Fairy Thimbles, Fairy's Petticoat. Though the foxglove is a favourite with bees, and other insects, who may be seen taking refuge from cold and wet in its droop-ing blossoms, no animals will browse upon the plant; and some steer well clear of it, instinctively recognizing its poisonous character. Yet, like most poisons, foxglove, if scrupulously administered, is a valuable remedy: distilled as digitalis, it is a cure for heartache and for dropsy. Culpeper says it is a gentle, cleansing herb, good for healing a fresh wound, the leaves being bruised and bound thereon; and the juice thereof is also used in old sores, to cleanse, and dry and heal them; it is a capital remedy for a scabby head. In large doses, the action of digitalis on the circulation causes various cerebral symptoms, such as seeing all objects blue, and various other disturbances, such as sensations of flying, and being able to hear what the wind says by way of the trees and chimney-pots. Should it be called for, atropine is an antidote to digitalis: *similia similibus curantur*, like is cured by like. For atropine is Deadly Nightshade, Atropa Belladonna, Devil's Cherries, Great Morel, Bad Man's Cherry, Devil's Herb. When Duncan I was king of Scotland, the soldiers of Macbeth poisoned a whole army of invading Danes by a liquor infused with Deadly Nightshade, as they drank a toast to the truce. Suspecting nothing, the Danes drank deeply and fell comatose, and were murdered in their sleep by the Scots. For atropine derives from Atropos, she of the Greek Fates who holds the scissors to snip the thread of life.

Belladonna dilates the pupils, and its juice was used by Venetian belladonnas to enhance the brilliance of their eyes, as they glided down the dark canals in gondolas, accompanied by silent escorts, gazing at the lamps reflected there. The Greek astronomers used belladonna to enhance the brilliance of the stars, and thus they traced their constellated diagrams of dot-to-dot. For everything, they reckoned, drugged by belladonna, must connect, since what has happened is forever, and behind the story that we tell today another story lies. So before we can discuss the fate of Ganymede, we must outline that of Orpheus.

GANYMEDE

Orpheus had won Eurydice. Taking up his lyre, he summoned Hymen to the wedding. He sang in the voice which had charmed lions and tigers, and played the music which had caused the very trees to shiver in an ecstasy of dance. Passing through the measureless expanse of air, the marriage-god alighted in his saffron cloak, brandishing his nuptial torch. But that day there was to be no happy flame; usually reliable at such festivities, the flambeau puffed and guttered, giving forth rank smells instead of light. The face of Hymen was obscure. Tears sprang to the eyes of guests and ushers blinded by the smoke. Worse was to come. Momentarily to escape the atmosphere, Eurydice strolled down to the banks of a winding stream. Here, willow branches trailed in the water and fireflies moved like finely broken starlight through the purple leaves. Then from a deep pool appeared

Aristaeus, god of bees, and olive oil, and wine: beneficent deity, son of Apollo by the nymph Cyrene. His wet shoulders glistened in the moonlight. He was smitten instantly by Eurydice's beauty. He would possess her there and then.

He stepped out naked from the darkness. He smiled at her. She held her breasts. She faltered back a step. She turned. Through moonlit groves and dew-drenched grass she ran. She heard the breathing of the god behind her. A snake was hidden in the grass. She stepped on it, and slithered over it, and instantly it flickered forth its fangs, and bit her on the heel. She fell. She died before the god of olive oil and wine could taste her living soul.

So Orpheus found her stone dead. He took up his lyre and sang his grief to all who breathed the upper air, both gods and men. He sang to the lions, whose animal ferocity might bring her back to life. He sang to the very trees, that they might, by their power of shoot and leaf, resuscitate her. He complained bitterly, with all his artistry of string and cord. It was all of no avail. When every plea had been rejected, he descended by the Taenarus portal to the Stygian realm. There, through unsubstantial throngs and ghosts of former beings long since buried, he moved, feeling them sometimes breathe invocations in his ear, or touch his eyelids with their clammy fingers. At last he reached the throne of Pluto and Persephone, the guardians of that dreary region of the dead. Then, taking up his lyre again, he sang once more:

– O gods who rule the nether world, to which we mortal beings must return, allow me this plain song that has no double meaning, for it speaks the unembroidered truth. I come not as a tourist of the dark abyss of Tartarus, nor do I wish to view Medusa's monstrous offspring. The reason for my journey is my wife, whose body was infected by the venom of a viper in the grass, who snatched away her budding years. I know I should endure her fate, and I have tried to do so. But the god of Love has vanquished me, a god well-noted in the upper world, but whether here or not I do not know; yet I surmise that he is known here as well; and if the story of that famous rape is true, you too were joined by Love. By these fearsome places, by these vast chaotic silent realms, I implore you to unravel what has been, and make my too-soon-taken-from-me Eurydice alive again. For we must finally attend to you, and whatever time we have on earth is your dominion. To you we must all make our way at last; this is our final home. She will be yours again when she has lived the years she should have lived. I ask her living body of you, who have power over life and death; but if the fates deny this privilege, I will not return. Praise then the death of two.

And as he spoke, accompanying his words with plangent music, the captive spirits of that realm wept to hear him. Tantalus gave up his everlasting quest for drink; Ixion's eternal wheel stopped dead; the vultures paused from pecking at the liver of the giant Tityus; and Sisyphus himself forgot to roll his monstrous stone uphill. Nor could the rulers of the underworld remain unmoved. Pluto and Persephone called Eurydice. She was but a new ghost, and came limping with her wounded foot. Orpheus received his wife on this condition, that he should walk before her as he took her from the dark world to the realm of light, but never to look back at her. They walked the upward-sloping path through stairs and corridors of utter silence, he pulling her behind him as they pushed against the horizontal wind of Hades, clouded by infernal lightless flame. And now, as they approached the margin of the upper world, afraid she might not make the final step, he turned round to encourage her, and instantly she slipped into the depths. He stretched his arms towards her, eager for her clasp again; he clutched the void. Now, dying for a second time, how could Eurydice complain? For what complaint had she, except that she was loved by Orpheus? She spoke her last farewell; but the words, dwindling away from him, hardly reached his ears. She fell back to the realm of the newer ghosts.

Orpheus was stunned by Eurydice's double death. He felt like someone turned to stone. He roused himself. He tried to cross the Styx a second time; but the dark ferryman repulsed him with his oar. For seven days he crouched there on that gloomy bank in squalid guise, with nothing to sustain him but his grief, with not a drop to drink except his tears. Then, complaining bitterly against the cruel gods of Erebus, he took himself to Rhodope and wind-swept Haemus. Three times the sun passed through the sign of Pisces; and Orpheus had shunned all carnal knowledge of the other sex. Many women made advances to him; but all were disappointed. And it was he who introduced to Thrace the art of loving tender boys, enjoying them before their bloom of youth had gone.

There was a hill, and on the hill a level plain luxuriant with green grass; but there was no shade in that verdant place. So Orpheus took up the lyre, and summoned shady trees to him. Here came the mighty creaking oak, the slender tamarisk, the pool-adoring lotus, and the ash-tree, good for spear-shafts; pussy willows came, and noble beeches, and the sisters Heliades, who'd been changed to poplars after Phaeton's death; the ilexes were there, and cedars from the distant Lebanon, accompanied by nervous hazels; the planes, whose spreading leaves afford the perfect cover for a festive party, made themselves at home; sloe-eyed myrtles danced attendance on the box-trees, good for tuning-pegs and flutes; the azaleas and rhododendrons spread themselves around; and aspens whispered of their happiness to meet the spindle-trees. Wisteria was there, and fondly twining ivy. Vines with grapes in blue abundance vied with plum-trees for the prize of soothing juice. The Ponderosa pine exuded amber odours over and above the aromatic bays. Emblematica of victory, the super-supple palm-trees wafted in to nod and bow before the seated poet.

Amidst this congregation was the cone-shaped cypress, now a tree, but once a boy, beloved by the god who strings the bow and lyre. There was a stag, the sacred pet of certain nymphs, whose broad-extended antlers made a mighty shade. Gold studs shone in his horns; an amber necklace fell from his shoulders; upon his brow, a silver bubble-ball, tied up with little straps. Pearly ear-rings dangled from his lobes. This noble animal was friendly, and devoid of fear. Often he would walk into a neighbour's house, there to be patted; he would even nuzzle up to strangers. But no one loved him more than Cyparissus, lovely boy of Cea. For you, O Cyparissus, led the stag to running springs and pastures new. You garlanded his horns with scarlet flowers; at other times, you'd be his bare-back rider, urging him to go this way or that, twitching his mouth with your purple bridle.

It was one high noon of a summer season, when the shore-adoring Crab lies stricken by the sun. The stag lay panting in the coolness of the woods. Cyparissus did not see him hidden in the ferns, and stumbled over him. His naked javelin went through the animal. He could not bear to watch him die, and begged for death himself; but Phoebus, god of noon, commanded him to rein his passion. To no avail: the youth had set his mind on death, and asked that he might mourn forever. The other gods were good to him, and granted him his wish: for now his blood became like chlorophyll, and his whole body was imbued with green; his hair became the spiky cypress crown beneath the starry sky. All tree finally, he creaks and groans, and grieves for those who grieve like him.

Such was the grove the bard had summoned to that place. There he sat in majesty, surrounded by the birds and beasts. And when he tried his lyre again, he found a strange new pitch; the hitherto impossible in music came to him, and so he sang: O parent muse, O mighty Jove, whose power I have often sung, inspire my song, and Titans, whom I oft invoke in order to be struck by lightning, give me now the gentler touch, for I would sing of boys beloved by gods, and maidens twice betrayed by wanton lust. For here is Zeus, who burned with love for Ganymede, the slender lad; so much he did adore him, that he had to change his shape, and take on wings. No ordinary bird was he: royal eagle, he descended from the sky, and snatched the Trojan boy away; and captured Ganymede is languishing in heaven still, obliged to bring the cups of wine to Zeus, who fondles him eternally.

*

Ganymede, according to the Ancients, became Aquarius, the constellation of the Water Bearer. In our astronomy, Ganymede is one of the four satellites of Jupiter (the others are Io, Europa and Callisto) first perceived by Galileo with his telescope, on the 7th of January, 1610. Before that, he had viewed the Moon, and discovered that it was not, as the philosophers maintained, a perfect sphere: on the contrary, it was full of inequalities, uneven, pitted and pock-marked; it had hollows and protuberances, like the surface of the Earth itself, which is varied everywhere by lofty mountains and deep valleys. Indeed, the prominences and depressions in the Moon surpassed in magnitude the ruggedness of the Earth's surface.

Galileo, it is said, constructed his telescope from hearsay, after descriptions of an instrument known as 'the Dutch trunk', or 'the Holland spectacles', which had been circulating in Europe for some years. According to one story, some time around the year 1600 two children were playing in the workshop of an obscure Dutch glasses-maker, Hans Lippershey of Middelburg (capital of Selandor, or Zeeland), when they put two lenses together and looked out the window through them. Terrified, they dropped the lenses, and ran in to tell the craftsman they had seen a monster cock at the window: this was the weathercock on the church steeple. Lippershey put two and two together, and constructed the first telescope. In another version, the children are his own; they are playing in the garden, and they see birds roosting in the far-off steeple. These anecdotes may have some relevance to the researches of John Henry van Swindon, who found documents among the government papers at The Hague that showed on the 2nd October 1608, the Assembly considered the petition of a John Lipperhey (*sic*) of Middelburg, inventor of an instrument for seeing at a distance. A commission was appointed to look into the matter, and the instrument was tested from the tower of Prince Maurice's house. The findings surpassed all expectations: the rigging of distant men-o'-war, bejewelled with the salt spray, appeared like close-up spiders' webs; the details of the sailors' apparel were clearly visible, down to the buttons; and, in one case, the smoke from a captain's meerschaum was the subject of a grand debate, as to whether the tobacco was Virginia or Maryland. Lipperhey was instructed to make three similar instruments, of rock crystal, and to keep the details of its manufacture secret. He was paid 900 florins for one. On the 15th December he exhibited a binocular instrument to the Commission, and was ordered to make two more; but as the invention had become known they did not give him the exclusive rights of manufacture.

However, van Swindon had also found in the library at Leyden, among the Huygens manuscripts, an original copy of a petition, also dated 1608, and addressed to the States General by Jacob Adriaanzoon, alternatively known as James Metius, a native of Alkmaar, in which he sought the exclusive rights to sell just such an instrument. This, he claimed, had been invented by him accidentally, and he had so perfected it, that it was as good, if not better, than the one lately offered by a spectacle-maker of Middelburg. He was told to perfect it still further; we have no record of the outcome.

Pierre Borel, physician to the king of France, disputes these accounts in his *De Vero Telescopii Inventore*, published in 1655. His chief witness was William Boreel, the Dutch Envoy to the French Court, who attributed the invention to a Zacharias Jansen of Middelburg, son of Hans Jansen, on the sworn evidence of Hans Jansen's grandson, who said his father had constructed a telescope in 1610, and also that of his grand-daughter, who gave either 1611 or 1619 as the date. Three other persons, notes Borel, claimed that Lipperhey had been the inventor, giving the dates as 1605, 1609 and 1610; but they were, he says, 'of unreliable character'. Boreel supports his claim by a somewhat rambling anecdote, which is here considerably abridged in the translation:

– It was the year 1610 or so, and many rumours were abroad regarding the wonderful invention, whereby it was possible to see gargoyles spouting water from the spire of a church in the next parish, or, indeed, if one were so inclined, to gaze into the parlour of a house across the canal and identify the place-names on a map of the United Provinces displayed on the back wall, not to mention the details of a piece of lace being worked on by the hands of a young girl sitting at the window in the sunlight. About that year, a stranger came to Middelburg. His appearance was much commented on by the populace. He wore the typical holland shirt of the time, reaching below the calf when first put on, but hitched up around the pantaloons so that six or seven inches of loose shirt would be bloused around the waist. Over this, the long knee-length waistcoat, all embroidered, with cloth-covered buttons down the front and the sleeves split at the wrist to turn back over the deep cuff of the full-skirted coat, with the flare of

the skirts commencing well below the hips, and the large pockets used as decoration, for, to tell the truth, they were so far
down to the hem that the stranger's hands would find it difficult
to find their bottoms, but a sharp pick-pocket might make light
work there. Rolled ribbon-gartered stockings over high-heeled
buckled shoes. The wide slabbering-bib cravat at the neck of the
shirt. The scarlet sash and the green morocco-leather sword-
belt. Over the long curly wig he had the grand beaver hat with a
peacock's feather in it, and the wide hard brim rolled up to the
side and turned down to the front, so the stranger's eyes were
shaded by it. And the bunches of ribbons all over the place from
shoulder to toe.

We have it on the evidence of the churchwarden's wife that the
stranger stopped in the middle of the main street in Middelburg
and produced a pair of green spectacles from out of his muff. She
distinctly remembers the jessamy gloves he was wearing, for they
were but lately in fashion in Amsterdam when she had visited
there the week before; and he put the spectacles up to his nose,
and looked about him, at the various signs on the shops, and the
inns, and what-have-you. Then, she says, he was approached by
van Tromp the candlestick-maker, and she thinks van der Vaal the
amber-dealer, and the stranger doffs his beaver and makes a low
bow, and conjures up a little silver snuff-box with the Lion of the
Netherlands engraved on it, and flicks it open, and he offers it to
the gentlemen concerned. The next thing, she says, she sees
them going into Lipperhey's shop close by.

Now – continues Boreel – comes the crux of the matter. For
it transpires that the stranger, on enquiring as to where he might

get the frame of his spectacles repaired, for the bridge of them
cut into his nose so, had been mistakenly guided by these wor-
thies to the aforementioned Lipperhey, when it was common
knowledge in the town that Jansen was the better man for optical
equipment, and had been established long before Hans Lipperhey
came in from Wessel with his two pairs-for-the-price-of one.
Van Tromp's evidence comes next. It seems the stranger, after a
great show of exhibiting the dents on the bridge of his nose to
Lipperhey, saying how much he would be in his debt, et cetera,
and taking out a silk purse from his muff, proceeded to casually
enquire about a new device he had good report of, that brought
the far horizon to a hand's breadth from the face, and so on.
Now Lipperhey might not have been the craftsman Jansen was,
but he was always good with words, and shrewd with it. So he
says to the stranger, Well, sir, exactly what sort of device would
you have in mind here, for we've quite a few models, and of
course, there's six months of a waiting-list, for there's a great
demand for these devices right now, and would it be the No. 1
you want, which is your basic nautical device, or the 3a, which is
very good for close-quarter spy-work, sir, says Lipperhey. Of
course Lipperhey didn't know a telescope from a hole in a dike
wall at this stage. So the stranger says, thinking he had the right
man here, O, you know, one of the simpler models, the ones
where you have the two lenses, and you have your basic concave
and your convex, and you put them together in a long leather
tube, and away you go, he says – and offers Lipperhey a pinch of
snuff – and, he says, of course I can get them ready-made back in
Holland, but I was passing this way on business, and had heard so

much about your establishment, I thought I'd drop in. The point being, says Boreel, that the rogue Lipperhey elicited from the stranger the information necessary to construct a telescope of his own, and was to thereafter claim he had invented it, and he made up some cock-and-bull story about the children playing with a pair of lenses in the backyard.

Here we will abridge Boreel's account further, as the company he has been describing adjourns to a nearby tavern, and some pages are devoted to a description of the various spirits, beers, and tobaccos available there, together with an analysis of the complicated round system then in vogue. However, returning to his main theme, Boreel gives the stranger's name as Cornelius Drebel, who upon his return to Holland (i.e. the province) met up with Adrian Metius (i.e. the aforementioned Jacob, or James Adriaanzoon, also called James Metius) and, learning of his mistake, was persuaded by Metius to go back with him to Zeeland, to Jansen's shop, where Drebel purchased several telescopes of him, including a very fine specimen mounted in amber. Q.E.D. Furthermore, says Boreel earlier on in the document quoted, *Jansen also invented the microscope* —

Middelburg, the capital of Selandor, is my native place, and I have many happy memories of playing in the shadow of its beautiful star-shaped fortifications, which, when scaled, afford a magnificent view of the city and the many twists and turns of its picturesque old *graachten*, or waterways, for the transportation of goods to and from the merchants' houses on their banks. Here you can admire the beautifully crafted brickwork of the *Kloveniersdoelen*, or Marksmen's Guild Hall, with its bas-relief representations of the *klovenier*, or long musket; or contemplate the grand façade of the *Stadhuis*, or Town Hall, with its figures of twenty-five Counts and Countesses of Zeeland and Holland, under canopies surmounted by fabulous animals, which have all, happily, survived the bombing in the recent war. I should mention also the magnificent *Onze Lieve Vrouwe Abdij*, or Abbey of Our Lady, established by the White Canons of St Norbert, founder of the Norbertine Order, of whom the Canons are its most august and spiritual expression: one can easily get lost in this picturesque and many-towered complex of buildings, when one thinks of its cloisters, chapter houses, chapels, choirs, and all the ancillary features of kitchens, galleys, cellars, stairways, alcoves, studies, libraries, printing-presses, dungeons, parlours, corridors, dormitories, bedrooms, boudoirs, closets, powder magazines, store-rooms, bays, oriels, sanctums, cloakrooms, landings, long-rooms, galleries, ateliers, herbariums, sick-bays, box-rooms, laboratories, vestibules, shops, dining-rooms, canteens, gun-rooms, refectories, and stables. Ah, how pleasant it was to wander the mazes in the ornamental gardens, and savour the fragrances of rosemary and purple basil mingled with parsley and thyme, the overpowering odour of yellow roses, the sweet waft of fresh hay!

Middelburg, my birthplace! Oft, as I grew to be a man, would I be invited to the traditional weddings held on the frozen Zuider Zee, or Southern Ocean; and I would shyly watch the women performing their round dance, wearing the *ryglyf*, or traditional bodice, either dark blue in colour or embroidered, part of which was allowed to show. Then I would wonder what that happy state of wedlock held in store for me. I could visualize the sunlit first-storey bedroom redolent with pressed linen, and the fresh buttermilk smell emanating from the dairy in the backyard, newly scrubbed by the wife, or perhaps she might have been assigned a maid who also looked to the general provision of the house, who would come in with her arms full of loaves in the morning, or warm rolls flecked with poppy seeds, and cone-shaped buns studded with white sugar crystals; I could hear the hiss of the smoothing-iron, and the sizzle of the pan, and the stock-pot boiling imperceptibly away on the hob. Zeeland hams hung from the ceiling. Alkmaar cheeses ripened in the cool larder. Beautiful pictures of the countryside surrounding Middelburg – its barns, its meres, its windmills – were arrayed on the newly distempered walls of every room, save the kitchen, which nevertheless contained an arbutus-wood spice-cabinet with forty-eight drawers, each labelled with names like cardamom, black pepper, cumin, coriander, nutmeg, foxglove, ergot, man-drake, caraway, and all-spice; and the drawers with little turned ivory knobs engraved with the heads of mythological beasts. I can tell you, sir, it was a very neat case for all its dimensions, much akin to a surgeon's box which, when opened up, reveals its vari-ous implements for cutting, sawing, drilling, clipping, piercing, snipping, all reposing in a boxwood maze, their steel ranks ready for action. Then again, it's like looking at a beautiful flute made in amber, with chased silver keys, and its four sections glowing in the blue velvet-lined chambers of their canteen; the instrument's embouchure is lined with gold, and you know if you put your lips to it and blow, a fundamental bass note will tremble there, the buzz of which you'd never felt before. Syrinx never knew this tune, nor did Apollo blow so nicely on the reed.

In the front parlour there is the pair of virginals, fingered deftly by one's mistress as the tinkling sound of spoons and coffee circulates throughout. Blue Delftware shimmers in the opened cupboards. Upstairs, holland shirts, chemises, blouses, stiff petticoats, whalebone stays and corselets reside in aromatic wardrobes. In the attic of the house is a doll's house inherited from one's mother-in-law, who inherited it from hers, and many ghostly generations hover over it. Could you unhinge its front wall, you could begin to grasp its overall dimensions, which are mighty particular, because all the requisites of a real home are there, down to the tiny mirror in the vestibule where you can see yourself reflected, if you could but put your eye to it; and a fly would do very well here, for all the items, such as the glass bell covering the knuckle-end of yesterday's baked ham studded with cloves, are appropriate to his scale of being.

There is a lady's boudoir in the doll's house, where the tiny lady doll regards and powders her face in the triple looking-glass. Microscopic jars of unguents imported from Arabia lie scattered on the shiny walnut surface of the dressing-table. Above the boudoir is the nursery where a baby rocks in an ancient cradle; and when it cries, I think of me, who might have been that very infant, swaddled in its winding-sheet and bawling mightily.

But then, how I envied the older men at those wedding ceremonies of long ago, puffing contentedly at their tobacco pipes and gazing into the constellations reflected in the ice! From then on I resolved I would be worthy of the burg of Middelburg, this star of Zeeland, star of the sea, harvester of all its fishy species, fount of scientific wisdom. Could I but see myself then as I am now, writing to you, my Lord, in my capacity as Envoy to the Court of France!

As I have said, Middelburg is my native place, and Hans Jansen, in 1591, when I was born, inhabited a neighbouring house, and I knew Zacharias, his son, and as a boy I was often in his shop. This Hans, that is, Johannes, as I have often heard, invented the first microscope, and gave one to Maurice the Governor, and head of the Belgian Army. Later a similar model was sent to Albert, Archduke of Austria, supreme ruler of the Belgian Kingdom. When I was an envoy in England in 1619, Cornelius Drebel of Holland, a man aware of many secrets of Nature, mathematical tutor to James the First, and known to me, showed me the very instrument, which the Archduke had given to Drebel, viz. the one made by Zacharias himself; nor was it (as they are now shown) with a short tube, but the tube was nigh a foot and a half long, made of gilt brass, I should say two inches in diameter supported by three dolphins in brass and a figure of Poseidon. The base was an ebony disc, on which were placed the most minute objects which we looked at from above enlarged almost miraculously.

But to go back: it was the year 1610 or so, and many rumours were abroad regarding the wonderful invention, whereby it was possible to see gargoyles spouting water –

And so on, as above.

Helicon

Galileo Galilei turned things upside-down and made his telescope into a microscope. On the 12th of November, 1614, he reported that he had seen flies which looked as big as lambs, covered with hair; they had very pointed nails which enabled them to walk on glass, although hanging feet upwards, by inserting the points of their nails in the pores of the glass – like walking on the Moon.

On the 12th of September, 1674, Antony van Leeuwenhoek, a draper of Delft, in the province of Holland, filled a glass vial with some greenish cloudy water – 'honey-dew', as it was known to the country people – from a marshy lake some two miles outside the town. When he examined it in the microscope he had made himself for inspecting cloth, he found 'very many small animalcules' in it. He then turned his instrument on a drop of pepper water as big as a millet seed: here were 'little eels, or worms, all huddled up together and wriggling; just as if you saw, with the naked eye, a whole tubful of very little eels and water, with the eels a-squirming among one another; and the whole water seemed to be alive with these multifarious animalcules'. No more pleasant sight had ever met his eye, he said, than that of these many thousands of living creatures, seen all alive in a little drop of water, moving among one another, each several creature having its independent motion. It was a vision of the ideal republic.

Vermeer of Delft, son of a silk-weaver, saw dots of light where none should be. Or one could say that everything is made of fluid dots of light. Look at his *Woman Holding a Balance*, sometimes called *Woman Weighing Gold*, or *Woman Weighing Pearls*. Under close scrutiny, the pans of the scales are empty, or they are weighing drops of light. Magnify the clear liquid eye of the girl in his *Head of a Young Girl*, also known as *Young Girl in A Turban*, or *The Girl with the Pearl Earring*; and it dissolves into a blur of chiaroscuro; the pearl, in close-up, is a tadpole fleck of white within a dark, ambiguous globule.

The white walls of his interiors, when looked at closely, are anything but white. They flicker with distempered blues, golds and ochres. They glow with yellows, violets and oranges. As light falls on the surface of a Vermeer wall, it moves continuously in diffuse harmonies of colour, shifting through the spectrum, swaying, bulging, exaggerating its own bumps and blemishes, making scumbled cloudscapes of them. There are delta rivulets and hieroglyphs of colour. These walls are as old as Egypt, and speak to their observer of their source: of stone being quarried, stone being pulverized by time, stone ground into sand, into grains, into atoms, into particles. They are made up of the dust of ages, which is everywhere; and all things of like nature, no matter if dispersed through aeons of time and space, lie cheek by jowl *sub specie aeternitatis*.

At 10.30 a.m. on the 12th of October, 1654, the powder magazine at Delft, crammed with 80,000 lb of explosives left over from the Spanish war, was accidentally ignited. The resulting explosion was heard in Germany. Whole streets were swept away, and hundreds killed. The famed autumn light of the Dutch Golden Age was temporarily dimmed in Delft, as dust-clouds obscured the sun for days. All that was left of the magazine was a pool of water some fifteen or sixteen feet deep. Among those who lost their lives was a pupil of Rembrandt, Carel Fabritius, who is thought to have influenced Vermeer. It is generally agreed that Fabritius's *View in Delft, with a Musical Instrument Seller's Stall* (1652) was painted with the aid of a camera obscura. Here, in the left foreground, a man sits with his chin propped on his thumb, framed by a lute leaning against the wall, a recumbent bass viol, and the unglazed slats of his stall; the right is taken up by a distant view of the Niewe Kerk and the surrounding houses. So great is the disparity between the two, that the cityscape has a dreamlike, ephemeral quality, as if it were an extension of the brooding man's thoughts.

The Sentry, painted in the year of Fabritius's death by explosion, is also a meditation on the transience of things, or a commentary on war. The dozing sentry, gun in lap, his helmet tilted over his eyes, is slumped on a wooden bench before an open gate, beneath a broken column. Just beyond his sprawled right leg a small black dog looks reproachfully at him. Above the archway of the gate is a bas-relief depicting an image of St Antony and his attribute, the pig: Antony, who is the patron saint of butchers, brushmen, and those given to hallucinations.

Van Leeuwenhoek was a great seer. Not only did he have brilliant eyesight, but he knew how to focus it. Many frankly disbelieved his visions of the seething life within a drop of water. Some dealers in cloth thought him a witch, because he could detect flaws in material that could pass the most discerning eye. Eminent scientists and philosophers, invited to peer into his microscope, could see only a vague granular motion. Emperors who saw nothing swore they'd seen myriads.

Some art historians assert a close connection between these two great contemporaries in Delft: van Leeuwenhoek, the microscopist; Vermeer, the observer and painter of light. In his capacity as clerk to the town bailiff, van Leeuwenhoek was appointed the administrator of Vermeer's posthumous estate: according to this 'mutual friends' hypothesis, van Leeuwenhoek dealt sympathetically with Vermeer's bankruptcy, and spent much effort in satisfying the demands of creditors. Not so, say others: he was cold, calculating, and bureaucratically efficient.

Then, say the first party, look at Vermeer's companion pieces,

The Geographer and *The Astronomer*: surely the long-haired scientist in these paintings is the image of van Leeuwenhoek. Not so, say the others, pointing to an attested portrait of the man: the real van Leeuwenhoek had coarser features, and a pencil-line moustache. And his sardonic pragmatic gaze does not match that of the myopic scholar poring over his terrestrial and celestial globes.

In his *View of Delft*, Vermeer mixed grains of sand into some of his paint to achieve the glittering highlights in some of the architectural detail. Microscopic bits of stone become light. Sand becomes glass. Van Leeuwenhoek, early on in his researches, took as his unit of measurement a 'sand grain', which he defined as a cube 1/80 of an inch on edge. Within this scope he counted his animalcules, like counting angels on the head of a pin.

To our eyes, a van Leeuwenhoek microscope looks like a child's toy, or an instrument of torture. Typically, it consists of a crudely cut brass lens plate some 40mm × 18mm in dimension, to which are connected two reciprocating wing-nut screws to bring the object to be studied into focus. The single simple lens is barely the size of a seed pearl. With this device van Leeuwenhoek looked at such things as the eye of a gnat, sections of an elephant's tooth, lambswool, blood corpuscles, the spinneret of a spider, a tinder-box flint, goat's semen, a tea-leaf, the embryo of a cochineal insect (commonly used for red pigment), a hair with adherent ring-worm, a section of nutmeg, and a silk thread. These were all discovered in thirteen boxes fitted into an Indian cabinet which he bequeathed to the Royal Society. He dissected and examined a whale's eye pickled in brandy, brought to him by a whaling captain. Among the specimens auctioned after his death were the muscles of a codfish and a duck's heart; the lens, bladder and tongue of an ox; hairs from a beaver, elk, bear, and a human nose; the thread, mouthpiece and eyes of a spider; red coral; the brain, optic nerve and feet of a fly; and scales from a perch, a roach, and human skin. Other items included ergot of rye; fragments of marble, rock crystal, diamond, gold leaf, silver ore, amber, and a variety of crystals; the eye of a dragonfly; and six embryo oysters.

On the 3rd of February, 1598, a fifty-foot sperm whale beached itself in the sandy shallows at Berckhey, a fishing village between Katwijk and Scheveningen. Lugged ashore by cables, it lay there twitching feebly for four days. When it finally expired, its bowels had burst, so infecting the air that many who went to see it were cast into diseases by the stench, and some died. The Exchequer of the Province of Holland, in whose domain it lay, immediately established legal claim to it, and its carcass was auctioned off for 136 guilders. The ominous significance of the whale was much debated; some saw it as a sign that the Hollanders would triumph over their enemies, others that it was a portent of disaster. It became an ikon; drawings and many prints were made of it, most of them based on a prototype by Jacob Matham. The whale is surrounded like Gulliver by Lilliputians: some of them well-dressed spectators on horseback, others clambering over it like mountaineers, or hacking at its corpse. People in working clothes are collecting its oil and blubber in takeaway buckets. Already it is being surveyed. Its various parts, including its fins and penis, will be measured, and its teeth enumerated.

But the LORD sent out a great wind unto the sea, and there was a mighty tempest in the sea, so that the ship was like to be broken.

Then the mariners were afraid, and cried every man unto his god, and cast forth the wares that were in the ship into the sea, to lighten it of them. But Jonah was gone down into the sides of the ship; and he lay, and was fast asleep . . .

And they said every one to his fellows, Come, and let us cast lots, that we may know whose cause this evil is upon us. So they cast lots, and the lot fell on Jonah.

Jonah is the archetype of lazy fellows and skivers everywhere. He could stand in for Carel Fabritius's dozing sentry. He would do well in Jan Steen's *The Drunken Couple*, or any of the Dutch genre paintings of disordered households, where the dogs and cats look imploringly at their unconscious masters. Or you might find him comatose in one of the bawdy-house interiors, a tobacco-pipe drooping in his hand, and the floor littered with broken eggshells. The taverns of the Dutch Republic were redolent with tobacco. And the tobacco, then, in the 1670s and 80s, had a high kick: dealers mixed the cut leaf variously with thyme, citron, aniseed, saffron, mace, black henbane, rosemary, dill, belladonna, and hemp. One 'drank' tobacco; and one got 'tobacco drunk'.

In these crazed interiors, household effects take on surreal still-life presences that remind us of the ergot-driven fantasies of Bosch and Bruegel. As serving-girls are pawed and ogled by old buggers, long-handled skillets glow blackly on the floor beside discarded mussel shells and broken pipe stems; walking-sticks, hats, basins, flap-can tankards, candlesticks, chamberpots are scattered everywhere in riotous, promiscuous abandon. Monkeys leer from mantelpieces. Goggle-eyed owls perch on open oven doors. Parrots dangle upside-down on high trapezes. Unscrewed paper twists of 'tobacco' are highlighted on wooden benches. Dogs piss under tables.

The Dutch Republic, meanwhile, was the cleanest place in Europe. Elegant tourists from all parts were terribly impressed. An important English lady reported that she walked almost all over the town yesterday, incognito, in her slippers, without receiving one spot of dirt. The Dutch maids washed the pavement of the street with more application than her maids would do her bedchamber. There was neither dirt nor beggary to be seen, and one was not shocked with those loathsome cripples so often seen in London.

The tall Dutch windows lay uncurtained for everyone to look in. Not only that, one of the first things to strike a stranger's eye in a Dutch town were the little mirrors projecting in front of the windows of almost all the houses. They consisted of two pieces of glass placed at an angle of 45° to each other, the one reflecting up, the other down the street. By means of this contrivance the Dutch lady could see all that passed outside, without the trouble of going to the window, or the necessity of exposing herself to the vulgar gaze; and while she sat ensconced behind the gauze blind, could continue her knitting or sewing uninterruptedly.

Furthermore, one of the essentials of comfort for a Dutch lady was the *vuur stoof*, a square box open on one side to admit an earthen pan filled with embers of turf, and perforated to allow the heat to ascend and warm the feet; it served as a footstool, and was concealed under the dress. The use of it was rarely dispensed with, whatever the season, indoors or out – the citizen's wife had it carried after her by her servant to church or at the theatre.

This, indeed, is the object depicted in the lower right corner of Vermeer's *Woman Pouring Milk*, also known as *The Milkmaid*, or *Maidservant Pouring Milk*. These different names must depend on the eye of the beholder, and there are worlds of difference between them. So with every description of the painting. For now, let us identify it as the one with the girl in the white headscarf (possibly a milkmaid's) and the yellow bodice and the red skirt with a blue apron tucked into the waistband. She's pouring white milk from a red earthenware jug into a brown glazed bowl and there's a loaf of bread in a wicker basket on the table and a lidded pitcher and other bits of broken bread on the tablecloth. There's a wicker basket and a shiny metal basket hanging up on the wall beside the window, which allows the apparent morning to spill across the room, transubstantiating the seeds or the granular crust on the broken bread, and the whole bread, into bits of broken-up-loaf-sugar light, which you feel you could pick off with a licked finger. Some have attributed these luminous dots to the 'circles of confusion' seen through a camera obscura, or in an out-of-focus photograph; but the same circles, or 'discs', are not to be witnessed on non-reflective objects, so if anything, Vermeer might have transferred them from the glint of the metal basket, or the window-glass; perhaps not. Nevertheless, the viewer can imagine Vermeer in his dark room wrapped in his black cloak of invisibility, observing the maid concentrate her gaze on the stilled unbroken stream of the milk from the lip of the jug, or asking her in a muffled voice like that of Beauty's Beast to hold this pose or that for all eternity to see; or perhaps this is only one moment recollected by him, or a resumé of many moments that he's run back through his mind, not knowing which was when; perhaps none of these. Perhaps this is an image of Tanneke Everpoel, his family's maid. Perhaps she is a woman in her own right.

Then we return to the *vuur stoof*, which seems to have crept in from another dimension, sitting at an odd angle to the skirting of blue and white Delft tiles and the red hem of the woman's skirt. This foot-warmer, once thought to be a mousetrap by some critics, is common enough in de Hooch's interiors, where we see it fulfil its very useful function, and we feel a palpable vicarious warmth when we see a matron resting her unslippered foot on the top of one. But this is the only time Vermeer depicts a *vuur stoof*, and, isolated from its mistress, it assumes a lonesome *gravitas* and presence, like some Platonic cuboid that resists direct translation to our world of known things. Even when identified by name, we do not know it from experience. It might well be a mousetrap. It is well known to Irish country people that mice are fond of warmth, and are often found jumping out of the ashes of a turf-fire when you go poking at it in the morning, and it is not unknown for mice to breed inside the big wire-grilled speakers of a radiogram, which emanates a warm hum when you turn it on. A student of musical instruments could easily take the *vuur stoof* for an early Wheatstone concertina, except the country and the period is wrong, and it lacks the little wing-nut keys to the sides. Then again, it might be a case for a small chamberpot, or a large pomander.

But let us take it as a little stove for warming feet. What is it doing here? Does it belong to the milk-pourer, giving a low glow of comfort at her back, or does it wait to be replenished for a higher employer, from a hearth we cannot see? Already we imagine coffee being brought upstairs, although no trays are evident. Would this maid – if such she be – carry in her arms the warm-box for her mistress to that morning's service in the Oude Kerk in Delft, where Admiral van Tromp reclines entombed?

These are imponderable questions, and the object lies beyond our ken. But it is pleasant to imagine the cool, damp church interior reverberating with prayer or sermon, and to visualize that monument of Tromp: 'a seafight cut in marble, with the smoke, the best expressed I ever saw', said Samuel Pepys, on being shown it in 1660 by a smith's boy of the town of Delft, 'who could speak nothing but Dutch'. This is the Tromp who, after his victory over the English, caused a broom to be hoisted at his mast-head, to signify that he had swept the Channel clean. They honour him in England as the Dutch Nelson; but this stout captain died a century and more before Horatio was conceived. He is buried in the Oude Kerk, with Leeuwenhoek and Jan Vermeer: companions of a vanished universe.

Meanwhile a spoor of turf-smoke clung to the ladies' linen petticoats, and it is difficult to resist thinking of what it would be like to be an infant hiding under them. Maybe the yellowed smell was the smell of all of Holland, concentrated – no, not Holland, as we call it in our Anglophone; it is Nederland in Dutch, a deeper name by far – the Nether Land, the land which lies below. Van Leeuwenhoek examined it in detail, and saw the flaws in silk that breed a thousand lovely crawling things. Rembrandt looked into its smoky alcoves, and he saw the light which shines in darkness. The doomed Fabritius saw visions of eternity. De Hooch died in the madhouse.

At funeral and all other services, the men drank tobacco in the pews of churches through their long-stemmed churchwarden clay pipes, while the women basked their nether regions in a footstool underglow. English travellers were appalled at the clouds of smoke that billowed into one's face if one was so much as to open the door of even a respectable tavern. The hansomboats were not exempt, for the Dutchmen would crowd into the below-decks cabins to light up immediately, preferring to confine their smoke among themselves, and not exhaust it to the open air. They chewed tobacco too, and snuffed it, so that any common beggar, before asking you for alms, would proffer you a pinch of it, and that from a nice receptacle carved in some exotic wood the Dutch imported from the East. It was no wonder that the English traveller would occasionally succumb to the practice, and secretly admire its vast collectabilia of implements for dealing or containing tobacco, as depicted in the genre paintings of tobacco memorabilia, in which clever *trompe-l'œil* masters absolutely convinced you that a painting of a pipe was the pipe itself, and all you had to do was pick it out of the picture and smoke it.

John Keats knew the magical connective power of nicotine. On 5th September, 1817, he wrote from Oxford to Jane and Mariane Reynolds –

My dear Friends,

You are, I am glad to hear, comfortable at Hampton, where I hope you will receive the Biscuits we ate the other night at Little Britain. I hope you found them good. There you are among Sands, stones, Pebbles, Beeches, Cliffs, Rocks, Deeps, Shallows, weeds, Ships, Boats (at a distance), Carrots, Turnips, sun, moon, and stars and all those sort of things – here am I among Colleges, halls, Stalls, Plenty of Trees, thank God – Plenty of Water, thank heaven – Plenty of Books, thank the Muses – Plenty of Snuff, thank Sir Walter Raleigh – Plenty of segars – Ditto – Plenty of Flat country, thank Tellus's rolling pin – I'm on the sofa – Buonaparte is on the snuff-box – But you are by the sea side – argal, you bathe – you walk – you say 'how beautiful' – find out resemblances between waves and camels – rocks and dancing masters – fireshovels and telescopes – Dolphins and Madonas –

And so he rambles on in his tobacco fantasy. Keats, I dare say, would have known Sir John Beaumont's 'The Metamorphosis of Tobacco', written in praise of the weed:

> By whom the Indian Priests inspired be,
> When they presage in barbrous Poetrie:
> Infume my braine, make my soules powers subtile,
> Give nimble cadence to my harsher stile:
> Inspire me with thy flame, which doth excell
> The purest streames of the Castalian well,
> That I on thy ascensive wings may flie

> *By thine ethereall vapours borne on high,*
> *And with thy feathers added to my quill*
> *May pitch thy tents on the Parnassian hill —*

Tobacco-smoke, inhaled by Cortez on the heights of Mexico! John Keats drank it, too, like blissful Hippocrene from Helicon, on first looking into Chapman's Homer, and its properties enabled him to chant the proper names that are the high peaks of his ultramontane poem: *Apollo — Homer — Chapman — Cortez — Pacific — Darien*. They are like the names of new-found planets; and John Keats knew the ancient history of Io, as told anew by Ovid in his *Metamorphoses*.

Io

There is a vale in Thessaly surrounded by steep-wooded slopes on every side. They call it Tempe. Here the Peneus River flows, and gathers force in its descent. Foam-flecked, lathered, dappled-horseback-brown, it throws off clouds of spray and steam into the upper branches of the trees, and snorts along at such a pace that neighbours miles away are kept up by its noise. This is the abode and inner sanctum of the mighty river: residing in a cavern measureless to man, Peneus gave authority to these, his waters, and to all the nymphs inhabiting his element. Here he was joined by all the other rivers of that country, and they sang his praises in their different voices: Sperchios, the poplar-fringed Aeolian; restless Enipeus, who makes a tinkled litany of pebbles shifting in his bed; sluggish, muddy Apidanus, whose *basso profundo* sounds like the fog-horn; Aeas and Amphrysus, whose music is as gentle as a perfume wafting through the meadows.

Only poor Inachus does not come. Hidden in his deepest grotto, he augments his waters with his tears; and, wrapped in gloom and utter wretchedness, bewails the loss of Io, his daughter. For whether she is still alive, or moves among the shades, he does not know. But since he cannot find her anywhere, he thinks she must be nowhere; and in his mind he dreads the worst.

Now, Jupiter had seen Io coming from her father's stream, and said: O maiden, worthy of the love of Jove, and destined to make some man happy, I beg you for your beauty's sake to seek the coolness of these woods – here, he pointed to a shady grove – for noon is nigh, when Phoebus throws his burning rays. But if you fear to go into the wood where wild beasts dwell, know that a god protects you – no ordinary god, I might point out, but Jupiter himself, who holds the lightning-bolts and hurls them where he pleases – but do not fly from me. For by now, she had left the pasture-fields of Lerna, and the wooded plains of Lyrcea. The lusting god then summoned up his powers of darkness, and drew a cloak of cloud across the land; and under it, he pounced on her, and raped her.

Meanwhile, his wife Juno, gazing down across the land, detected the unnatural cloud, and wondered what had caused it: it was not like river-vapour, nor did it emanate from a bog. And then she looked around to see where Jupiter might be, for well she knew his ways, and what he might be up to. She scoured the heavens; he was nowhere to be found. Either I am wrong, or I am being wronged, she said. Gliding from the stratosphere, she alighted on the earth, and bade the cloud disperse. But Jupiter had seen Juno coming, and had changed Io into a white heifer. And even in this form, she still was beautiful. Now, Juno had an eye for cattle, and regarded this fair heifer with a grudging admiration; then she asked whose she was, from whence she came, or from what herd — as if she didn't know full well. O, she sprang from the earth, says Jupiter, thinking to evade these awkward questions. So Juno asked for the white heifer as a gift. What could he do? Cruel it would be, thus to surrender; not to do so would arouse suspicion. Shame persuades him on the one hand; lust dissuades him on the other. Desire might well have conquered shame; but to refuse so poor a gift to one who shared his pedigree and bed would make it look as if the cow was not a cow at all.

The rival being given up to her, Juno's fears were not allayed. She knew that Jupiter might try to steal her back. So she put the snow-white heifer in the care of Argus, son of Aristor. This Argus had a hundred eyes encircled around his head. Two eyes would rest and sleep at any given time; the other ninety-eight would do sentry duty. Whatever way he faced, he looked towards Io; and even when his back was turned, Io was before his eyes.

In the daytime, he allowed her to graze; at night, he harshly tethered her. She fed on the leaves of the arbutus tree, and bitter herbs; her bed was the cold earth, and she drank from muddy streams. Suppliant, she would try to stretch her arms to Argus; but she had no arms. She wanted to complain, but she could only moo. How terrible, to be startled by the sound of one's own voice!

Then she would wander to the banks of her father's stream, where she used to play as a child; but when she saw her drooling muzzle and her horns reflected there, she was totally bewildered by this image of herself, and fled. Her Naiad sisters knew her not; and Inachus himself, her father, did not recognize her. But still she followed them like some obedient beast, to be petted and admired. Old Inachus had plucked some grass, and held it out to her; she licked his fingers, and she tried to kiss his palm. Tears came to her eyes: if only she could tell her sorry altered state, and beg for help! No words came, but with her hoof she traced the letters of her story in the dust.

– O wretched me! exclaimed Inachus, clinging to her horns and snow-white neck. O misery! are you indeed the daughter I have sought upon the plains of Abyssinia, and the Afric shore, and in the hills of Zanzibar? Not to have found you would have been a lighter sorrow. For you are dumb, and cannot answer me. You groan at me from deep within you; you do not speak, you moo. Before you went, I had prepared the bridal suite and honeymoon for you. I had a prospect of a son-in-law, and grandchildren. But now I must look to the herd to find you a husband; and my grandchildren will be calves. Nor will death end my grief. It is a dreadful thing to be a god: for the gates of death are closed to me forever, and my sorrow will endure eternally.

As they wept together, star-eyed Argus separated them, and drove the daughter, torn from her father's arms, to higher pastures, there to keep a better eye on her.

But now the highest god of all cannot endure to see these further tortures of the heifer Io, and calls forth his son Mercury, born of the bright Pleiad, and orders him to do the Hundred-eyed Thing to death. With hardly a delay he puts on the wingèd sandals, and takes up his sleep-inducing wand, and dons the magic broad-brimmed hat. Thus arrayed, he springs down from the sky. He alights on earth. He removes his hat and wings, and hides them. He keeps the wand. Disguised as a shepherd, he drives a flock of nanny-goats along the country paths, and plays his reed pipe as he goes. Argus, hearing him, is greatly taken by his music, and he says to him, Sit down my friend, whoever you might be, upon this stone with me, for here the grass is good for goats like yours to graze; and as you see, the shade is very good for shepherds like yourself.

So the son of Atlas sat down, and talked the hours away beguilingly with Argus, and he played him many tunes to overcome those watchful eyes. Wanting to sleep, Argus allowed some of his eyes to sleep; but the others looked on. And he enquired how the reed pipe came to be thought of; for at that time, it had been just invented.

Then the god began: In the cold mountains of Arcadia, among the Hamadryads of Nonacris, there dwelt a Naiad very famous, known to her sister nymphs as Syrinx. On more than one occasion had she slipped the grasp of the lusty satyrs and minor deities with which the fields and shady groves abounded. She had dedicated her way of life – most especially, her maidenhood – to the Delian goddess; and, when dressed like Diana, could deceive a casual beholder, who would take her for Latona's daughter, had Syrinx not a bow of horn, whereas Diana bore the gold. And even then, mistakes were often made.

One day, Pan, wearing his crown of spiky pine leaves, spied

her coming back from Mount Lycaeus, and addressed her in these words:

Here, Mercury was about to repeat the words of Pan, and go on to tell of how the nymph, declining his suit, had fled through verdurous glooms and winding mossy ways until she came to Ladon's sandy banks; that here, checked by the water, she implored her sisters of the stream for metamorphosis; how Pan, thinking he was on the verge of seizing Syrinx, caught instead a bunch of marsh reeds; and, as he sighed his disappointment, a low wind stirred the reeds and murmured like a soul complaining; and how, very taken by this new discovery, and by the beauty of the sound, he said: This marriage, at least, shall I have with thee – and, accordingly, these pan-pipe reeds have since retained the name of Syrinx.

As I say, the Cyllenian God (Mercury, that is) was about to get into this part of the story when he noticed Argus snoring, and he saw that all his hundred eyes were fast asleep. So straightway he breaks his narrative, and strokes the languid constellated eyes with his magic staff. Without delay he takes his hookèd sword, and smites the nodding monster in the jugular. Then he kicks him off the rugged cliff, which drips with gore.

So, Argus, were you laid low. So the blazing starry night was snuffed; and one darkness fills your myriad of eyes. Then Juno took those liquidated eyes, and set them like so many jewels in the feathers of her pet peacock.

As for Io, she will eventually regain her human shape; and that's another story.

Meanwhile, for us, her name is the name of a moon of Jupiter, first seen by Galileo. What he could not have foreseen were the close-up images of Io broadcast by Voyager, in 1979. In these, Io glows like a translucent amber ball, throbbing with sulphuric oranges and yellows, pitted by the gaping throats of boiling black calderas. Gravitationally perturbed by Ganymede and Europa, two other moons of Jupiter, Io's orbit is eccentric: hence its oscillating tidal bulges, and the movement of the magma in the satellite's interior, which is massive. Io is kneaded and stretched like molten glass. Io's fires are stoked primarily by Jupiter, which constantly throws forth lightning bolts the size of terrestrial rivers.

Io is forever boiling, gulping, bubbling, seething, changing. Her whole being is a realm of metamorphosis. Volcanoes vent symphonic batteries of sulphur, whose light and noise blend like obsidian. The horizon glimmers with the noise of clashing armies. Liquid tries to become solid; solid is already liquid. The secret of glass is discovered a million times and more, except the moments are but fleeting glances, seen by no one, and already the window of time is dissolved. Billions of particles per second explode into the stratosphere; and the huge magnetic field of Jupiter sucks in these outbursts like reversed tornadoes. Brilliant auroral patterns flash from Io to Jupiter in shimmering intensities of colours, pulsing, throbbing; the two globes exchange spectral dialogues of immense electrical charges that build up, struggling for release, which comes finally in a supercharged titanic blast, as bolts of lightning miles wide are hurled mutually between them, and Jupiter and Io are joined by fire.

After the climax, the fall-out drifts back slowly to Io's surface.

Innumerable motes accumulate a centimetre in three thousand years. And yet, when miles of such evaporated time have been laid down, those solid layers too will melt back into Io, whose fires will burn as long as Jupiter's.

The volcanoes, calderas and paterae of Io are named after gods of fire and mischief: hence, Marduk, Pele, Loki and Prometheus, among many others. An exception is Inachus Patera: the river-god has been transformed into a lake of fire, and Io now contains Inachus, her father.

As it happens, I had outlined the gist of Io's story to my own father as I drove him to the Cranfield Inn to relate the story for the third night in the lady's mansion; and I'd remembered that, following her metamorphosis, she had run like a mad thing over the continents of Europe, pursued by a gadfly sent by Hera to torment her; and each of the straits she swam across was called Bosporus, or Ox-ford. Now, *bó* is the Irish for cow; and after we had remarked on this collusion of the Irish and the Greek, my father fell silent for a few minutes. When he spoke again, it was to tell me that he'd decided to substitute another story for the usual one in the sequence, which he'd never liked that much anyway. The one he would tell involved a cow-girl; not that the cow factor itself was important, but the story told of metamorphoses: so why not swap one thing for another? For the storyteller is allowed some liberty within the known framework. So, when his audience was assembled, he began:

Once upon a time there was a girl lived near Tobarnaveen. She was only a small girl, about fourteen or fifteen years of age. Her people had a cow and they told her to drive her to pasture one morning. But she strayed off the path into a wood full of blue-bells, and the girl was seated in a glade while her cow chomped at the grasses of the forest's ferny floor. It wasn't long till a frog came out of a pool and hopped towards her and sat down and looked into her face. For the girl had the most beautiful blue eyes, as blue as hyacinths or bluebells. The frog had a very big belly, and for devilment the girl said, May you not give birth to your burden until I am with you. And the frog hopped away and jumped back into the pool.

The girl went home. She forgot all about what happened. Just a month to the day, herself and her father and mother were asleep one night, when they heard the sound of a horse's hooves approaching the door. There was a knock at the door, and some-one cried, Open up! The girl's father jumped out of bed, and opened the door. The finest gentleman they had ever seen walked in. He wore a black beaver hat with a peacock plume in it, and a swallow-tailed coat of parrot-green over a popinjay waistcoat, and pantaloons of canary yellow, and raven-black riding-boots.

— I don't know you, sir, said the man of the house.

— No blame in that, said the gentleman, for I come to ask you to do something for me.

— There wouldn't be much I can do for the likes of you, said the man of the house, for I'm a poor man.

— It's your daughter I want. I want her for twenty-four hours.

The father didn't like the sound of that, nor did the small girl, who whispered from her bed that she wouldn't go with him.

– Ah, you will, said the gentleman. I give my hand and my word to yourself and to your father and mother that you'll be home here again safe and sound, within twenty-four hours.

– Well, sir, I'll take your word, said the father. She can go with you that length.

– Thank you, said the gentleman.

– Get up, said the father, and go with him now.

So the girl got up, but she was very reluctant about it.

– Good girl! said the gentleman, and he took her hand in his, which had an ostrich-skin glove on it, and he led her out of the house.

He got up on his horse and he caught hold of her shoulder and he lifted her up behind him, and as they rode along, he talked to her.

– There's no need to be afraid, he said. There's no need for it, for I'll bring you home safe and sound tomorrow night. Give the back of your hand to the first food offered to you, said he. Say that you won't eat it. But you may eat the second food offered to you, and any food after that.

They rode along till they came to a hill. A great door opened in the hill, and they entered the finest court that ever rose to the sky. There was a throng of people moving around and chatting to each other at their ease, drinking out of crystal goblets, and they were all dressed to kill in costumes gorgeous as the plumage of the golden oriole, or bird of paradise. As the gentleman and the girl walked along the crowd parted for them, till they came to the inner sanctum of the court. There were three nurses there, tending a woman who was ill in bed. There was a huge fire blazing and crackling in the grate. The moment the two of them entered, the woman gave birth to a child. Immediately two of the nurses took the baby from the mother, and the third started to poke the fire, making a shallow hole in it. They put the child into the hole in the middle of the fire and raked the hot coals over it. The mother bawled and cried, but it was no use.

The baby wasn't yet fully burned, when in came a man and a woman. The woman was carrying a baby in her arms. She handed it to the woman who had just given birth to the burning baby. The baby latched on to the woman's nipple, and began to drink. For this was a baby they had stolen from the human world. All this time the other baby was roasting away, till it was reduced to ashes. There was a big trough by the side of the wall near the door you'd go out by. They sprinkled the baby's ashes on the water in the trough till it was full to the brim.

The girl who'd been brought there by the gentleman watched all of this with wonder. Now they laid a table of fine food before her, with roasted partridges, and guinea-hens, and nightingales, and little skewered larks, and all sorts of fowl imaginable. But she turned it all down, saying she wasn't used to that kind of food. So then they brought her fine millet cakes, and roast hazelnuts and chestnuts, and poppy-seed buns sprinkled with nutmeg, and blackberries and sloes and wild cherries. And she ate her fill, and washed it all down with dandelion wine. The gentleman had not left the room all this time, and he watched the girl closely.

– Good girl! said he, when he saw her eat the second food.

Just then, three pipers struck up music for dancing. The chamber was full to overflowing. They danced the whole night long, but not one of the guests spoke a word to the girl. Then daylight filtered in through a tall window and the crowd started to take their leave. One by one, as they left the room, they dipped their fingers into the trough and touched the water to their eyes. The girl watched them doing this. She spent the day in the house with the gentleman watching over her, until it was almost night. The gentleman left the room ahead of her and put some of the trough-water to his eyes as he went out. Now, the girl was at his heels, and she wondered what to do about the water; so she decided to rub one of her eyes with it, so that if anything should go wrong, she would have the sight of the other eye.

– I may as well give you a present before you leave, said the woman with the baby in the bed, since you were so kind as to come when I sent for you.

The woman turned about and rummaged under her pillow, and pulled out a silken neck-shawl, and a stocking full of gold and silver coin, and she gave them to the girl. No sooner had she done so than the gentleman came back into the room.

– It's time to go, said he to the girl. I must leave you safely back to your father and mother.

So the girl left the room behind him, and as she did, she dipped her fingers into the trough and she put the water to one of her eyes. She went out. The gentleman jumped on to his horse, and he lifted the girl by her shoulder up on the horse behind him. As they rode along, he talked to her, until they came to a wood a good distance away. They rode into the wood.

– Did my mistress give you a present? he asked.

– She did, and very grateful I am to her, said the girl.

— I see, said the gentleman.

They were passing a huge oak tree in the wood, when the gentleman jumped down from the horse and lifted down the girl in his arms.

— Go now, like a good little girl, and wind the silken shawl around that tree.

The girl did as she was bid. No sooner had she done so, than the tree split in two halves.

— Leave the silk shawl there! said the gentleman.

She left it there. They mounted the horse and rode on.

— Did my mistress give you any other present? he asked.

— She did. A stocking full of gold and silver.

— Good, said the gentleman. Now, as soon as ever you reach home, you must go to all the fine houses and shops, and change that money into their money, for within six nights from now, any premises that has my mistress's money in it will be burned by next morning. But your money will be safe. Do this not for me, but for your own sake.

Within a minute they were at the door of her father's house. The mother and the father were sitting by the fire and poking the ashes and talking about their daughter when they heard the sound of a horse's hooves approaching the door. The horse stopped at the door. The gentleman dismounted, and he swung the girl down from the horse and he put her two feet on the ground. He entered the house with her.

— Here is your daughter back safe and sound. I am very grateful to you. Good night!

He went out of the house. Next morning, the small girl got

up, and she went around all the big houses asking for change for her gold and silver. After six days, she had changed it all. On the sixth night, all the big houses were burned to the ground.

The girl now started to buy up land and cattle. She was to be seen at all the fairs, dealing with the strong farmers and the horse-traders. One day she went to a big fair down in the West of Ireland, far away from home. It wasn't long till she noticed people moving in the crowd, dressed like popinjays and parrots, and some of them with ostrich-plumes in their hats, and others wearing gloves of ostrich-skin. They were flitting here and there among the crowd, twittering and talking to each other at their ease. Then she saw the gentleman who had taken her from home and brought her back again.

— I must speak to him, she said to herself. She walked through the crowd, who parted for her, and she shook his hand.

He shook her hand too.

— I'm very glad to see you, said she.

— Wasn't it quick of you to recognize me? asked he. Did you see me with both eyes?

— No, only with the one.

— Might I be so bold as to ask with which of your beautiful blue eyes did you see me? he asked.

— Of course, said she.

— Put your hand to the eye you saw me with, said he.

She did. He stuck his finger into that eye and tore it from her head.

— You'll never see me more, he said.

And it was true. She never laid eyes on him again. The people still talk about the one blue eye of the old woman who used to be a small girl, especially when they walk in dark woods floored with hyacinths, or bluebells.

— That was a good story, said one of the men. May we expect another one tomorrow night?

    — You may, said Jack, if I am still here tomorrow night.

So the men and women walked out the door in the wall as they had on the other nights. But of course Jack didn't know the way out, and he spent that night as he had spent the other nights, and the morning the same way as the other mornings.

So, afterwards, I put my father in the Vauxhall Astra, and I drove him home, imagining the bluebell glades as the road parted before the headlights like a tunnel into a dark wood.

JACINTH

Jacinth is zircon. Jacinth is sapphire. Jacinth is Hyacinthus, the fallen youth. She is Jacinta. Jacinta is the bluebell, or the nodding squill. From early in April till the end of May – as often as the Ram succeeds the watery Fish – the wild hyacinth blooms perennially in woods. The pendulous bells are bluish-purple, composed of six leaflets. They have a slight starch-like scent. The cultivated hyacinth is grown extensively in Holland. One variety is called Delft Blue.

Zircon is colourless, or yellowish. Sapphire is the tincture blue or azure. Zircon is midium, or red lead. Sapphire is the name for certain kinds of humming-birds. Zircon is a crystal. Sapphire is lapis lazuli. Jargon is a smoky zircon found in the former Ceylon.

Bluebell bulbs are poisonous in the raw state. The viscid juice abundantly contained in them was used for starch in days gone by.

The stiff ruffs depicted by Rembrandt were achieved by bluebell juice. It is also used for fixing feathers to an arrow. The bluebell, flower of mourning, tolls quietly in the dark woods.

Like Ganymede, Hyacinthus might have been a constellation: but so sudden was his death, that Phoebus had no time to fix him to the sky. But he too is immortal as he blooms each year.

Apollo loved this beautiful youth. Zephyrus, the wind god, loved him too. One day, Apollo, bored with his zither and his lyric bow, called up his dogs and ranged the mountains with his comrade Hyacinth. At noon they came to a plateau. Here they stripped beneath the bronze sun and took out the shining discus. They smeared each other with olive oil till they gleamed. Then ensued the discus-throwing competition. First one, then the other threw, each throw longer than the last. At each throw they stepped back, anticipating yet a further throw. Then Apollo wound himself up like one almighty spring, and threw his best. But Zephyrus, invisible spectator, was jealous of their friendly rivalry, and puffed his cheeks, and blew with all his force against the flying object, so that it fell short. Hyacinthus, in his boyish eagerness for sport, sprinted towards it. But alas, the keen-edged discus, ricocheting off the stony mountain soil, caught him full in the face and laid him low.

The god of music grew deadly pale as he ran to the falling boy and caught him in his arms. Vainly he tried to staunch the dreadful wound. Just as in a garden, when you break off a violet or a stiff poppy and, deprived of their stalks, they droop so suddenly, and cannot keep their heads erect, so the dying face of Hyacinthus drooped, all strength gone in his neck and shoulders.

– You are gone, deprived of all your bloom, O Spartan youth, Apollo cried, and in your wound I see my guilt; I am the author of your death. And yet, what is my fault, unless my playing with you can be called a fault, unless my loving you is called a fault? If only I had been in your place, you in mine, then I would gladly die instead of you! But since the laws of fate decree that you should die instead of me, I will make you live forever. You will be forever in my music. Every note I play will be for you, and you will be an admirable flower.

So, where the youth's blood stained the earth, a blue-veined flower sprang. Not satisfied with this accomplishment, the music god inscribed the letters of his grief upon the leaflets, so that the flowers bore these words, *Ai*, *Ai*, as they do to this day.

But on the English hyacinths no such words appear, so they are known as *Nonscriptus*, or 'not written on'.

The hyacinth is naturally the emblem of St Hyacinth, whose patronage of Lithuania was confirmed by Pope Innocent XI on the 24th September 1686, which day is celebrated at the feast of Our Lady of Mercy, who is also the patron of the Argentinian army. It is worth noting in passing that Innocent XI is alleged to have privately funded William III of Orange's campaign to depose the Catholic James II of England, and that the victory at the Battle of the Boyne was thus due to papal intervention; but some authorities hold this to be an atheistic fiction, contrived for the purpose of discrediting both Orangeism and the papacy.

Hyacinth is, by way of *jacinthus*, a spurious Latin form of the Polish Jacek, Jaczko, or Jacko, a form of John or James, as in Spanish *Iago*. A member of the noble family of Odravag, he was born at Camin in Poland in 1185, and studied at Cracow, Prague and Bologna, at the last of which universities he took the degree of Doctor of Laws and Divinity. On his return to Poland he benefited from the nepotism of his uncle Ivo Konski, and was given an important administrative position in the cathedral at Cracow. At this stage in his life he was devoted exclusively to worldly things; but all this was to change when his uncle, following the resignation of the bishop of Cracow, St Vincent Kadlubek, in 1218, became bishop himself, and was summoned to Rome on ecclesiastical business. He asked Jacko to accompany him. At that time St Dominic was in Rome, where he had recently received the blessing of Pope Honorius III for his establishment of the Order of Preachers. This is the Dominic whose legend has survived to this day, as witnessed by the song 'Dominique', composed and performed by the French Dominican 'Singing Nun', 'Sœur Sourire', which attained the distinction of reaching no. 7 in the popular music charts on the 7th December 1963; coincidentally, this is the feast day of St Ambrose, who was declared by John Paul II to be patron of the French Army Commissariat.

In Rome in 1218, St Dominic was a figure of majestic austerity. His bureaucratic skills were unparalleled, having been initially exercised in his ruthless suppression of the Albigensian heresy which had devastated his native Castilla; and his Order was a model of religious surveillance, which could not help but commend itself to those who ruled the Vatican. He was often to be seen striding purposefully around the Holy City in his habit, exhorting all he met to shun the fleshpots of the Forum, creating daily reformations by his hermeneutic presence. It was on one such peripatesis that Dominic met Jacko Odravag; or rather, Jacko Odravag met him. He had just emerged from a trattoria in the shadow of St Peter's after concluding some valuable church business. It was a beautiful April day, the 19th to be exact, the feast of St Expeditus, patron of urgent cases, and matters of reluctance to deliver, or procrastination; and Odravag felt an inner glow of wine and sanctity at having successfully invoked the patron's name, for the suit of a third cousin laying claim to a minor prelateship, which had languished for years in the toils of a serpentine legalistic process, had now suddenly recommended itself to the cardinal responsible for the taxing of the Polish beet industry, since Jacko had casually dropped the name of a notorious courtesan known to have associations with the cardinal's sister. As he emerged, arm in arm with the chief negotiator, into the cool block of shade below the awning of the trattoria, the piazza was a blaze of white light traversed by parasoled cardinals, wimpled nuns, well-horsed noblemen, bookmakers scribbling in pocket-books, itinerant tinkers bearing trays of holy relics, wandering minstrels, three-card trick men, clowning saltimbancos, posture-masters, wheelers, dealers, one-legged men on crutches, legless men on little trolleys, ice-cream vendors, statue-mongers, hooded monks, and kings of Ethiopia. Then, as Jacko feasted his eyes on the magnificent scene, like a bolt of lightning hurled by Jupiter into the throng appeared the dynamic Dominic, his stark black habit contrasting severely with the elaborate high couture outfits on show. He happened to materialize immediately before a cavalcade of minor Roman nobles; the lead horse shied at the apparition, and its rider was unhorsed on the spot. His gorgeous ostrich-feathered headgear afforded no protection as he struck the granite flags of the piazza head-first, and was killed before he knew it; though, for an instant, as he fell, the whole of his life flashed through his mind, and he remembered especially the pleasurable sensation of drinking water as a child from a glazed earthenware cup whose inner lip bore a motto he was too young to be able to read, but now he saw and understood the letters clearly, which said *Who drinks from me shall* – but he died in mid-sentence. Dominic was unperturbed. He stooped, and from a pocket in the folds of his drab garment he produced a handful of oatmeal. From another pocket, a sharp knife with which he opened a vein in his wrist. He mixed the blood and oatmeal, and thrust this concoction between the dead man's lips. The minor noble's eyes sprang open immediately, and he rose from the dead like a gymnast in full possession of his faculties.

The surrounding crowd began to bay the praises of Dominic, but he quelled them with a glance of his querulous eyes. He spoke about the resurrection of the body, and the life of the world to come, and his words resounded through the dazzled amphitheatre, entering the vestibule of Odravag's ear like drops of paregoric distilled in eternity. As he drank in Dominic's tirade, Jacko felt himself go all limp; he fell into a swoon; when he recovered, opening his eyes, he found he'd been bewildered into being born again; and he scorned his former occupations.

Now, Jacko became the most avid of Dominic's followers, and wholeheartedly enjoined his rule of chastity and obedience. After a brief novitiate of six months, he was appointed Superior of the Polish Mission, for many of his people still maintained the old pagan gods, whose loose-limbed wooden dolls adorned the cabins of the poor. Arriving in Cracow with his team of Dominicans, he was received with much fervour, and his sermons proved miracles of conversion. He founded convents of his order at Sandomir, and at Ploksko on the Vistula. Then he rapidly passed through Poland, remonstrating, preaching, carrying the gospel imploringly into far-flung Pomerania and Prussia. He boarded the fastest boats of the time to Denmark, Gothland, Sweden, Latvia and Norway; and he entered Lithuania at lightning speed, causing havoc among the Odin worshippers, and devotees of Juraté, the mermaid goddess. Then he visited Red Russia, where he combated the Eastern Church, and persuaded its prince to desert it for the Roman communion. Everywhere he went he built convents, and enlisted suitable virgins as nuns. He built them at Lemburg, and at Haletz on the Mester, and then invaded Muscovy. With noble tolerance, the Duke Vladimir IV, son of Ruric II, allowed Jacko to establish a convent at Kiev; but he was deaf to his entreaties that he should become a Roman Catholic, for the ways of his fathers were too deeply ingrained in him. Regrettably, the preaching of Jacko in Muscovy left no appreciable results.

While Jacko was at Kiev, a terrible Mongol invasion occurred. The princes of Russia, distracted with rivalry, their strength broken by internal squabbles, failed to put up an effectual resistance. The Mongols swept all before them, raping and pillaging, swarming into the fantastic churches of Russia on horseback, shattering the gorgeous glass with arrows; they tore the ikons from their tiered iconostases, and spat on them, and burned the libraries of unreadable books. Then, having reached the river Kalka, in the year 1224, the barbarians mysteriously retired; but innumerable hosts gathered under Bathi, the grandson of Genghis Khan, and in 1236 they burst on Russia again, streaming in unstoppable hordes across the steppes. In 1237 they turned their attentions to the Ukraine: Kremenchuk, Poltava, Zolotonosha, and Pereyaslav were sacked in quick succession. Now the Mongols surrounded Kiev: even they paused before its antique beauty – its green and scarlet and gold and blue cupolas, and spires hung with shining chains, reverberating carillons of bells all day long – and offered to spare it, if it would open its gates. In the absence of the princes of the Russian Empire, the citizens of Kiev rallied under the leadership of the minor noble Demetrius, preferring a glorious end to the disgrace of slavery. After a bloody siege, the walls of the city yielded to the barbarians' onslaught; and now every tower, every stately church and monastery were converted into fortresses. The magnificent cathedral of Hagia Sophia, the church of the Tithes, the monastery of St Michael, and the Pecherskoi monastery: all were taken by storm, and looted, and torched. John the Metropolitan, it is believed, perished in the general massacre amidst his flock. Jacko escaped by walking across the river Dnieper: according to the account of Severinus of Cracow in the *Acta Sanctorum*, when word came to him that Kiev was taken, he made ready to flee; but the alabaster statue of the Virgin called out to him, Jacko,

Jacko, are you fleeing from the Mongols, and leaving me behind? Whereupon he answered, You are too heavy to carry – and the image answered, Try me. He then discovered she had become miraculously weightless; he carried her all the way to Cracow, where she afterwards became an object of great veneration.

Jacko now preached to the Jazyges on the Danube, and baptized many thousands. He then travelled to Tibet, where, although his mission was comparatively unsuccessful, he acquired the arts of levitation and astral projection; these were to stand him in good stead upon his return to Russia, where he wrought many miracles. For instance, on one occasion he was crossing the Vistula when his boatman told him that he had been praying for two weeks to the Blessed Virgin for wine to celebrate the Epiphany. Jacko said, Your prayers are answered, whereupon an enormous fish jumped into the boat, which lucky catch the fisherman sold for an abundant supply of wine. Another time, a nameless rascal determined to steal three beehives from a convent founded by Jacko: to compound the crime, he first got drunk in a nearby inn, then stole a boat in order to transport the bees to his home, for the apiary was in an orchard that ran down to the river's edge; but he was found dead the next morning two miles downriver, stretched out in the drifting boat, covered in swarming bees. Then there was the case of the locksmith who made a key on a Sunday; the next morning, the fingers on both of his hands had stiffened, and before long his fingernails pierced his hands, so that the man who made a device for locking a door had his hands locked. For four months the fingernails pierced his flesh like alien invaders, and his palms festered. By good luck, Jacko was passing that way and made to shake hands with the man, till he saw his predicament; whereupon he pulled out a key from his habit, and inserted it into the man's fists, and turned, and the man was healed. This, indeed, is not unlike the story of the reckless man, who, not respecting the holy day of the Lord's resurrection, took his harvest to a millstone, and started to grind the grain by hand, when he found his hand irremediably stuck to the wooden lever. So they had to saw him free, and the lever remained stuck to his hand for three months before he met Jacko, who fed him a handful of rye flour, which released him immediately from his bondage, and he stretched his right hand to God and gave praise. I could mention many similar incidents, besides examples of the blind being made to see, and the dumb to speak, and the deaf to hear, and of the dead being raised from their sepulchres.

Jacko had a book, which was miraculously preserved from fire. He had loaned it to a disciple, for the salvation of his soul, and the correction of his life. When night fell, the monk lay down on a bed filled with old straw, and placed the book beneath his head. As he slept, a man appeared in a dream, and said, Do not sleep on this straw, for it is cursed by blood! That is to say, that some unspeakable crime had been committed on this very straw, and that it was not a proper resting-place for such a holy book. But the monk turned over in his sleep and promptly forgot the vision. Then the man appeared in a dream a second time, and said, Do not sleep on this bed, for it is cursed by blood! And in the dream the monk found himself hovering over the bed as he watched the straw heave and pullulate with millions of maggots. But he turned over in his sleep and forgot what he had seen.

Then the man appeared in a dream for the third time, and said, Do not sleep in this bed, for it is cursed by blood! And he revealed himself to the monk in an unmentionable way. The monk woke, greatly perturbed, and he ordered a servant boy to take the straw from the bed, and burn it in a fire; but he forgot about the book. The servant boy set fire to the straw, book and all. About an hour later, the monk realized his loss, and ran to the scene of the fire. Everything was in cinders, save the book, which was untouched.

This was the book to which Jacko confided his innermost soul, writing in a nervous delicate hand with a crowquill pen using oak-gall ink on parchment manufactured from the skin of an aborted calf, and we are fortunate that some relics of his thought remain to us, for fragments of some pages of the book have been preserved in various locations in Lithuania, in the Ukraine, in Bohemia, in the former Yugoslavia, in Latvia, in Poland, in Muscovy, and in Estonia:

– putting one foot before the other on the water, forgetting how to wade, I proceeded like a man walking on a rope across the water, and I thought of its miraculous shoals of fishes glid-ing under my feet. I could see the Lord clearly at the other side, as he beckoned me towards him. The moon was up, and I felt at my back the heat of the city on fire, and I heard the cries of the abandoned –

– I was born an Odravag, a Polish prince. At the age of thir-teen I lost my virginity to my uncle's whore. At fifteen, I knew the use of a knife, for I stabbed a cousin. At seventeen, speaking fluently in Latin, I impressed the doctors of the church. At nineteen –

– cold air, long distance. Gazing over folded snow-capped mountains. Vultures circling in the sky, I drink freezing water from a cup –

– at thirty-three, I saw a man raised from the dead. That man was me. –

– I feel Prince Caloman will listen to my solicitations. I have not used as yet the threat of the Teutonic Knights. For he must abandon the Orthodox communion. Pope Innocent demands it. –

Jacko Odravag, as he was once known, died on the feast of the Assumption in the year 1257. Some of his relics are preserved in Cracow, in a chapel dedicated to St Hyacinth. Many posthumous miracles have been attributed to him: for example, the story of the man who suffered from a blister and was in pain. He asked some men whether any of them had visited the church of the blessed Jacko at Cracow; and one of the bystanders replied that he had, indeed, been there. The blistered man then asked him what he had taken away from the church as a blessing, and the bystander replied, Nothing. The sick man asked him what clothes he had been wearing when he visited the holy church. The other man said he'd been wearing the very clothes he was standing in now, whereupon the man with the blister confidently snipped off a piece of the other man's clothes with a little scissors he had somehow concealed about his body, and placed it on his blister; and as soon as he had done so, the blister burst, and the man was immediately relieved. It is related by another authority that this particular remedy was so effective that anyone who suffered from a blistering sore would rush into the church dedicated to Jacko, and had only to seize the curtain over the door, or a bit of the draperies that hung on the walls, to be restored to a blisterless state.

In Jurbarkas, in Lithuania, until recent years, a holy well of St Hyacinth, or Jurko, as he is known to the Lithuanians, was traditionally maintained. Here, on the eve of his feast day, the inhabitants would congregate to dance, and drink copious libations of their local aquavit, and make conversations with the saint throughout the August night. At dawn, they would let nets on long handles down into the well, and draw up pebbles of amber, which were prized as amulets against death by fire or water, which leads us to the shores of Lough Neagh, and Cranfield, in County Antrim, where such a custom also used to reign, and might still, for all I know.

KIPPER

Behind 'Cranfield' lurks the ghost or garbled echo of an Irish name. Cranfield has nothing to do with cranberries, nor fields. It has nothing to do with cran, a measure of capacity (37½ gallons) for herrings just landed in port, from the Irish *crann*, a measure; nor is it even connected with the primary meaning of *crann*, a tree, let alone its derivatives, a step in dancing, an ornament played on the Irish pipes, a piece of stick used in casting lots. Cranfield is from *creamhchoill*, wild-garlic wood, where the nasalized *mh*, pronounced somewhat like English *w*, has mutated into *n*, and the guttural *ch* has become *f*. This verbal metamorphosis is appropriate: the native woods of the Lough Neagh shore have long since been replaced by fields, and the Irish language supplanted by English, or Scottish. I do not know if wild garlic still grows in Cranfield.

Deirdre Shannon, my wife, was walking with her parents one day in the vicinity of the Holy Pool at Cranfield church. Two elderly couples were out walking there too. As Deirdre described them, they looked like they might be golfers, or at least people with a common aspiration to some minor grandeur. They were casually well-dressed. All four wore Hush Puppy suede shoes. Behind their modulated English lurked a glottal burr of Scottish. She overheard them telling each other stories of their youth. How they used to come here and fish. How they would ramble the fields, picking wild flowers, sloes and blackberries. Remembering their play of hide-and-seek among the long grasses and the tall hedgerows. How the summer air was drowsy with the scent of sweet briar, eglantine, and dog-rose. The buzzing of the bees. How they would fish for amber in the Holy Pool, in those days long ago. They'd tie a tin can to a pole cut out of the hedge and they'd dredge up nuggets of amber from the murk, which items made valuable media of barter, and were reputed to have magical powers.

I confess I was sceptical about Deirdre's story. So I thought I'd look it up, and found it corroborated by the *Ordnance Survey Memoirs of Ireland*, in an account given by a T. C. Hannyngton, in 1835:

There is a holy well 94 yards to the east of Cranfield church. It is fine spring water and produces amber crystals. The country people assemble there on May Eve. There is much drinking of the local *aqua fortis* which they distil from potatoes, and dancing to the bagpipe. At dawn, they drain the well and take out the crystals, which they believe to grow only on May Eve.

These they take with them to America: their tradition is that
no ship can be wrecked in which they are; neither can it go on
fire. In previous times, it is said, the well was attended by an
important fly, whose movements were studied by those desir-
ing to know the outcome of their wishes. The guardian fly was
supposed to be exempt from the laws of mortality. To the eye
of ignorance he sometimes appeared to be dead, but it was
only a transmigration into a similar form, which made little
difference to the real identity. Every movement of the sympathetic fly was regarded with silent awe, and as he appeared
cheerful or dejected, the anxious votaries drew their presages.

Reading this passage again, I picture this guardian as a daddy-
long-legs, or crane-fly, which comes from the Old English *cran*;
here English and Irish meet in an etymological blur. The Lough
shore is notorious for flies: millions of midges emerge here in
summer. Clouds of them viewed from a distance look like the
smoke from bonfires. Sometimes the sun is darkened by their
swarms. So, to be significant, the fly that guards the well must be
solitary – more visible – a thing whose fragile long-legged stum-
blings we both pity and admire.

The common Lough Neagh fly has a bit-part in the etymology
of the old graveyard called Templemoyle, in the Barony of
Toome, not many miles away from Cranfield. Here is T. C.
Hannyngton again:

The old graveyard called Templemoyle is situated in the town-
land of Kilvillis – *cill mhilis*, that is, sweet church – on the farm

of Laurence McKeown. Tradition has it that St Bridget intended to build a church here, but could not succeed in raising it higher than the foundation, on account of the workmen becoming drunk on beer distilled from heather, which had no froth on it until Bridget ordered them to take froth from the mouth of a boar which was pursued by a swarm of gnats, which was to pass that way; and to cast the same froth into the cauldron which contained beer, and which caused it ever after to froth plentifully. When St Patrick heard of the conduct of Bridget, in allowing the workmen to get drunk, he ordered her to wander about till she could find two birds perched on a deer's horns, and which she found at Duneane Church, and there she was desired to build a church, which now stands without a steeple, a 'moyled temple', for 'moyled' comes from the Irish *maol*, bald. And Duneane signifies in the Irish language Dughen or Deahen, 'two birds perched on a deer's horns'.

This somewhat garbled account puts us in mind of *Sliabh Dá Éan* in County Sligo, the Mountain of Two Birds; *Bealach an Dá Éan*, in Monaghan, the Route of the Two Birds; *Dún Dá Éan*, in Donegal, the Citadel of Two Birds; and *Snámh Dá Éan*, on the banks of the Shannon River, Swim Two Birds.

> *The Shannon bore me to thy bosom wide:*
> *I wandered with it on its winding way*
> *By fields of yellow corn and new mown hay,*
> *And far blue hills that rose on either side,*

And low dark woods that fringed the ebbing tide;
And ever as its waters neared the west,
Out of the slumber of its broadening breast
Faint momentary ripples rose and died: —
And rose again before the breeze and grew
To wavelets dancing in the noonday light,
And these were changed to waves of ocean blue,
And creek and headland faded from the sight,
And oh! at last — at last I floated free
On the long rollers of the open sea.

E. G. A. Holmes

Sometimes Lough Neagh, on a stormy day, billows like the open sea with waves. Sometimes a considerable extent of its surface freezes over. In the winter of 1878–9 the thermometer, for weeks on end, stood many degrees below the freezing point, and during a large portion of the time, there was a dead calm. The snowflakes fell languidly, enveloping the face of nature in a beautiful, fleecy winding-sheet, thus shielding many plants from death. The birds became tame with hunger, and many lame from frostbite, while thousands died a lingering death. In the streets of Antrim, large flocks of larks were observed.

But though the aspect of nature was wintry in the extreme, it was an aspect which will have impressed itself on many minds by the singular beauty of the scenes witnessed. Every tree, shrub and plant which rose above the great winding-sheet was for a time a striking picture, an artistic study. The snowflakes had gently fallen and alighted in a fairy-like manner upon the strongest branch and tenderest twig; and as they appeared to come from a warmer region to a colder one, they adhered tenaciously to whatever they touched – every branch and leaf and spray becoming coated with the most delicately beautiful ice-crystals it is possible to imagine. Nature donned a silvery armour infinitely passing the skilful manipulation of the worker in the precious metals. Every object was studded with an infinity of diamonds, whose dazzling beauty as they caught the first rays of the morning sun filled the spectator with admiration and delight.

On the Lough itself, skaters from Belfast and other places congregated in considerable numbers, many of whom had penetrated to the outer border of the great ice-sheet, probably two-and-a-half miles from the Antrim shore. On making one's way out, the scenes beheld were truly novel. Group after group of skaters and sliders, picnicking parties and onlookers, who had, in consequence of the haze, been previously invisible, came into view, while those who had reached the outer extremity, and when not more than half-a-mile distant, appeared no bigger than nine-pins moving about on the horizon. The effect was most peculiar, the distance being magnified in a most remarkable manner. These had pushed on until they discovered a skater's Eldorado – a belt of beautiful, glassy ice, on which not a single snowflake rested – while beyond appeared gurgling waters, mist, chaos. Some of the skaters had brought sails with them, and were being blown about at a terrific speed to and fro like miniature tea-clippers. Indeed, some connoisseurs of the noble leaf, 'which vanquisheth heavy dreams, easeth the brain and strengtheneth the memory', brewed libations in tin pots on little turf-braziers, which they had set on the ice, where one could overhear them sip the steaming amber liquor and discuss the heterozygosity of tea.

How pleasant and delightful it was, to bandy words like Ceylon Orange Pekoe, Keemun, Lapsang Souchong, Rose Pouchong and China Caravan, to appreciate the merits of a Lady Londonderry! One sniffed the icy air appreciatively, for it bore their warm aromas: fragrant as of flowers; fruity as of lemons; spicy as of cloves; resinous as of pines or burning amber; burnt as of tar; and putrid as of fish or eggs. 'There are a thousand and ten thousand teas,' says the sage Lo-yu. Of these we may single out for praise the Irish Breakfast Tea, a black India variety, with a blaze of golden tips; the famous Gunpowder tea – young leaves, tippy, rolled in balls ranging from Pin Head to Pea Leaf, the best grade of China green tea; and English Breakfast Tea, with its high Ceylon content, whose taste is as delicate as the thinnest of cucumber sandwiches.

Fresh cucumber might have been out of season; but the ladies had packed in their hampers some jars of the pickled Dutch variety. Indeed, the convivial scene resembled nothing so much as those favourite Dutch pictures of winter pastimes. While the female of the species prepared the abundant post-match repast, the males exhibited their prowess at a novel game of hockey, using the lid of a tea-canister in lieu of a ball, and inverted walking-canes as sticks. The boys and girls skidded each other about on tea-trays, too busy to indulge in the adult comestibles, which included, besides the Dutch cucumbers sliced as a side-dish, Randalstown sausages and Cullybackey bacon sizzled in a griddle on the brazier, and the famous kippered pollan, that fish indigenous only to Lough Neagh. This pollan, from the Gaelic *pollán*, a thing found in a hole or lake, is a unique freshwater herring, and its flavour is impossible to describe if not experienced, but many who have known both have favourably compared it to the Black Sea sturgeon, which yields caviar and isinglass. The kippered pollan is a delicacy among the Dutch, as are the Lough Neagh eels, which flourish here in great abundance. They are principally of two kinds: the sharp-nosed (locally called worm eel), and the broad-nosed kind (locally termed the gob eel): the former is more common, and is taken in great quantities at Toome in the north-west, where the water discharges itself into the River Bann. So prodigious are the catches – some 70,000 have been landed in one night – that the local markets are unable to absorb them, and so the excess are smoked and exported to Holland, together with the pollan. In this way an amicable aquatic fellowship has been cultivated between the Irish and the Dutch, and a reciprocal trade in tobacco and meerschaum pipes has been established, much to the satisfaction of adherents to that 'luscious leaf of fragrant savour'. Hollands gin is also imported in some quantity. The local Dutch agent, a Mr Jan Both, is well known in these parts as a convivial host, who takes great delight in conversing with the fishermen and exchanging piscine anecdotes. He is especially interested in the local legends concerning mermaids and water-horses, and it is to him that we are indebted for the following account.

In 1630, Holland was visited by a storm that carried away dikes and forced the sea into the meadows. Some market-women, crossing the mere in a boat, saw a human head above the water. When they got nearer they found it was a mermaid floundering about in the mud. The woman-fish made some resistance, but they speedily conquered that; and by kindly usage taught it to wear woman's clothing, to eat bread and milk, and to spin. Even more remarkably, she displayed a singular predilection for the art of painting, which was at that time entering its Golden Age in Holland, as its masters vied with each other in the accurate depiction of everyday reality. Being shown the uses of brush, pigments, palette, canvas and easel, and all the other accessories of the craft, she took them up with alacrity, and within a matter of days was able to reproduce a likeness of a merman, and those who saw it swore it breathed, it looked so real. She then, over the sixteen years of life that remained to her, after she had been taken from the drowned meadow, proceeded to paint an extraordinary series of canvases of marine life. At the time she was residing in the Town-house at Haarlem, with a woman attendant, but it was impossible to teach her to speak. It is reported that she made her reverences very devoutly when she passed a crucifix, and had some notion of a deity. Indeed, some interpreters of her art saw in her depiction of fishes a reflection of the bountiful Creator; for some of the species painted by the mermaid were hitherto unknown to man, until a specimen would be discovered in some serendipitous trawl for herrings, and what had been dismissed as fantasy became an intimation of reality.

The amber-fish – also called the amber-jack, the sea-bream, or dorado – was not sighted until the year 1639, and that in the sub-tropical Atlantic; yet the mermaid had accurately forecast the beauty of its near-translucent golden skin, and had registered exactly the odd Vermeer blue of its eyes, and its carp-like mouth, in 1634. This fish is not to be confused with the dorado of the Indian Ocean, which the mermaid is unlikely to have known; but it is worth observing in passing that my compatriots, the navigators Pieter Dirkszoon Keyser and Frederick de Houtman, bestowed the name Dorado on a small southern constellation which is notable for containing most of the Large Magellanic Cloud, a small neighbour galaxy of our own Milky Way. Among the other constellations which they traced was Pavo, the Peacock, the sacred bird of Hera, wife of Zeus; and how the peacock came to have eyes on its tail is another story, which if I were to relate now would detain us too long from the matter in hand.

To continue: painting the scenes of her former habitat was the mermaid's chief delight. She would happily labour for hours at her canvas, using the finest camel's hair brushes to achieve her effects of meticulous delicacy. Such colouring! — slate blues, coral pinks, pale amphitrites, the wet cobblestone blue of mussels, frail sea-forget-me-nots, anemone yellows and carmines, emeralds and eau-de-nils! No scale of being could escape her microscopic gaze. In some of the mercurial pupils of her fishes' eyes she would paint a tiny portrait of her self-reflection, invisible except to whomsoever sought it. Or she would paint her keeper, whom she appeared to love devotedly. Indeed, this woman of the Haarlem Town-house was of a most tender disposition; and the pair were often seen sharing a celebratory repast of oysters, tangy-fresh, and Amber beer, with its undercurrent of burnt honey, after the mermaid had successfully navigated a particularly difficult passage of her current work. I have said that the mermaid never learned how to speak Dutch; but so deep was their bond that the woman of the House was able to manage to communicate to some extent with the creature, and came to be her interpreter. By various movements of her tail and flutterings of her eyelashes, the mermaid made her wishes known to the woman, to the extent that she conferred on her the role of naming her pictures. It was marvellous to watch the pair in action, as the woman tried one word, then another, carefully scrutinizing her partner all the time; to see the light dawn in her eyes as she realized the mermaid's beautiful intentions. Then the mermaid would reciprocate with joyous thrashings of her tail. How she could name a thing! So we have titles like *Underwater Grotto with Echinoderms and Cod*, *Although the Star-fish has No Brain*, *Years before Kippering*, *Sea-mouse Evading Catfish*, and *Why Smoke a Haddock, When There are the Pipe-fish and the Sea-gar?*

Merchants enriched by tobacco, beer and herrings, patrons of the arts, astronomers and microscopists, natural philosophers and fish economists, all flocked to her dank quarters in the Haarlem Town-house. All wanted to buy a piece of her art; but the mermaid steadfastly refused, and would not be coerced for any price, for she never learned the use of money. In this she was aided and abetted by the older woman, who made their mutual wishes forcibly known. So, over the years, the Mermaid's Grotto, as it came to be known, grew more and more elaborate, more labyrinthine; and gradually, the light grew more sub-aqueous. Mesmerizing schools of herrings glinted patterns of eternity.

Gurnards and latchets wove their sapphire blues. There were glimpses of the underwater palace of the plaice.

I forgot to mention that the mermaid learned to smoke, as evidenced by one of her titles above; and she was especially fond of the meerschaum pipe for its ostensibly aquatic origins. Mischievously, she would sometimes paint a pipe as a throwaway item in the corner of one of her canvases. Its bowl would be marvellously modelled to resemble the face of some curious fish, and would emit bubbles instead of puffs of smoke: some connoisseurs interpreted these as symbols of the transience of life, others as portrayals of eternal pleasure.

One day in the Year of Our Lord 1646, the older woman fell down dead of an embolism. While she was being buried, a sudden conflagration burst out in the Town-house. When its smouldering ruins had been sifted through, it was concluded that the mermaid, who had been left alone in her chamber while the obsequies were in progress, had knocked over with her tail one of the votive candles that had been left burning in the chamber to signify that the soul of the deceased was in transit to a higher realm; that the volatile oils of the paintings had immediately responded; that the fire had spread to the kitchens above, with all their tremendously combustible comestibles of fat bacon, sugar, lard, cod-liver oil, et cetera; that the refectories above the kitchens, with their resinous pitch-pine tables, had immediately blazed up, carrying the fire to the gentlemen's smoking-rooms above that, to the ladies' chambers, to the private cubicles lined with plush, to the amber museum; and when the flame reached the powder magazine at the top of the Town-house, the explosion was not as loud as might have been expected, for the powder-stock was low, owing to its expenditure in the current war. Nevertheless, all who remained there were consumed – thank God, there were not many, since most were at the funeral!

All that remained of the mermaid was her skeletal anatomy, which, when touched, crumbled into ash. Therefore we have no physical record of this prodigious creature, and no evidence of the wonders of her art. But her legend lives on, and wherever Dutchmen go, they will tell her story, because it is true, and beautiful, and as your English poet John Keats says in his 'Grecian Urn', *'Beauty is Truth, Truth Beauty: That is all ye know on earth, and all ye need to know.'*

LEYDEN

— Yes, continued the Dutchman, it is a curious paradox, that the
sea, our educator and provider, is also our eternal enemy; yet
sometimes, even as she overwhelms us, she saves us, as in the
story of the Siege of Leyden, which I might relate to you on
another occasion. I myself am a Leyden man, and as I speak to
you, my inward eye lights up with its charming prospect of red
roofs, its labyrinthine *graachten*, and the splendours of its Natural
History Museum, which has representative specimens — stuffed,
pickled, or anatomized — of every living animal, from the smallest cheese-mite to the great skeleton of a sperm whale suspended
from the pitch-pine rafters of the ceiling: for you must remember
that the whale was an important mammal to the Dutch, not least
for its very bones, which furnished buttons, combs, hair-clasps,
corset-bones, pill-boxes, the decorative rings on flutes, and the

little draughtsmen-shaped containers for joint-grease for the said flutes. It reminds me that your esteemed writer Oliver Goldsmith was observed to be a passable flute-player, and that he had a walking-stick flute with an amber screw-top in the figure of Bacchus, which, when you twisted it, disclosed a crystal receptacle for *aqua fortis*, set into the head of the flute: this was a marvellous machine, combining three functions in one article, and it is displayed to this day in the Museum of Musical Curios in Leyden.

It was in the year 1755, I think, that your Goldsmith came to Leyden to acquire a medical degree. Some of his general impressions of Holland, I am pleased to say, are recorded in his mighty poem, 'The Traveller', which I understand also to be the title of an Irish jig, but which is a perfect description of his state of mind and body, for, as the poet Keats says, 'Oft have I travell'd in the realms of gold'; and Goldsmith is a most appropriate name for your poet, and these lines make me quite homesick:

> To men of other minds my fancy flies,
> Embosm'd in the deep where Holland lies.
> Methinks her patient sons before me stand,
> Where the broad ocean leans against the land,
> And, sedulous to stop the coming tide,
> Lift the tall rampire's artificial pride.
> Onward, methinks, and diligently slow,
> The firm connected bulwark seems to grow;
> Spreads its long arms amidst the watery roar,
> Scoops out an empire, and usurps the shore.

148

When the pent ocean, rising o'er the pile,
Sees an amphibious world below him smile;
The slow canal, the yellow-blossom'd vale,
The willow-tufted bank, the gliding sail,
The crowded mart, the cultivated plain,
A new creation rescued from his reign.

Goldsmith was drawn to Leyden to hear the great Professor Albinus, whose discourses were at the cutting edge of medical philosophy, and whose researches, using the resource of the newly invented Leyden jar, as it is now known, promised a solution to the eternal question of the origin of the vital spark of life. The Leyden jar, you will recall, is an electrical condenser consisting of a glass bottle coated inside and outside with tinfoil, and having a brass rod surmounted by a knob, passing through the cork, and communicating with the internal armature. With this apparatus Dr Albinus anticipated the experiments of the Italian, Luigi Galvani, who had seemingly, in 1792, brought life to the body of a dead frog; but Albinus had gone further, and was reputed to have made dead cats, dogs and monkeys move in a convincing semblance of their natural gait. Why the publication of these results was suppressed is a story I do not propose to go into now, for it is a long one, and would divert me from the train of my original thought.

Once Goldsmith had determined to go to Holland, he characteristically took a passage in a vessel bound for Bordeaux. At Newcastle-upon-Tyne, however, on going ashore to be merry, he was arrested as a Jacobite and thrown into prison for a fortnight.

The result was that the ship sailed without him. It was just as well for him and for us, for the ship sank at the mouth of the Garonne. Goldsmith forever attributed this escape to the benign influence of the amber knob of his flute, for this material is considered a preventative against death by fire or water. By what route, circuitous or otherwise, he finally reached Leyden, we do not know; but we do know that he wrote a long letter to his Uncle Contarine from that town, in the year 1755. Luckily I have in my inside jacket pocket a little pocketbook compendium of your Goldsmith's works, which carries a printed extract from that very letter, in which he observes my country with a sometimes sympathetic, sometimes jaundiced eye. I quote from it at random:

A Dutch lady burns nothing about her phlegmatic admirer but his tobacco. You must know, sir, every woman carries in her hand a stove with coals in it, which, when she sits, she snugs under her petticoats; and at this chimney dozing Strephon lights his pipe . . .

In winter, when all their canals are frozen, every house is forsaken, and all people are on the ice; sleds drawn by horses, and skating, are at that time the reigning amusements. They have boats here that slide on the ice, and are driven by the winds. When they spread their sails they go more than a mile and half a minute, and their motion is so rapid that the eye can scarcely accompany them . . .

Physic is by no means here so well taught as in Edinburgh; and in all Leyden there are but four British students, owing to all the necessaries being so extremely dear and the professors very lazy (the chemical professor excepted) that we don't much care to come hither . . .

But the same professor is a joy, and makes his lectures fervent and intelligent with wit, and he is magnanimous with it, for he afforded me the great privilege of inviting me to his chambers once. Here I saw sights that would dazzle the eyes of any Irishman: a room packed with complicated apparatuses, retorts and tubes all a-bubbling, and dynamic sparks quivering in glass jars; the air seemed charged with ozone, and all the various surfaces trembled with experimental energy. He has conjured me not to speak further of these processes, but I can let you know that he is probing the very nature of existence, and the metamorphoses by which we live. For without change, there is no life . . .

Here, Mr Both paused reflectively, and began to fumble the pockets of his several waistcoats, which were ranged around his considerable girth like archaeological layers. I had witnessed these operations before, and knew from experience that the search would conclude with the Dutchman's finding a pipe and the other prerequisites for a smoke. I also knew that his lighting up demanded further prior conditions, a series of discoveries whose sequence altered hour by hour, or, more accurately, at those times when the Dutchman felt the urge to replenish his nicotine levels; for the act of smoking implies incremental dimensions of time, and is a kind of sacramental thing, because it pauses time; the smoker, particularly the pipe-man, sits outside

of himself as he contemplates the puffs which measure his existence. And the complicated lull of looking for a smoke is an
important device in the storyteller's vocabulary, as it allows him
to consider the possibilities of the narrative thus far, as if he hesi-
tated at a crossroads late one dusk, finding it difficult to read the
fingerposts. Even when he manages to trace their names, they
mean little to him, for he has not been there before, and only
knows these villages by hearsay, if at all.

So, the Dutchman would initiate his pat-and-fumble routine,
one hand circling clockwise, the other anti-. With the thumb
and first two fingers of either, or both, he would extricate an
interesting diversity of objects from the fobs, slits, manifolds and
deeps of the waistcoats: coats of green shagreens and multi-
coloured silks embroidered with fantastic patterns, or dull slubs
in which an awry thread or brack or two spoke many volumes.
He'd pull out a fish-hook. He'd put it back. He'd pull out a pill-
box whose lid was inlaid with a lion motif. He'd open it,
examining its contents briefly, then put its lid back on and put it
back. What can I say of the cough drop stuck with granules of
tobacco, the nub of chalk, the bits of string, the broken comb, the
pencil stub, the foreign coins, the beads, the swirly marble, the
clutch of iron keys which fitted nothing, the folded buff envelope
scrawled with measurements for a bookcase he would never
build, a watchmaker's screwdiver, the Bible the size of a postage
stamp, all scrutinized, perused momentarily, and put back?

For one thing leads to another, as it does in Holland. The cities,
by means of canals, communicate with the sea; canals run from
town to town, and from them to villages, which are themselves

bound together with these watery ways, and are connected even to the houses scattered all over the country; smaller canals surround the fields, meadows, pastures and kitchen-gardens, serving at once as boundary wall, hedge and roadway; every house is a little port, in which you might hear stories from the seven seas. One can drift from any place to anywhere.

Eventually the Dutchman produced, in no particular order, a short clay pipe, a plug of tobacco, a pen-knife with a tamping device on the end of it, and a box of vestas. These he juggled in a predictable routine; he lit up, and when the pipe was drawing to his satisfaction, he continued:

– Yes, your Goldsmith was a charming fellow. It was with his good Uncle Contarine's money that he had travelled to Leyden. The time came to leave, and Oliver was again without resources. He borrowed a sufficient sum from Dr Ellis, a fellow-countryman living there, and prepared for his departure. But on his way from the doctor's he had to pass a florist's, in whose window there chanced to be exhibited the very variety of tulip which Uncle Contarine had so often praised and expressed a desire to possess. And, though the market at that time had considerably depreciated from the excesses of the great Tulipomania of a century previous, these flowers still commanded considerable prices. Goldsmith, nevertheless, never one to interrupt a generous impulse, plunged into the florist's house and despatched a costly bundle of bulbs to Ireland. The next day he left Leyden with a guinea in his pocket, no clothes but those he stood in, and a walking-stick flute in his hand. For the rest, you must see his story of the Philosophic Vagabond.

The good nature of Goldsmith puts me in mind of my fellow Leydener, Jan Steen, whom some have characterized as a jocular sot, a hapless ne'er-do-well, constantly in financial straits, while admitting that he was unsurpassed as a master of a lower, comic mode of painting. Born in 1626 the son of a brewer, Jan Steen seems to have intended, as one commentator puts it, 'to make brewing his staff and painting merely his cane; but sociability and a terrible thirst were too much for him'. But others have pointed to instances of circumstantial misfortune in his affairs: in 1654, for example, his father set him up as manager of the Snake Brewing Company in Delft; this was the very year that the Delft arsenal exploded, devastating the town; not a house, it was said, was left undamaged, and it can be presumed that Jan Steen's business was not unaffected by the disaster. At the same time, there are many witty anecdotes about Jan Steen's improvident nature, of which the following is a typical example:

Instead of brewing beer, which is a laborious and finicky task, Jan was wont to purchase wine instead of malt, so that one day his beloved wife came to him and said, 'Jan, trade is dwindling; the customers come in vain. There is no beer in the cellars, nor enough malt for a brew. What is to be done? You are meant to keep the brewery lively.' 'I'll liven it up,' said Jan Steen. So he told the men to fill the largest vat with water, and he went to the market, where he bought some live ducks. He poured what remained of the malt into the water, and let the ducks swim around in it. The ducks were not used to such treatment, and flew like crazy through the brewery, making such a racket that his wife came to see what was the matter, whereupon Jan said,

'Well, the brewery is lively enough now, is it not?' And his wife, loath though she was to do so, could not help laughing at his merry prank.

So, to this day, we Dutch have a proverb, 'to liven up the brewery', a saying which is applicable to many circumstances in life. In fact, as you are aware, we Dutch are a most proverbial people. Even a sailor may sometimes fall overboard. Wise is he who is always wise. Never hunt the hare with a drum. The doctor and the sexton are rarely intimates. The herring does not fear the sprat. The amber-fisher eagerly awaits the storm. As the old sing, so pipe the young.

Jan Steen painted several pictures illustrating this latter proverb. The best of these, in my opinion, is that which resides in the Royal Cabinet of Paintings, Mauritshuis, The Hague. I remember it as a generous and ardent composition, whose spontaneity is enriched by the artist's warm palette. The scene is of a family gathered around a table draped with a rug and set with a pewter plate of oysters, a huge half-peeled lemon, and bunches of grapes. To the viewer's left, a woman sprawls indecorously in her armchair, holding aloft a glass to be filled. Above her is a parrot on its perch. Behind her, a grandfatherly old man with a benevolent expression like that of your Irish poet Michael Longley. Next to him, a woman with a babe-in-arms. Standing above her, a servant pouring wine from on high into the first woman's glass. Facing her across the table, an old woman – presumably the old man's wife – displays a song sheet on which is inscribed a version of the proverb. I translate loosely: 'As it is sung, so it is piped, as everybody knows, so everybody sing it with me, be you young or old.' Behind the old woman's back is a group consisting of Jan Steen himself and three of his children: Cornelis, who is learning to smoke a long-stemmed clay pipe held to his mouth by his father; Thadeus, who is playing the bagpipes; and little Eva, who looks out from the picture at us. A cocker spaniel stands in the foreground.

These are the broad outlines of the Mauritshuis *As the Old Sing, So Pipe the Young*, in which Jan Steen's use of red to unify the composition is very striking. The parrot is mostly red: emblem of docility and the ability to learn, he nevertheless seems to regard the merry company with bemused resignation. The wine filling the woman's glass is red: she has been identified as Steen's first wife, Margriet van Goyen, whom he got pregnant while apprenticed to her father, the painter Jan van Goyen. They married in October 1649. The red ribbon at her bodice is undone. The dull red of her slipper rests on a foot-warmer, in which we can see the red glow of the coals exposed. To some, this lady's accessory, known in our country as the *vuur stoof*, implies lasciviousness, especially when depicted thus under the lady's raised hem. The sleeve of the old woman's undershirt is red. The bagpipe-player's hat is red: typically, the bagpipe is considered as the instrument of fools and lechers. The noses of the characters are red, particularly that of Michael Longley, who is wearing, at a tipsy angle, a *kraamherenmuts*, the embroidered hat traditionally worn by new fathers.

For in this picture, everything is slightly skewed. Since every gesture, every thing depicted has at least a double meaning, the picture can be read in many ways. The proverb is itself ambiguous. Our Calvinist poet Jacob Cats, writing in 1632, used it to support his argument that human nature is inborn, and thus we cannot change it; our Jesuit apologist Adriaen Poirters, writing in 1646, advised parents not to indulge themselves, especially in front of children, since nature could be changed by nurture. The parrot is an emblem of a human being. The family is setting bad example: the family is happy. The painter is a father and a fool. Jan Steen the Catholic: Jan Steen the Protestant. Jan Steen puts himself in his pictures again and again. He is the lecher in the tavern tugging at a wench's skirts. He is the rich boor quaffing wine and oysters in a fancy whorehouse. He plays the clown as he plays the lute. He lets his pocket get picked by a smiling girl while he plays the fiddle for an old crone and the smiling girl. In his only known non-role-playing self-portrait, arrayed in sober black and white, Jan Steen looks at you mock-seriously: you feel he finds it difficult to keep himself from bursting out into a fit of laughter. He is wise who always plays the fool. Consider the dog in the foreground, then, who might be innocent of everything. I forgot to mention the two birds in a cage which hangs on the wall above the traditional hat tipped over the left brow of the benevolent Longley. Even the enormous lemon which accompanies the opened oysters is not beyond reproach, for its half-divested dangling peel displays a perfect nipple at its blossom-end, or bosom-end.

Everything is sleight-of-hand. You can see this in *The Cardplayers*. The scene, again, is probably the interior of a fancy whorehouse. Two figures play cards at a table. One is a soldier who might be a young Steen. The other is a young woman. She holds the Ace of clubs in her right hand, while, knowingly and covertly, she shows us the Ace of hearts held in her left. The Ace of spades lies on the floor. Obviously the young officer is being well beaten: his expensive sword hangs on the back of the young woman's chair. A cocker spaniel sleeps on the floor behind her. A man in black proffers the officer a glass of wine. A maid presents a dish with a lobed rim, containing pieces of red fruit, to a woman dressed in black, seated to the left of the table where the cards are being played. Watching all this is a man like myself standing in front of the empty dark fireplace, filling his pipe from a pouch of tobacco. Through an archway to the right, an open door invites us to look through to a second room where a man is attempting to pull a woman on to his lap; by her expression, he should not have too much difficulty. A long-necked cittern hangs on the wall to the left of the arch. Above the monumental fireplace is an overmantel which depicts a darkened landscape with a horseman, distant mountains, and an army tent.

As the Old Sing, So Pipe the Young: coeval with this parable, the Calvinist and Jesuit, Cats and Poirters, quoted its companion: ' *'t wil al muysen wat van catten komt*: the offspring of cats incline to catching mice.' And in his masterpiece, *The Family of Cats,* painted in 1675, Jan Steen shows himself surrounded by a merry, music-making family, one of whom proudly displays a litter of kittens . . .

But here, I had to leave Mr Both, for his story of Jan Steen put me in mind of the story I'd been meaning to tell you, which is the story for the fourth night in my father's ongoing story told by Jack the Lad, which, as you will remember, is preceded by the lady's blowing her whistle, and the door opening up in the side wall, and the twelve men marching out of it with twelve ladies on their shoulders, each of whom carried a black knife in her right hand, and their all sitting down peaceably to hear the next episode, or story in the series, which goes as follows:

MARIGOLD

Long ago there was an old hag living alone between the hills of Dog Big and Dog Little. She had dwelt there as long as anyone could remember. They said she had maybe been around since the days of the Ancients. And indeed, she was withered and bent to the ground with age. No one would approach her house for fear of her. Some said she was a witch. No one had been seen coming from or going to her house for two score years; but she could be seen standing at her door daily, surrounded by her coven of cats. These cats were all her worldly goods, and her only means of livelihood. Of course, everyone wanted to know what she and the cats got up to; but no one had the courage to ask.

One day a gather-up of fellows were out playing hurling. Among them was a half-wit, Pat the Lad by name. He was well known for wandering the counties of Mayo and Galway.

— You're welcome here, Pat, says one of them. Have you any news?

— Indeed I have not, says he, unless I get some from you.

— Well, there's the old witch up there living with her cats between Dog Big and Dog Little, and I double-dare you to go up and talk to her, for if you do, you're the bravest man in Ireland.

— By golly, and by gosh, I will talk to her, and I'll get a kiss off her too, if you'll give me that fine hurley stick you have when I get back, said Pat the Lad.

— I will surely, said the young man.

No sooner said than Pat the Lad shot off, and didn't stop till he got to the hag's house. He walked straight in. The hag was sitting in the corner. As soon as she saw Pat she jumped up and asked him his business.

> — Just a kiss
> From my pretty miss —

said Pat the Lad.

— If you don't get offside I'll give you a kiss that'll sicken your mouth forever, says she.

— Damn the foot will I stir till I get to chat you up, says Pat, and he made a step towards her.

— Keep off, says she, or it'll be the worse for you.

— Take it easy, my good woman, there's a fine hurley for me if I get to kiss you and chat you up. There's not a girl in the country wouldn't kiss Pat the Lad, for we Pat the Lads are the nicest bunch of lads you'd find anywhere. Do you not know that much?

— Who told you to come to my house?

— A friendly fellow who's playing hurling down below, says Pat, and he's the one that's going to give me the hurley.

— If it weren't for the fact that you're a half-wit, you'd pay a pretty price for coming here, says she. With that, she put her hand into the chimney-nook and pulled out a ball.

— Here, says she, give this to the lad who promised you the hurley.

— But I won't get the hurley if I don't get a kiss, says Pat.

— You can kiss my big toe, says she, now be off with you.

— Bad cess to you! And did you think I'd kiss your ould gob? says Pat, and off he went.

When the fellows saw Pat coming, they ran up to see what news he had. Did you see the witch? they said.

— Arrah, hold your whisht till I tell my story. I saw the witch but I saw no cats. By gosh and by golly she's the strangest witch in the world. Look here, she gave me this ball. He showed them the ball. One of the fellows grabbed the ball and kneaded it in his hands to test it. No sooner had he done so, than the ball exploded in a cloud of dust and blinded every mother's son of them, save the half-wit.

So there they were, blinded, screeching and roaring, and within half an hour the whole neighbourhood had gathered around, commiserating with them, curious to know the cause of their sudden loss of sight. When they heard the story, they swore they'd burn the witch and her cats. They took the fellows home. They armed themselves with pitchforks, sticks and bales of hay, and started off for the witch's house.

When they got there they roared at the witch and demanded that she come out, or they'd set her house on fire. The witch appeared at a little upstairs window and asked them their business.

— We're here to kill you, they said.

— Because of the fellows that were blinded? says she. They only got what they deserved. Why should they send a half-wit to poke fun at me, that never harmed them? And if you don't go home this instant, you'll find you'll be the blind leading the blind. But if you do go quietly, I'll restore the sight of the fellows in seven days.

So the folk discussed this proposition, and the oldest and the wisest of them reckoned that it would be best not to bother the witch until the week was out, to see if she was as good as her word. This seemed like sound advice. They all went home.

A week later, the fellows all got their sight back. You can be sure they never bothered the witch again.

One night, a man called Larry the Red was going home from the fair. It was a dark night, and he went astray. And where did he find himself, but in the witch's house! There was no one at home, and since he didn't know where he was, he went into the bedroom, lay down, and fell fast asleep. He didn't know how long he'd been asleep, but when he woke, he heard voices. He raised himself on one elbow, put his hand to his ear, and he heard someone saying,

— Now that you're all gathered here, tell me how you got on since you set off.

Larry jumped out of the bed. He looked through a crack in the door, and saw the witch, surrounded by a cluster of cats.

One of the cats spoke up: I was in the king of Connaught's castle, and I had my fill of griskins. I stole a fine spool of thread for you, and I've left it in your room, my queen.

Another cat spoke up: I was in the house of a big farmer, and I drank my fill of milk straight from the cow. I stole a fine spring lamb, and I've left it in your room, my queen.

Another cat spoke up: I was in a nobleman's court in Galway City, and I drank my fill of cream. When I'd had enough I thought I'd steal a pig's heart. I was creeping out of a hole in the wall. The hole was too small. I knocked a candlestick off the table, and it woke two men who were sleeping on the floor, and they caught me and hanged me from a tree till they thought I was dead. Then they threw me in the ditch. Somehow I managed to crawl out. I came home empty-handed.

Another cat spoke up: O, look at me! I lost half my tail. I was in the king of Leinster's castle. I'd stolen a fine salmon, but the king's daughter saw me as I was making good my escape. She threw a knife at me and took off the half of my tail. But I got my own back on her. There was a posset warming by the fire in her bedroom. I sneaked in and breathed my bad breath over it. She's lying sick to death now, and she'll not be cured till she gets the herb that grows at the bottom of Larry the Red's garden, that lives below — and that's something that she'll never get.

— Larry the Red's! said another cat, that's the very place I was in. His wife had a fine chicken prepared for when he came home, and I stole it, and I've left it in your room, my queen.

— The same Larry would be a rich man, said another cat, if he knew about the pot of gold beneath the tree that grows beside the well at the back of his house.

— Much good would it do him, if he did know, said another cat, for isn't the same pot guarded by the Great Wildcat of the Belly-boys. He wouldn't be able to lay a hand on it.

— But the Great Wildcat died yesterday, said another cat.

Another of the cats was about to speak, when a little bell rang, and the witch called out, Time for bed! Larry the Red lost no time, and was out the bedroom window like a shot. He ran as fast as his legs would take him till he reached home.

His wife was sitting fretting by the fire. She was overjoyed to see him, and asked him where he'd been.

— It was dark out last night as I was coming home, and I got lost, says he, and maybe I fell asleep under a thorn bush.

— I had a chicken killed for you, says she, and nicely roasted, but a stray cat got in and stole it.

— Maybe the poor cat had greater need of it than me, says Larry, and I won't blame him for it.

Next morning, at the scrake of dawn, Larry went out and he found the pot of gold in the very place the cat had mentioned. Then he knew that every word the cat had spoken was true. He took some of the gold from the pot and left the rest where he had found it.

Then he looked about, and he saw a great yellow flower growing at the bottom of his garden. That flower wasn't there yesterday, he said to himself, and surely that must be the remedy for the king's daughter's sickness. If I can cure her, there'll be great fortune in store for me.

When he'd got his breakfast he went into the town and bought a suit of gentleman's clothing. He dressed himself up as a doctor. He bade his wife goodbye. He took the yellow flower with him, and set off for the king of Leinster's castle. When he arrived there, there were doctors from all over Ireland gathered there, but none of them could do a thing for the king's daughter. The general opinion was she wouldn't last another day. The king had put up a bag of gold for anyone who could cure her.

Larry the Red went up to the king and said, I can cure your daughter within the hour, if you'll allow me.

— Go ahead, says the king, but if you do her any harm, I'll have your guts for garters.

Larry went up to the daughter's room and told her he was about to cure her. He put some of the yellow flower in her mouth and told her to chew three times and swallow. This she did, and she rose within the hour, as healthy as she'd ever been.

The king was overjoyed. He gave Larry the bag of gold, and a grand coach and horses to bring him home. The neighbours were amazed when they saw Larry with his coach and pair.

— Didn't I often tell you, says he to them, that there was a power of healing in wild herbs, and you'd scoff at me, but the scoff's on the other side of your face now, for I'm after curing the king of Leinster's daughter, when not a doctor in the whole of Ireland had a cure for her, and that with a herb from my own garden, and it was the king of Leinster himself bestowed this coach and pair on me!

Larry the Red bought a big parcel of land, and built a fine house, and lived at his ease. He only lived another twenty years after making his fortune. When he died he left his wife and his relations rich. One night before he died he told his story to the neighbours, and it was from the same neighbours that my grandfather got the story, and I got it from him. The day Larry the Red died, a hole opened in the ground and swallowed the witch's house. It's likely she and her cluster of cats were in it when it was swallowed up, for no one has set eyes on her, nor on her cats, to this day. The hole of the house of the witch of the cats can be seen to this day, between the hills of Dog Big and Dog Little. And if you'll allow me, said Jack the Lad, I'll have another story for you tomorrow night.

The twelve men rose, as did the twelve women. Good story, they said. The door opened up in the side wall, and they walked out. The lady bade Jack goodnight and vanished. The doorman came in. Jack was fed, and went to bed. The next morning, he got up and spent the day as he had the other days, until he was summoned to the big room. The lady was already there. She asked if he was ready with his story. He said he was. She blew her little golden whistle, the door opened in the wall, and the same company came in. They all sat down, and Jack began his story . . .

It is possible that the yellow flower Larry the Red found growing at the bottom of his garden was the Common Marigold, for an infusion of the freshly gathered flowers is employed in fevers, as it gently promotes perspiration and throws out any eruption. A conserve made of the flowers and sugar is good for trembling of the heart; and it has been asserted that a Marigold flower, rubbed on the affected part, is an admirable remedy for the pain and swelling caused by the sting of a wasp or bee. A lotion made from the flowers is most useful for sprains and wounds, and a water distilled from them is good for inflamed and sore eyes. The leaves when chewed at first communicate a viscid sweetness, followed by a strong penetrating salty taste. The expressed juice is a cure for warts. A poultice made with the dried flowers, turpentine, rosin, and hog's grease, applied to the breast, is efficacious in pestilential and other fevers. Taken internally, an infusion of Marigold is useful in chronic ulcer, varicose veins and migraine.

It was once thought that Marigold should be taken only when the moon is in the Sign of the Virgin, and not when Jupiter is in the ascendant, for then the herb would lose its virtue. The gatherer, who was to be without mortal sin, had to say three Paters and three Aves. Merely to look on Marigolds would draw out evil humours from the head and strengthen the eyesight. The wearer of Marigold would receive a vision of anyone who had robbed him. In this, the Marigold is allied to Dog's Mercury, for Mercury is the patron god of thieves, and it was he who revealed the uses of this latter herb, which has similar properties to the Marigold. Dog's Mercury is a remedy for sore eyes, warts, scabs, tetters, ringworm, and the itch.

The Marigold is said to bloom on the calends of every month, hence its Latin name, *Calendula officinalis*; and one of the names by which it is known in Italy – *fiore d'ogni mese* – also countenances this derivation. Its golden orange flowers open and close with the sun, as Shakespeare observes in *The Winter's Tale:*

'The Marigold that goes to bed wi' th' sun / And with him rises weeping.' Hence it is also known as *solsequia* and *solis sponsa*.

The Marigold was formerly much cultivated in Holland for its use in winter broths, and barrels full of the dried flowers were to be seen in grocers' and spice-sellers' shops. It was an essential ingredient of the seventeenth-century Dutch hotchpotch known as *olipotriga*: other components included capons, lamb, rams' testicles, calves' heads, coxcombs, chicory, marrowbones, artichokes and asparagus, together with many exotic spices from the burgeoning Dutch empire. The brilliant dye obtained from the boiled Marigold flowers was especially popular for its association with the House of Orange, and ladies rinsed their hair with it, in emulation of the legendary amber-coloured locks of Berenice of Cyrene. Marigold was used to dye Dutch cheeses, thus producing an edible orange bloom; and Marigold was fed to hens to enhance the yolks of their eggs; egg-yolks were employed as a binding agent in *olipotriga*. For a while, the Marigold Market in Amsterdam was the focus of all commercial and cultural business in Holland. Scholars, merchants, fishwives, poets, painters, lawyers, growers, sailors, whores, tailors, nailers, tilers, roofers, stuffers, horticulturists, and deep-sea divers, captains, stokers, lens-men, architects, hooks, philosophers, priests, pawnbrokers, nuns: all congregated and rubbed thighs and shoulders in the teeming square, as the high-pitched gabbled mantra of the rising prices of that morning's Marigold consignment was chanted out by wheeling dealers. Prospective buyers dipped their hands in oaken barrels full of Marigold, and sniffed their fingers, or they'd pinch a leaf and contemplate it with their nostrils before chewing and digesting it. A bag of Marigold could buy a whore. Crumbled Marigold was wrapped in tobacco-leaves and smoked, and passed around the jolly crowd. Red-cheeked girls wearing clogs and elaborate head-dresses dispensed glasses of Marigold wine from Delft pitchers. Gentlemen snuffed Marigold-dust from amber boxes, provoking copious discharges of mucus. Hence another name for Marigold, Snot-herb.

On the other hand, it is perhaps more likely that the flower at the bottom of Larry's garden was the Marsh Marigold, *Caltha palustris*, i.e. bog goblet, also known as Fire-of-gold, Gilty-cups, Meadow-bright, Butter-blobs, Bull's Eyes, Leopard's Foot, Meadow Routs, May-bubbles, Water-bubbles, Molly-blobs, Hobble-bobbles, Billy-buttons, Mary-bud, and Horse Blobs. It shares many properties with the Common Marigold, and is called *Verrucaria* for its efficacy in curing warts. When a large quantity of Meadow Routs were put into the bedroom of a girl who had been subject to fits, the fits ceased. An infusion of the flowers was afterwards successfully used in various kinds of fits, both of children and of adults. A tincture made from the whole plant when in flower may be given in cases of anaemia, in small, well-diluted doses. The leaves are highly toxic when raw, but can be eaten like spinach after being boiled, usually in two changes of water. The young buds have occasionally been used as capers, but rather inadvisedly; the soaking in vinegar may, however, remove the acid and poisonous character of the buds in their fresh state.

Marsh Marigold is also called Drunkards, Crazy-bet and Soldiers' Buttons. It is called the Water-caltrops, because of its supposed resemblance to the caltrops, an iron ball armed with four sharp prongs, placed so that when thrown on the ground it has always one prong projecting upwards, used to impede cavalry; the term is also applied to a trap, gin, or snare for the feet. Marsh Marigolds sometimes grow very thickly together, and might conceivably entrap the feet if stumbled into.

Common Marigold and Marsh Marigold follow the course of the sun; and they are flowers of the Sun.

NEMESIS

Phaeton, the Shining One, goes to see his father the Sun, who has not yet acknowledged him. Through the double folding-doors of silver. Great workmanship: made by Mulciber the Mighty. Reliefs of waters, land and sky carved on them. Dark-hued gods in the sea: Triton, Proteus and Aegaeon, his strong arms clutching a pair of whales; Doris and her daughters, some swimming, some sitting on a rock drying their green hair, some riding on fishes. The land full of men and nymphs and other deities. Full of beasts and cities. Then a picture of the sky: six signs of the zodiac on the right-hand doors, six signs on the left.

Phaeton enters the radiant presence, blinded momentarily. Phoebus clad in purple sits on his emerald-embroidered throne. To right and left stand Day and Month and Year and Century, and the hours set incrementally. The Sun doffs his blazing crown and says, Come closer.

– Are you my father? Phaeton asks.

– I am indeed, says Phoebus, and you are worthy to be called my son. And so that you may not doubt me, ask me for whatever gift you want, and I will grant it; this I swear. The words are barely out of his mouth, when Phaeton asks to drive the winged horses. Already the Sun repents of his oath, and says:

– Your words have proved me even more rash than yourself. For this is the last thing I would give you, could I eat my words. But let me strive to dissuade you. You have no conception of the danger of this thing. You are mortal. Zeus himself could not drive this car. The uphill road is mighty tough, even for fresh horses. Even I tremble when I reach the zenith, and look down on the distant earth. Then there's the downhill, trying to hold back the steeds. All this time the vault of heaven spinning. Stars whizz dizzily. I drive contrary to the revolution of the universe. What will you do? Against the whirling poles on axes of quicksilver? There are temples there, you think, and cities of the gods? You did not contemplate the beasts of prey that lie in wait for you? The horned Bull, the keen Archer, the Lion's maw, the curved-arm Scorpion, the Crabwise cut? And the steeds breathe fire from their nostrils. They are not an easy number. I fear for you. Be wise.

But the son is not wise. He demands to see the chariot. Vulcan work. Very fine. Gold axles, gold pole. Gold tyres. Silver wire spokes. Yoke set with chrysolites and amber. The whole thing gleaming. Phaeton runs his fingers over it. Then Aurora springs her purple gates. Stars begin to disappear, as the Hours lead out the horses from their stalls, breathing fire from their bellies well-fed with ambrosia.

Again Phoebus says, Be wise. But the boy must have his spin. He scorns to ask for directions. But the god gives them anyway: Don't take the straight way through the five zones. Your road lies slant. Take a curve inside the three zones, well outside the northern and the southern heavens. Look for the track of my wheels. Avoid the writhing Serpent, and the Altar. And the best of luck to you.

Scarcely has he taken the reins than the horses take off like four bats out of hell. They sense the car's unusually light. It feels driverless, destabilized. Off the beaten track with them. Phaeton's panic-stricken. Can't handle it. Can't see the road. Horses buck-mad. Chariot Armada remnant blasted by hurricane. Pilot abandons useless rudder. What to do? Some sky lies behind, but more looms large ahead. Tries to measure it. Mind boggles. Can't hold the reins. Can't let go. Doesn't even know the horses' names. Pyrïs. Eoüs. Aethon. Phlegon. Steeds reverting to the wild, becoming what they were before their names. Just a few syllables whinnying. And scattered everywhere the figures of huge beasts. Here Scorpio embraces a major part of the dark with his curved arms and tail. Reeking toxic sweat. The sting in the tail. Fear. Drops the reins.

Horses feel them slack on their backs. Now no check. Horses crazed with freedom. Follow impulse. Knock their knees against the stars. Their backbones against constellations. Tails flailing the universe. Mouths devouring nebulae like hay. Horses plunge like rockets towards Earth. Moon amazed. Earth spits and splits. Roasting apple. Global warming. Meadows ashes. Trees torched. Cities perish. Nations rubble. Heather blazing. Glaciers thaw. Mountains burn. Lava flows. Alps, no snow. Bare Himalayas. Harbours drowned.

Boy lost in smoke. Coming or going? Doesn't know. White-hot chariot beneath his feet. Thus the black people of Ethiopa, and the Ind. Thus the Abyssinian desert. Thus Sahara. Thus the nymphs bewailed their wells and fountains. Argos. Amynone. Boeotia, the loss of Dirce. Corinth, her Pierian spring. Not a river left unscathed: Ganges, Phasis, Danube, Nile, Hebrus, Rhine, Po, Strymon, Tiber, Rhône, Don, Ismenus, Seine, Xanthus: all of them parched dry. Great cracks yawn everywhere. Fishes dive to the lowest depths. Dolphins refuse to leap. Dead manatees float belly-up. Even Doris and her daughters feel hot, reclining in their underwater grottoes. Neptune, too, feels the heat, and stays well below.

Can you imagine it? Poor Earth! She lifts her hand to her brow. Wipes off the sweat. Sinks down on a couch. Speaks. I'm talking to you, Zeus. God of the gods. What have I done to deserve this? I can hardly breathe. I'm choked. See my singed hair? The ashes in my eyes? This is a reward? Year in, year out, men plough and harrow me. I'm tormented by their spades. Sheep shit sheep-shit on me. Cows dung. Horses not so bad. Pigs. I grow grain and vines. The eats and drinks are always on me. People piss on me. I don't mind. It's a job. Somebody has to do it. You want to end it like this? If this goes on, we're looking at serious chaos. Stop whatever's going on.

So speaks Mistress Earth. Then her mouth dries up. A shadow of her former self. Jupiter appears. He mutters thunder. Takes a lightning-bolt from his right ear. Throws it at the driver of the car. Meets fire with fire. Throws him from the car. Driver Phaeton loses life. Horses leap apart. Wrench necks from the yoke. Scatter. Here the reins amid the stars. There the axle torn from the pole. The spokes of broken wheels. The thrown golden tyres. The Vulcan body-work all shattered. Brilliant chrysolite and amber fragments splintered far and wide. Ghost horses in the sky.

Fire ravages ruddy hair of Phaeton. Burning rocket hurled headlong. Falls with long trail through the air. Star that does not seem to fall, yet falls. Falls eternally, then falls. In western lands he fell. Found by nymphs. Buried by them. His body smoking still from that forked thunderbolt. Carved epitaph upon a stone:

HERE PHAETON LIES: IN PHOEBUS' CAR HE FARED,

AND THOUGH HE GREATLY FAILED, MORE GREATLY DARED.

Sick with grief, his wretched father hid his face. One whole day went without sun. But the burning world gave some light. Mother seeks bones of son. Found on riverbank in foreign land. Weeps. Daughters Heliades beat naked breasts. Four times Moon full orb. Heliades mourning still. One sister lying on the grave complains. Her feet cold stark. Second sister tries to come. Her feet held fast as roots. Third sister makes to tear her hair. Plucks leaves. Fourth sister's ankles encased in wood. Fifth's arms branches. Bark surrounds loins. Waists. Breasts. Shoulders.

Hands. Then lips. The mother tries to kiss, to tear the bark away. But blood flows from the wounds.

    – Spare us, mother, and now, farewell. So the bark grew over the Heliades' final words. They became all poplar. Still they weep tears of resin, which are turned to amber by the Sun. This is the priceless story of the origin of amber, as told to us by Ovid. Of amber, Pliny has this to say:

I am glad to have this opportunity of exposing the falsehoods of the Greeks. For it should be known that not everything recounted by the Greeks is true, nor worthy of our admiration. Among others, the poets Aeschylus, Philoxenus, Euripides, Nicander, and Satyrus have recounted the story of Phaeton stricken by the thunderbolt, and of the grief of his sisters; how the sisters' tears turned into amber, known to the Greeks as 'electrum', since they call the sun 'Elector', or 'Shining One'; and how this amber is deposited in the River Eridanus, which we call the Po. Any Italian will tell you this story is bullshit, for there is no amber in the Po. Other Greeks mention islands in the Adriatic called the Electrides, to which amber is carried by the Po. But there are no such islands situated there. In fact, there are no islands anywhere within reach of anything carried downstream by the Po.

    Aeschylus places the Po in Spain, and says that it is also called the Rhône. Euripides and Apollonius maintain that the Rhône and the Po meet on the Adriatic coast. Considering their ignorance of geography, we may more readily forgive their ignorance of amber. Less reckless but equally misled writers have described in some considerable poetic detail how, somewhere in the Adriatic, there are inaccessible rocks on which grow trees which, at the rising of the Dog Star, shed this gummy stuff. Theophrastus states that amber is dug up in Liguria, while Chares asserts that Phaeton died in Ethiopia on an island called by Greeks the Isle of Ammon; here is his shrine and oracle; here is the source of amber. The comedian Demonstratus calls amber 'lyncurium', alleging that it is formed from the urine of the wild lynx. The males produce a tawny, fiery amber, the females more of a lemon yellow. The grammarian Zenothemis calls these beasts 'langes', and assigns to them a habitat on the banks of the Po. Sudina says that the amber-producing tree of Liguria is called 'lynx'. Metrodorus holds the same opinion. Sotacus has a splendid passage in which he describes amber oozing from the British cliffs known as the Electrides.

Pytheas comes nearer the truth when he speaks of an estuary of the Ocean named Metuonis, the shores of which are inhabited by a German tribe, the Guiones. From here it is a day's sail to the Isle of Avalon, 'apple island', to which amber is carried by the spring currents, being an excretion of solidified brine. Timaeus shares this theory, but says the island is called Basilia. Nicias has an elaborate proposition in which amber is generated from moisture from the sun's rays; I will not trouble you with its details. The physician Xenocrates holds that amber is washed up on the capes of the Pyrenees. Theomenes tells us that close to the Gulf of Sidra is the Garden of the Hesperides, and a pool called Electrum, where there are amber-producing poplar trees. The amber is gathered by the daughters of Hesperus, and distributed in some mysterious fashion.

And this is not the half of it. The world abounds in amber pundits. For such is human nature, that people believe what they want to believe, or are inveigled into lies. But let me tell you that all these experts are models of objective observation when compared to the great Greek poet Sophocles; I am most surprised that Sophocles, whose tragedies are of such high seriousness, and whose military and political exploits are universally esteemed, should come out with such nonsense. Amber, he tells us, is formed in the land beyond the Indies from the tears shed for Meleager by the birds known as Meleager's Daughters, or Penelope Birds. Can you believe this? That they weep every year? That they shed such large tears? That they once migrated from Greece, where Meleager died, to mourn for him in the land beyond the Indies? No. Yet many do believe it, because Sophocles tells it so. This, of a substance readily available in amber markets everywhere. The whole story is an insult to the intelligence, and an insufferable abuse of our freedom to tell lies.

It is well established that amber is a product of islands in the Northern Ocean. It is known to the Germans as 'glaesum'; so, one of these islands, known to the natives as Austerevia, was dubbed Glaesaria, or Amber Island, by our troops, when Caesar Germanicus was conducting naval operations there. Germanicus has a fine description of an amber harvest, in which he summons up the wild and stormy atmosphere of those regions, the freezing mist and fog, and the billows crashing on the shores of amber islands, through which the amber-fishers wade intrepidly with nets and tridents, dressed in greased leather to keep out the cold; he tells of the great fires burning in iron baskets hung from gibbets on the shore, and evokes pity and terror by his account of the ragged women and children, some barely able to walk, who, searching for the precious nuggets, pick over the tangled sea-wrack hauled in by their men, as they are whipped on by their overseers.

To resume, amber is formed of sap or resin of a species of pine. This exudation is then transformed by frost, or perhaps heat, or else by the sea, and it finds its way to the sea, where it is harvested. We know that the tree it comes from is a pine because it smells like pine when burned. There is still living a Roman knight who was commissioned by Nero to procure amber, by whatever means, from Germany, for use in a display of gladiatorial skill. Such was the amount of amber he brought back that the cages of the beasts were studded with nuggets of it, and the gladiators' outfits were sequinned with amber. The shields and the weapons and the stretchers for carrying away the dead were all ornamented with amber. And Nero had the corridors and stairways of his palace paved with pulverized amber.

There are several kinds of amber. The palest yellow has the finest scent, but little worth. The tawny is more valuable, especially if transparent, but not too much fire in the colour: what we want in amber is the merest hint of fire. The best specimens are the Falernian, which evoke the colour of the wine; they have a low transparent glow, a mellow tint of burnt honey. When rubbed with the fingers, amber attracts straw, dead leaves and linden-bark, as the magnet attracts iron. Amber chippings steeped in oil give off a steadier and brighter flame than pith of flax. So luxurious a commodity is amber that a figurine of it, however small, is more expensive than a batch of healthy slaves. But what use is amber? I can understand Corinthian bronze because, alloyed with gold and silver, it looks really well. The chased metalwork we admire for artistry and inventiveness. Fluorspar and rock crystal have their integral and practical beauties. Pearls can be carried about on the head, and gems on the finger. But what use is amber? All it gives us is the private satisfaction of knowing we have spent a lot of money on it. Domitius Nero bestowed the name of amber on the hair of his wife Poppaea, for every defect can be termed an asset; and from that time, fashionable ladies aspired to dye their hair with amber.

Amber, however, has some pharmaceutical properties, though that is not the reason why women are attracted to it. It is useful in cases of diseases of the pharynx, and is of benefit to babies when attached to them as amulets. Callistratus says it is good for people of any age as a remedy against attacks of wild distraction and for strangury, both taken internally and worn as an amulet. Powdered and mixed with honey and rose oil, it is good for infections of the ear. And amber is the basis of many fake gemstones, particularly amethyst; but it can be dyed any colour.

So much for amber, says Pliny.

In Ancient China, it is related that somewhere there are cliffs – the cliffs of Ning Chou – in which dwell thousands of bees. When the cliffs crumble, as they do from time to time, the bees swarm out. People catch them, burn them and make them into amber. Honeybees are fried and eaten in China; chocolate-covered bees, and bees in amber barley-sugar are prized by gourmets. Bee vinegars exist, and there are bees in alcohol. Bee marmalade, and bees in honey, have some devotees; for the curative and talismanic powers of honey, which are similar to those of amber, are thus enhanced. Gladiators and athletes of Ancient Rome were well fed with honey; and they ate the larvae of bees to relieve constipation. The Assyrians ground and mixed locusts with honey and dates, which they spread on bread in lieu of butter. Alexander the Great was embalmed in a honey and beeswax amalgam, for honey is a natural preservative of all organic matter. Bees are embedded in the most valuable of amber pieces. Propolis, the stuff exuded by bees to seal up the walls of their hives, is used by man in some varnishes. You will remember varnish is derived from Queen Berenice, she of the amber locks. And the Modern Greek for amber is *beronike*. Miniature boars made of amber are deemed especially lucky, particularly when St Antony, one of whose emblems is a pig, is invoked.

In Lithuania, on whose shores much of the prized Baltic amber is found, they tell of the mermaid goddess Juraté, who lived in an amber palace at the bottom of the Baltic. She fashioned this many-chambered turreted structure herself, taking her inspiration from the spiral shells of the sea; and she is therefore the patron of architects in Lithuania and its hinterlands. Her influence is visible in the church spires of Vilnius and other towns of Lithuania, whose principal industry is peat. By extension, Juraté is the patron of craftsmen and painters; and thus she is sometimes identified with St Veronica, who occupies a similar role in

Christian eschatology. The typical Lithuanian genre interior study shows a room of a Lithuanian log cabin whose fourth wall is us, and whose ceilings and beams have been ambered by peat-smoke. Here sits the father by the fire, smoking his thoughtful pipe-clay pipe, and the mother filleting the herrings, while the children disport themselves on the floor beneath the festive fir, as the smoulder-glow of the lowly burning peat lights up their pastimes of spinning pine-cones and fresh-firecoal-fallen chestnuts. The dog slumbers on, dreaming of the cat, who dreams of mice, who dream of the many-holed Lithuanian cheese whose leftovers adorn the plain pine table; the beautifully depicted bottle of amber spirits has but one transcendental inch left in it, and the knuckle-bone of the ham is pearly visible. All this is glimpsed through a palette patina of amber smoke.

Many miraculous ikons have been attributed to Juraté-Veronica; these are considerably prized by foreign connoisseurs, and the Lithuanian authorities have found it necessary to put armed excisemen in place at all the points of exit from the country, especially the sea-ports. The officials are led by trained dogs who recognize the scent of the ikons' amber varnish at twenty paces, in the manner of the truffle-hunting pigs which root beneath the spreading oaks of Italy. When a dog snuffles about a prospective smuggler's luggage, its exciseman will grab the guilty person in two shakes of the dog's tail; then, the game is up; guy says it's a fair cop; same dogs get rewarded with nuggets of barley-sugar, which they gulp gratefully. The typical Juraté-Veronica ikon shows her sitting in her glory on an amber throne beneath the waves, naked save for some wisps of seaweed strategically placed about her body. Amber halo about her head. Her hands extended, pointing to a great variety of marine species. Sea-slugs. Telescope fish. Electric rays. Skates. Sometimes she rides a smiling dolphin, or a grinning whale. Rarely is she portrayed in the arms of an octopus.

One day, or night – we cannot be sure which, for fishing often happens at night, with blazing torches held above the dark waters – the mermaid goddess Juraté saw a fisherman fishing fish from the Baltic sea, which was her habitat, which she had freely swum for all recorded time, which she regarded as her place. She'd never seen a fisherman before, and she resented his presumed dominion. She saw him silhouetted in his little boat, letting down the complicated nets. Things full of rope and holes. She watched him catch some. Then she spoke:

O man, or thing, whatever you might be, why do you want to catch my cousins, fish that never harmed you, schools that move in perfect unity, or solitary beings wandering my sea? If you catch them, do you not know that you catch me?

He never answered, not hearing her amid the wavy noise. He sailed home and sold his fish, and got the market price. He fed his family. Every dawn or night he sailed out once again into the Baltic blue or grey, and Juraté called out to him, Stop, stop, stop.

Then she fell in love with him. She loved his body stooping trance-like into the ocean, and the knotted cords of his arms hauling the nets, and the veins of his neck standing out. She loved his spear and trident, and his wet protective leather outer garments gleaming wetly, or starred by dried salt. She understood what courage was from him. When she declared her love, the fisherman reciprocated. He left his family for the eternal sea.

Above in his high mansion, the thunder-god, Perkunas, watched all this with a yellowed hateful eye. Eye of the storm. For until now he could not admit that he too loved the mermaid amber goddess Juraté. Mad with jealousy, he fired a thunderbolt at her amber palace. The fisherman, who was lying exhausted in an amber chamber, was killed. The underwater palace was demolished. Perkunas had Juraté chained to its ruins by his myrmidons.

To this day, emprisoned Juraté weeps tears of amber which are gleaned like beads from the Baltic shores by amber fishermen after storms. And the amber bits of her palace are also still flotsam and jetsam; sometimes they include tendrils of seaweed, microscopic fish and fossil molluscs, thus enhancing their prices in the amber market, which delights in such inclusions. To Lithuanians, these things are expensive; to us, tourists with strong currencies, they are cheap at twice the price.

OPIUM

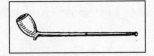

— Yes, said Jan Both, the story of the mermaid goddess has a special resonance for us in Holland; and your tracts concerning amber are both useful and entertaining.

It had grown dark since we last conversed, and we had abandoned the frozen stony surface of the Lough for the warm snug by the fire of the Cranfield Inn. Fortified by port mulled with lemon, cloves and cinnamon, the Dutchman was expansive and relaxed.

— You will have remarked, he continued, on your few visits to my country, that from time to time its moist changeable atmosphere attains a kind of amber glow; and it is to be supposed that such light was more prevalent in the so-called Golden Age of Dutch painting, or that its masters were more responsive and attentive to these fugitive effects. I am thinking of the golden ochres of van Goyen's landscapes, for example, and the shifting tones of the vast skies which subordinate the land as they reflect the waters; or Aelbert Cuyp, of whom it has been said that he saw the world through sunglasses. Into my inward eye springs his *Herdsman with Five Cows by a River*, which bears his autograph of stillness and serenity: estuarine light floats in the clouds above, and the fore-shortened boat with fishermen in the foreground draws our attention to the series of sailboats that carry our eyes to the far horizon. The cows huddle architecturally, and their backs form a straight line. So the atmospheric perspective rises naturally from the moist atmosphere; and I am reminded, here, that our Dutch language has four words for 'horizon', each distinguished by its different properties and depths.

Horizon: this word bears many of your English associations of the line at which sky and earth appear to meet, or the boundary or limit of any sphere of thought. We, too, sometimes think of it as a great circle of the celestial sphere, the plane of which passes through the centre of the earth and is parallel to that of the sensible horizon in a given place; and the broad ring in which our early artificial globes were fixed is also distinguished by the word *horizon*. We are familiar with the concept horizontal. More specifically, a poetic usage of *horizon* is 'where Holland ends'.

Kim: this keen word is found in the jargon of mariners, and is like your English 'rim' or 'edge'. One could apply it to a pewter plate as easily, or to any like vessel, but it is more congenial to a seascape: here, one easily imagines brisk days, and the sails whipping and slapping, outward boats leaving the cold harbours, bound for the Spice Islands. Your English painter Turner, who spent some profitable time in Holland studying our Dutch masters, displays a transcendental grasp of *kim* in his dramatic *Antwerp: Van Goyen Looking for a Subject*. Here, the far-off cloud-capped palaces and spires of Antwerp float on the edge of the sea, illuminated by a sun-shower, like a vision of the New World. Everything else is tossed about by the breeze, including the yacht in which van Goyen stands, identified by his plumed hat. This is one of Turner's many tributes to the Dutch. I recall that when, towards the end of his life, Turner would still receive the odd visitor on his home-made roof terrace in Chelsea, he would point inland, saying, 'My English prospect', and downriver whispering, 'My Dutch prospect.'

This leads us naturally to a contemplation of our next word, *verschiet*. *Verschiet* is indeed 'prospect', with all its attendant ambiguities and implications of futurity. It is the direction in which an object, such as a building, faces; an outlook. It is something presented to the eye: *a pleasant prospect*. It is a thing expected, or the chances of a thing's success or failure: perhaps *not a pleasant prospect*. It is the act of surveying. It is to search for mineral deposits: to prospect for gold, or amber. It is the thing which flits incessantly into the future, and is found in market-places thronged with prospective buyers. Without it, there would be no profit, for promises could not be made. The paintings of the Golden Age are redolent with *verschiet*; and even in interiors its rule is manifest. When, in 1694, the microscopist van Leeuwenhoek dissected the eye of a dragonfly and looked through it with the aid of a candle placed nearby, he saw its *verschiet* clearly: the great steeple of the New Church in Delft, which was 300 feet high and about 750 feet distant from his house, appeared no larger than the point of a small needle seen by the naked eye; and he could tell whether the doors and the windows of the neighbouring houses were open or shut.

Lastly, the increasingly archaic *einder*, the end of sight, as far as the eye can see. We note its Biblical connotations: *the end is nigh*, *to the last syllable of recorded time*, *world without end*. Turner manages to portray both *kim* and *einder* in his *Dutch Boats in a Gale: Fishermen Endeavouring to Put their Fish on Board*. To our left, an ink-dark squall – *einder* – blown straight out of Apocalypse, threatens to capsize the central fishing-boats with their ill-advisedly full sails, and the crew of the smaller vessel, busy gathering their catches into baskets, is unaware that they are on a collision course with the other boats; only by backing his jib could the helmsman avoid a crash, but the wind needed for this manœuvre is in any case stolen by the bulging sails of the other boats. To the right, a *beurtschip*, or Dutch packet-boat, lies close-hauled on the star-board tack in a strong south-easterly, while two other ships, also close-hauled, diminish in the long perspective towards a strip of yellow between sky and water not yet overwhelmed by the cloud – *kim* –

Here, the Dutchman paused and spat a gob of rheum and nicotine into the fire. Warming to his theme, he went on:

– Perhaps I do not exaggerate when I propose that these four words reveal much about our genre paintings of the Golden Age. For the frame itself imposes limits to the sight, and there are further frames within the painting – mirrors, other paintings, maps; marine light streaming through an open window; a door opened to a courtyard, and a brick wall beyond that, and a little roofscape above; the bolder perspective of the tiled floors; skirting the walls, tiles depicting miniature tradesmen out of doors, or windmills. By this means, the eye is always drawn to a new horizon, and is forced to invent from what it sees or cannot see. So the truth of any matter is not readily discerned.

Look at Emmanuel de Witte's *Interior with a Woman Playing the Virginals*: a series of rooms telescoping through open doorways one into the other. In the first room, the woman sits at her instrument with her back to us; above her is an ornate ormolu mirror, in which her face is nearly hidden by a mob-cap. In the second room, beneath a section of a wallhanging map, stand a pump and a bucket. In the third room, tiny in scale, a maid sweeps the floor. Beyond her, an alcove with a tree-blurred casement window. Preoccupied by this vision, we failed to notice at first the fourposter bed to the right of the door in the first room. Now that our eye recedes back into the room from the blur at the end of the passage, we note how the fourposter's hanging half-drawn curtains resemble the vertical folds of the stone window embrasures, and the towel draped on the table beside the lidded pewter wine-jug, placed there to show the gleam of the outer light. Our eye wanders back to the bed, and it's then we notice the man's face looking at us from the dark between the curtains, for he's lying in the bed, and he's been there all along, except we didn't want to see him, not expecting a man to be concealed in such a proper household. Not only a man, but a soldier; for now we clearly see – how could we have missed them? – the unbuttoned trousers, the military jacket flung on the chair, the pommel of the sword beside. Now, the mercury dark in the ormolu mirror looks more threatening, for it looks like a window into another world, which might be ours. And we cannot see ourselves in it at all.

We still can't really countenance the man in the bed. The pump and the bucket have become accomplices, and the purely imagined music of the virginals is compromised. Yet we still imagine unheard fingered harmonies. The tiled floor is lit like a keyboard with red notes between the blacks and the whites so it looks like a stretch of polder with its strips of white lilies and red cabbages and black earth. And yet the world beyond the glass is kept at bay; the soldier in the bed is not at war.

For war is not depicted in the paintings of the Golden Age. There are no canvas panoplies of banners; no armoured regal countenances. A rare naval battle might be manifested; but it is not about the war, it is of sea-craft, and of *kim*. All we see of soldiers is their presence in lounges and parlours and bedrooms; their command is always undermined, or compromised, by female company. Swords sprawled uselessly by chairs and fires. Soldiers blown in from the cold like dogs. Drinking from glasses and pitchers. Smoking long-stemmed pipes and blowing the smoke at the women, or sometimes the pipes lie broken on the tiles. So much for the war. More release to be had from tobacco, I should think, especially when cut with opium, or hemp –

*

Here, the Dutchman paused to take a swig of his mulled port and a glug of his pipe.

— Tobacco! National drug of the Dutch, emblem of the free! Kings prohibited it. Popes excommunicated it. In the East, Sultans condemned smokers to cruel and unusual deaths. What could they know of its catholicon of medicinal properties? For it is used as a sedative, diuretic, expectorant, discutient and siala-gogue, and internally as an emetic, when all other emetics fail. The smoke injected into the rectum or the leaf rolled into a sup-pository has been beneficial in strangulated hernia, also for obstinate constipation; also for retention of urine, spasmodic urethral stricture, hysterical convulsions, worms, and in spasms caused by lead, for croup, and inflammation of the peritoneum, to produce evacuation of the bowels, moderating reaction and dispelling tympanitis, and also in tetanus. Tobacco is an excellent relaxant. The leaves, combined with belladonna or stramonium, make an application for obstinate ulcers and painful tremors. The inspissated juice cures facial neuralgia when rubbed along the tracks of the affected nerves. A pipe smoked after breakfast assists the action of the bowels.

I am fond of a pipe myself, as you see, and I have never had any trouble that way. It will not surprise you to know that when the Dutch, under Johann van Riebeck, took possession of the Cape of Good Hope in 1652, they immediately began growing tobacco. Tobacco rapidly became a currency, for the Hottentots were will-ing to sell their cattle for rolls of tobacco, and the price of a cow was the length of tobacco-twist rope that would reach from its horns to its tail. From there it was only a matter of time before the drug was prevalent throughout the continent of Africa. Some of the native pipes are most ingenious, sometimes of ivory, beautifully bound with brass wire; sometimes with bowls of earthenware and reed stems, as among the Bambalas. Among the Fangs, the stem is a yard-long rib of banana-leaf. For length is an asset to coolness of smoke, and in Cameroon the pipes are so long that a servant is required to apply a light to the bowl. Schweinfurth, travelling among the Bongos of the Congo basin, found them much addicted to the pungent *Nicotiana rustica*, which they sometimes smoked through a rifle, using the touch-hole as a bowl and the muzzle as a mouthpiece. The Bushongo people of the south-west have an appealing philosophy regarding the value of tobacco, which goes as follows:

When you have had a quarrel with your brother, you may wish to kill him. Sit down and smoke a pipe. By the time it is finished, you will think death too great a punishment for your brother's offence, and you will decide instead on a flogging. Relight your pipe. Smoke on. As the smoke curls upwards, you will think the best thing to do is to give him a piece of your mind. Light your pipe once more. Smoke. When the bowl is empty, you will be ready to go to your brother and forgive him, or to ask him to forgive you.

— And this is why, said the Dutchman, the soldiers in the paintings do little else but drink and smoke; for ours is a peaceable nation. After many years smoking, I have come to appreciate more fully your delightful essayist Charles Lamb's saying that he toiled after tobacco as some men toil after virtue. I have smoked with many men, sometimes in distant parts of the world, and never a cross word troubled our company as we puffed content-edly and talked of this and that. Stories would be told after dinner, sometimes on a verandah draped in motionless foliage and crowned with flowers, in the deep dusk speckled by fiery cigar-ends. Now and then a small red glow would move abruptly, and expanding light up the fingers of a languid hand, part of a face in profound repose, or flash a crimson gleam into a pair of pensive eyes overshadowed by a fragment of an unruffled forehead: and with the very first word uttered, the storyteller's body, extended at rest in the seat, would become very still, as though his spirit had winged its way back into the lapse of time and were speaking through his lips from the past.

I have smoked with natives too, and I have ingested their tabloids of cannabis pounded with sesame seeds and honey. I have known the gargled music of the hubble-bubble. Then, evenings of pupil-black mingled with a scent of lemons, olives and patchouli oil: standing in a cool doorway, we would look beyond the snow-capped Atlas mountains to the freezing stars, and contemplate the stories of their constellations. I'd hear my partner whispering in my ear of gods to whom everything is permissible because they are not men. One night, I remember – how could I forget? – I imbibed excessively of pipes of opium. Reclining on my couch, I fell into a pensive mood. All of a sudden the gold silk curtains at the glassless window began to sway slowly, revealing their woof and warp in shifts of muted trumpet music, tapestries of colour I had never witnessed until then, for gold is not just gold. Many hints and glints of other honey shades resided there – topaz, amber, marigold and green – speckles of the humming-bird, and dust of the bee. It took a while for me to absorb all this, as I got lost in the depths of the fabric. When I emerged, the oranges and russet pomegranates spoke to me from their Venetian bowl with promises of juice. When I bit into a peach, I felt the rasp of its skin on the fuzz of my tongue like cat's fur or velvet rubbed the wrong way.

It was then that I became a still-life. I have studied the paintings of Willem Claeszoon and Pieter Claeszoon, of Jan Davidszoon and Abram van Beyeren; the works of Balthasar van der Ast and Floris van Dijck are not unknown to me. The elaborate flower pieces, full of morality and sometimes crawling with insects. The breakfast pieces: apples, bread, cheese, herrings, glasses of beer. The increasingly baroque arrangements of lobsters, butterflies, skulls, candlesticks and drinking-glasses, pewter-ware, fruit, flowers and vegetables, of course, and the occasional pocket-watch, showing its intricate mechanism but never its face. The meticulously dangling lemon peel with microscopic pits and dimples in its zest. Fiddles, oysters, silver cruets, champagne flutes, and cut-glass goblets: in many cases the sumptuous appurtenances are closely bunched on a table-top partly draped by a crumpled Oriental carpet, the better to show the master's virtuosity in paint; and it must have been the rug in the nook of the opium snug where I lay that led me to lose myself, as I tried to fix my vision to its ever-changing patterns. The more I looked, the more I swooned into its universe of loom.

Just as I entered the rug, I saw through the eyes in the back of my head my body sprawled on a couch. The body shimmered briefly; then I became all textile. I'd been made up hundreds of years ago: sometimes woven on the back of a camel, and I felt it with every thread of my being, sometimes woven by a camp-fire of camel dung, while the stars blazed like algebra, and frost glittered on the violet-black roof of the tent. I was sifted by infinite sands. I was the smell of mint tea, mutton-fat and olives. Coffee, cardamom and cinnamon. Pigeon giblets, orange-flower water, garlic. Cumin, parsley, icing sugar, almonds, lentils, raisins, ginger, sweet red peppers, hot red peppers, chick peas, onions, aubergines and watercress: I was all these odours. I remembered the welcome smell of rain. I could practically taste myself: such a hubbub of competing buds! I was a sweet and sour bitter salty peppery self, all shivering tufts and knotted alleyways.

I was privy to many yarns and confidences: I became their compendium. After centuries, I realized that all stories are the same. I was walked on by jackboots, and silk slippers. I was stabbed on three occasions. I felt my stitches. Men and women bled on me. I was copulated on. I was hung on walls for admiration. I was bartered many times: a bag of salt to begin with, then a knife. Later, an ivory snuff receptacle in the figure of a charmer holding two snakes to his head; a small Greek ikon of St George; a scimitar; a book containing all the alphabets in the known world; a pair of bejewelled duelling pistols; an amber bee, attributed to Phidias. My last transaction was a knife again, for I had recently come down in their world; but I had endured generations of them, and would endure more. Possession was their fantasy, not mine. Their habitats are fleeting, and the dogs bark forever.

Now I knew I was a rug for definite, I proceeded to create elaborate accoutrements for myself. Unwittingly, I took as my model the paintings of Willem Kalf. If you are familiar with this work you will know that Kalf is a genius of the Still-Life on Turkish Rug sub-genre, where a selection of appropriate subjects is artfully mastered on to the said rug, both dull and glittering, sometimes inlaid with a mirror-image of the painter in the crystal boss of a cup, and the whole thing deadly accurate in its opacity and sheen. I took it on myself to array me with such items, breathing life into the bloom on a grape before proceeding to fill it with flesh and sap. Encouraged by its palpability, I conjured up a bunch of them, bursting with gooseberry reds and greens. A gutted mackerel occurred to me next, then a pineapple, faceted like the eye of a fly, the inevitable spiral of lemon peel, ladybirds with different numbers of dots on them, fancy hyacinths, and variegated tulips, the conch of a sea-slug, a statuette of Ganymede, a frog, a moth, two butterflies, a sponge, a goblet borne by an amber figurine of Neptune, and some opened oysters: I became these things.

Then I realized I was not a rug at all, but a still-life by Willem Kalf. Now I apprehended the picture of myself without seeing eyes, from within the flat planes of my apparent two dimensions: I comprehended sumptuous red cochineal vermilions, melon-yellows, orpiments, live lobster blues, green malachites, starch whites, oranges, crushed velvet blacks, and imitation pearls. I breathed them together with the earthy tones of raw sienna, ochre, and oak-gall black, above the needle-piney scent of turpentine and linseed oil. I detected microscopic galaxies of amber in the varnish glazed on me. I quickly established the order of the multitudinous brush-strokes which composed me, and from their dabs and dashes and touches began to infer a portrait of the mental Kalf: sometimes nervy, delicate; sometimes assuredly grim and sombre; fastidious; collects fiddles; clever; not necessarily voluble, but given to sententious parables; collects sea-shells; might have made a good preacher, had he not taken up the brush; proud; collects knives; speaks five languages, and all dialects of Dutch; given to occasional depression; outwardly religious; prudish, but fond of good food, especially fish; reads books; hands permanently flecked with paint; smokes; rarely frequents brothels; collects walking-canes; charges high prices; bathes frequently; likes wearing hats, and gloves; goes walking after Sunday service; grinds his own pigments; owns a microscope; myopic; does not remember his dreams; liberal when the occasion demands it; likes cats; has a cast in his left eye; dines out; collects stones; likes wearing cloaks; prepares his own canvases; has the fire in his studio lit for him by a maid; drinks coffee; owns three clocks; has a strawberry mark on the inside of his right wrist; presses flowers; occasionally insomniac; dabbles in music, and can accompany himself on the cittern.

Then I woke up. I was looking in a mirror at myself.

PEGASUS

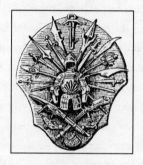

Here, the Dutchman's story ended; for, after uttering the last sentence, he fell into a profound doze. It was no wonder, given the amount of mulled South African port he had consumed, which might well have been inspired by his remembered images of still-lifes with their plethora of half-drunk wine-glasses, flutes and goblets; or perhaps it was the other way about. For memory, as his fellow Dutchman Benedict, or Baruch, Spinoza stated in *The Ethics*, is simply a certain association of ideas involving the nature of things outside the human body, which association arises in the mind according to the order of the manner in which the body has been affected; and one can read 'mind' for 'body' in this instance; so that we can see how the mind is able to zip from one thing to another which has no tangible connection to the first; in particular, if an Ancient Roman thought of the word *pomum*, he would directly arrive at the thought of the fruit of an apple-tree, which bears no approximation to the sound of the word, and looks nothing like it; but the body of the man has often been affected by these two things; that is, he has often heard the word *pomum* when reflecting on a bowl of the fruit, wondering whether to eat one before lunch, perhaps, munching into its possibilities and thinking of the juice dribbling down his chin, and his bad tooth, and should he wear his new toga to the Forum that morning, and maybe he should commission a fruit-painting for the dining-room, remembering the imminent visit of an important dignitary, thinking how his nubile wife will charm the visitor, for the word *pomum* now sounds round and comfortable in his mouth; in like fashion, every man according to his bent will go from one thought to another, for everything in life is habit-forming. A soldier, when he sees the tracks of a horse on the beach, will instantly leap from the hoof-prints to the thought of a horse to the thought of a horseman, and thence to the thought of war; he both pities and admires the armoured rider, splendid in his newly acquired carapace; or maybe he remembers himself setting out for battle long ago. A country farmer will allow himself to be led from the thought of a horse to the thought of a plough to the thought of a lovely corduroy-like polder in which he intends to plant cabbages or spuds or tulips, depending on crop rotation; and he'll inevitably think of horse-shit for its value as a fertilizer, and remember how, in his young day, the lads would follow the horses on the road and shovel up their droppings and bring them back home still steaming in a bucket for their mothers to manure the vegetable and herb and flower beds in the kitchen garden with. The horse-dealer will proceed from the thought of a horse to the thought of money to the thought of an inn where a tulip auction is being held between bouts of tobacco, wine, dice, cards, fights, dance, women and song. Thus everyone, according to their own experience, will jump on this or that express of thought, not knowing where it takes them, thinking it to be a grand adventure; but their destinations have been preordained; and all things are contained in what they are.

As for me, I often go from the thought of a horse to a memory of the famous *Réamhrá*, or Preface, to Séan Ó Ríordáin's collection of poems, *Eireaball Spideoige* (*A Robin's Tail*). He begins with a question: *Cad is filíocht ann?* – which one might translate as 'What is poetry?'; but the English lacks the tangibility of the Irish, and one needs some circumlocution to get into its deep grammar – 'Where does poetry reside?', for example, or 'Poetry consists of what?' Ó Ríordáin continues, as I translate his words:

The mind of a child? Imagine two people in a room, a child and its father, and a horse going past in the street outside. The father looks out and says: 'There's Mary's horse going by.' That is a narration. From all appearances the father loses the horse because he remains outside it. Say a horse is a disease. The father doesn't catch that disease. The horse does not enrich the father's life. But as for the child – he perceives the sound of the horse. He savours the sound of the horse for the sake of the sound itself. And he listens to the noise grow dim – diminishing – finally becoming mute. And silence and noise are wonderful to him. And he gets the horse by its hind legs and ponders their antique authority.

And the world blooms with horsiness and the magic of reins. It's like – like having another countenance. And that, I think, is poetry. The child dwells in his apparition of the horse. Let us say that the mind of a child is a die. Everything that emerges from that die must be stamped with . . .

– And so on, for many pages. Translating it, I have become conscious of how weird this passage is: who else but Ó Ríordáin, obsessed as he was with bodily and spiritual ill-health, would think of a horse in terms of a contagion? And who is this shadowy father-figure saying things like, 'There's Mary's horse going by'? Thus rendering the horse, it seems to me, riderless; or else the father's social skills are as stunted as his attributed imaginative faculties, and he has failed to register that Mary is indeed riding her horse, to what purpose we will never know, but it is nice to speculate on her going to market, and maybe the horse is carrying wickerwork panniers or creels full of produce, but not eggs, we hope, reckoning them too fragile for the journey; and I see Mary in a red cape of the style once popular among the colleens in a now-forgotten class of Irish fiction. At any rate, my English translation seems to have been infected by some Ríordáinese disease, and I am reminded that Ó Ríordáin was fond of playing with his name, for *dáin* is the genitive of 'poem'; so he reckoned that his aspirations to Parnassus were preordained, and the name was a stamp or a die from which he emerged like a Swammerdam butterfly from its pupa, or a tulip from its bulb. So I bore that in mind when I was doing the translating, and became, I think, more conscious of what I think he might have been driving at.

Nevertheless, my English spin on it is sometimes inadequate, sometimes verbose, for language can be registered in many ways; and bringing one language to bear on another is like going through a forest at night, where there are many forking paths, and each route is fraught with its own pitfalls. Take, for instance, *Agus éisteann leis an bhfuaim ag dul i laghad agus i laghad agus ag titim siar isteach sa tost*, which I have rendered as 'And he listens to the noise grow dim – diminishing – finally becoming mute', whose tackily impressive rhyme does not do justice to the simple repetition of *ag dul i laghad agus i laghad*; nor does 'finally becoming mute' adequately convey the strangeness of Ó Ríordáin's use of *tost*, which is ordinarily attributed to people, for it is the condition of being silent. Here it becomes disembodied, a thing in itself like a void, or a bottomless pit, a portal to another time-warp into which the noise sinks irrevocably.

I could have said, 'And he listens to the musical note going diminuendo till it falls into the mute condition', or 'And listens to the sound growing fainter and fainter till it happens to be silent', or 'And understands the noise as it weakens and weakens and falls west into the wordlessness'. These are all plausible readings.

So, Ó Ríordáin's *Réamhrá* has become, for me, an exploration of translation, and I stumble about in the maze of its dark garden. Somewhere a quince tree blooms gold with original paradisal fruit, and sometimes I get its scent. But there are many distracting odours, and the trail is far from clear. And whatever he says about poetry, if you believe it, can be applied equally to translation. I know now that if I were called on to translate that passage again, I would do it differently, because I would have changed my mind by then; and that, too, is an inevitable outcome, given the paths I would have to choose to get there.

So, when I countenance the *Réamhrá*, I proceed to a thought of Ó Ríordáin's poem 'Malairt', which is as much about translation as anything. The word *malairt* itself can mean translation: it is change, barter, dealing, traffic, metamorphosis, destruction: and one can have a change of religion or clothes; one can duel with this word, or take opposing sides. Here it is in a new translation:

Contract

'Come over here,' said Turnbull, 'till you see the sorrow
    In the horse's eyes,
If under you were hooves as cumbersome, there would be gloom
    In your eyes too.'

And it struck me, that he'd so realised the sorrow
    In the horse's eyes,
So deeply had he contemplated it, that he'd been wholly
    Steeped in the horse's mind.

I looked at the horse, that I might see the sorrow
    Looming in its eyes,
And saw instead the eyes of Turnbull peering at me
    From the horse's head.

I looked at Turnbull, then I took a second look,
    And saw beneath his brows
The over-big eyes that were dumb with sorrow —
    The horse's eyes.

And when I think of Turnbull, I think of the ox-man of Giraldus Cambrensis, as translated from the Latin of his *Topography of Ireland*:

People still talk of the amazing man who was once to be seen in the neighbourhood of Wicklow not so many years ago, if indeed it is correct to call him a man. He had all the parts of a Christian body save the end bits, which were those of an ox. From the wrists and ankles he was all ox-hoof. He was bald as an egg with some duck-fluff on it. His eyes were like an ox's eyes, huge and round and liquid. He had this face flat as far as the mouth. No nose as such, just two holes for nostrils. He could not speak; he lowed. He was a great fixture at the court of Maurice fitzGerald, who owned Wicklow at that time, and he came to dinner every day. He could manage his cleft hooves like hands, and he ate everything that was put in front of him. He met an undeserved fate when the bog-Irish put him down because they were fed up being taunted by the Norman invaders for their supposed inclination to beget such beings on cows. Actually, the Irish are well known for this particular vice of bovine intercourse, for it is a matter of historical record that before the Normans ever came to Ireland, a woman living in the Wicklow hills gave birth to a man-calf. He was that rare conundrum: a man half ox, and an ox half man. At any rate, it spent about a year with the other calves following their mother and latching on to her teats, and then, because it had more of the man than the beast to it, it was taken in by a childless couple, who apparently looked after it very well, and taught it to write, for like most man-calves, it could not speak. But what happened after that, or how it ended up, I couldn't tell you, for that part of the story got lost.

Translation is a kind of monster, and its seeming master is a Dr Frankenstein, whose Creature gets to recognize himself in the distorting language mirror of a puddle. He also sees the stars down there, in the deep bottom of beyond, and he weeps at the sight of his face. Yet our pity is confounded by our admiration, for he is impossibly noble. He moves in the aura conjured up by John Keats, in his 'Ode to a Nightingale': 'Darkling I listen; and, for many a time / I have been half in love with easeful Death' –

> O for a beaker full of the warm South,
> Full of the true, the blushful Hippocrene,
> With beaded bubbles winking at the brim,
> And purple-stainèd mouth,
> That I might drink, and leave the world unseen,
> And with thee fade away into the forest dim –

And Hippocrene, 'the horse's fountain', is the gush of inspiration sprung from Mount Helicon when Pegasus landed there and stamped his authoritative hoof on its stony soil. Such horses' stories lie in wait behind many magic wells and springs. Hence aspiring poets take Pegasus as their emblem. Not content with Keats's 'viewless wings of poesy', they want to mount this horse that's powered by fabulously embodied wings. But such a horse is hard to bridle: this is Pegasus who sprang from the butchered body of a

Gorgon: Medusa, most terrifying of that grim sorority of Gorgons. You will recall that Perseus, tracking down the Gorgon, saw statues of men on the road who'd been turned into stone by her gaze. But someone had told him that mirrors veil the soul, so he was able to catch her reflection in his highly burnished shield, and thus – not being taken by her naked gaze – behead her with his sword of Mercury, because mirrors are made of mercury. Pegasus was born out of the hole of her neck. 'Pegasus' means 'spring'.

Perseus had been given the bronze shield by Minerva, whom the Romans identified with the Greek goddess Pallas Athene. The story goes that Zeus, her father, had swallowed expectant Metis, his first wife, who knew more than all the gods and men combined; for he feared she would bring forth a son more powerful than himself. Prometheus – some say it was Hephaistos – cleft the head of Zeus with an axe, and Athene sprang out from the wound, yelling a terrible battle-cry, clad in bloodied gold armour, brandishing her javelin. But other narrators contend that one of her many epithets, Tritogeneia, that is, 'born of Triton', points to water as the source of her being; and the worship of Athene, and the story of her birth, are accordingly connected with many sacred brooks, lakes and springs. Athene is associated with Poseidon, bearer of the mighty trident, with which he stirs up the sea and cleaves rocks, making fountains and horses spring from them: it was she who taught men to tame the horse, and to yoke the ox to the plough. Also under her aegis, to the Roman mind, were most accomplishments and arts. She was the patron of fullers, doctors, fiddlers, sculptors, cobblers, painters, dyers, poets and actors. Most of all she was the goddess

of spinning and weaving, as practised by women. The story goes
as follows:

Arachne came from humble stock: her father was Idmon of
Colophon, a Phoacean Purple dyer. He used to dye her wool for
her. Her mother was dead, but she too had been a nobody.
Nevertheless, the girl Arachne was winning increasing fame for
her skill at the wheel and the loom throughout the Lydian cities,
for all that she lived in Hypaepa, which was off the map. Often
the mountain-nymphs would filter down through the vineyards to
be spellbound by her magic work; to see her weave, the water-
nymphs would leave their aqueous abode. To see the finished
article was brilliant, but to watch her spin was to begin to realize
the majestic deftness of her hands: whether winding the raw yarn
into a new ball, or rubbing it in twists between her fingers, reaching back to the distaff to grip more of the cloudy fleece, drawing
long soft threads from it, or giving a practised flick of the thumb
to the elegant spindle, or doing fancy needle-work: it was all a
treat to behold, and everyone declared that Pallas herself must
have taught her. There was no higher praise. But Arachne was
offended at the very thought that she had learned from a goddess.
So Arachne challenged Pallas to a weaving contest: winner take
all.

Then Athene turned herself into an old woman and put on a
grey wig. She propped herself on a stick, tottered up to Arachne's
door, and spoke to her straight: I may be old, but I'm not stupid.
With age comes experience. Old head on old shoulders. Some
day you'll know all about it. Take my advice: show off to your

mortal clientele all that you want; you'll never lack admirers. But don't push yourself too far. Bow to the goddess, say you're sorry that you dared to think yourself as good as her. You'll see she can be generous. But Arachne bared her teeth, and glared at her, and dropping her needle-work, she drew back her hand as if to slap the disguised goddess, but spat out these words instead: You silly old bitch, who do you think you are? Your trouble is, you've been around too long. You'd think they would have put you down by now. Away back home and talk to your daughter-in-law, or your daughter, if you were ever able to have one, which I doubt. I'm well able to advise myself. Where is this goddess of yours, anyway? Is she scared to meet me?

Then the goddess exclaimed: She has come! And throwing off her wig and her old shawl, revealed Athene in her golden glory. Then all the nymphs who'd been watching fell down and worshipped her, and the Mygdonian women: but Arachne drew herself up to look dignified, and though she did blush a little, she soon regained her composure; as when the sky goes crimson when the dawn appears, and then when the sun is up it pales again. Still she would persist in her unruly challenge. Tight-lipped Minerva contemptuously shrugged her shoulders. So the contest began. They set up the looms in no time, getting the set of the warp just right. They bound the web to the beam. Threaded the reed through the warp, and threw the woof from the shuttle through the threads of the warp as the whole loom trembled and clacked like electricity as they began to weave the stuff. They'd bared their arms and hitched up their skirts for the job, but they hardly broke sweat, for you could see there was a rapid practised ease about their work. There they interwove the famous Tyrian Purple, and shades of other purples verging on the bloom on plums, or violets, or indigo. As when after an April shower, a rainbow glazes the air with all the colours of the spectrum; as how or where one colour shades into the next is problematic to the human eye; so did the colour-schemes of these two geniuses of weaving blend. The colours were a code through which they wove a thread of gold, and traced some ancient tale.

Pallas depicts the hill of Mars, and the ancient dispute about what the country should be called. There sat the Heavenly Twelve, one of them herself, on big thrones, Jupiter amongst them; each god shown with his proper features. There's Poseidon, smiting with his wonted trident the rugged rocks from which sprang seas and horses. Herself is depicted with shield and spear, and the plumed gold helmet; and from her spear stuck in the earth there springs her gift to men, the olive tree with juicy olives growing on it; and the other gods admire her for her bounty. Then, just to show Arachne what might lie in store for her, for daring to presume, she weaves four scenes of contest in the corners of the web, each done meticulously, in microscopic detail. Rhodope and Haemus, now bleak mountains, who had dared assume the names of gods. The Pygmy Queen, whom Juno changed into a crane. Likewise Antigone, who is now a stork. Lastly, the daughters of Cinyras, who, insolent with good looks, challenged Juno to a beauty contest: she changed them into the steps of a minor temple, and made their father an accompanying stone. The goddess then wove an olive-wreath, her special emblem, around the whole work, and sat back triumphantly.

Arachne showed Europa being raped by the god in the shape of a bull. You'd swear the bull and the waves were real when you looked at them. Then Asterie, raped by the eagle. Leda, raped by the swan; the struggling wings. Jove disguised as a satyr, raping Antiope. Jove in the form of a gold shower entering Danae; Jove entering other women in the form of a flame, or as a spotted snake. And many more such godly metamorphoses, all rendered in uncanny detail in appropriate surroundings: to look at it, you'd think you'd been there yourself. Then, in the middle of these lusting shapes, she depicted Aphrodite, goddess of true love, with her hands holding emblematic golden apples. She wove a commentary of wild flowers and winding ivy all about these images.

It was flawless work. Pallas knew it, even Envy had to admit it. Jealous Pallas tore the web asunder in her anger. She took her boxwood shuttle and beat Arachne about the head with it. Arachne could not endure such treatment. Swiftly she made a noose for her neck and strung herself up. As she hung there, Pallas took some kind of pity on her, and said: Live on, wicked girl, but long may you hang; may all your kind dangle forever. So saying, she sprinkled her with wolfsbane. All Arachne's hair fell off, infected by that herb of Hecate. Her nose and ears dropped off. Her head shrank. Her body dwindled. Her breasts withered. Her slender fingers clung to her as legs. All the rest was belly. Still Arachne weaves, and spins her thread eternally.

QUINCE

Many authorities agree that the golden apple of Greek Aphrodite – Venus to the Romans – is a quince: this was the gift she received from Paris. Quinces were the golden apples of the Hesperides, which feature in the story of Atalanta:

Atalanta was the fastest runner of her day. There wasn't a man alive could beat her in a foot-race. When she consulted the oracle about a husband, the god replied: A husband's not for you. Flee from all potential husbands. And yet, there will be no escape; though living, you will lose yourself; for what will be, will be. So Atalanta lived a maiden in the shady woods. To the many who proposed to her, she laid down these terms: whosoever was to win her, he would have to win a race against her; the swift would be rewarded with a wife and wedding-bed; the slow would suffer death. Such was her beauty, that men still dared to take her on. Invariably, they lost, and paid the ultimate penalty.

Now Hippomenes had taken his seat as a spectator at one of these predictable contests. He was saying to his neighbours how he couldn't for the life of him understand how anyone would want a woman so much that they'd put their lives on the line, and what idiots such men were, when he saw her in her running strip, and his jaw dropped. Forgive me, boys, he exclaimed, I take it all back, now that I've set eyes on her. For he was dazzled by her beauty; and, mad with jealousy, hoped that none of the contenders would receive the prize. Then it struck him that he too should have a go; for the gods help them that dare.

As he was turning all this over in his mind, the girl fluttered by like an arrow, and he admired her figure all the more. Her hair floated behind her, exposing her ivory shoulders; her breast heaved; her limbs glowed beneath the hem of her short slip. He was drinking it all in when the race came to an end. Atalanta was the unsurprising winner. Groaning, the losing youths were executed in the customary fashion.

Undeterred by this spectacle, Hippomenes spoke: You call it victory, to beat these sluggish fellows? Try me. And if fortune favours me, you need not take it badly. For I am somebody. My father was Megareus; his father was Onchestius and his grandfather was Neptune, which makes me great-grandson of the king of waves. And I am every bit as noble as my breeding. If I should be beaten, then your name will gain all the more credit.

So he spoke, and Atalanta was visibly disturbed. What god, she replied, wishes to undo this youth, and make him risk his life for me? Am I worth so much? Not that I'm moved by his good looks; but then again, I could be, given time. No, it's because he's a mere boy, that I feel sorry for him. Still, he's brave enough; and the Neptune connection is not to be overlooked. But why should I care for him, when so many others have already died for me? And so she debated with herself, and warned him to begone; but Cupid had smitten her, just as he had Hippomenes.

Now the crowd demanded the usual race. Hippomenes offered up a silent prayer to Aphrodite, asking for her help; and the goddess was moved by his plea. Invisible to all but him, she gave him three golden apples, and told him how they were to be deployed. Then the trumpets sounded, and the runners were off like a shot. Such was their pace, had they been running on the sea, you'd bet on them to have dry feet; or in a field of standing corn, they'd skim along the crests of the unbent ears. The crowd loved it. Come on, Hippomenes! You can do it, Hippomenes! Go for it! they shouted. They were all for Hippomenes; but it's a moot point who was most encouraged by the great support, for Atalanta, when she could have passed him, would slacken her pace to gaze at his handsome features. Meanwhile Hippomenes is finding the going tough; and the finish is still a long way off. So he drops one of the golden apples; Atalanta, as if mesmerized, turns from her course to pick it up. Hippomenes takes the lead. The stadium reverberates with applause. But before long the two are neck and neck again. Hippomenes drops the second apple. And not to make the story longer than the race, Hippomenes ends up winning.

But that's not quite the end of the story. For Hippomenes,

flushed with victory and passion, forgot to offer thanks and incense to the goddess for her intervention; and Aphrodite was not one bit pleased. As the happy couple were passing through a dark wood, they stopped to rest by a temple of Cybele, goddess of the Earth. Aphrodite took the opportunity to excite Hippomenes to the point of wanting Atalanta there and then. Near the temple was a shrine carved out of the native pumice-stone, sanctified by centuries of ritual. Hippomenes entered this dim cave. Lying down with Atalanta, he committed the forbidden crime. The holy statues turned away their eyes. Cybele, enraged by sacrilege, was about to plunge the pair into the Styx. But that would be too light a punishment. So tawny manes shot from their hitherto smooth necks; their fingers and their toes sprang claws; their arms became legs, and their legs hind legs. Their tails swept the sandy floor. They did not speak; they growled. No bridal chamber for them now; forever they wander the dark woods, except when they are yoked to Cybele's chariot. Nor can they ever join in love again; for it is well known that lions only mate with leopards.

Such were the consequences of the quince. Pliny speaks of the exquisite scent of the fruit, and mentions that quinces were placed 'on statues that share our nights with us'; that is, images of deities placed in the bedrooms of that time. The expressed juice of the seeds is, he says, an excellent remedy for dysentery, thrush and gonorrhoea. It may also be used to ward off the influence of the evil eye. The fruit is often found depicted in the wall paintings and mosaics of Pompeii, where quinces are almost always to be seen in the paws of a bear; for Apollodorus, in telling the legend of Atalanta, alleges that her father abandoned her in a desert, where she was found and suckled by a she-bear. She was eventually discovered by some hunters, and hunting became her favourite pastime. She shot and killed two centaurs who tried to rape her.

The Northern European quince, unlike the Greek or Latin fruit, has a harsh and unpalatable flesh, with an astringent, acidulous taste; but it may successfully be made into a marmalade or jelly. For quince jelly, pare and core some ripe quinces, weigh them and put them at once into part of the water in which they will be cooked. Put the quinces on the fire, with 1 pint of water to each pound of fruit, and let it simmer, but not long enough to change the colour to red – it should be quite pale. Strain through a jelly-bag. Weigh the juice the next day and put it in a preserving pan and boil it quickly for 15 minutes. Then take it from the fire and stir into it 12 ounces sugar for each pound of juice. Boil for another 15 or 20 minutes, till cooked, stirring all the time, and remove the scum. Quinces and apples can be mixed; this makes a good combination.

The quince was called *cydonea* by the Greeks, from Cydoneum, a city in Crete; and the English name is a corruption of this word – except that it was originally a *coyne*, then a *quin*, and the plural *quins* is now our singular. In like manner, the singular *chess* is derived from the plural of *check*; and there are other such interesting cases of number confusion, too numerous to mention here. And *cydonea* has got nothing to do with *cider*, which comes from another root altogether.

216

The quince was especially popular in Palestine, and many commentators consider that the *tappuach* of Scripture, always translated as apple, was the quince. It is also supposed to be the fruit alluded to in the Canticles, '*I sat down under his shadow with great delight and his fruit was sweet to my taste*'; and in Proverbs, '*A word fitly spoken is like apples of gold in pictures of silver.*'

Another thing about this famous fruit is that it features in yet another story, which is the story for the fifth night, as told by Jack the Lad, as related by my father, as translated here by me:

Once upon a time, but not so long ago that the story would be forgotten by now, for then I wouldn't be here to tell it, there lived an earl in the mountains of Kerry. He had an only son. The son was called Earl Minor. Now the old earl was pretty rich, and when he died he left everything to Earl Minor. Earl Minor was a great man for sport and repartee; a great fisherman, and a great rider to hounds. He would be seen at practically every meet in the district.

One day a great hunt party set out in GlenBrock. All the high society was there. The horn blew, the hounds howled, and a fine doe jumped out of a wood. Posse-like, the riders followed it, and it led them a merry dance over hills and through glens till the sun was high in the sky. Earl Minor was on a superlative steed, and it wasn't long till he looked over his shoulder and saw that he was way ahead of the pack. There was not another horseman in sight. He followed the track of the doe till the sun was declining beneath the blue mountain. When the sun went down, he found he didn't know where he was.

He was thinking of making his way back when he spotted a big house at the foot of the blue mountain. He was wild thirsty after the day's hunting and he thought he might get something to drink if he went up to the house. So off he set, and landed at the front door. A maiden came out and said, A hundred thousand welcomes to you, Earl Minor.

— And a hundred thousand thanks to you, says he, but I would have thought no one would have known me in this neck of the woods. I've no idea where I am, but I'd be eternally grateful to you if you could give me a drink, for I'm half dead with the thirst.

— You're in GlenSpell, says she. Come in and I'll get you a drink and welcome.

She called out to a groom and told him to stable Earl Minor's horse and give it plenty of oats and water. Earl Minor walked in the door, and when he gazed around he was amazed, for he'd never seen a finer place in his life. There was a solid gold table in the middle of the room, and gold chairs around it, and a gold chandelier hanging from the ceiling, and the table settings were all twenty-four-carat gold. The maiden filled a crystal goblet with some fine wine, and handed it to Earl Minor. He took one big sup out of it, and said, I was parched with the thirst, but I don't seem to be thirsty any more, and my thanks to you again.

— Sit down, says she, you must be starving after the long day you've had at the hunt.

He sat down, and these three butlers came in bearing dishes. There was mutton and beef beyond belief, and heaps of venison and hairy bacon. There was boiled parsnips and carrots and cabbages, and mussels and winkles and potted herrings. There was a big dish of sliced beetroot in sour cream, and I nearly forgot the potatoes steamed in their jackets, with the floury insides bursting out of them. Then there were the sweet puddings and the custards and the jellies, all that kind of thing. The maiden sat directly opposite Earl Minor, and scrutinized him as he got tucked in. Occasionally he'd glance up at her to meet her gaze and think to himself he'd never seen one half as beautiful. So they ate and drank away quite merrily, and every time he looked at her, she grew more lovely. He ate up the last bit of his grub and thanked her again, and he asked her if her father and her mother were still living.

— God rest them, says she, they are not, for they died a while back, and I'm more or less alone, except for the attentions of this giant they call the Black Rogue who wants to marry me. It seems I've no way out unless I get me some sort of hero to put him down, and that's a hard job, for there's no sword in the world that can kill him except this one sword owned by the king of Greece, and the king has it under lock and key in a box in a chest in a wardrobe in a recess of one of the innermost rooms of one of his castles in Greece, or it might be on a Greek island, for his rule extends over archipelagos.

— Is there any way of getting hold of this sword? said Earl Minor, for if I had a sword like that I'd soon put an end to the Black Rogue.

— There's one way, she admitted, but it's very dangerous.

— What care I for danger, says he, show me the way, and I'll get the sword, or lose my life in the attempt.

— Go out the back door tomorrow morning, says she, and go to the bottom of the garden, and you'll find a quince tree there. Pick the first quince that comes to hand, and eat it. It will be bitter as hell but you must swallow it. You'll have the pit in your mouth by now. Spit it into the midden nearby, then take it out. You'll find it's turned into a jewel. Then go to the top of the blue mountain and you'll see an old man sitting on top of a rock. Give him the jewel, and he will ask you what you want. Tell him, and do what he orders you to do, and you won't go amiss. You are tired after your long day, and you should go to sleep now.

She showed Earl Minor to a room at the back of the house.

— Now, says she, can't you hear the snoring of the Black Rogue? The way his chest whistles between snores? He's in a room at the top of the house, and he won't wake up till sundown tomorrow.

Earl Minor went to bed, but couldn't get a wink of sleep. He'd doze for a minute or two before the snores of the Black Rogue got to him, and he'd come to with a start, thinking it was thunder. Damn the bit of sleep did he get. He rose before dawn, but the maiden was already up. There was a great breakfast cooked for him, and the three butlers dashing around, serving it from silver salvers, but Earl Minor's appetite was bad, for he felt kind of nervous, and he didn't eat that much. He got up from his gold chair and bade goodbye to the maiden, and she was sorry to see him go.

He went out the back door and down to the bottom of the garden and he picked a quince from the tree. He bit into its bitter flesh and he felt the pit sear his tongue. He spat it into the midden and the pit jumped out of the midden back into his mouth and when he took it out he found it was a jewel. He went up the mountain, and before long he discovered the old man sitting on top of his rock. He gave him the jewel, as instructed by the maiden.

— What do you want, what is your need, or what is your will? said the old man.

— I want the Greek king's sword, the only sword in the world that's fit to kill the Black Rogue, said Earl Minor.

The old man gave him a little bell, and said, Go to the wood that lies to the south of GlenSpell, tinkle the bell, and a white gelding will come to you, and you do what he tells you to do.

— Earl Minor thanked the old man. He took the bell and went to the wood. He tinkled the bell. He saw the white gelding. It came up and nuzzled him and said: I know your needs, jump up on my back, for we've a long way to travel.

So Earl Minor mounted the steed, and no sooner was he on its back than the gelding sprouted wings, and off the pair of them went into the air. They proceeded thus till they came to the shore of a sea. Then the gelding said, Hold tight, we're going under. So in they dived, under the waves, and on they went for what seemed like an eternity, but at last they reached dry land again. Earl Minor was half-drowned, but he kept his grip, and on they went again till they came to a fiery mountain. Hold tight, said the gelding, we're going over. And with one leap it flew over the mountain. The soles of Earl Minor's feet were a bit scorched, but otherwise he was fine. On they went till they came to a Greek island, and they landed at the gate of a castle. The walls were forty feet high. There were two lions, one on either side of the gate, with instructions from the king not to admit anyone without his permission.

— Now, said the gelding, put your hand in my left ear, and you'll find a little sharp knife there. Kill me, and skin me, put my hide over you, and you can walk past the lions without them seeing you. When you get into the castle, go down the hall, take the spiral staircase on the right down to the lower level, take a left, and a right, and another left, and you'll come to a door. You'll find the key under the stone. Open the door and walk in. There'll be a wardrobe in the corner of the room. It won't be locked, but open the drawer the king keeps his shoes in and you'll find a key in the toe of the left shoe of the third pair from the right. This is the key to the chest in the top half of the wardrobe, and if you open it up, you'll find the sword in a golden case. Take it out and come back to me. Quick! And don't forget to lock everything behind you and to put the keys back where they belong.

— Indeed, said Earl Minor, I could never kill you, after all you've done for me, and in any case, if you were dead, what use would the sword be to me, for I'd never be able to find my way back to GlenSpell.

— Do as I say, and have faith, said the gelding, and when you get back here with the sword, throw my hide over me, and see what happens.

Reluctantly, Earl Minor did as he was told. He killed the gelding, skinned it, and put the hide over himself. He walked in past the two lions, who saw nothing. He followed the gelding's directions to the letter, got the sword, and locked up after him. When he got back out he threw the hide over the gelding, and the gelding sprang up as good as new.

— Jump up on my back, said the gelding, it's time to be off.

Earl Minor jumped on, and they went back the way they had come, across the fiery mountain, under the sea, over hills and through glens, till eventually they arrived at GlenSpell. The gelding alighted, Earl Minor got off, and the gelding said, Goodbye for now, and may you get the better of the Black Rogue, and may you win the hand of the loveliest woman in the world.

— Seven thousand thanks to you, old friend, said Earl Minor, and goodbye to yourself.

So in he went to the maiden's house, and she was overjoyed to see him. A hundred thousand welcomes, says she, and did you get the sword?

— I did, said Earl Minor, now where's the Black Rogue? For I've a bit of business to settle with him.

— Wait till you've had a bite to eat and a drop to drink, said she, for he won't be here for another hour.

So Earl Minor ate and drank all that was put before him, and he was telling the maiden all about his adventures, and the wonders he had seen, when they heard the giant approaching. Earl Minor went out and confronted the Black Rogue coming up the path.

— I'm here to cut the head from your shoulders, said he.

— You must be joking, said the Black Rogue, you'd be better off milking your cows back in GlenBrock.

With that, they set to. The maiden stood in the doorway, with her heart in her mouth. When Earl Minor gave the Black Rogue an especially telling blow, she clapped and cheered. The Black Rogue wasn't one bit pleased by this, and he roared out, I'll give you something to cheer about when I've finished with this young buck!

— Indeed you will not, said Earl Minor, and a couple of moments later he cut the head from the giant's shoulders. The head tried to jump back on to the body, but Earl Minor gave it another blow and it rolled on to the floor.

— Oh! said the head, that's the Greek king's sword, that you stole off him, and you haven't been playing fair. But there wasn't another peep out of the head, for Earl Minor had it chopped in four with two blows of his sword. He took the body then, and hauled it over to a dry well. He threw it in, and threw stones on top of the body into the well till it was full to the brim. By now, it was nightfall.

He went back into the house, and you can imagine the welcome he got.

— I never thought, said the maiden, that things would have turned out so well when I turned myself into a doe and you started me out of the wood in GlenBrock, and I beg your pardon for it, for it wasn't a doe that you chased that day, but my very self. The Black Rogue had bewitched me, and I'd been told that the spell would never be broken till Earl Minor of GlenBrock came to GlenSpell. I am an earl's daughter myself. My mother died a while back, and my father was killed three years ago by his enemies.

Earl Minor kissed her, and asked her to marry him. Come live with me and be my love, said he, come to GlenBrock, and leave GlenSpell and its black magic behind you forever.

— I will, said she, for the spell is broken now. I have a coach and horses waiting for us, if you know the way back.

— Come to think of it, I don't, said Earl Minor, for I don't know exactly where I am, nor how I got here.

— Perhaps one of my servants would have the directions, said she, for whatever sense of direction I had when I was a doe, I lost when I regained my human form. But if Virgil's about, I'm sure he can tell us the way. She called for Virgil, and an old grey man entered the room.

— Do you know GlenBrock? said she.

— I do indeed, said the old man, and why wouldn't I, for I was born there a hundred years ago.

— I'm for GlenBrock in the morning, said she, see that the chariot is ready.

The next morning, Virgil had a fine coach and four ready for them. The young couple got on board, and the young woman brought all her gold and silver with her, and all her gems and jewels. Virgil clicked his tongue at the horses and off they went at a spanking pace. Onwards they travelled, till the sun was low in the sky, and at last Earl Minor recognized his whereabouts. I'm home now, said he.

— Great, said she, let's stop here a while before we enter the glen. They stopped, and she said to the old man, Go back to GlenSpell; my house and its contents are all yours. For it's unlikely that I'll ever be back.

The old man set off, and Earl Minor brought his bride-to-be to his court. There was a great welcome for him. Everyone had thought he was dead.

Next morning the couple were married. The celebrations lasted seven days and seven nights, and each night was better than the one before. They lived in GlenBrock as happy as the day was long, and they reared a houseful of children. They died of old age, but some of their descendants are there to this day.

That is my story, and if you'll allow me, I'll have another for you all tomorrow night.

— A good story, and a true one, said one of the men. Good story, chorused the rest of the company. They rose, the door opened in the wall, and they left as they had come. The lady bade Jack goodbye, and off she went. The doorman came in. Jack went to bed. He spent the next day as he had spent the others. Night came. He was shown into the chamber again. The lady asked him if he was ready to begin his story. He was. She blew her little gold whistle, the door opened in the wall, and the twelve walked in with the other twelve on their shoulders. They all sat down, and she said, Begin your story.

RAMIFICATION

When I woke up it was broad daylight, and I didn't know where I was. The window was wide open and I could hear waves lapping. Then I remembered I had been with the Dutchman, Jan Both, in the Cranfield Inn, on the shores of Lough Neagh. We had sat up late, and he had fallen asleep, when one of the company produced a little metal pipe and a lump of dope, and we began telling each other stories, of which I had contributed more than my share. Some kind soul must have put me to bed; or maybe I had negotiated the journey upstairs myself, for it's amazing what a body can do when it's stoned out of its mind.

There was a great smell of bacon frying in the air, and I got up eagerly and cautiously. I was already fully dressed. I went downstairs and who was sitting in the breakfast room but the Dutchman and a Polish sailor.

— Sit down, my friend, said the Dutchman, and enjoy some of these excellent bacon and eggs. My companion has been relating me a most engaging story called the Amber Room Mystery. May I introduce you to Mr Jarniewicz? I am sure he will be only too pleased to recommence his adventure from the beginning, for your benefit.

I sat down, and Mr Jarniewicz began:

— As you can see, sir, I am a Polish sailor. How I came to be here is immaterial, for the story which concerns us began many millions of years ago, when the great forests of the Baltic *Pinus succinifera* were oozing their resin over insects and pine-needles, over slime moulds and bacteria, parasitic fungi, higher fungi such as mushrooms, lichens, mosses, ferns and flowers of nearly a hundred species in addition to hundreds of arthropods. This would be to begin at the very beginning; one could then go on to describe the metamorphosis of resin into amber, before launching on an exhaustive enquiry into the prevailing climatic conditions in the early Pleistocene era, and how the ambered pines lie many fathoms deep, petrified in the Blue Earth stratum underneath the Baltic. I could tell you how this amber has been venerated through the ages, and of the Emperor Elagabalus, who paved a portion of his palace with pulverized amber. Antony brought Cleopatra armbands of amber. A figurine of amber cost more than five slaves. Pliny scoffed at Demonstratus, who alleged that amber was formed from lynxes' piss; but there are stranger stories about the origins of amber. Suffice to say that it is known as the Golden Gem of the Ages.

Look into a piece of amber. Let us pretend that it is not one of the more desirable insect repositories, but a relatively cheap piece with a few fragmented pine-needles in it. But marvel at the iridescent discs you see within the amber gem, these spangles of sparkly light, which, it will interest you to know, were not visible until the amber was carefully heated to a precise temperature, whereupon the constellation came into being; for these discs, so like the 'circles of confusion' apparent in images seen through a camera obscura, as the light is diffused and refracted in its different wave-lengths, are nothing more than droplets of trapped water, or tiny air-bubbles, pressurized and volatilized, and tempered into gorgeous sequences of sequins. It is easy to be mesmerized by them; and one understands why some fortune-tellers prefer an amber ball to gaze into, instead of the standard crystal. The colour, too, is beautiful, is it not? And there are many shades of amber, from the lemon yellow or primrose to a near-opaque toffee black, but I need not look too closely at the amber spectrum at this moment, for such an exploration would distract us from the main thread of our story.

We could begin, then, in 1312, in my home town of Gdańsk, when the amber fishing rights to the neighbouring coast were granted to the fishermen of Gdańsk, with similar rights contracted to the Monastery of Olivia in 1340; but the only way of receiving such rights was through the Grand Marshal of the Teutonic Order. As amber increased in value and amber prospectors came to Poland in their thousands, staking out bits of the beaches, the Order rescinded these treaties, and by the middle of the fifteenth century had gained complete control of the amber harvest and the amber trade. These Teutonic Knights were known as the Amber Lords, and they maintained a harsh dominion. Why amber became so gradually valuable is a moral tale itself: throughout this period, most of Europe was ravaged by periodic outbreaks of ergotism, or St Antony's Fire, an affliction caused by eating bread made from rye infected by a small but powerful fungus, and whose many symptoms included loss of major limbs, and religious visions of the hallucinatory variety. It was thought that amber, with its many attested healing properties, would also prove efficacious in the case of ergotism; and such efficacy, it was argued, would be all the more powerful if the amber was made into rosary beads, and prayed with. So there was a boom in amber rosaries; and the Grand Marshal of the Amber Lords, in 1394, wanting to monopolize the trade, issued an edict forbidding anyone except authorized personnel to possess raw amber. All collecting of amber was henceforth to be done under the supervision of a Beach Master; and all amber was to be delivered to the Amber Lords. This order was brutally enforced. Any unauthorized person observed picking up amber was summarily hanged.

Picture the scene for yourself: all along the amber-bearing Baltic coast, at regular intervals, gibbets have been erected. Hanged individuals in various stages of decomposition dangle at intervals as examples to the local populace. Some are being picked over by birds. There are many skeletons. Also worthy of comment are the gibbet-like structures with wire fire-baskets hanging from them, for the focus of amber harvest-time is winter, when the storms disturb the ocean floors, and dislodge

nuggets of amber from their fossil status in the deep seam of the
Blue Earth underneath the Baltic Sea, and winter is cold; the
amber fishermen have built these fires to thaw out by, wading
ashore in their leather amber-fishing gear, with their nets and
tridents, looking like so many minor Neptunes. Meanwhile, their
wives and children pick over the bladder-wrack and other bits of
flotsam and jetsam, whipped by the Beach Masters, whose myrmidons immediately seize any bit of amber thus discovered. At
the end of the day the amber slaves receive their wages: they are
paid the amber's weight in salt.

Permits were needed to walk on a beach where amber might
be found. Every third year, fishermen were made to swear the
Amber Oath, which required them to denounce any harbourer of
amber, or any amber-smuggler, even if they should prove blood
relatives; so the community was riddled with suspicion, and
anyone at all unorthodox would be denounced as an amber-
witch. The Amber Court had a special Amber Oath for priests to
administer to anyone suspected of owning amber. Armed horse-
men known as Beach Riders were sent out after storms to deter
the inhabitants from beachcombing for amber. To this day stories
are told of the ghosts of cruel Beach Riders and Masters who
were forced in the afterlife to haunt the scenes of their crimes.
Anselmas of Lozenstein, one of the more notorious Masters, was
condemned to wander the Baltic coasts eternally on stormy
nights, crying out, 'O my god, free amber! Free amber!'

By the middle of the fourteenth century the Teutonic Order
had assumed complete dominion over all the inferences and
implications of amber. It forbade independent amber works at

source, and the raw material was shipped under armed guard to warehouses in Bruges and Lübeck, from whence, under close surveillance, it was distributed to selected groups of amber workers, who were known as paternoster-makers. During this period the first Paternoster-makers' Guild was organized in Bruges; they were assigned their own church there, and given their own patron saint, Adalbert of Prague. Remind me to relate the story of Adalbert to you when we have greater leisure, for it is full of interesting morals and historical details; and we may contemplate in passing the fact that Adalbert is conventionally represented bearing an amber-fisher's trident, for this was the instrument of his martyrdom.

By now, the Bruges and Lübeck guilds produced rosary beads for the whole of Christendom. These became increasingly more elaborate in design. As you know, the use of beads on a string or chain to help the memory in those devotions where repetition or set numbers of prayers are involved is not an exclusively Christian practice, for Hindus, Buddhists and Mohammedans use them; but of course, in modern Europe, they are perceived as a distinctively Roman Catholic accoutrement. It is not widely known, perhaps, that various arrangements of such beads exist: in addition to the common Dominican rosary, there are those of St Bridget, of the Seven Sorrows, of the Five Wounds, of the Immaculate Conception, the Camaldolese chaplet of our Lord, the Franciscan crown of our Lady, and the Byzantine rosary, used principally by monks. Here, it is helpful momentarily to ponder the etymology of the word 'bead', which is simply Old English *bede*, a prayer: this is a case where the intention has become fossilized into an object, or where the thing translates the thought, becoming an unwitting relic.

But let us return to the standard rosary, traditionally held to have been revealed by Our Lady to St Dominic, who propagated its use: the word is from Latin *rosarium*, a rose-garden, whence a wreath, garland or ramification. The rosary is a string of beads consisting of five sets (decades), each of ten small and one larger bead (a crucifix with two large and three small beads is ordinarily added); it also means the prayers said on these beads. Each decade is associated with a Mystery of the Faith, as follows: the Joyful Mysteries, consisting of the Annunciation, the Visitation, the Birth of our Lord, the Presentation, and the Finding of the Child Jesus in the Temple; the Sorrowful Mysteries, which comprise the Agony in the Garden, the Scourging at the Pillar, the Crowning with Thorns, the Carrying of the Cross, and the Crucifixion; and the Glorious Mysteries, which are the Resurrection, the Ascension, the Coming of the Holy Ghost, the Assumption, and the Crowning of the Blessed Virgin. As you know, the method of saying the Rosary, in public or private, is to recite an 'Our Father' (large bead), ten 'Hail Marys' (small beads), and a 'Glory be to the Father' (large bead), while meditating on the appropriate Mystery; theoretically, the essence of the devotion should consist in a loving and intelligent meditation, and not a mere mechanical repetition of the prayers. But I need not tell you how difficult this is in practice; and I remember vividly mumbling the family Rosary as a child or a youth, kneeling with my back end to the fire and my face buried in a cushion, while my ostensible contemplation was disturbed by a string of

inappropriate thoughts. These might take the shape of idle recol-
lections of the salient points of the school day, or, more
dangerously, proceed from the memory of a garter-strap
glimpsed under the skirt of a passenger climbing the stairs to the
upper saloon of the double-decker tram I took home. For it was
easy to enter the realm of distraction, that is, lack of due attention at prayer. When voluntary, this was considered a venial sin of
disrespect; but it was comforting to know that when involuntary,
it need not deprive the prayer of merit; that indeed, the imaginative disturbance might be the occasion of an increase in merit,
especially when the distraction is persistent, because then the
will has to make much more deliberate and sustained efforts to
keep united with God than when the prayer goes easily. But I
doubted whether the apparition of a mental garter-strap fell into
this category.

At any rate, one can appreciate the plethora of symbolism
which lay at the paternoster-makers' fingertips, and the wealth of
ornamental possibilities thus afforded; for the Rosary was a powerful devotion, though it still remained to be given its special
feast-day, that of the Most Holy Rosary, which is celebrated on 7
October, in commemoration of St Mary of Victory – which Pope
Pius V ordained to be observed yearly in memory of the great victory secured on this same day, in 1571, by the Christians over the
Turks in the naval battle of Lepanto. But I can tell you that the
amber rosary deployed on that occasion by the commander of the
Christian forces, John of Austria, was made some 250 years ear-
lier, by a master paternoster-maker of Lübeck, known to us as the
Master of Lübeck, who had emigrated from my home town of

Gdańsk, and who learned his craft as a boy on tiny pebbles of smuggled amber contrabanded by his amber-fisher father, and thus was all the more meticulous for it, for he knew that the price of its possession was death. He was also fond of studying insects, and would spend long hours rambling the suburban fields of Gdańsk, or in the crevices between the bricks in his own back-yard, collecting specimens which he would pin to a board to be examined and dissected. He was reputed to own a beryl stone through which he looked to magnify the insects' interiors, and he would spend hours wandering their labyrinths of veins, capillaries, and glands. Hence the German for magnifying glass is *Brill*. As a result, he suffered from steadily progressive myopia; but as his long vision diminished, and the greater world grew blurred, so he saw deeper and deeper into the mystery of small things. His amber carvings were gems of microscopic detail: a tiny buttercup, for instance, with an almost-invisible bee embedded in it, correct in every bit of its anatomy, and its wings trembling convincingly, so delicate was their amber structure; or an apple the size of a bead, invaded by a fruit-fly; or an opened amber oyster mouth the size of a pearl, with a seed-pearl on its palate. Thus he was an exem-plar of the proverb, 'God never shuts one door, but he opens another': for he made a virtue of his handicap. We have numerous examples of this throughout history, as Pliny relates. To take the converse: Strabo of Sicily was notoriously long-sighted, and could not read at arm's length a parchment with letters written on it three times normal size; but, during the Punic wars, he was in the habit of telling from the promontory of Lilybaeum in Sicily the actual number of ships in a fleet rowing out of Carthage harbour, a distance of 123 miles; not only that, but he could identify the numbers and configurations of the oars deployed by the same vessels, for they reminded him of the legs on insects. Cicero records that a parchment copy of all the books of the *Iliad* was enclosed in a nutshell by an anonymous master. Callicrates used to make such small models of ants, earwigs, spiders, fleas, and other creatures, that to most people their parts were invisible. Myrcenides won fame in the same department by making a four-horse chariot of ivory that a fly's wings could cover, and a fully-manned quinquereme so tiny a baby wasp could hide it beneath its wings. All these artists were known progressive myopics.

Of a similar order of delicacy was the superb craftsmanship of the Master of Lübeck. Let us take as an example one of his trademarks, his interpretation of the image of St Veronica on the boss of the rosary, that important focal point where the five decades meet the Morse code of the one large bead, three small beads, one large bead, which lead up to the culmination of the crucifix. Typically, the boss occupies about the area of a baby broad bean; but in this limited scope the Master could depict a mass of narrative corroborating detail. Here were the steps of Jerusalem, and spectators leaning out of windows, and Christ carrying the cross, sweating blood and tears, and the occupying forces of the Roman military, and Pontius Pilate wringing his hands in a barely visible upstairs room, and then the central figure of Veronica appearing in the wings holding her napkin; Veronica again, approaching her Lord to wipe his face with the napkin; finally, Veronica displaying the image of Christ thus imprinted on the napkin. This would be one version, for the Master never repeated himself, but found ever subtler correspondences within the implications of the text.

You can imagine, then, the opportunities the Master grasped when it came to making the beads. Each was interpreted as a tiny visual prayer. He made three main models of rosaries, corresponding to the three categories of Mysteries: Joyful, Sorrowful, and Glorious; and each bead in the appropriate Mystery of the Mysteries illustrated a telling point in the story of that decade. For example, the Third Joyful Mystery, the Birth of Our Lord, might proceed as follows: one, the three astronomers discovering a new star; two, them loading their camels with gold, frankincense and myrrh; three, Mary and Joseph learning about the imminent census; four, the three astronomers getting on the camels; five, Mary and Joseph wandering Bethlehem; five, the angel appearing to the shepherds; six, the Massacre of the Innocents; seven, a tavern scene with gambling Roman soldiers; eight, a ladder; nine, the Miracle of Loaves and Fishes; ten, the birth attended by the animals, all lit by the amber glow of the baby beaming from the gold straw of the manger, and the haloes of the holy ones composed of the discs of confusion within the amber itself. Such was one order of his intelligence, for this sequence was negotiated differently each time around. Similarly with each of the other Mysteries.

The crucifix occupied a lot of the Master's time. This was usually designed as an openable cruciform box, on hinges of silver wire, with a complicated fretwork lid that partially concealed the underlying structure with patterns of relatively opaque amber; when opened, it revealed an image of Christ as a butterfly emerging from a pupa, or a grub from an amber egg,

or some such visible parable. Sometimes the interior would consist of a beautifully carved olive tree, or a copy of the Ten
Commandments with one deliberate mistake in them. At other
times a veritable Noah's Ark would be depicted. No wonder the
victor of Lepanto attributed the success of his campaign to the
rosary beads of Mary manufactured by the Master of Lübeck.

I say all this to press on you the importance of amber and its
immense religious and economic ramifications, which must necessarily have been examined briefly before we could proceed to
the next part of the story of the Amber Room Mystery.

The year is now 1701. King Frederick of Prussia has commissioned, for his main palace in Berlin, a banquet room made
entirely of amber. His inspiration has been derived from the holy
caskets and house altars of inlaid amber, sometimes of incredibly
elaborate miniature architecture, which were in vogue in the
houses of the nobility of Königsberg and Danzig – Gdańsk, as I
would naturally prefer to call it – in the late seventeenth and early
eighteenth centuries. For I am pleased to say that by now the
working of amber, by whatever circumlocution of historical route,
has passed back into the realm of the amber-bearing regions, such
as my own home coast of Poland, and the master amber carvers of
Gdańsk are world-renowned. The room was therefore assembled
laboriously at the king's command from many oak-based panels
meticulously inlaid with over 100,000 individual pieces of amber,
comprising mosaics of floral designs, dolphins, mermaids, royal
heralds and profiles. Each panel bore the Prussian coat-of-arms of
boars surmounted by crowned eagles. The task was thought
beyond the ingenuity of man; but the craftsmen of Gdańsk, like

Titanic builders mesmerized by magnitude, successfully concluded the contract in eleven years, and the Amber Room was
officially opened in 1712. There was much applause, and the fame
of the Amber Room reverberated around the known world. Tsar
Peter I, known as Peter the Great, saw it shortly after its com-
pletion, and admired it greatly. In 1716, Frederick William I of
Prussia signed the Russo-Prussian Alliance with Peter the Great
against Karl XII of Sweden, and one year afterwards the room was
presented to Russia to commemorate the alliance. Its first home
was the old Winter Palace in St Petersburg; in 1755, it was moved
to the Ekaterinsky Palace in Tsarkoye Selo. Here, hired master
amber carvers continued to work on the room, producing *objets
d'art* such as small chests, candlesticks, snuff-boxes, insect repositories, cups, saucers, knives, forks, crucifixes and tabernacles.
They made a mirror with an amber frame which showed the
Imperial Russian crown held by two armed men, and amber
pedestals carved with the figures of war and peace; beneath them,
figurines of Neptune and a dolphin, signifying Russia's power at
sea; at the foot, carvings of soldiers and arms, signifying her power
on land. They constructed little boxes of amber inside amber
boxes, where scenes from Ovid's *Metamorphoses* were graphically
depicted. This is not to mention the allegories of Russian bears
bearing amber apples in their paws; for the Room became more
and more an embodiment of the Russian Empire, as if it had been
geologically predetermined; and foreign dignitaries admitted to
the Amber Room were suitably impressed.

And where is the Amber Room now? cried the Polish sailor,
and he paused dramatically.

SUBMARINE

So Mr Jarniewicz paused; then, with a practised gesture, he produced from an inside pocket a meerschaum pipe with a sailor's head for its bowl, unlidded its cap, rapidly stuffed the hollow head with a thumb-and-fingerful of a pre-rubbed aromatic mix relinquished from a suddenly disclosed tobacco-pouch, whereupon he lit a match from nowhere with a click of his other thumb and finger, and applied it to the bowl. When the pipe was puffing aromatic smoke to his satisfaction, he proceeded:

— But perhaps I am asking the wrong question, or maybe the right question at the wrong time, for there is more to the Mystery of the Amber Room than the present whereabouts of the Room. I feel, for example, I have not sufficiently emphasized the importance of amber in fossil studies, and I could speak at length about the possibilities of insects being resuscitated from the amber capsules of their tombs, thus probing the very secrets of existence, which puts me in mind of a bit of poetry I could have quoted earlier, but which might be more appropriate at this juncture, as an opportunity for meditation:

> An ant beneath a poplar found,
> An amber tear has covered round;
> So she that was in life despised,
> In death preserved, is highly prized.
> In the bright tear Phaeton's sister shed
> A bee is seen, as in its nectar, dead.
> Its many toils have earned a guerdon high,
> In such a tomb a bee might wish to die.

Lines translated by one of your English poets from Martial's Latin. Or should I say, resuscitated? For we disinter things from their bed of antique Latin, as princes translate the relics of the saints from this holy place to that, there to be venerated again under a different dispensation. The dream of the Catholic Church was not a petty one, for it sought to embrace the world by the dominion of an almost universally unintelligible language; it knew the dialects of men could not express things apprehended by the soul, as incense is not savoured by the ear, nor candlelight by tongue.

And as I speak to you, I realize how foreign and salty your English lies on my tongue, though it seems I have forever been accommodated to it, and I am enraptured often by its lack of cases, its plethora of synonyms, and its ambiguity of preposition. In Poland I was born, and Polish is my mother tongue; many occupying empires failed to subjugate it; and, in spite of all opposition, I think I am correct when I say that more people now speak Polish than ever before. In my language we have a tense for ongoing incompletion of an undertaking. This leads me to acknowledge that before enquiring into the whereabouts of the Amber Room, I should have related the necessary Prologue of the Green Star, which goes as follows:

The year is 1905. The place, Boulogne, France. The month, August. The day, the fifth. The time, eight o'clock on a balmy evening. The Boulogne Theatre has been generously placed at the disposal of the First International Congress of Esperantists. The venue is packed to capacity with delegates from more than twenty nations: some are experts, some are beginners; but all, save a very few, must be alike in this – that they have all learned their Esperanto at home, and, as far as oral use goes, have only been able to speak it (if at all) with members of their own national groups – that is, with compatriots who have acquired the language under the same conditions as to pronunciation, etc., as themselves. The acid test of mutually international comprehension has yet to come.

Dr Zamenhof, the author of the new language, has left his eye-patients at Warsaw and has come to preside at the coming-out of his *karo lingvo*, now well on in her teens, and about to leave the academic pupa of scholastic use and emerge like an imago into the larger sphere of social and practical activity. The unique assembly of that audience is pervaded by an indefinable feeling of expectancy; as in the lull before the thunderstorm, there is a hush of silence charged by electricity, the premonition of a vast force about to be let loose on the world. The preliminary speeches – thanking the various committees who made it all possible, and the Mayor of Boulogne for the use of the hall, and the suppliers of the various complimentary refreshments, and the people who'd laid out the chairs, and the designer of the very fine banner which adorns the platform, on which is depicted a portrait of Dr Zamenhof – are relatively short; but the audience is getting restless, and the hush is becoming a buzz of Chinese whispers. Can it be, they ask each other, is it possible? It is now twenty to nine, and it is getting dusky in Boulogne. The new electric chandeliers are suddenly switched on by the stage crew of the Boulogne Theatre, and the crowd gasps collectively, seeing each other for the first time, illuminated like rows of Romans in an amphitheatre. Still the stage is in darkness. Then a spotlight goes on, stage left. You can hear two thousand people hold their breath. A small man appears in the spotlight. He faintly resembles his somewhat abstract portrait. He is wearing a carefully groomed goatee beard and, at the age of forty-five, is going very bald at the temples. Held to his ears with wire armatures is a pair of oval-shaped pebble-lensed rimless glasses through which he peers at his audience. He looks a bit like Lenin. He also looks like what he is, a working oculist. Still there is silence. Was it all a dream, a chimera, a hopeless fantasy? He coughs. He reads from his prepared speech:

– *Gesinjoroj* (Ladies and gentlemen) – the great audience leans forward as one, straining ears and eyes towards the speaker – *Kun granda plezuro mi akceptis la proponon* . . . The crowd drink the words in with an almost pathetic agony of anxiety. Gradually, as the impeccably cut sentences pour forth in a continuous stream of perfect lucidity, and the audience realize that they are all listening to and understanding a really international speech in an international tongue – a tongue which secures to them full comprehension and a sense of comradeship on equal terms with all users of it – the anxiety gives way to a scene of wild enthusiasm. Men and women shake hands with perfect strangers, or embrace them in a delirium of communication, and all cheer and cheer again. Zamenhof finishes with a solemn declamation of *La Espero*, the Esperanto hymn, embodying the lofty ideal which has inspired him through the many difficulties he has had to face. When he comes to the end, the fine passage beginning with the words, *Ni inter populoj la murojn detruous* ('We shall throw down the walls between the peoples') and ending *amo kaj vero ekregos sur tero* ('love and truth shall begin their reign on earth'), the whole concourse rises to their feet with prolonged cries of *Vivu Zamenhof!*

– Such, I imagine, said the Polish sailor, would have been the account of an enthusiastic Esperantist eye-witness of that momentous occasion. I forgot to mention the flag which was proudly waved by the local Esperanto group in Boulogne, for they had designed it the night before in a frenzy of conviviality, and their wives had sat up till dawn, quilting it: a green flag, with a green star on a white background in the top right-hand corner. The concept was not entirely original: the green star had long been an emblem of Esperanto. It had appeared as a colophon on Zamenhof's first booklet, *International Language*, published in 1887 in Russian under the pseudonym Doktoro Esperanto, or Dr Hopeful; and shortly afterwards, an enterprising Esperantist in St Petersburg, tacitly approved by Dr Esperanto, had a batch of enamel green star lapel-pins run up, which were rapidly adopted by Esperantists everywhere. Thus an Esperantist was given permission by his or her badge to walk up to a stranger wearing the same device, and initiate a conversation with him or her. In this manner the most unlikely couples met: a Czech brewer with a French traveller in lingerie; an English philologist with a Polish sailor; a Scottish spinster typist with a renegade Russian count; an Alsatian dog-breeder with a Lorraine quiche-baker; an Italian prima donna with a Lithuanian ballerina; an Irish postman with a Chinese laundryman. The permutations were endless. Sometimes it was not necessary to speak at all, but the newly-met would hold each other at their two arms' length and gaze into each other's eyes, plumbing the wordless depths of brotherhood and sisterhood within each other, inhabiting their mutual worlds. Then they would leave each other joyfully, promising to correspond: many long-standing correspondences were initiated, photographs of growing families exchanged, and the never-to-meet-in-the-flesh families would think of themselves as cousins.

Such was the power of the green star. From whence did it come? Let us begin in the city of Bialystok, then situated in Russian Lithuania, hence in Russian Poland, where Ludwig Lazarus Zamenhof, as he would be known, was born on 15 December 1859. It was a freezing cold night – it was, indeed, the

feast of St Valerian, who is invoked against cold and exposure –
and his father, a censor for the Jewish press in the city, was going
through a particularly difficult time with his employers. The child
looked puny when it came out, and failed to bawl when slapped;
they thought it would not survive. But the child confounded all
expectations, and proved tenacious. Even so, Ludwig Lazarus
did not utter his first words until the age of four. On the occasion, the family – the censor, his wife, and the child – were sitting
around the dinner table when Lazarus, as he was known in the
family, gravely spoke, and said, Mother, this soup is cold.
Whereupon his delighted parents enquired why he had not
spoken until then, and he replied, Because up until now the soup
was always warm. From then on in, there was no stopping him,
and his linguistic skills proceeded by leaps and bounds, till by the
age of nine he knew, in this order, Russian, Polish, Yiddish,
German, and some Lithuanian. His father taught him Hebrew
and Greek.

– You must, said the Polish sailor, recognize the peculiar ethnic
complications of life in Bialystok at that time. Short-sighted from
an early age, Zamenhof was anguished that men and women
everywhere looked much the same, but spoke differently, and
thought themselves to be Poles, or Russians, Germans, Jews,
and so on, instead of human beings. Thinking that grown-ups
were omnipotent, he resolved that, when he was grown up, he
would abolish this evil; for no one, he said afterwards, can feel
the misery of barriers among people as strongly as a ghetto Jew,
and no one can feel the need for a language free from a sense of
nationality as strongly as the Jew who is obliged to pray to God in

a language long dead, receives his upbringing and education in the language of a people who reject him, and has fellow-sufferers around the world with whom he cannot communicate. So he resolved to become an oculist, and the inventor of a universal tongue, by which means he'd correct the vision of the world. Before leaving school in 1879, he completed his first effort at a planned language. He left it in the hands of his father when he went off to study medicine in Moscow. The censor in the father immediately recognized the danger of possessing such a document, written by a poor Jewish student in a secret language, so he destroyed it, lest it be discovered by the authorities.

But the student Lazarus, as he was known to his fellows in the university, became increasingly active in the Zionist movement Khibat Zion, and reinvented the principles of his language from memory, writing them down in a new notebook. In 1884, he was sent to take a semester in the School of Ophthalmology in the Department of Clinical and Forensic Medicine of the University of St Petersburg. As chance would have it, it was the long-established custom of the School to celebrate the conclusion of such semesters by a dinner at which the Professor, tutors and students were given permission to get drunk together; and it so happened that the Professor of the School at that time had significant connections with the imperial authorities, and had somehow managed to book the magnificent dining-chamber of the Tsar, the Amber Room of Tsarkoye Selo, for the occasion. You can imagine the scene: the nervous students huddled in a corner, clutching and sipping their unaccustomed preliminary drinks, the tutors standing looking over their shoulders at incremental distances from each other and talking loudly to no one in particular, the beaming Professor gazing around in splendid isolation underneath an amber chandelier. Then the ice is broken to some degree when an imperial butler in full regalia appears and calls for attention: before they sit to dine, he is to be their guide to the legendary magnificences of the Amber Room.

– Here is the amber throne of the Tsar which your Professor has so generously occupied. Here is the little chair of the heir to the throne. Here the amber button-boxes of the princesses. The student Ludwig finds himself at the back of the guided crocodile of the tour, and wanders off on his own. He comes across an ornately carved cabinet. Surreptitiously, he opens it. Within it is a little amber statuette of a mermaid. He puts his hand in and takes it out, and looks at it. Its eyes are two green stars: sidereal splinters of pine-needles, serendipitous inclusions within the amber body.

The party sat down to dine, somewhat confused by drink and splendour. Zamenhof excused himself to his neighbours, and sidled up to the Amber Room guide-tour butler, who was standing to attention by one of the magnificent double folding doors with portals of the Russian Empire depicted on them. Let me introduce myself, said Zamenhof, I am a poor student of ophthalmology, but I am most interested in the mermaid figurine I just witnessed when I took her out of her gorgeous cabinet and met her eyes, for they are most unusually formed. Do you, sir, perchance, happen to know anything of her history? And the butler replied:

– Long, long ago, way back in the depths of time, the Baltic Sea from whence all this amber comes was ruled by a mermaid goddess. In Lithuanian, which is my native tongue, she is known as Juraté. Other nationalities have other names for her; but she is the same deity everywhere, for all stories are the same. My people tell me that this Juraté once met a fisherman who fished her seas from his little rowing-boat relentlessly. At first, she resented him for invading her dominion, and she asked him to desist; but he could not understand her fishy language. Then she fell in love with him, because his body was not like hers. She wove a spell of sea-foam round him, and dragged him, so cocooned, to a chamber in her underwater amber palace. There she divested him. Naked as a grub, he looked into her eyes. It was not long until the two strange beings met, and lingered about each other's newly discovered bodies for hours, while plankton dust-motes drifted in the green gloom light that slanted through her amber bedroom window. Meanwhile Perkunas, the thunder-god, looked on. He had long lusted after Juraté, but she had repelled all his advances. He was deadly jealous when he saw her wind herself about a mortal. He let go a bolt of lightning at her palace, and demolished it. The fisherman was electrocuted immediately. Juraté he could not kill, so he had her chained to the ruins of her palace by some spider crabs enslaved to him by promises of even richer pickings. Still, she retained some of her former power, enough to change the eyes of the fisherman – before the crabs could get to them – into two green stars to gaze at her eternally beneath the waves. And this is why the little fig-urine you held a while ago has two green stars for eyes; for it is believed by our people that a lover looks at the world through the eyes of the beloved. So spoke the Lithuanian butler.

— Zamenhof, said the Polish sailor, met Klara Zilbernik, the daughter of a prosperous fishmonger, in 1886, the year he matriculated in ophthalmology, and the following year he established a practice in Warsaw. That year, 1887, was also the year he published his first booklet on his international language, and the year he married Klara Zilbernik. For a wedding present he gave her a pair of earrings in the shape of green stars. What they mean, he told her, is beyond words.

— Brothers and sisters, Zamenhof said in his speech before the Boulogne Congress, according to the Polish sailor, Brothers and sisters created on a single pattern, brothers and sisters who should have helped one another and worked together for the happiness and glory of the human family — these siblings of the world have become strangers to one another, and they have divided themselves, apparently forever, into hostile camps, and among them an everlasting war has begun.

— Ludwig Lazarus Zamenhof, deeply depressed by the disintegration of his ideal of universal peace, died on 14 April 1917, having jotted down, in Esperanto, his last thoughts on paper: 'I have begun to feel that perhaps death is not disappearance . . . that there exist certain laws in nature . . . that something guides me to a higher end.'

Mr Jarniewicz fell silent.

Your recitation thus far, I said, has impressed me deeply. You will scarcely believe it when I tell you that my own father, who was born on 14 April 1916, exactly one year before Zamenhof died, was also an Esperanto enthusiast, and a postman; and I remember being taken by him to upstairs chambers in an obscure part of Belfast where these odd bodies from different persuasions and walks of life would meet and talk to each other considerately, and one of the Esperantist's wives would make tea. And it is true that he met many people through the medium of Esperanto, as you have adumbrated it. I recall a certain Chinese sailor who sent him the *Thoughts of Chairman Mao* in Esperanto, as he responded by sending the Gospels in Esperanto. On one of his postman's walks he accosted a Russian sea-captain in the street, and was invited on board his merchantman by him, and entertained by all his crew. One time he met an English actress for whom he bought tea and buns in the Ulster Dining Rooms. Then there was the time two Esperantist Mormons came to our door, and my father was only too pleased to bring them into the front room to dicuss in Esperanto the finer points of Biblical interpretation. He once met a man who told him he was a millionaire. And for years he corresponded with a Dutch tobacconist.

Here, the Dutchman stirred himself. Your conversation is also music to my ears, he said, for our nation has been one of the most hospitable to Dr Esperanto's brain-child. And in our Golden Age, the notion of a universal language seemed not impossible. Van Leeuwenhoek saw in his microscope the tiny eels that breed within us all. Fabritius depicted the dust-motes in the light of Delft. Swammerdam dissected a caterpillar and found a pre-formed butterfly folded within it. Spinoza wrote his *Ethics*. Huygens invented the pendulum clock, and was the first man to measure the refraction of light. Vermeer painted walls pitted and dimpled by light. Meanwhile the Dutch herring industry was a common market for all of Europe, and the Dutch were renowned throughout the world for breeding cows, cabbages, pigs and flowers.

The restless energy and curiosity of that age was singularly epitomized by the figure of Cornelius Drebbel, whom many claim as the inventor of the microscope, though I have my doubts on that account; but it is documented that he made a compound microscope – as opposed to the simple, single-lens instrument used by van Leeuwenhoek – as early as 1619. Born in 1572 in the cheese market town of Alkmaar, Drebbel was apprenticed, at the age of thirteen, to the famous engraver and alchemist Hendrik Groltzius. In 1589, at the age of seventeen, he built an impressive fountain for the burghers of the town of Middelburg in Zeeland, which included automata of mermaids and mermen, with moving parts, and a water-clock which chimed the hours as various cherubs urinated into a series of bowls. He constructed a perpetual motion machine, an elaborate toy which operated on the basis of changes in atmospheric pressure. His ingenious thermostats, much in demand among the makers of Delftware for use in their kilns, operated on the same principles: as the temperature rose, air expanded and pushed a column of mercury to the point where it would close a damper valve; the same idea was applied to an incubator for hatching chicken and duck eggs. The fame of his mechanical inventions eventually reached the ear of James I of England, and he was soon taken into the special service of Henry, Prince of Wales, to whom he was enjoined to teach physics, Latin, astrology, and posture, in the palace of Eltham. It was there that he was visited by Emperor Rudolf II and the Duke of Württemberg; he was subsequently invited to visit Rudolf, and in 1610 he was installed in Prague with the imperial family. Here he displayed his *perpetuum mobile* and conducted experiments in alchemy. After Matthias, Rudolf's brother, had conquered Prague and deposed Rudolf, Drebbel was imprisoned; but at the intervention of Prince Henry, he was freed to return to Eltham in 1613. It was during this second royal residency that he was encouraged to design and build the first workable submarine, which he successfully sailed below the Thames in 1620, reputedly with King James and Prince Harry on board.

TACHYGRAPHY

Here, I was inescapably reminded of the life and works of John Wilkins, who is the subject of a brief essay by Jorge Luis Borges in his *Otras inquisiciones*, first published in Spanish in 1952, and published in an English translation by Ruth L. C. Simms in 1964, under the title *Other Inquisitions*, by the University of Texas Press. As Borges puts it, Wilkins 'abounded in happy curiosities' – among his interests were cryptography, theology, the possibility of a trip to the moon, and the possibility and the principles of a world language. It was to this latter problem that he dedicated his *Essay towards a Real Character, and a Philosophical Language*. Borges's essay is an exploration of some of the implications of such a language. And, impressed by eye-witness accounts of Cornelius Drebbel's submarine voyage in the Thames, Wilkins examined the potential of such a submersible vessel in his book *Mathematical*

Magic; or, the Wonders that may be performed by Mechanical Geometry, to which we will return in due course.

A biographical note in his *Mathematical and Philosophical Works* describes John Wilkins as follows:

He was born in 1614, son to Walter Wilkins, citizen and gold-smith of Oxford, described by John Aubrey in his *Brief Lives* as 'a very ingeniose man with a very mechanical head; he was much for trying of experiments, and his head ran much upon the per-petuall motion'. Such was his early proficiency in Latin and Greek that at thirteen years of age he entered a student in New-Inn, in Easter-term, 1627. He made no long stay there, but was removed to Magdalen-Hall, under the tuition of Mr John Tombes, and there he took his degrees in arts. He afterwards entered into Orders, and became Chaplain to Charles Count Palatine of the Rhine, and Prince Elector of the Empire.

Upon the breaking out of the Civil War, he joined with the Parliament, and took the solemn league and covenant. He was afterwards, in 1648, made Warden of Wadham College by the committee of parliament appointed for reforming the univer-sity: this was also the year of publication of *Mathematical Magic*. In 1656, he married Robina, the widow of Peter French, formerly canon of Christ-Church, and sister to Oliver Cromwell, then Lord Protector. In 1659, he was by Richard the Protector made head of Trinity College in Cambridge, the best preferment in that university.

After Charles II's restoration, he was ejected from thence, and became preacher to the honourable society of Gray's-Inn, and minister of St Lawrence Jury. About this time he became a member of the Royal Society, and proved one of their most eminent members and chief benefactors. Soon after this he was made Dean of Ripon, and by the interest of the Duke of Buckingham he was created Bishop of Chester, and consecrated in the chapel of Ely-house in Holborn, the 15th of November, 1668: this was also the year of the publication of his *Essay towards a Real Character*.

He was, according to one biographer, a person of great natural endowments, and by his indefatigable study attained to a universal insight into all, or at least most parts of useful learning. He very much advanced the study of astronomy. He was as well seen in mechanics and experimental philosophy as any man in his time; and in divinity, which was his main business, he excelled. He treated sometimes on matters that did not properly belong to his profession; but always with a design to make men better and wiser; which was his chief aim in promoting universal knowledge. He was never eager in pursuit of dignities; but was advanced to them by his merit. He contemned riches as much as others admired them; and spent his ecclesiastical revenues in the service of the church from which he received them. His conversation was profitable and pleasant, and he was particularly careful of the reputation of his friends. After the Restoration he conformed himself to the Church of England, and stood up for her government and liturgy; but disliked vehemence in little and unnecessary things, and freely censured it as fanaticism on both sides.

John Wilkins died of strangury, or suppression of the urine, on the 19th of November, 1672. He knew from Pliny's *Natural History* that Callistratus recommended amber for such cases, and advised his doctors accordingly; but they applied it to no avail. He lies buried under the north wall of the church of St Lawrence Jury.

Before we proceed to Wilkins's thoughts on underwater travel, and his universal language, it may be useful briefly to peruse his book *Mercury; or, the Secret and Swift Messenger: shewing how a Man may with Privacy and Speed communicate his Thoughts to his Friend at a Distance*, published in London in 1641.

Angels, says Wilkins, talk with their whole beings; therefore they need no spoken language. But for men, that have organical bodies, nature has designed instruments for the conveying and receiving of knowledge; that is, the tongue, and the ear; and the communion between these is called speech or language. And a man is equally disposed for the learning of all, according to how education shall direct him. Nor is there such a thing as a natural language, as some fondly conceive.

As language is artificial, so is writing. The first inventor of the art of making speech permanent is thought to be the Egyptian Mercury, who is therefore styled the messenger of the gods. To which purpose the poets have furnished him with wings for swiftness and dispatch in his errands. Parables are basic codes. Fables both disguise and show their meanings. For gods are difficult to understand. For our part, we may proceed by inventing a new secret language, as in canting, and conjuring; or we may change the known language, by inversion, transmutation, diminution, or augmentation. Examples will follow.

As for conveyance, there are many methods. The belly of a hare is one. Tablets of wood with the letters covered with wax, another. Writing on leaves that are then used as a poultice for some sore or putrid ulcer. Writing on one's body. Shaving a servant's head and writing the message on it, unbeknownst to him; then ordering him to grow the hair again; sending him off to be shaved again. Some Jews at the Siege of Jerusalem, the more securely to carry away their gold, melted it down into bullets which they swallowed, venting it afterwards amongst their other excrements. Now if there were a tachygraph who could, by diminution, write the *Iliad* of Homer in so small a volume as might fit into a nutshell, it were an easy matter for him by this trick securely to convey a whole packet of letters.

Then there is the whole question of the many invisible inks: milk, urine, raw egg, or the distilled juice of glow-worms, visible only in the dark. There are others: the glutinous slime of the entrails of a beast, for one. Essence of snail, another.

Then the hieroglyphs. Plutarch speaks of a temple in Egypt dedicated to Minerva, in front of which there was placed the image of an infant, an old man, a hawk, by which they did represent God; a fish, the expression of hatred; and a sea-horse, the common hieroglyph of impudence: the construction of all this being this: O ye that are born to die, know that God hateth impudence.

As for swiftness of communication, none are better than the angels. For there is nothing in their nature which retards them from their courses. If a man could be familiar with an angel, and send him on an errand, that would be a most swift dispatch.

Dolphins are very quick, as are trained runners, or horses. But the latter are primitive methods, for messages can be sent with the speed of sound, or light. There are divers methods of semaphore, employing significatory torches, flags, or smoke; and in the Dutch wars windmill sails conveyed simple messages with rapidity. And it is easy to conceive of a language that may consist only of tunes and musical notes, without any articulate sound. Trumpeters standing on platforms at intervals of a mile or so could thus relay information across a kingdom.

These are but a few of the ideas considered in *The Secret and Swift Messenger*, which is a resumé of all the methods of enciphering and encryption known to seventeenth-century man. Wilkins's proposal of a musical language was fully realized in 1817 by a French music master, François Sudre, who was struck by the fact that the notes of the scale were known with a definite syllabic value, namely *do, re, mi, fa, sol, la, si*, all over the civilized world. With these seven syllables only, he proceeded to make up his vocabulary, according to the principles of classification. Initial *do* indicated a class or key, that of Man, moral and physical; *dodo* gave a sub-class, *dododo* a third sub-division, and so on. With words of not more than five syllables a goodly dictionary could be composed: arithmetic tells us that we could have 7 monosyllabic words, 49 of two syllables, 336 of three; as for longer words, Sudre was satisfied with 2,268 of four syllables, and 9,072 of five. By shifting the accent from one syllable to another, he formed with a single stem the verb, the noun of the thing, the noun of the person, the adjective, and the adverb corresponding to a given idea. Sudre called his language Solrésol, and its resources were practically unlimited, not least when we consider that such a system lends itself to all possible forms of graphic, phonetic, and optical expression. If the seven syllables of the musical scale are pronounced in the ordinary way, you can speak the language like any other: *dore do milasi* sounds as well as 'I do not love'; but you can sing it, or play it on an instrument, if you prefer; with bells or horns, you can communicate to a ship in distress; substitute the seven colours of the rainbow for the seven notes of the scale, and you have an optical language, to be spoken by means of flags, lanterns or rockets. One can readily imagine spectacular communications of *son et lumière*, not to mention banquets in which the guests would eat the speech, or in some instances regurgitate it, for the system can as easily appeal to the gustatory senses; and elaborate flower displays could make statements in perfume and colour. Solrésol also lends itself admirably to stenography or tachygraphy, for the seven simple signs can be reduced further, to *d*, *r*, *m*, *f*, *so*, *l*, *s*. In short, it is truly universal in its applications; and in the nineteenth century, it was favourably reported on by committees of the French Institute, rewarded in international expositions, and endorsed by writers, artists and scientists of no mean repute, such as Victor Hugo, Cherubini, Jules Verne, and Émile Burnouf.

Whether Sudre had read Bishop Wilkins is open to debate: many other attempts to construct such *a priori* languages exist; all of them presume to catalogue the universe and its contents; and since all men, in all ages, tend to have similar thoughts, accusations of plagiarism are irrelevant. Wilkins's own invention, developed fully from the suggestions contained in *The Secret and Swift Messenger*, was announced to the world in 1668 by the publication of *An Essay towards a Real Character*: in it, following a system suggested by the *Ars Signorum* of the Scots gentleman scholar George Dalgarno, he divided the universe into forty categories or classes, sub-divisible in turn into species. To each class he assigned a monosyllable of two letters; to each difference, a consonant; to each species, a vowel. For example, *de* means element; *deb*, the first of the elements, fire; *deba*, a portion of the element of fire, a flame.

Borges, noting that all classifications of the universe are arbitrary and conjectural, ends his consideration of Bishop Wilkins's system by quoting from the English Roman Catholic Chesterton:

> Man knows that there are in the soul tints more bewildering, more numberless, and more nameless than the colours of an autumn forest . . . Yet he seriously believes that these things can, every one of them, in all their tones and semi-tones, in all their blends and unions, be accurately represented by an arbitrary system of grunts and squeals. He believes that an ordinary civilized stockbroker can really produce out of his own inside noises which denote all the mysteries of memory and all the agonies of desire.

Yet the dream of Bishop Wilkins was a logical one: one of the chapters of his book contains a digression concerning Noah's ark, wherein he maintains the truth and authority of the

Scripture, against the objections of atheists and heretics, that a vessel of such dimensions could not contain so vast a multitude of animals, with the whole year's provision for them. If a vessel built by man could hold such plethoras, how much more would a language constructed by man contain! And it was to this Biblical precedent that the Bishop returned in the second book of *Mathematical Magic*, entitled *Daedalus; or, Mechanical Motions*. Chapter five is subtitled, *Concerning the possibility of framing an Ark for submarine navigations. The difficulties and conveniencies of such a contrivance*.

I have said that Jules Verne espoused the cause of Solrésol; for it accommodated his encyclopaedic vision of the world, in which balloonists and submariners performed taxonomies of exploration. We do not know if Verne read Wilkins, but he was familiar with the work of Cornelius Drebbel, whose legend on the continent of Europe far exceeded his posthumous reputation in his adopted home of England. Drebbel – scholar, scientist, engineer, engraver, alchemist, inventor – was a notorious eccentric, habitually to be found wandering the streets of London in midsummer wearing eleven waistcoats, with various formulae and objects of scientific curiosity distributed within their many pockets; yet he epitomized for Verne, and many others, the restless spirit of the Victorian age, which sought to place everything within the category of the known. And if Verne had not read Wilkins, then Wilkins's list of the advantages and conveniencies of a submarine contrivance are curiously precognizant of those put into practice by the Captain Nemo of Jules Verne's *20,000 Leagues under the Sea*:

1. It is private; a man may thus go to any coast of the world invisibly, without being discovered or prevented in his journey.

2. It is safe; from the uncertainty of tides, and the violence of tempest, which do never move the sea above five or six paces deep. From pirates and robbers which do so infest other voyages. From ice and great frosts, which do so much endanger the passages towards the poles.

3. It may be of very great advantage against a navy of enemies, who by this means may be undermined in the water, and blown up.

4. It may be of special use for the relief of any place that is besieged by water, to convey unto them invisible supplies; and so likewise for the surprisal of any place that is accessible by water.

5. It may be of unspeakable benefit for submarine experiments and discoveries.

Among Wilkins's work we find many other such speculations: one essay concerns the art of flying, and the four several ways whereby this flying in the air has been, or may be attempted, namely: by spirits, or angels; by the help of fowls; by wings fastened immediately to the body; and by a flying chariot. More practically, he contemplates the Sailing Chariot, that may be without horses driven on the land by the wind, as ships are on the sea; such a device was already a reality in Holland, where it had been made by the direction of Stephinus, and was celebrated by many eminent authors. This wheeled chariot was a development of a craft known in Holland for centuries: 'They have frequently in Holland,' writes Wilkins, 'other little vessels for one or two persons to go upon the ice, having sledges instead of wheels, being driven with a sail; the bodies of them like little boats, that if the ice should break, they might yet safely carry a man upon the water, where the sail would still be useful for the motion of it.'

Stephinus's vehicle was remarkable for its dimensions – it could accommodate twelve passengers and a crew with ease – and its speed. The eminent philosopher Peireskius, having travelled to Scheveling for the sight and experience of this sailing chariot, would frequently afterwards speak with awe of its capabilities and specifications: though the wind were in itself very swift and strong, yet to the passengers it was not at all discernible, for they went as fast as the wind itself; men that ran before it seemed to go backwards; and things which seemed at a great distance would rapidly be overtaken and left behind. In the space of two hours it would travel from Scheveling to Putten, a distance of more than forty-two miles. Wilkins's suggested improvement to the design is an ingenious one: I have often thought, he says, that it would be worth the experiment to enquire, whether or no such a sailing chariot might not be more conveniently framed with moveable sails, whose force may be imprest from their motion, equivalent to those in a wind-mill; in which the sails are so contrived, that the wind from any coast will have a force upon them to turn them about; and the motion of these sails must needs turn the wheels, and consequently carry on the chariot itself to any place (though fully against the wind) whither it shall be directed.

The most fantastic device of all those treated by Wilkins merits only a brief anecdote at the end of Chapter XIX of *The Secret and Swift Messenger*:

> I have heard a great pretender to the knowledge of all secret arts, confidently affirm, that he himself was able at that time, or any other, to shew me in a glass what was done in any part of the world; what ships were sailing in the Mediterranean; who were walking in any city in Spain, or the like. And this he did aver with all the laboured expressions of a strong confidence. The man, for his condition, was an Italian doctor of physic; for his parts, he was known to be of extraordinary skill in the abstruser arts, but not altogether free from the suspicion of unlawful magic.

This glass is no other than a version of the strange sphere which features in the story called *The Aleph*, by Jorge Luis Borges, with whom we began this chapter. The full details of the story need not concern us here: suffice it to say that its protagonist is neither the 'Borges' who is its first-person narrator, nor Beatriz Viterbo, who died in February 1929, and with whom 'Borges' had been in love, nor her first cousin, the minor poet Carlos Argentini Daneri, in whose cellar the Aleph is to be found, under the nineteenth step of the stairs, nor Zunino and Zungri, owners of the saloon bar next door to Daneri, who want to expand their premises into his, and thus deprive him of the source of all his inspiration, for he is writing a poem called *The Earth*, which will set to verse the entire contents of the planet, with regard to flora, fauna, hydrography including the art of dikes, orography, military and monastic buildings, and any other conceivable category; no, the protagonist is the Aleph itself, for in it is included everything, including 'Borges', who yet fails to glimpse himself in its mirror. For the Aleph is one of the points in space which contains all other points. It is the only place on earth where all places are, seen from every angle, each standing clear, occupying its own space unconfusedly; and Daneri had found it as a child when he stumbled and fell down the cellar steps in the dark.

'Borges' gets to see the Aleph. In it he sees a catalogue of things desolated by each other's incredibly persistent, detailed memories of themselves; of things implying past events, and narratives; of things which bring to mind the perfume of another age; of things so small or big as to be incomprehensible, and therefore lacking in names; of things resembling other things; and among these things, a summer house in Androgué and a copy of the first English translation of Pliny, that by Philemon Holland, whose name leads us to the protagonist of our next biography.

UNDINE

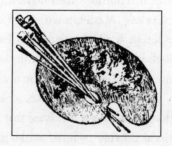

John Philip Holland was born in Liscannor, Co. Clare, on the 29th of February, 1840, the son of a prosperous farmer. As a child he was known to his family and friends as Johnny Jump, on account of his having been born on a Leap Year day. As he grew up, he found himself the butt of many jokes concerning his age; but such a birthday was considered auspicious by the old country people, and they marked him out for future fame. He showed great promise from an early age, and passed rapidly through primary school. He was proficient in Greek and Latin by the age of ten, whereupon he graduated to the Christian Brothers' school in the nearby market town of Ennistymon, where his natural bent towards philosophical enquiry was much encouraged by the faculty. He was a notably devout boy, and was often observed telling his beads in a corner while reading a book. He

267

had a special devotion to St Brigid, whose holy well in Liscannor is the chief ornament of the village; and indeed, it is arguably the most distinguished of the many wells throughout Ireland dedicated to St Brigid, such as those in Ardagh, Co. Longford; Buttevant, Co. Cork; Castlemagner, Co. Cork; Cliffony. Co. Sligo; Dunleer, Co. Louth; Inismagrath, Co. Leitrim; Kilranelagh, Co. Carlow; Marlerstown, Co. Louth; Mullingar, Co. Westmeath; Outeragh, Co. Leitrim; and Tully, Co. Kildare. The St Brigid's Well in Faughart, Co. Louth, is perhaps a close rival of that in Liscannor, for it includes many remarkable features, including the Head Stone, the Knee Stone, and, most importantly, the Eye Stone; for it is related that Brigid was often importuned by a local chieftain, who desired her, whereupon she asked him what feature he liked best about her, and he replied, Your eyes. So she plucked out her eyes and threw them down on a stone and told him he could have them. Whereupon he retired from the contest. Then she bathed her empty sockets in the water that ran from the well, and her sight was restored.

John Philip Holland, then, was an ardent devotee of the cult of St Brigid, and her magnificent shrine in Liscannor afforded him a convenient station for contemplation of her many gifts and consequences, for she was generally held to be the patron saint of writing and invention, as demonstrated by her intervention in the making of the Book of Kells. From an early age he knew how to weave a St Brigid's cross from the green rushes of the field, and he was especially fond of attending those annual occasions, when, on the eve of the first Sunday in August, the people of the village and its hinterland would gather to perform a special ritual in honour of St Brigid. Here they would go their rounds, repeating their prayers and adorations aloud, fortified by copious draughts of poteen, dancing, and making conversations with the saint till dawn. Then, as the first rays of the sun appeared on the rim of the mountain, they would dip long-handled nets into the well and withdraw pebbles of amber from the innumerable supply at the bottom of the well; for no matter how many were taken from it, their number always remained the same.

It was at such a pattern that the young John Philip Holland experienced the vision that was to sustain him for the rest of his life. From an early age, listening to the stories of underwater realms told by the old people, he had often entertained the notion of the possibility of a contrivance which would enable its driver to travel underwater, and experience the magical events thus narrated. He had often prayed to Brigid to inspire him to conceive the practicalities of such a thing. He was fourteen – or rather, three, if you take into account his Leap Year birth – when on the eve of the first Sunday of August, 1854, he cast a St Brigid's cross woven by himself on to the waters of the well, and asked a special favour of her. When he opened his eyes, he found he was suspended above the well, in whose pellucid depths he could discern the shape of a golden trout. As he gazed at it wonderingly, it began to transform itself: its scales changed into tiny transparent amber plates, through which the young John Philip saw in perfect detail all the inner workings of its engine-room, and the microscopic valves and tappets pulsing at the command of its small submariner engineer. He saw its many herringboned compartments. Then he was its captain, looking through its fish-eye lenses at the other world: he saw himself, peering down enormously at his other self within the deep fish.

He was marked out for future sanctity by the Christian Brothers. In 1858, at the age of eighteen, he was enjoined by them to teach in their most important educational establishment, the Christian Brothers School, Limerick. He spent some years there, before proceeding at his own request to take up positions in other schools around the West of Ireland. Meanwhile he read avidly, and was often to be seen buying books in the county town of Ennis and in the city of Galway. Within a few years he had managed to absorb every detail of the admittedly scanty literature of undersea effort, including the work of Bishop Wilkins, and of the pioneers Bourne and Bushnell. He made a particular study of the career of Robert Fulton, born to Irish parents in the Pennsylvanian town of Little Britain (now known as Fulton in his honour). Fulton was implacably opposed to war and dedicated himself to a means of neutralizing the warship, the principal means of transmitting aggression around the world; hence he was determined to destroy the British Navy. An expert gunsmith while still in his teens, he became a briefly celebrated painter of still-lifes, and a highly skilled draughtsman. In 1794 he emigrated to England to study engineering, supporting himself by working as a navvy in the canal-building boom; in 1797 he was in France, working as an engineer under Napoleon Bonaparte; and in 1798, the year of the Rebellion in Ireland, he designed the *Nautilus*, a hydrodynamically sophisticated submersible craft, shaped like an enormous slug, powered by a hand-cranked propeller, and armed with a 'torpedo'. She had an audacious conning tower; a horizontal rudder which anticipated the diving-plane of the modern submarine; ballast tanks; and glass scuttles in the hull for illumination, to obviate the need for air-exhausting candles. Her crew of three was often enchanted by the sight of odd fishes swimming by as the *Nautilus* was put through her paces in the Seine. Regrettably, we cannot manage an account of Fulton's subsequent trials in so brief an editorial space; suffice it to mention that before his death in 1815 he completed for the US Navy the world's first steam-powered surface warship, the SS *Fulton*.

To return to Holland: in 1869, just before the outbreak of the Franco-Prussian War, Jules Verne published the most successful and influential book of his career, *20,000 Leagues under the Sea*. An English translation appeared in 1870; John Philip Holland was arguably the first person in Ireland to read it. To his dying day he was able to recite by heart the passage in which Captain Nemo rhapsodizes about his adopted element.

The sea is everything. Its breath is pure and healthy. It is an immense desert where man is never alone, for he feels life palpitating around him on every side. The sea does not belong to despots. On its surface iniquitous rights can still be exercised, men can fight there, devour each other there, and transport all terrestrial horrors there. But at thirty feet below its level their power ceases, their influence dies out, their might disappears. Ah, sir, live in the bosom of the waters! There alone is independence! There I recognise no masters! There I am free!

It is not the purpose of this brief enquiry to examine the political climate at that time: suffice it to say that for Holland, as for many of his compatriots, Ireland was not only the utopian future and the intolerable present; it was a narrative of mythological dimensions, whose structure had been disturbed almost irreparably by the depredations of the invader. Holland, like Fulton, proposed to shift the action to the underwater sphere, where the greatest navy in the world would be powerless. By 1871, he had drafted plans for a submersible, but he lacked the means to proceed. For many years he had made discreet and tentative enquiries to those in the clergy and religious orders whom he perceived as sympathetic to his cause; increasingly, he became disillusioned, as he realized that he was considered an impractical idealist, and that the Church, far from aiding and abetting revolution, was happy to maintain a tacit equilibrium with the temporal realm. As Holland endured an elaborate series of deferrals and procrastinations, his religious thinking became more introspective and unorthodox, and he turned more and more for succour to the primitive elements of Irish Christianity. Brigid, as ever, occupied his meditations; and he often contemplated the feats of the water saints, such as Comgall, who harnessed four otters to a chariot and drove it under Lough Neagh, and Colman Mac Luachain, who as a child spent a day and a night under the Brusna River, where the water animals included him in their sport. As his interest in these matters grew, he was often to be seen walking the roads of the West of Ireland, enquiring after old men and women who were noted repositories of ancient wisdom. It was on one of these excursions that he made the acquaintance of an itinerant tinsmith called Frank O'Connor, to whom Holland had been initially attracted by the superlative riveting of his tin vessels. They met seven times; and on each occasion, the crafty tinker would divert the talk from the finer points of tinsmithery, and their possible application to submarine technology, by reciting to Holland the story of an ingenious storyteller who tells a story of seven episodes which are told over seven nights. At first Holland took this to be an elaborate joke, and he humoured O'Connor accordingly. When, on the sixth night, O'Connor began the story told by the storyteller on the sixth night, Holland was about to make some perfunctory excuse and leave, when he was arrested by some detail in O'Connor's voice, for the words emerged in an unusually low timbre, as though his spirit had winged its way back into the deep lapse of time, and was intervening in the past, and spoke through his lips. Holland leaned closer over the embers of the fire; the story that he heard that incandescent night, as he remembered it years later, went like this:

– Long ago, there was this old king who lived in the province of Ulster, and he had only one son. The queen died giving birth to him.

The king loved the young heir very much, and when he grew up and entered his teens, he let him have his way with everything. Some might have called him a spoiled brat. He was full of bad devilment. Many's the mean trick he played on the palace staff. There was no use complaining to his father; the king's mind was closed on that subject.

Thomas was this prince's name. When he was about fifteen he took a great notion of fishing. He fished all the lakes and rivers in the neighbourhood, till he thought he'd try his hand at sea-fishing. So the king ordered him a little curragh, with a sail and oars, and that was fine by the young prince.

One day he rose early, unbeknownst to the king and all the household. He got into his curragh, hoisted the sail, and off he went till he came to Malin Head in Inishowen. Then a sudden sea breeze brought him into the lee of a big rock. When he looked up, he saw a beautiful young woman sitting on the rock. She had a gold mirror in one hand, and a gold comb in the other, and she was combing the locks of her long amber hair. It occurred to the young prince that he'd never seen anyone as beautiful. He spoke to her, saying, Are you Venus, or the morning star, or why otherwise are you up so early, on the bare rock?

— I am not Venus, nor the morning star, said she, only a poor girl without father nor mother, who has nobody belonging to her in this world.

— If you come with me to my father's castle, said young Thomas, you can live there merry and contented all your life.

She rose without a word and boarded the curragh. He hoisted the sail and made for home; but he had not gone far when a squall blew up from nowhere. The little curragh was tossed about by the waves as though it was made of straw.

— By my troth, said he, I'm sorry I ever brought you on board; it looks as if we won't come out of this alive, for the waves are oh-so-rough and the wind is oh-so-high.

— Fear not, said she, we're in no danger of death by drowning. I am a mermaid. I have a castle under the deep blue sea; and since you are prevented from your father's castle, I'll take you to mine.

274

No sooner had she said these words, than the curragh was lifted high by a wave, and as it teetered on its crest, she pulled out a wand from her breast, and struck Thomas with it. He was instantly turned into a fish. He felt himself swimming in the wave, yet he retained his former mental faculties. The curragh was capsized. Then Thomas saw the mermaid swimming alongside him. No sooner said, than a monster of a whale appeared, with its jaws agape to swallow them; but the mermaid put its eye out with her wand, and it swam off. They went on for many leagues, till they came to another land under the sea. The mermaid struck him again with her wand and he regained his human form. All around him was a bright green landscape. There was a sun, and a moon, and stars, just as we have.

She brought him into the castle. He gazed around amazed, for he had never seen the equal of the décor. His father's palace was a cow-shed by comparison. Most of the furniture and fitments were of amber-studded gold, and he reckoned that all the wealth of Ireland couldn't buy this place.

— You can rest easy here, said the mermaid, for there's no one here to stop you having your own way with anything. You can do what you please. You are to stay here for seven years, and when the seven years are up, I'll return you to your home in time to see your father before he dies.

She blew a whistle, and a crew of waiters appeared with platters and salvers. They laid them on the table; they were arrayed with every delicacy known to man. She blew her whistle again. Seven warriors appeared, and sat around the table without so much as a word. They began to eat and drink. Sit down with these men, said the mermaid to Thomas, they are all of noble birth. Thomas sat down, but wasn't fit to eat nor drink, he was that full of wonder. When the warriors had eaten and drunk their fill, she said to them, This is a son of a king of the North of Ireland, Thomas by name.

— You are welcome, said they all; and with that, they all arose and walked out.

— Now, said the mermaid, I can see you are amazed by all you've seen, but you haven't seen the half of it, nor the quarter of it. There are many other wonders yet in store for you. Come with me till I show you what my warrior élite can do, men and women both.

She took him to the big courtyard in the centre of the castle. There were seven men and seven women there, and she said to them, Show the prince some of your disciplines.

One of the men went into the castle and came out with an enormous sharp-pointed spear. He stuck the butt of the spear in the ground, stood back from it, took a leap twenty feet up in the air, and landed chest-first on its point. He stayed like that for a couple of moments, then leapt back down again unhurt. Another man came up and took a leap and came down jaw-first. The spear went through his mouth and out at the base of his neck. He stayed there for a few moments, then jumped down unharmed. Another hero took a leap and the point went through his backside, and came out the crown of his head. He stayed there for a few moments, then jumped back down unharmed. Another soldier took a leap and also landed jaw-first, except he caught the point of the spear in his teeth, and he fired it back into the ground again about twenty paces away from where it had been. Another knight scooped up one of the women, took a flying leap, and landed foot-first on the point, where he pirouetted for a moment before swooping down again unscathed. Then another spear was got and stuck in the ground beside the first spear. Two warriors jumped up and balanced on the tips of the spears. They drew their swords and started to fence with each other till the sparks flew. After a while, they flew back down again without a scratch on them. Then the women got started, and they did everything the men had done. Thomas was truly amazed by all this.

– What do you think of my men and women? said the mermaid.

– I've often heard tell of the exploits of the Fianna, said Thomas, but they never matched such tricks as these; and what's more, the women are every bit as good as the men.

She took Thomas to a little parlour within the castle, where she showed him all kinds of everything, each one more beautiful than the last. Then she asked him if he was fond of music.

– Indeed I am, said he, and I have a fine harp back home.

– If you're fit to play, said she, I'll get you a harp, or I'll send for your own, if you like.

– Indeed, I'd rather have my own, said he, for I don't know if I could handle an instrument I'm not used to, and anyway, how could you send for mine?

– Hold on, said she. She tinkled a bell, and a little man appeared. Go, said she, and bring me the harp that's in the prince's room in the king of Ulster's castle.

She opened a window and, swift as Ariel, the little man flew out. He was back in an hour and a half with the harp.

– By golly, said the prince, this is a most express dispatch.

– Now you have your harp, said she, we'll adjourn to the music room.

She went out, and Thomas followed her. She took him to a magnificent chamber where there were at least two score musicians with every sort of instrument imaginable: there were trombones, balalaikas, clarsachs, crumhorns, bassoons, rackets, ocarinas, ukeleles, serpents, dulcimers, euphoniums, viols, cimbaloms and psalteries, not to mention cymbals, congas, bodhráns, glockenspiels and bones. The Master of the Music swept off his hat and bowed to the mermaid.

– This is the son of the king of Ulster, said the mermaid, and he's very interested in music. Play something for him.

The Master took up his viola d'amore, tapped his foot three times, and the ensemble all began as one. Such music! Human ear could barely comprehend its labyrinth of ornament, its many interweaving parts, its interplay of modal possibilities, in which triumph vied with tragedy, and happiness with sorrow, till at last the piece concluded with a plangent chord that seemed to linger in the air forever.

– What do you think of my musicians? said the mermaid.

– I think they must be the best in the world, said Thomas.

– I'd like to hear you play now, said she.

– Indeed, said he, I'm ashamed even to try after what I've heard; but since you sent for my harp, and wish to hear me, I'll try my best.

He played his best piece; but his music was like the buzzing of a bee in a tin box compared to the golden harmonies of the court musicians.

When he came to the end, she said, You don't play too badly, my friend; but don't worry, you've plenty of time for improvement before you get back home. Then she took him to a beautiful garden. The branches of the trees kissed the ground, weighed down with their bounty of strange fruit; and there were flowers whose blooms no human eye had ever seen till then. The king's son tried to voice his wonder; but he fell silent.

That evening the warriors were all seated at the table, and the mermaid on her amber throne, when a stranger warrior all dressed in black appeared, and said, Your ladyship, I have been sent by the Mermaid of the Baltic Sea, and I have bad news for you. She desires to know how many warriors you can put up against hers, and the place and time of combat.

– I have seven fighting men; the place, Lifford in Tyrone, in the North of Ireland; the time, tomorrow night. That is my message for your queen.

The mermaid appeared unperturbed while the black knight was in her presence; but when he had gone, a cloud came over her features. No one has ever beaten the Black Knights of the Baltic Sea before, said she, and I am sore afraid that my warriors and I will fall in the battle tomorrow; but so be it, if that's the way it has to be.

– I know the venue for the battle well, said Thomas, and I'd like to be there, if it please you, and may God protect you from all harm.

– You will be there, said she, and should I fall, you will find your curragh in the lee of the rock where first you beheld me.

The warriors spent the first third of that night singing, the second third relating Fenian lore, and the last third in the deep sound slumber of the comatose, till the sun rose the next morning. They spent the day honing their swords and fixing their armour in preparation for the battle that lay ahead. Then they set off, taking the prince with them; and no one knew how they left, or how they came; but they were all present and correct at Lifford, a minute before midnight.

The Baltic Queen and her seven black knights were there already, drawn up in battle formation. Not a word was spoken; no salute was made. The two sides drew their weapons. For three hours, they waged an awful war. The night sky was lit up for miles around with the forked lightning that ran from their swords; the clash of their shields resounded through the mountains, and in the wilderness the wolves howled hungrily. Then, bit by bit, the Black Knights of the Baltic gained the upper hand; no quarter was asked, nor given; the Irish mermaid and her seven warriors were slain. When they had made sure that they were dead, the Black Knights threw the bodies into the Lifford River. Then they went as they had come, leaving Thomas grieving sorely for his comrades.

When he came to, he set off, and didn't stop till he came to the spot where he had first seen the mermaid. He found his curragh in the lee of the rock, as the mermaid had predicted. He set sail for home.

The king was overjoyed when his son landed home, for he

thought that he'd been drowned. He held a feast in his honour that lasted seven days and seven nights.

From then on, Thomas never went near the sea. To this day, fishermen and sailors give the Mermaid's Rock off Malin Head a wide berth, and will not approach it for love nor money.

That is my story.

VERONICA

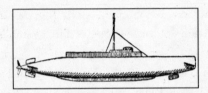

John Philip Holland visited Frank O'Connor for the seventh time on the 3rd July, 1873. It was the feast of Thomas the Apostle, patron saint of the blind, and of shipwrights. He listened courteously as O'Connor related the final episode of his story, then thanked him for his time and his patience. As a parting gift, he awkwardly presented the tinker with a tin whiskey flask in the shape of a submarine, saying that he hoped O'Connor would not look too unkindly on his workmanship; for it represented the first stage in the battle against the Black Knights, be they of the clerical or British variety. Then they laughed, shook hands, and parted forever.

On the eve of the first Sunday in August, Holland paid his last visit to the shrine of St Brigid in Liscannor, where he was granted permission to take an amber pebble from the holy well. After settling his affairs he proceeded to Cobh, from whence, on the 25th of the month (it was the feast day of Louis of France, patron of French soldiers, and button-makers), he sailed on a packet-boat bound for America. He had the amber pebble with him in a waist-coat pocket, for it was considered a powerful amulet against death by fire or water. When he got to the other side, he rapidly found employment as teacher of mathematics in St John's Parochial School in Paterson, New Jersey, a city founded in 1791 as an industrial settlement of the Society for Establishing Useful Manufactures. One New Year's day (it was the feast of Clarus the Abbot, patron saint of the short-sighted) he slipped while walking on the frozen Passaic River, and broke his leg. He was laid up for three months, in which time he was able to bring his plans for a submersible to perfection. In 1875 he was persuaded by some friends to submit these to the scrutiny of the Secretary of the US Navy. They were rejected out of hand as the crazed fantasy of a civilian. Private sponsorship would therefore have to be found: it was done so rapidly, for within days of the rebuff, Holland was approached by an emissary of a high-ranking member of the Irish Revolutionary Brotherhood, who gave him to understand that a profitable meeting could be arranged, for this was an organization even more implacably opposed to English rule in Ireland than Holland himself. Recently reformed from the shambles of the Fenian Society, which had engineered, among other débâcles, the abortive invasion of Canada in 1866, the Brotherhood had mem-bers in high places, and had means at their disposal. That they were still known as the Fenians in popular parlance only enhanced their cause.

After witnessing a splendid demonstration with a 30-inch clockwork model, the Fenians advanced Holland $6,000 from their slippage fund. In 1878, on the 11th July (it was the feast of Benedict the Abbot, patron saint of speleologists) *Holland I* was launched. She sank immediately. Holland had intended to launch her with himself at the controls; he decided at the last minute to let her go unmanned; for, just before the final preparations, he had fondled the amber pebble in his waistcoat pocket and had felt a palpable electrical jolt which convinced him to abandon his original thought. When *Holland I* was hauled up and examined, it was discovered that two small screw-plugs were missing from the bottom. It was widely rumoured that the craft had been sabotaged by a known British agent who'd been seen lurking in the vicinity of the shipyard; and the Fenians, greatly encouraged by the interest of the enemy in their experiments, gave Holland further backing. They now moved to the second phase of their plot, and resolved to have Holland build a number of well-armed submarines that could be smuggled into merchant ships by way of specially constructed watertight holds. The mother ships would then cross the Atlantic and proceed from harbour to European harbour, stalking the enemy within its lair, releasing their lethal submarine children when least suspected.

Holland's response to the scheme is not known; but, after making a complete survey of the design defects of *Holland I*, he stripped her of her assets, scuttled her shell, and began work on his legendary masterpiece, the *Fenian Ram*. She was launched in the Hudson River from the Delameter yard in 1881, on 3rd May. It was the feast day of the Apostles Philip and James, patrons of

Uruguay. The *Fenian Ram* was thirty-one feet long, with a six-foot beam; nineteen tons displacement; powered by a one-cylinder internal combustion engine, developing fifteen horse-power; fitted with a pneumatic cannon, eleven feet long, with a nine-inch bore, which would fire a six-foot torpedo underwater. Admittedly, the torpedo had a habit of shooting straight up out of the water, and on one occasion narrowly missed a dozing fisherman; nevertheless, the *Fenian Ram* represents the single most important moment in submarine history, for she married underwater boat and gun.

For the next two years the *Fenian Ram* was often to be seen manoeuvring in the Hudson River, as Holland put her through painstaking trials, seeking for an ever higher pitch of submarine perfection. Meanwhile, the Fenians were becoming impatient. To them, Holland, in his obsession with the thing itself, seemed to have lost sight of the ultimate objective. In 1883, on 4th December (it was the feast of Barbara, patron saint of gunners and artillery, of Italian marines, military engineers, and firemen) the Fenians took possession of Holland's creation, and towed her to New Haven, Connecticut, where, after a few unsuccessful attempts to master the intricate controls, they ran her aground. The furious Holland severed all connections with the Fenians.

All alone once again, having neither money nor influential friends, Holland was forced to take employment as a draughtsman with the Pneumatic Gun Company of New York. Before long, he had persuaded some of his colleagues to finance another submarine adventure, and with their aid he founded the Nautilus Submarine Boat Company. In this he endured many setbacks and trials. His designs were proposed to and accepted by the relevant committees of the US Navy time and time again; yet other interests seemed to conspire against him, and he became accustomed to the standard letters elucidating the budgetary restraints which made it impossible for the authority to proceed as it would have wished, given the superlative quality of his application. Then, in 1898, on 5th February (it was the feast of Agatha, patron saint of bell-founders, and of volcanic eruptions) he unveiled the submarine which has always been known simply as the *Holland*. Fifty-three feet and ten inches long, ten feet in diameter, with a submerged displacement of seventy-five tons, her armament consisted of two torpedo tubes, one bow pneumatic dynamite gun, and several Whitehead torpedoes; she had a gasoline engine for surface propulsion, and electric storage batteries and motor for submerged cruising. All these factors made it the most efficient submarine of its day. A number of severe tests followed. In 1900, on 23rd April (it was the feast day of Adalbert of Prague, patron saint of amber workers) purchase was authorized by the Government of the United States of America. Holland received $150,000 and a commission for a fleet of submarines. His struggle had been vindicated; and he is regarded almost universally as having deservedly earned the title of 'the father of the modern submarine'. He designed two submarines for Japan during the Russo-Japanese War of 1904–5, for which service he received the Mikado's Order of the Rising Sun.

Nevertheless, his tribulations were by no means over. He was forced – again for financial reasons – to merge his interests in a new firm, the Electric Boat Company; his last years were spent in ruinous litigation over copyright, and in aeronautical experiments. John Philip Holland died penniless on 12th August 1914, the eve of the feast day of Cassian of Imola, patron saint of shorthand writers and stenographers. Holland's model submarines were auctioned off. His clothes were given to a local charity, and they say a vagabond inherited his waistcoat with the amber pebble in its pocket.

The 13th of August is also the feast of St Hippolytus, patron of prison officers, and of horses. The Revd Baring-Gould, folk-song collector, composer of hymns, and hagiographer, admits that there is great difficulty about St Hippolytus: Prudentius the poet, writing more than a hundred years after Hippolytus's supposed martyrdom in the year 258 (or 235, according to another source), states categorically that St Hippolytus was commemorated on this day at Rome, and that he was torn to pieces by being attached to the tails of wild horses; but on 22nd August St Hippolytus, Bishop of Portus, is commemorated, who suffered martyrdom by being attached to the tails of wild horses; and Hippolytus, the son of Theseus, died a very similar death. Moreover, we must also consider Hippolytus, priest of Ostia, and Hippolytus, Bishop of Portus, the eminent ecclesiastical writer of the third century; and some authorities are of the opinion that at least three Hippolyti have been run into one by the poetic licence of Prudentius.

Here, in a nutshell, is the Greek story of Hippolytus. After the death of Antiope, Theseus married Phaedra, sister of the deserted Ariadne, daughter of Minos, king of Crete and owner of the labyrinth which hid the Minotaur. But Phaedra lusted after Hippolytus, the son of Theseus, for he was the image of his father, but much younger. One night, in her husband's absence, she tried to drag the youth into his father's bed; but he repudiated her advances. So when Theseus returned, there was a letter waiting for him, accusing his son of trying to rape his wife; and when he questioned Phaedra, she, with seeming blushes of reluctance, confessed that it was true. The son was banished from his father's house; and as Hippolytus drove his chariot angrily along the sea-shore, Theseus called on his father Poseidon to avenge him. Summoned up by the sea-god, a huge bull exploded from the waves; the horses panicked, ran amok, and dashed the chariot against the rocks; the axle snapped, and Hippolytus, falling, legs entangled in the reins, his body pierced by a broken spoke, was dragged to bits, and died a martyr's death. When Phaedra heard the news, she hanged herself, too late repenting of her crime. We have this story from the mouth of Hippolytus, who was afterwards brought back to life by Apollo's son, Asclepius, the god of medicine.

According to the *Acts and Martyrologies*, St Hippolytus is said to have been the soldier in charge of the jailed St Laurence, who was broiled to death on a gridiron. It is said that Laurence, as he underwent this torture, asked to be turned, 'for the other side was quite done'. Hippolytus, impressed by the saint's demeanour, was converted, and helped to bury his body. When brought before the Emperor Decius, he boldly professed his faith, whereupon Decius asked him if he was not ashamed to so disgrace his uniform. Hippolytus answered that he had passed to a higher service. 'Same old story,' said the Emperor, and shrugged his shoulders wearily. He ordered Hippolytus to be done to death in the manner of his classical namesake. He was tied to the tails of horses, and dashed over the rocky roads, and through thickets of brambles, till he disintegrated, and became a saint. The Christians followed the cavalcade, picking up bits of Hippolytus where they could. His relics are scattered throughout Christendom.

As for Cassian, we have even less information. No one knows when he lived or died; but it is certain, according to some, that he was a calligraphist and writing master to the sons of the bourgeoisie of Imola, near Ravenna in Italy. There was a major persecution going on, and Cassian was lifted and interrogated. He refused to bow to the indicated gods. The ironic judge, asking what his profession was, pronounced an appropriate sentence. He called on Cassian's young scholars – some 200 of them, by all accounts – and commanded them to stab the Christian to death with their pens. At the time it was the custom in schools to write upon wax laid on a boxwood board, in which the letters were incised with a stylus, a piece of metal needle-sharp at one end but blunt at the other, to erase what was to be effaced. The scholars, 'by whom', says the *Martyrology*, 'he had made himself disliked by his teaching them', threw their tablets and pens at his head; some cut deep into his flesh, while others ripped and tore it; the more sophisticated carved graffiti on his body.

It is known that before he died St Cassian had prepared a secret document, an apocryphal life of St Veronica, to be circulated in the Christian underground. This he had written with an immaculately fine-nibbed crowquill pen on a piece of parchment made from the skin of an aborted calf, in characters so minuscule that the whole of the known life of the saint, when wrapped up small, made a perfect fit for a nutshell. If such a feat is not to be believed, one only has to turn to the testimony of Isaac Disraeli, son of the English Prime Minister Disraeli, who records Holinshed's chronicle of the calligraphist Peter Bales, who was famed at the time when the taste prevailed for writing what none could see. He presented Queen Elizabeth with a manuscript set in a ring of gold, covered with a crystal; he had also contrived a magnifying glass of such power, that, to her delight and wonder, her Majesty read the whole volume, which she held on her thumb-nail, and recommended it to her lords of the council. He also enclosed the Bible in an English walnut the size of a hen's egg. Then there is the artist cited by Aelian, who wrote a distich in letters of gold, which he hid in the rind of a grain of corn. Cassian's microscopic effort is long since lost to us; all we can do is try to reconstruct the legend of St Veronica from a modern perspective.

In an account given in the *Mors Pilati*, a matron called Veronica, wanting to have a souvenir of Jesus, was taking a linen cloth to a studio to have a picture put on it, when she happened to meet Jesus. He, hearing what she wished, took the cloth from her, and caused his features to appear on it. In later versions, he pressed his face on it. Then it was thought that this must have happened during the bloody sweat in the garden. Not until the fourteenth century did the story of the compassionate woman wiping the face of Christ on his way to Calvary begin to circulate. This woman is identified with the Veronica of earlier legend. She is venerated in many places as a saint, under a number of variants of her name – Berenice, Bernice, Venice, Venisse, Vernice, Veronce, Verone, etc. – but she does not appear in any known martyrology.

Some say that the legend of Veronica is of Oriental origin, and in art she is portrayed wearing a turban. She holds on her hands, before her breast, a transparent veil of the cloth on which is printed the face of the Saviour, generally in brown because of its customary appearance in Byzantine ikons, which have been blackened by time and the smoke of candles. Sometimes sculptures of Veronica represent her sitting naked in a medieval bath-tub. Some of the clergy, scandalized by this depiction, had her breasts planed off.

In the fifteenth century Veronica became a prominent figure in the French Mystery Plays. To explain the fact of the veil in her hand, they make her into a draper. She is blind, but recovers her sight when she sets eyes on the image of the Holy Face; and with this miraculous sudarium, or sweat-cloth, she later heals the Emperor Tiberius of cancer of the face. She donated free of charge the linen for Christ's shroud.

The Gascons, following an example of the Provençal legend of St Madeleine, created a legend of Veronica which greatly profited a church at the mouth of the Gironde, and she became the patron saint of the Médoc. It is related that after the Crucifixion she followed St Amateur, who is identified with Zaccheus, and married him. She built a hermitage in the sand dunes of Soulac-sur-mer, at the remotest point of the Médoc peninsula; and her relics are preserved in the church of Notre-Dame-de-la-fin-des-terres, which is under the constant threat of shifting sands. She donated to the town of Bazas a purificator (the linen cloth used to cover the ciborium) which was stained with the blood of John the Baptist. She distributed locks of the Virgin's hair to the people of Clermont, and gave the Virgin's shoes to the towns of Rodez and Puy. After this, all that remained to her was the One and Only Milk of the Virgin; which is *solum lac* in Latin, hence the name of Soulac.

Anyone who looks at an image of the Holy Face is guaranteed not to suffer violent death on a journey: in this Veronica corresponds to Berenice, whose amber hair was sacrificed to bring her king safe home; and this reminds us of the legendary Irish amber pebbles, amulets against death by fire or water. Missals and Books of Hours are interleaved with pictures of Veronica holding the Holy Face. Like St Christopher, she has a power of granting a last Confession to anyone who dies a violent death.

In Normandy, women have recourse to St Venice, who is identified with the woman with the bloody flux in Matthew IX: 20–22: 'And, behold, a woman who was diseased with an issue of blood twelve years came behind him, and touched the hem of his garment . . . and the woman was made whole from that hour.' St Venice is prayed to by women who have difficult or copious periods, who wear a white or red ribbon on their necks in her honour. She can cure sterility. She is the patron saint of linen-drapers. She is invoked by laundresses. More recently, she has become the patron saint of photographers, who ingeniously compare the print of the Holy Face to a photographic proof.

Among others, Giraldus Cambrensis alleges that Veronica is derived from *vera icon*, a true image. Some say Veronica is *berenike*, 'victory-giver'. And a *veronica* is also a manoeuvre in bull-fighting, where the matador stands with his feet fixed and his back arched as he brushes the bloody face of the bull with his cape. As to Veronica's veil or bit of linen cloth, it is preserved intact in three locations: at Milan Cathedral, St Sylvester's in Rome, and St Bartholomew's in Genoa. Such multiplication of relic should not surprise us, for it is a common circumstance, as witnessed by the fate of St Bartholomew himself:

Bartholomew, or the Son of Tolmai, is reckoned by St Matthew, St Mark, and St Luke, as one of the Apostles of our Lord. The Gospel of St John mentions no Bartholomew, but speaks of a Nathanael. The Gospels which mention Bartholomew make no mention of Nathanael; so from this, and other internal evidence, we may conclude with probability that they are one and the same person, the former being his proper name, and the latter a patronymic, as Simon was called Peter. St Epiphanius maintains that Nathanael was the young man, the son of the widow, whom our Lord raised from the dead at Nain; but he stands alone in this improbable conjecture. Bartholomew is held to be the apostle of India, of Arabia Felix, of Byzantium, and Armenia; and he is said to have been flayed alive by order of the Armenian Prince Polymius, or by Astyages, the brother of Polymius; or, according to the Armenian historians, Sanatrug, whose daughter he had converted to the faith. When flayed, Bartholomew was suspended on a cross, and left to die with his raw flesh exposed to the flies. His remains were afterwards translated, in 508, by the Emperor Anastius, to the city of Daras in Mesopotamia, which he had built and fortified as a stronghold. How they got there is a long story.

Longer still is the story of how the body turned up in Lipari, and was translated thence, in 839, to Beneventum, where it was authenticated by Pope John XIII; stranger still is the story of another body of the saint being found by Pope Paul IV, in 1560, in the church in Rome dedicated to St Bartholomew; it reposes entire in the high altar. Yet bits of St Bartholomew are shown and venerated at Lyons and Liège. An arm was taken to Canterbury by St Anselm.

There are other relics in the church of St Bartholomew at Bergamo; and in those of the Apostles, St Eusebius, St Laurence outside the walls, St Mary of the Angels, St Cross of Jerusalem, St Sabina, St Praxedis, and St Pudentiana, at Rome. Others at Monte Cassino. A head at Naples, an arm at Amalfi; a great part of the skin of St Bartholomew at Riotorto near Assisi. A foot at Genoa, with flesh and skin dried on it; a tooth at St Maria Liberatix in Genoa, a large part of the skin also in St Blase de Cataldo in Venice. At St Symphorian, Reims, 'a part of the body of St Bartholomew'. Some of the relics anciently enclosed in the leaden weathercock of Sauvemajeur, as protection against lightning, were removed to the choir; but as a monk was killed by lightning in the church shortly afterwards, the relics were restored to the weathercock. Flying ants when they approached the weathercock became paralysed, and fell dead on the roof of the church. A head of St Bartholomew at Toulouse, and an arm and a hand at Gersiac, near Paris; another arm, with the flesh dried on it, at Béthune; part of another arm, 'nobly proportioned', at Foppens; other relics at Ogniac on the Save; a knuckle at Rutille on the Meuse. At Brussels, in the Court Chapel, part of an arm; some bones at Bruges in the cathedral, others at Parc near Louvain, at Tongres, and Utrecht; a shoulder-blade at Maastricht, a finger in St Servais, and part of the skull in St Mary's. At St Charles at Antwerp part of the chin; at Mosaic some of the skin; at Cologne, some of the skin in the church of St Severinus, a double tooth in that of the Apostles, an arm in the church of St Maria in the Capitol, part of an arm in St Pantaleon, a jaw in the Augustinians' church, a jaw in the Jesuit one. An arm at Ebers, at Steinfeld an upper jaw; one of the knives used in flaying the saint in St Stephen's at Mainz. An arm at Andechs; the crown of the head and part of the jaw, and three large leg or arm bones in St Veit, at Prague; another crown of the head at Frankfurt; a lower jaw at Murbach; some of the hair of St Bartholomew at Aix-la-Chapelle. Some bones and skin at St Dominici de Silos, near Toledo, a rib at St Maria de Maxara; an arm bone, part of the skin, and a rib in the Escorial.

In works of art, St Bartholomew appears in the Greek types as a man with an incipient beard; Western traditions represent him in the prime of life, with a quantity of vigorous black hair and a bushy grizzled beard. His peculiar emblem is a butcher's flaying knife, which he holds in his hands; sometimes he carries over his arm the skin of a man with a face attached to it. Michelangelo depicts him thus, in his *Last Judgement*; the face is Michelangelo's.

WHEREABOUTS

— Your narrative, said the Dutchman, is a fascinating one, and, in its multiplication of possible truth, reminded me at times of another tale of human gullibility; but you will recall that our friend Mr Jarniewicz was relating to us the Mystery of the Amber Room, before your train of thought interrupted him; and I would like to know how the story ends.

— Indeed, said the Polish sea captain — before I could apologize — there is not much to relate, for I had almost got to the point of the mystery, which is that no one knows the present whereabouts of the Amber Room, for it was stolen by the Nazis in the Second World War. I understand that there are many competing theories as to its location, which I would be better able to elucidate, were I in complete possession of the available knowledge, but alas! I am not. Just last year my boat, the *Spirit of Łódź,* was docked in New York; we had three days ashore. Rather than spend my time in jazz joints, or perusing the extensive menus of New York's countless restaurants, or going up the Statue of Liberty, for that matter, I resolved to devote my time to piecing together more bits of information about the Amber Room, in addition to those told to me by my father, a former amber worker – how he used to talk! His memory, clear as a bell! His beautifully embroidered details of the detours! His vivid wit, his flashing eyes, his floating hair, God rest his soul!

Had I his gift – but I will proceed. I was directed by our Embassy to that admirable repository of knowledge, the New York Public Library on Fifth Avenue, between Fortieth and Forty-second Streets. Approaching its magnificently proportioned classical façade, deciphering the zenith of its pediment, measuring my steps on the numerical order of its immense broad stairs, I felt myself diminish in its enlightened shadow. Pleasurably, I pushed in through the noiselessly pneumatic revolving doors into resounding marble, stifled by the scent of books laid in archaeological layers, and crumbling chlorophyll; pine-forests of books oozing amber resin, with sunlight slanting through them from the stained glass windows of their limitless cathedral. From the studiously appointed Information Desk I was directed by a kindly grey-haired lady who reminded me of my grandmother to the relevant catalogues in their oak apothecary's cabinets, enumerated and inscribed with Dewey decimals and alphabets. I grasped a knob, and slid open a long thin drawer weighted with reams of printed cards packed infinitely tighter than sardines, drilled and held by a metal spine. I riffled through them with difficulty, imprinting the ghost of my thumb on the numberless smudges of others. I spent many hours at this activity. When I discovered a relevant reference point, I would write its details with one of the many pencil stubs so thoughtfully arrayed in cardboard boxes by the Library staff on a pink request slip with a yellow carbon backing. This I would bring to the Reading Room's issue point, an extensive mahogany desk behind which officers of the Library smilingly engaged you. I watched with interest as the pink top copy of the slip was rolled up and inserted into a cartridge which was then tamped into the orifice of a pneumatic tube and torpedoed to the bowels of the Library, where, I imagined, it would be deposited like a helter-skelter bullet for some underling to pick up. I knew from the plan of the Library provided by Information that the ostensible edifice of the Library concealed a depth of knowledge which ran to eight floors beneath its surface; here, minions laboured ceaselessly among the labyrinthine shelves, climbing long ladders that ran on rails through the narrow aisles, descending like hodsmen with books on their shoulders, in order to accommodate your hope of knowing what you'd never known until then.

I could speak volumes about the Library's systematic splendour. Suffice it to say that books miraculously appeared before your very eyes, some tomes so ancient and disintegrating that they came in special boxes tied with ribbons, that you undid reverentially for fear of further damage to the thing within; and as you disengaged the volume from its cardboard folder, it exhaled musty perfumes of a bygone age – defunct inks and fonts, bindings of linen stitches and fish-glue, rag-paper made from torn veils, washed bandages and worn shirts, the sticking-plaster smell of Rexine, and the snuffy pungency of bookworm dust. I'd take a deep breath before even opening the book. Then I'd stick my nose into its pages. Sometimes they were yellowed, sometimes white with age.

On my first day I had come across a card in the catalogue which announced the existence of a book called *The Amber Room Mystery*, by one Victor Krolevskii; this, I thought, would be the answer to my dreams. I do not remember the publisher, but I have a vague recollection that it was printed in Moscow. I dutifully filled in the request slip, and bore it to the relevant assistant of the Library. I was informed that the book was held in an annex of a remote part of the system, and would take two days to be retrieved and brought to the issue point. This was a setback and a disappointment, but I had no choice but to endure it. Meanwhile I proceeded in my researches and uncovered many details about amber, some of which I have been privileged to share with you. When the appointed day came – the last day of my three days' leave in New York – I marched up anxiously to the issue point and presented my carbon slip for the book. The assistant riffled through her many similar corresponding slips. There was no sign of the request. For some reason, the book had not come through. I was advised to check with the person to whom I had made the original request. Her name was Dante Joyce, as I found out later, for she gave me her name after an elaborate apology, saying that she had put the slip through the normal channels, but that her colleague at the annex had searched high and low, and had phoned her up, saying that he could not find the book in its allotted place on the shelf. If I could perhaps wait another day or two? Perhaps it would turn up, and she would do everything within her power to make sure this was the case. What was I to do?

I did something I had never done till then, and have not done since: I held up the boat, on the flimsy pretence of a sudden bout of influenza. I was the captain of the *Spirit of Łódź*. The boat could not move without me. Dante Joyce gave me the number of her private line, and advised me to phone her at intervals to see how the search was faring. I did so; each time, I was told there was no sign of the book. On the sixth day of my extended leave, I went to her in person. She was beautifully bereft of excuses. She could not account for it; the book had disappeared. I thanked her profusely. She asked if I might be in New York for some more days; I replied, in a reluctant tone, that I was bound to go. I trailed around the bars and brothels of New York for a night and a day, assembling my erstwhile crew, and left for Gdańsk the next day.

All I know about the fate of the Amber Room is this: in 1941, when the Nazis invaded Leningrad, as St Petersburg was then known, the Russians transferred all the movable objects in the Room – the chests, the candlesticks, the cabinets of curiosities, et cetera – to a secret location. They papered over the amber panels to hide them. When the drunken soldiery of the SS burst into the former splendour they found nothing lootable, and resolved to burn the Room; but they were restrained by their commander, a certain Koch, a known connoisseur of art, fine wines and Havana cigars, whose trained nose alerted him to the smell of wallpaper paste. With a black-gloved hand he fastidiously peeled off a corner of the paper to reveal a fragment of the underlying amber glory; he lit a celebratory corona, and ordered the whole room to be stripped. The soldiers drew their bayonets and set about their task with the fervour of a gang of boy vandals, and within minutes were festooned and bedecked like May queens with swathes and ribbons, some of them tripping with their feet entangled, or rolling around on the floor till they became like mummies. Gradually, as more and more of the magnificence was laid bare, their whoops and hollers diminished, until the whole room was gazed at in silent wonder. Koch then dismissed his troops and spent some hours alone in the room, studying its monumental beauty. That night the Amber Room witnessed its last dinner party, as Koch and others of the SS élite gorged themselves on looted caviar and vodka on the gorgeous premises.

It is supposed that over the next day or so Koch procured a detail of men sworn to secrecy to disassemble the panels and stow them in a safe place. In any case, the Amber Room was soon an empty shell. Some think it was Koch's intention eventually to restore the Room to Berlin, its original location, as an emblem of Germany's domination of Russia; some say he was moved primarily by financial gain; others, that his motives were aesthetic. We shall never know for certain; Koch is dead, and where the Amber Room resides is anybody's guess. Perhaps the panels are stacked in a lost subterranean ice room of the brewery that Koch used to frequent; perhaps they were wrapped in oilskins and dropped into an ornamental lake; perhaps they languish in an annex of a labyrinthine salt mine. And that, my friends – concluded the Polish sea captain – is all I know of the Story of the Amber Room.

We were silent for some minutes as we contemplated the implications of this mystery. The Dutchman lit a pipe, and when it was going to his satisfaction, he began:

– Your story is a moral one, and true, in its acknowledgement of the limits to human knowledge; and it puts me greatly in mind of the tale I was about to relate before you embarked on the denouement of your narrative. It concerns my countryman, Han van Meegeren, possibly the most famous forger of all time. You will recall that when the war was over the Allies discovered innumerable looted articles hidden by the Nazis in various venues all over Europe; one such notorious location was the Alt Aussee salt mine, near Salzburg, in Austria. Here were found some 6,750 works of art, among them a hitherto unknown painting ascribed to the Master of Delft, Jan Vermeer, a depiction of Christ and the Woman taken in Adultery. There was consternation in the art world, for, given the paucity of Vermeer's *œuvre* – some thirty or forty pictures, depending on how you reckon it – discovering a new Vermeer was like discovering a new planet in the solar system. Admittedly, some six or seven 'new' Vermeers had come to light in recent years, but this only added to the immense interest in the case. A bill of sale was found with *The Adulterous Woman*, and consternation turned to anger when it was revealed that the painting had been bought by the Nazi propaganda chief, Hermann Goering, in 1942, for the then incredible sum of 1,650,000 guilders. The seller was a middle-aged, once-popular Dutch artist, Han van Meegeren. On 29th May 1945, van Meegeren was arraigned on a charge of collaboration with the enemy by conspiring to sell him a national treasure. For weeks he maintained an impeccable silence to all that was put to him, until finally, on 12th July, interrogated for the umpteenth time, he exclaimed, 'Fools! You are fools like the rest of them! I sold no great national treasure – I painted it myself!'

He then proceeded to claim that all the 'new' Vermeers discovered in the previous eight years, and authenticated by the most eminent art historians of the day, were also his work. He was frankly disbelieved. The case went to trial: all known precedents were turned topsy-turvy, as the defendant wished to be found guilty of forgery. He offered to paint another 'new' Vermeer in the confines of his prison cell; he was supplied with the necessary materials, and before the eyes of eminent observers, he went to work. Overnight, he became a celebrity, and progress on the painting was reported daily by the media. The public were delighted: here was a little man – van Meegeren was frail, and slight of build – proving what they had always suspected, that the art establishment knew nothing more about art than they did; in short, that its emperors had no clothes. Rapidly, it emerged that van Meegeren – for once in his life – was speaking the truth. While painting the 'Vermeer', he gave exhaustive descriptions of his working methods and techniques. The evidence was incontrovertible: all the recent Vermeers were van Meegerens. Within days, works that had been praised for their realization of eternal beauty became worthless daubs – not quite worthless, for they achieved a certain curiosity value; but now it was apparent to everyone that the expressions on the faces of the figures were wooden and lifeless, that their hands were badly painted, and that overall, the compositions were banal. Van Meegeren, far from collaborating with the enemy, had duped him, as he had duped his fellow countrymen.

The history of van Meegeren – like that of any person – is a long and complicated one, and it would require some volumes fully to throw light on his motives and psychology; and there are dark alcoves of the soul, that we can never penetrate. All I can do in the space allotted to me is to sketch a few salient details of the whole picture.

Han van Meegeren was born in 1889 in the pleasant old Hanseatic town of Deventer, which lies on the right bank of the IJssel. Should you ever find yourself in Deventer, you should take the opportunity to visit the town hall, which contains a very fine group portrait of the burgomasters and councillors of Deventer by Gerard ter Borch, one of the masters of the Golden Age of Dutch painting which van Meegeren so admired. Also of interest is the Late Gothic Weigh-house, together with the adjoining House of the Three Herrings, now the Municipal Museum of Antiquities; on the outside wall hangs a copper cauldron in which counterfeiters used to be executed by being boiled in oil or water, depending on the severity of the offence. You should also look into the delightful Toy and Tinware Museum.

Van Meegeren was christened Henri, in honour of his father, who soon took to calling him 'little Han' – more out of pity than affection, it would seem, for he was a puny child. The father was a rigid Catholic and a strict disciplinarian who ruled that his children were not to speak in his presence without his first addressing them; and he would march them in crocodile formation to early Mass every morning in Lent, as well as on the obligatory Sundays. He was a teacher of English and History in the local teacher-training college, and he held a relatively prestigious degree in mathematics. Little Han was not a distinguished scholar, but from an early age he showed a remarkable facility for drawing. Nothing pleased him more than to make pictures of his dreams, in which he was a king and his subjects were lions; his father, when he discovered these, would tear them up, appalled that a son of his should have artistic leanings. So Han learned to conceal his work, and became familiar with the spaces under floorboards and within wainscots. Thus began his circumvention of his father; and in later years, he was pleased to relate anecdotes of his skirmishes with authority. On one occasion, coming home by the police station, he noticed that the key had been left in the front door; he promptly locked the policemen in their own station, threw the key into the canal, and retired to a safe vantage point to watch them climb to freedom through the window. On another, he bribed his brother Herman, an altar boy whom his father had destined for the priesthood, to steal the communion wine. Van Meegeren's account of this drunken escapade would then often lead to the story of how Herman, when ensconced in the seminary, ran home one day, pursued by the bishop. He was forced to return, and later died of a mysterious ailment.

Such were van Meegeren's early years. Naturally, against his father's wishes, he took up the study of art. He easily won the coveted gold medal awarded by his college in Delft for the best painting by any student of the past five years. He was patronized by a coterie of rich collectors, and moved within a circle of admiring imitators. His one-man shows of 1916 and 1918 attracted stunning reviews; and his painting *Deer*, a likeness of a pet fawn of the Dutch royal family, was the most widely reproduced image ever in Dutch art. He seemed destined for a brilliant career. Then, bit by bit, van Meegeren's reputation started to decline. His temper had been always nervous and erratic; now, he found it increasingly difficult to finish anything he began, and his studio became littered with abandoned canvases. To supplement his income, he turned to commercial agencies, producing posters and Christmas cards. When he did manage to assemble enough work for a show, it was savaged by a pack of critics. His work was deemed banal and meretricious. It exhibited the worst tendencies of nineteenth-century studio art. What had seemed an impeccable technique now looked a dubious facility. Van Meegeren was pronounced a competent hack, and was held in almost universal contempt. All this only served to drive him more and more to a conviction in his own genius. He had always prided himself on his application of the methods of the masters of the Golden Age: he ground his own pigments, sized and stretched his own canvases, rigidly adhering to antique techniques. He saw himself as a bearer of the Holy Grail, in an age of ignorance and apostasy. Now his presence in the long dark bars of Delft became endemic, and he was often seen in the company of two or three equally embittered men, drawing up manifestos of revenge. They launched a magazine which excoriated the whole of twentieth-century art for nine issues before it sank without trace. Then verbal abuse became the order wherever they congregated. Bouts of fisticuffs were not uncommon. So it continued for some years.

Of his marital affairs at this time I will not say much, save that there were many extras: van Meegeren's smallness, and his air of petulant fragility, made him attractive to many women, who were willing to indulge his fantasy of genius. Throughout all this, his second wife stayed with him; perhaps she really did believe in him; perhaps she loved him.

By 1932, it is believed by many experts that van Meegeren had reached an advanced stage of certifiable paranoia. In that year, he left to take up residence in the Midi of France, swearing never to return to the Netherlands. Fortified by sun and wine, he would create the masterpiece that would confound his enemies. He endeared himself as a mild eccentric to the populace of the little Midi village, who liked to see him sporting his beret and pigment-stained garments. They addressed him as 'maître', and often shared their rough country wine with him as he regaled them with anecdotes of the great masters. No questions were asked when it became known that he had purchased an electric oven that was implausibly large, given the smallness of the van Meegeren ménage. No questions were asked when the postman revealed that he had delivered many mysterious packages to van Meegeren. No questions were asked because van Meegeren perfectly fitted his image of himself.

We cannot know at what stage van Meegeren decided to become a forger, but there were inklings of it in his former career. You will recall that as a student he won the coveted gold medal in Delft. The painting in question, a meticulously studied seventeenth-century church interior, had sold for a considerable sum; and shortly afterwards, van Meegeren made a perfect copy of it, proposing to sell it as the original. He intimated as much to his first wife, and was somewhat puzzled when she spoke of beauty, truth and ethics; but he acquiesced to her, and sold it as a copy by van Meegeren. It realized barely one-twentieth of the original sum.

At any rate, some time around the year 1933, van Meegeren began his exploration of the art of make-believe. He had an encyclopaedic knowledge of Dutch seventeenth-century art at his fingertips, and was confident that he could reproduce an image in the manner of any of its masters. He chose to imitate Vermeer. Here, his judgement was correct. Vermeer's *œuvre* was remarkably small – thirty-six canvases, some of those doubtful – and it was supposed that many of his works must have been lost. Dealers dreamed of finding a Vermeer in some forgotten attic; professors longed for another work which would bolster their pet theories; and even the general public were mesmerized by the legend of the Sphinx of Delft, the artist who retires unknowably behind his perfect creations. Moreover, Vermeer's reputation had suffered a catastrophic decline after his death; even in his lifetime, he was known only to a handful of connoisseurs. By the eighteenth century, Vermeer's name meant so little that his work sold more easily if passed off as a ter Borch or a de Hooch, or even a van Mieris. So, many of his pieces were fraudulently signed. It was not until the 1860s that his reputation was revived, and Vermeer became gradually acknowledged as a supreme master.

For van Meegeren to fake a Vermeer was in itself a comment on the mutability of taste.

Next, the subject; again, an impeccable choice. Rather than basing his composition on the famous Vermeer interiors, van Meegeren decided on a Biblical theme, in the manner of Vermeer's early works, such as *Christ in the House of Martha and Mary*, thought to have been painted around 1654 or 1655. You must remember that as a child van Meegeren had the Bible beaten into him, and even now, almost forty years later, knew large sections of it by heart. His chosen subject, the apparition of Christ at Emmaus, was eminently appropriate. The source is Luke 24, and the story goes as follows:

On the Monday after Christ has been crucified, his women followers come to the tomb bringing spices. They find the tomb empty. Two men in shining garments appear, and ask the women why they seek the living among the dead. For Christ has risen, as he said he would. The women bring the news to the apostles, but their words seem to the men 'as idle tales'. Peter goes to investigate himself, and finds the linen wrappings of Christ; but no Christ. He doesn't know what to think.

That same day, two of the disciples go to a village called Emmaus, on an unspecified mission. They are walking along, discussing the mysterious event, when Jesus appears by their side in the guise of a stranger. He asks them why they appear so bothered. Where have you come from, that you haven't heard the big news? they reply. And they proceed to give a resumé of the events of the past week, and their significance. As they draw near the village, Jesus chides them for their lack of faith, and is about to depart, when they insist on him joining them in a tavern. He sits down with them. He takes bread, blesses it, breaks it, and shares it round. Their eyes are opened, and they know him, whereupon he disappears.

Such, then, were to be the themes of van Meegeren's masterpiece: death, resurrection, disguise, revelation, disappearance. He decided he would paint the denouement of the story, where Christ breaks the bread and reveals himself to the two wondering disciples. All that remained to him now was the problem of ageing.

XEROX

– So, said the Dutchman, as I have related, van Meegeren, inspired by the boldness of his conception, was absolutely confident in his ability to paint the *Christ at Emmaus* in the manner of Vermeer. He saw the picture vividly in his mind's eye, and knew which colours to deploy. He would have to obtain the raw materials and grind them by hand, as Vermeer had done, so that their particles would appear heterogeneous under the microscope. The most important were the blues, the yellows and the whites – above all, the blues, which dominated Vermeer's palette. Vermeer sometimes used indigo, the violet blue obtained from the leaves of plants of the genus *Indigofera*. Indigo is one of the prismatic or primary colours defined by Newton in 1622, and the colour is also sometimes obtained from woad, a decoction of which was used in former times to quench St Antony's Fire, as noted by your English herbalist Culpeper. But Vermeer's blues were chiefly based on ultramarine. Nowadays this is always prepared by a synthesis of sodium chlorate heated with kaolin, charcoal and sulphur; Vermeer ground it from the fabulously expensive lapis lazuli, 'blue as a vein o'er the Madonna's breast', as your English poet Browning delicately puts it. Van Meegeren, after many enquiries, managed to purchase a sufficient quantity of this exotic substance from the London firm of Winsor & Newton, as witnessed by a contemporary bill of sale that was later to be produced as evidence at his trial.

The yellows were usually gamboge, which derives from Cambodia; occasionally, yellow ochre. The whites were based on white lead. Vermilion and bright red came from cinnabar and burnt sienna. He acquired these without difficulty. The task that now lay before van Meegeren was how to age his painting in a manner that would convince the eye of the most scrupulous expert. The canvas itself presented no problem: in his earlier career, van Meegeren, I forgot to say, had formed a relationship with a shady dealer in antiques, and was consequently familiar with the second-hand art market. Nowadays any painting from the Dutch Golden Age, no matter how incompetently executed, is worth a considerable sum: such are the vagaries of fashion, when a mediocre 'Whore in Brothel' piece, once exchanged for a sack of potatoes, is now seen fit to grace the drawing-rooms of the bourgeoisie. But no matter; van Meegeren procured a painting of the right period and dimensions for a few florins. Significantly, perhaps, this was a depiction of the Raising of Lazarus. He would scrape off the surface paint down to the original ground, on which his masterpiece would be built. But the most difficult thing of all – more difficult than Christ's eyes, more than the love and astonishment of the apostles, more than the broken bread, more than lapis lazuli, or gamboge – was to emulate the hardness and crackle of old paint. Oil paints take at least fifty years to dry, as the volatile substances imprisoned within them slowly relinquish their hold on reality and vanish into the atmosphere. Even after half a century, evaporation might not be complete. But all along, the painted surface has been dividing itself into many islands, into a vast archipelago of colour, as the diminishing volume of paint causes crackles to appear like a maze of tiny Canaletto canals threading through the topic. In these spider's-web-thin channels, the silt of centuries is embedded: tobacco-smoke, turf-smoke, the scent of herrings, the aroma of warmed cheese, microscopic flakes of human skin, wool-dust from a Persian carpet, dandruff, soot, chalk, and the impalpable corpses of mites. Meanwhile, the paint gets harder as it dries. There is a simple test for detecting a fake of an old painting. Dab a mild corrosive on the surface, and the paint, if relatively new, will dissolve. But a really old painting is immune to this treatment.

Van Meegeren knew all this backwards. Here the industrial-sized electric oven came into play. For months he experimented with baking carelessly made paintings at various temperatures. All his tests proved unsatisfactory: sometimes the colours lost their brilliance, or were changed; sometimes the surface blistered; several daubs caught fire. Then came van Meegeren's one true stroke of genius. He looked at his radio, which was playing a Bach cantata. There was something about its bodywork that made him think of amber and of tortoiseshell, of ancient varnish. The cantata descended the scale of being and climbed up again in parables of things lost and found, as he watched the sunlight play on the shimmery body of the radio. A summery bee droned past the open window. As he stared mesmerized at the red blip illuminated by its station, he felt himself become calmer than he'd ever been. The voice of the singer probed his veins, and entered them. His being throbbed to its pulse. Then the radio hummed to him about its body, which was Bakelite.

Van Meegeren had glimpsed a hitherto ignored property of Bakelite: it looks like solidified varnish. Here was the key. He rapidly established that Bakelite is a compound of phenol and formaldehyde, and began to experiment with various ratios of these substances. Eventually, after painstaking trials, he arrived at a phenolformaldehyde resin which he could incorporate into an essential oil which would be further mixed directly into the ground pigment. With this formula, a painting, if baked at a mild temperature, could age centuries in days. There was only one drawback: because of the rapid drying process, the paint had to be worked extremely swiftly; and once the strokes were made, there was no going back. But van Meegeren had no fears on this score: by now, he felt he could paint the Vermeer blindfold.

Now for the crackle. Here, again, van Meegeren showed his ingenuity. A lesser forger, presented with an old canvas on which to paint, would have dipped it in a solvent, thus erasing every trace of paint from its surface. Van Meegeren, with meticulous patience, scraped the layers of paint which depicted the painting back to the white painted ground, to which the crackles of the surface paint had penetrated. He guessed correctly that if he wound his painting on a roller, the surface would craze according to the pattern of the crevices below. In a normal old painting, the crackles spread from the top down; van Meegeren simply reversed the process. To simulate the dust of ages, he brushed the whole piece with Indian ink, and wiped it off again. In this manner the depths of the crackles were appropriately blackened. He would end by incorporating some fly-specks into the whole design.

Now everything was in place. Rapidly, driven by the power of his paranoiac rage for vengeance, attaining a realm of inspiration he had never known till then, van Meegeren painted his first and best Vermeer, the *Christ at Emmaus*, or, as I would prefer to call it, the *Supper at Emmaus*. After he had exposed himself as a forger, he liked to tell the story of how, one night in the little Midi village where he made his masterpiece, a passing Italian itinerant had knocked on the door of his villa in search of charity; van Meegeren opened the door, and found himself staring into the eyes of Christ. Van Meegeren took him in. He broke bread with him, and gave him wine. After a while he asked the tramp if he would be so kind as to act as a model for Christ in a painting he had in mind. The tramp took superstitious fright, and was about to run out of the door, but van Meegeren managed to restrain him. He sat him down in a chair and proceeded to disabuse him of all ideas of blasphemy, supporting his argument with precedents from Michelangelo and Titian, and quotations from the Gospels. The dazed tramp agreed to van Meegeren's conditions, and stayed with him for three days while van Meegeren painted his portrait, which he then incorporated into his grand design, which shows Christ with his right hand poised to bless the bread, watched by two men and a woman. The story is all the more extraordinary when we consider that in the finished painting, Christ's eyes are almost completely concealed by their heavy lids.

So van Meegeren painted the picture that would amaze the world, and confound his enemies. The next step was to have it authenticated. For almost fifty years, the word of Dr Abraham Bredius had been law in the field of Dutch Golden Age painting. He was a pioneer in Vermeer studies, having systematically read his way through most of Delft's notarial archives between 1880 and the 1920s in search of any scrap of information that might shed light on Vermeer's circumstances. Bredius, in 1937, was eighty-three years old, and half-blind. Van Meegeren knew that if Dr Bredius pronounced his work to be a Vermeer, then, to all intents and purposes, it would be a Vermeer. The story of how van Meegeren 'discovered' his own creation, and brought it to the attention of the unfortunate Bredius, is in itself a long and an interesting one; but I must press on. Bredius took one look at the picture, and was immediately convinced. For here was the fulfilment of his dreams: a new Vermeer. Later, van Meegeren was to say that his most difficult job was to forge Vermeer's signature, for it had to be accomplished in one stroke: this was not accurate, for Vermeer's signature is made up of carefully composed isolated letters. But it was noticed by some at the trial that the names van Meegeren and Vermeer – sometimes known as van der Meer – were not entirely unlike; and a smart journalist, tempted by this appropriate conjunction, dubbed the forgeries 'Vermeergerens'.

At any rate, Professor Bredius was hooked at first glance.
Within days he wrote van Meegeren a certificate of authentifi-
cation. Abraham Bredius was a mild, respectable, eminently
respected, much decorated, plausible man, who had worn out his
eyes in the service of Dutch art, which he loved passionately.
Had he not set his eyes, behind their pebble-lensed glasses, on the
first 'Vermeergeren', he would have found a modest place in history as a careful scholar of a subject infinitely bigger than him.
Instead, he is famous for being the first fool to be taken in by van
Meegeren:

> This glorious work of Vermeer, the great Vermeer of Delft,
> has emerged – thank God! – from the darkness wherein it lay
> for many years, undefiled and just as it left the artist's studio.
> Its subject is almost unique in his *œuvre*; a depth of feeling
> springs from it such as is found in no other work of his. I
> found it hard to contain my emotions when this masterpiece
> was first shown to me, and many will feel the same when they
> have the privilege of beholding it. Composition, colour,
> expression – all combine to form a unity of the highest art, the
> highest beauty.
>
> Bredius, September 1937

This document is interesting in many respects. I will take but one
example: Bredius's use of the word 'undefiled'. Now, van
Meegeren knew that every old painting has suffered wear and
tear; so he deliberately took a knife to his creation, and then
repaired the damage in the manner of a hack restorer. In fact,

when the *Supper at Emmaus* was eventually bought by the Boymans Museum in Rotterdam, for the unprecedented sum of 550,000 guilders, it was found necessary to restore the restorations; even then, no one suspected the fraud. Yet Bredius, in his purblind enthusiasm, failed to detect these flaws.

Of course, he was not the only one. Van Meegeren went on to construct another five 'Vermeergerens', each of which was received with more enthusiasm than the last; they were all authenticated by the most eminent historians of Dutch art, who appeared to be under the spell of a mass hypnosis. Van Meegeren began by painting his childish dreams; perhaps he ended by painting the dreams of others. Yet we should not be too quick to condemn in retrospect; we are all prisoners of time, and can never dream how the future will change the past.

Han van Meegeren died of a heart attack on 30th December 1947, worn out from years of morphine addiction. I will leave you with one last anecdote of his career. When the *Christ at Emmaus* was bought by the Boymans Museum, it was proudly exhibited in a special room, with a roped-off section immediately before it to safeguard the treasure from the attentions of the throng which had queued to see it. Van Meegeren joined the queue like the rest, and when he came to confront his creation, stooped over the ropes to examine the details of the restoration. He was sternly pushed back by an armed guard and told to be on his way. He gazed at the guard briefly, smiled, and left obligingly; for how was the guard to know that he had looked into the eyes which had looked into the eyes of Christ?

*

Listening to the Dutchman's recitation, I was reminded of the real Vermeer which had been discovered in the Alt Aussee salt mine in 1945, together with the fake. *The Art of Painting* had been acquired by Adolf Hitler in 1940, as part of his intention to establish a museum of art in memory of his mother, in the Austrian town of Linz: a pamphlet published on his birthday, 20th April 1945 (the feast day of St Peter Martyr, patron of inquisitors), outlines the project; its frontispiece is a colour reproduction of *The Art of Painting*. In 1813, the work, then thought to be a de Hooch, was sold by an Austrian saddlemaker to a Viennese aristocrat, Count Czernin, for the modest sum of 50 florins. In 1866, the French critic Théophile Thoré, writing under the pseudonym William Bürger, published a series of articles on Vermeer which were to be the first steps in his rehabilitation to the canon. As a radical democrat, Thoré viewed politics and art as being inseparable: 'all history is a perpetual insurrection against the powers that rule the world', he declared. Elected to the legislative assembly after the 1848 Revolution, he became involved in an abortive leftist *coup*, and was forced to leave France; his alias, German for 'citizen', was adopted during a stay in Belgium, where the secret police of Napoleon III operated unrestrained. Thoré/Bürger authenticated *The Art of Painting* as being the work of Vermeer. Today it hangs in the Kunsthistorisches Museum in Vienna; it is known to have been among Vermeer's household effects at the time of his death.

Jan Vermeer died suddenly, probably of a stroke or a heart attack, on St Lucy's Day, 1675, leaving behind eleven children. He was forty-three, and bankrupt. His widow, Catherina Bolnes, wrote that her 'late husband, Johannes Vermeer, during the long and ruinous war with France, not only had been unable to sell any of his art, but also, to his great detriment, was left sitting with the paintings of other masters that he was dealing in. As a result and owing to the very great burden of his children, having no means of his own, he had lapsed into such decay and decadence, which he had so taken to heart that, as if he had fallen into a frenzy, in a day had gone from being healthy to being dead.' An inventory of movable goods, drawn up on the Leap Year day of 29th February 1676, includes 21 children's shirts, 'so good as bad'; 11 children's small collars; four beds, one bedstead, and two cradles; and 26 pictures worth about 500 florins in total. *The Art of Painting* was not included in this latter item, for Vermeer's widow had signed it over to her mother five days before, to prevent its being seized as an asset. What happened to it between then and its turning up in the possession of an Austrian saddlemaker remains a mystery.

St Lucy's Day, the 13th of December, is traditionally regarded as the shortest day, the Winter Solstice, as the sun enters Capricorn, and 'the world's whole sap is sunk', as John Donne puts it in 'A Nocturnall upon S. Lucies day'. In the Baltic countries this day is celebrated as a Feast of Light, possibly because the name of Lucy is suggestive of light and clarity; in like manner, she is the patron saint of glaziers. She is thought to have been martyred under the persecution of Diocletian, in the year 304. It is related that she had dedicated her virginity to God; and on being approached by a pagan suitor, she asked him which bit of her he found most attractive. When he replied, 'Your eyes', she tore them out and presented them to him on a platter. She is depicted holding a dish containing her eyes in many paintings, including that by Domenico Veneziano in the Uffizi gallery in Florence. She is therefore the patron of those who suffer from eye diseases. In other versions, the disappointed suitor exposes her as a Christian to the imperial authorities, and she is condemned to spend the rest of her life in a brothel; but she is miraculously rooted to the spot, and her captors cannot move her. They then try, unsuccessfully, to burn her. Finally, she is killed by having a sword thrust through her throat; she is therefore the patron of cutlers, and of those who suffer from sore throats.

It is appropriate that Vermeer, the painter of light, should die on such a day:

> Study me then, you who shall lovers bee
> At the next world, that is, at the next Spring:
>> For I am every dead thing,
>> In whom love wrought new Alchimie.
>>> For his art did expresse
> A quintessence even from nothingnesse,
> From dull privations, and leane emptinesse:
> He ruin'd mee, and I am re-begot
> Of absence, darknesse, death; things which are not.

To the astronomer Johannes Kepler, whose theories of light influenced the Dutch painters of the Golden Age, the eye was a pin-hole camera; a camera obscura. Of van Eyck it has been said that his eye operates as a microscope and a telescope at the same time; this is equally true of Vermeer. We perceive it, in *The Art of Painting*, in his handling of the chandelier, made up of blips and lentils of light, and the more distant light which moves across the elaborate map of the Netherlands which hangs on the back wall. This is a map so meticulously depicted, that when an original map came to light, it could only be authenticated by comparing it to the Vermeer painting; paradoxically, Vermeer shows an antique map, so carefully representing its cracks and blisters, the oblique waves caused by the hanging weight of the object, that its information is obscured by zones of shadow.

The original map is by Nicolaes Visscher: in its surround, he represents a fisherman with a surveyor's tool, thus making a visual pun on his name. There are frames within frames. Let us take the classic Albertian definition of a picture: 'A framed surface situated at a certain distance from the viewer who looks through it at a second or substitute world'. So, seventeenth-century picture frames were designed like window surrounds, or mirror frames. Many of Vermeer's interiors invite the viewer to look in past a pulled-back curtain to the *mise-en-scène*: *The Art of Painting* includes the figure of man sitting squatly with his back to us as he paints the figure of a woman we take to be an allegory of Fame, or Clio, Muse of History. She is dressed up like a novice actress in an amateur drama, holding a brass trombone on one hand, and a yellow book in the other; she is swathed in a blue robe based on lapis lazuli, nearly the mysterious blue of the laurel crown on her head, which is the same blue as the leaves on the richly patterned curtain. Or were the laurel leaves originally green, in which the yellow has oxidized, leaving only blue behind? If so, does this change our reading of the picture?

Of laurel, we may say this: laurel is chaste Daphne, who, praying to the gods to deliver her from the hot pursuit of Apollo, was turned into a bay tree. But even in this new form Apollo loved her, and placing his hand upon the trunk, he felt the heart still fluttering beneath the bark. He embraced the branches as if human limbs; but the wood shrank from his touch. He then cried out, Since you can never be my bride, at least you will be my tree. My quiver and my lyre will always be entwined with you, my lovely laurel. Roman generals will wreathe their heads with bay leaves, returning from the wars, when long processions climb the Capital, beneath the triumph of their hyacinthine days. And the beauty of your leaves will be perpetual. So he spoke, and Daphne's new crown of leaves seemed to nod in assent.

Laurel was sacred to the Pythoness of the Delphic Oracle, and her votaries were commanded to wear it. For laurel is the source of prophecy and poetry. Hence, prospective climbers of Parnassus place laurel leaves under their pillows for inspiration. It was thought that bay laurel is antagonistic to the stroke of lightning; but Sir Thomas Browne, in his *Vulgar Errors*, says that he knows a man who disproved this theory by personal experience. A laurel wreath was the top prize in the Pythian games of the Greeks. Here, at Delphi near Parnassus, the gymnastics and foot-races took second place to the musical event, whose rubric demanded a new composition on an old theme, the *nomos*, to be played on the flute; in it, the competitor would celebrate the battle of Apollo with the dragon Python, and his triumph. Hence you can imagine elaborate serpentine melodies, marked throughout the hot blue Greek August afternoon by shady judges under canopies; and, borne on the wind from far-off, you can hear the sinuous chant of the minstrels praising Apollo in wine-tents pitched below Parnassus, and the low twang of their self-accompanying citharas.

Nowadays, the laurel retains shadows of its former power. A test for true love is to prick your sweetheart's name on a laurel leaf and wear it next your heart: if the writing turns red, he loves you; but if black, he loves you not. A laurel leaf is used for writing secret letters on. The berries of the laurel have been used to promote abortion. Oil of bays is sometimes dropped into the ears to relieve pain. An infusion of laurel cures most agues.

In *The Art of Painting*, Vermeer significantly depicts his artist beginning his picture of Clio by painting her laurel crown: a most unlikely procedure, according to most critics, who think that artists normally begin with the body, for ornament is what is added on. But there remain the controversially blue leaves of the laurel on the canvas on the easel painted on Vermeer's canvas; the head and body of the model, whom we view indulgently within the first frame, has yet to be depicted by the pictured artist. Delft, which contains the Vermeer studio, is contained by the Visscher map of the Netherlands painted by Vermeer. Is Vermeer painting himself? All we can see is the squat bum in its bulging black pantaloons, and the back shoulders of his black and white slashed doublet, and the loose hair, and the black cap, and the strange balloon of the painter's brush hand, which looks as if it has been broken and swollen beyond its normal dimensions into something barely capable of holding a brush.

YARN

On the 24th May 1921, at 9.15 a.m., the hour at which he normally retired to sleep, Marcel Proust sent his chauffeur Odilon Albaret to fetch the critic Jean-Louis Vaudoyer as his escort for a visit to an exhibition of Dutch art at the Jeu de Paume in the Tuileries.

Returning with the critic, Odilon parked, and kept the engine running as Marcel, wearing a black Homburg hat, dark one-button cutaway jacket and pinstripe trousers over chisel-toed black shoes, descended from his apartment above the boulangerie at 44 rue Hamelin, leaning on an elegantly thin silver-mounted African blackwood walking-stick with a curved handle. As he stepped on board the throbbing open-topped cabriolet and greeted his friend Jean-Louis, Marcel caught the whiff of gasoline – *l'essence* – that percolated through the warm freshly baked bread aroma, and was reminded of how years ago, strolling the boulevards with a companion, he could shut his eyes and, playing blind, identify his whereabouts from the smells that leaked from the many odiferous trade outlets of Paris: the cheesy tang of a fromagerie; the blood and sawdust of a butcher's; the clinic-sharpness of a pharmacy; the snuffy air of a tobacconist's; the crumbled odours of a dealer in old books. By a parfumier's foyer, he would be sometimes moved to catalogue the art: first, the bases or fixatives – ambergris, from the sperm whale, the pleasurable stink of civet, from the civet cat, musk from the musk deer; the floral group of odours, such as jasmine, rose, lily-of-the-valley, and gardenia; the spicy blends, featuring carnation, clove, cinnamon, and nutmeg; the woody smells of vetiver, sandalwood and cedar; the mossy family, dominated by the nose of oakmoss; the herbal rush of clover, new-mown hay, and sweet grass; male whiffs of leather, tobacco, birch and tar; not to mention spiritual balm, myrrh, frankincense and spikenard; complex combinations of these woven together in elaborate rugs of smell, which bring back reminiscences of others, like the kaleidoscopic motifs of a huge, dimly remembered symphony –

Here, a woman brushed past the writer, and his reverie was disturbed, for the waft of her garments recalled an indoor gown his aunt had worn – such a curious smell! – dark, fluffy, speckled, streaked with gold like a butterfly's wings, seeming to breathe by itself when hung on a hook on the boudoir door, with its arms folded by its sides. He opened his eyes. He was in the car, spinning along in the bright sunlight which cast spokes of zoetropic chiaroscuro through the wheels to flicker on the audible Braille of the bumpy *pavé*. A tram clanged briskly as it thrummed past; Odilon parped his horn in reply.

It must have been some time after ten o'clock when, arm in arm, they entered the Jeu de Paume, the ailing writer supported by the critic. Vaudoyer had recently published, in *L'Opinion* of 30 April and 14 May, two articles celebrating the art of Jan Vermeer, whose three pictures in the exhibition he regarded as its highlights: *A View of Delft*, *Head of a Girl*, and *The Milkmaid*. He had rhapsodized especially about *A View of Delft*, which till then he had only known in a reproduction. When Proust had seen it almost twenty years before in The Hague, at 9.15 a.m. on the 18th October 1902, he thought it 'the most beautiful picture in the world', and he wanted to renew his memory of it.

Now they stood transfixed by the *View of Delft*: by the stretch of rose-gold sand that takes up the foreground of the canvas, where a woman in a blue apron creates around her, by this blue, an intense harmony of colour; by the dark, moored barges, glittering with herring-scales of light; by the red brick houses; by the immense sky over the roofs of the town which gives an almost vertiginous impression of infinity; by the palpable breath of the climate, that hits you like a shock of ozone when you wind down the window of the closed compartment you've been travelling in, and realize your seaside destination has arrived. As the two companions more closely examined the locale, many other details came to light: Vermeer's craft, it seemed, had a Chinese patience, an ability to hide the minutiae and processes of work, that one finds elsewhere only in the lacquers and carved stones of the Far East. Take, for instance, the little oblong of yellow wall to the extreme right of the canvas, which, if concentrated on, looks like an ivory name-plate with nothing written on it, or a slip of ceramic inlay, or a bridge to the Delft not painted, for there is something otherworldly and uncanny in its abstract glow of yellow: it hints at how Vermeer's craft resides in the sheen of passages and linkages between things, of colours just about to shift but spellbound by the places occupied by others, of silent figures reading missives from beyond the window, of other pictures within mirrored rooms. Sometimes it looks like the work of a coach-painter, who lays coat upon coat on the panels, sanding and buffing, painting and repainting, in order to achieve that glossy finish in which every brush-stroke is eliminated. The technique is inscrutable.

— Vermeer's painting, said Vaudoyer, makes us think about things that one can touch, like enamel and jade, lacquer and polished wood, then about things that result from complicated and delicate recipes, like a crème, a coulis, a liqueur, before leading us to reflect on the living things of nature: the heart of a flower, the skin of a fruit, the belly of a fish, the agate-like eye of certain animals; and especially, it causes us to ponder the very source of existence, to reflect on blood. Yet Vermeer rarely used red. Blood is evoked here not by nuance, but by its essence. It can be, if you please, yellow blood, blue blood, ochre blood, since we are dealing with a magician. This heaviness, this thickness, this sluggishness of the material in the pictures of Vermeer, this cruel depth of tone often gives us an impression such as when we see the shiny surface of a wound, covered as it were with a rich varnish, or, perhaps, a spot made on the kitchen tile by the blood that drips and spreads itself beneath a suspended carcass —

Vaudoyer was, in fact, mistaken when he said that Vermeer rarely used red: one has only to think of the red brick and the red window-shutter in *The Little Street*, the red of the man's coat in *Officer and Laughing Girl*, and of the woman's dress in *The Glass of Wine*, not to mention the admittedly allegorical blood trickling on the tiles from the mouth of the crushed serpent in *The Allegory of Faith*. Then there is the recurrent motif of tables draped with elaborate Turkish rugs whose dominant colour is red, which remind us that Vermeer's father was a master weaver of the silk fabric known as caffa. Vermeer himself is obsessed with fabric: drapes, curtains, cloths, the texture of cloths and furs, especially when set against cool tiles, glassware, waxy knobbly items of fruit, or the neutral sheen of maps and paintings. He paints these contrasts of feel so convincingly you do not want to touch them, for they feast the eye, and not the fingertips. You are beguiled by their mesmerizing folds and puckers and crumples and pleats. If you look closely at the left-hand sleeve of the lady in *Lady Writing a Letter with her Maid*, it looks like a block of carved snow, or a geological formation, like a mountain painted by Cézanne; you can almost hear the creak of starch, and yet you cannot figure out the artifice. Then you feel with your eyes the ponderous weight of the huge chocolate-brown brushed velvet curtain at the window before you register its flimsy white cotton lining blown away from it by the gusting light. Vermeer loved doing fabrics.

Vermeer's father, Reynier Janz. Vos — which we might anglicize as Reynard Johnson Fox — also kept an inn, *Die Vliegende Vos*, The Flying Fox, on the north side of the Voldersgracht in Delft; sometimes, for reasons best known to himself, he maintained the alias of van der Meer, or Vermeer, i.e., 'of the lake'. From the documentary evidence, he appears to have been crafty, tight, but sometimes impulsive to the point of generosity; intelligent, with a good eye for art, in which he dealt intermittently, sometimes keeping a favourite picture for himself; a good flute-player; in debt more often than not, but usually on the right side of the law; a minor public figure, who wanted his son to do well in painting. He was more of a listener than a storyteller, but on occasions could relate a good anecdote to a regular; and as he helped out with the bar, the young Vermeer — John o' the Pond, as we might call him — must have heard some yarns.

The word 'yarn' derives from the same root as 'gut', the Indo-European *ghere*, which also gives us 'chord', and Latin *haruspex*, 'a reader of entrails', i.e., a diviner, or a storyteller. Yarn is the thread of the ropes that sailors splice together, and 'to spin a yarn' was nautical slang not so long ago. The yarns of old sea-dogs are notorious, for the yarn is a long, often elaborate narrative of real or fictitious adventures. Yarn is perfume-blenders' argot for the narrative dimensions of a scent, and its potential to seduce the public. It is measured in inches and feet.

I return to my father's yarn. You will recall that this is a story about a storyteller who relates a series of stories on successive nights to an audience which emerges from a secret door in a room in the house of a mysterious lady. The seventh story in the sequence goes as follows:

Jack the Lad spent the next day as he had the other days. Evening came, and he was summoned to the big room. The lady put up her gold whistle and blew it. The door in the wall opened, and the same team entered, each man with a woman on his shoulders, and a baby at the breast of each woman. They all sat down and the lady asked Jack to begin his story. So he did.

Once upon a time, but maybe not that long ago, there lived near Tobarnaveen an upstart of a fellow who was always arranging marriages between himself and some girl or other, but in the end he never married any of them, for he thought himself above them. They called him John the Fog. One day, there was a funeral, and when John the Fog came back home, he'd a fair few drinks taken. So when a neighbour man called by and asked him would he ceili with him, he was only too pleased. They got to the ceili house and the place was packed with young men and women, and some of his own cousins too. They asked him had he any notion of marrying.

– I have, says he, and every notion, but I don't know what kind of wife would be best for me.

– You could marry me rightly, says one girl.

– Don't, but marry me, says a second girl.

– I'd be a better wife than any one of that pair, says a third girl.

— Well, says he, I'd a nice blackthorn stick with me when I was above in the graveyard today, but I left it stuck in the ground near the grave of the old woman we buried. I'll marry whichever of ye will go up and bring me back my stick!

— You may go to the devil, said two of the girls, for we wouldn't go into the graveyard for all the sticks in the wood, never mind your piddly little blackthorn!

— I'll go, said the third girl, and I'll bring you back your stick, if you keep your promise to marry me.

— I promise, said he.

They called this girl Sally Gardens. Off she set for the grave-yard. She had no fear. In she went, and she was looking about in the dark for the stick, when a voice spoke from one of the graves.

— Open this grave! called the voice.

— I can't, and I won't, said Sally Gardens.

— You'll have to open it! said the voice.

And before she knew it she was digging away with a spade that one of the grave-diggers had left behind, and in two ticks she hit the lid of the coffin. It opened up, and there was a man inside.

— Take me out of this coffin! said he.

— I can't, and I won't, said Sally Gardens.

— You can very well, said the man.

So she had to take him out of the coffin.

— Now take me on your back! said he.

— Where to? said she.

— I'll direct you, said he.

She had to take him on her back, and she took him to the house of one of the neighbours. He told her not to go any further.

She carried him into the kitchen. The family were all in bed asleep. The man stirred up the fire.

— See can you get me something to eat? said the man.

— And where could I get you something to eat, said Sally Gardens, seeing I don't know my way about this house any better than you?

— Go! There's oatmeal in the room! Bring it here! said he.

She found the room, and the oatmeal was there.

— See can you get me some milk? said the man.

She looked high and low, but there was no milk to be found.

— And in case you're going to ask, said she, there's not a drop of water about the house either.

— Light a candle! said he.

She lit a candle.

— Hold that candle for me now! said he.

He made off to a room where the two sons of the man of the house were asleep. He took a knife and cut their throats, and he drew their blood into a basin they had by the side of the bed. He came back with the blood, and mixed it with the oatmeal, and began to eat it. He told Sally Gardens to eat up as well, but she only pretended she was eating, and she let the blood and the oatmeal fall into the pocket of her apron.

— It's a great pity, said she, that such a thing should happen to those two nice boys.

— It wouldn't have happened, said the man, had they kept some nice clean water about the house; but they didn't, and they must take what has happened!

— Is there no way of bringing them back to life? she asked.

— There is not, said he, for you and I have eaten the stuff that would have brought life back into their bodies. If some of the oatmeal that was mixed with blood was put into their mouths, then they'd jump back to life, all right, and the two of them would have a good life, if they had lived. Do you see that field their father owns?

— I do, said she.

— Well, there's not many knows it, but there's pots of gold in the bushes yonder, said he, and now, said he, you must take me back to where you found me.

She took him on her back, and when she was going out the yard gate, she took out the oatmeal from her apron pocket, and she let it fall by the wall. She took him along, and she never stopped till she took him to the grave she'd taken him from.

— Put me in the coffin! said he.

She put him in the coffin.

— I'll be going home now, said she.

— You will not! said he, for you must cover my coffin with earth, the way you found it!

She started filling in the grave, and after a while, a cock crowed in a house nearby.

— I must be off now, for the cock is crowing, said she.

— Pay no heed to that cock! said he. He isn't a March cock! Finish your task!

She had to keep on filling the grave. After another while, a second cock crowed.

— I must be off now, for the cock is crowing, said she.

— Off you go, said he, for that's a true March cock, and the

334

March cock is the only cock with power over me; and if he hadn't crowed just now, you'd have to stay with me forever.

She went home, and by that time, the ceili was over. She went to bed and slept late till her mother called her.

— Have you no shame to be lying in your pit and the bad news we have near us at the neighbours! said the mother.

— What news is that? asked Sally Gardens.

— Why, this neighbour of ours found his two sons lying dead in the one bed this morning, and their throats slit open!

— How can I help that? asked the girl.

— I know you can't, said the mother, but you might be a good girl and get dressed, and go to the wake.

She went to the wake. She remembered every word the dead man had told her. All the people at the wake were in bits crying, but Sally Gardens didn't cry.

— Would you give me one of them as a husband, if I brought the two boys back to life? she asked their father.

Now, John the Fog was at the wake, and he wasn't one bit pleased when he heard this.

— I thought you said you'd marry me, he said.

— Marry you! said she, you and your blackthorn stick! Do you know what I went through last night? I wouldn't marry you for all the tea in China!

— Don't be joking me! cried the man of the house, how could a slip of a girl like you put the life back into them? Can't you see I've trouble enough without you making fun of me!

— I swear to God I'm not joking, said Sally Gardens. I'll put life back into their bodies if I get one of them as a husband, and all I'll ask along with him is the little field above the house, the one with the bushes in it, and you can leave the rest of the farm to the other fellow.

– I'll give you that field gladly, said the father, if I saw that you'd put the life back into my two boys, the way they were before.

She went out and she fetched the oatmeal that she'd let fall the night before. She went into the room, and put some of it into the mouths of the two boys. No sooner had she done so, than they sprang up out of the bed as alive as they'd ever been.

After a while she married the better-looking fellow, and she told him the whole story about meeting the dead man. She told her husband to go dig among the bushes, that he might find something there. So he did, and he came up with a pot of gold. He took it home and emptied it, and he put the gold in a safe place. They put the pot on a shelf in the dresser as a conversation piece, for there was a bit of strange writing on it that no one could read.

About nine months later, a poor scholar called in to the house and he saw the pot.

– Who put that writing on the pot? he asked.

– We don't know, they said, and nobody else knows, either.

– I don't know either, said he, but I know what the writing says.

– That's more than we know, said they. What does it say?

– It says that on the other side there's three times as much, whatever that means, said the poor scholar.

So that put them to thinking, and that night they went back to where they'd dug up the pot, and they dug around the eastern side of where they'd found it, and they found three other pots, all full of gold. Then, you may be sure, they had a great party for seven nights and seven days, and each day and night was better than the one before. They raised a house full of children and lived happy and contented until it came their turn to die.

— And that, said Jack the Lad, is how Sally Gardens got her husband and her gold because of the blood-and-oatmeal man, and it's a true story, for before she died she told her story to my grandfather, who told it to my father, and I got it off him.

And now, O mistress of the house, ladies, gentlemen, honourable listeners all, I have come to the end of my stories, and the time has come to bid you goodbye. I know my mother and father are worrying about me, as they usually do when I've been away so long, and I'll be off home now. All the stories I told you are true; I only regret that I've no proof of their veracity.

A big black-bearded chap rose from the seated company. 'Twill not be long before the proof is out, said he. I am Mr Fix-my-tooth, that you met in the graveyard, and every word concerning me in the first night's story is true.

A fine-looking woman got to her feet. Only then did Jack notice she had only one eye. Indeed, said she, for I'm the girl that met the fairy frog, and I own half of Connemara, and every bit of what you said about me's true.

A fine fellow in a swallow-tailed coat and a dicky bow came to the fore. And I'm the King of the Fairies, said he, that plucked the eye from the head of herself, and your fairy story's absolutely true.

A gawky-looking individual stood up. And I'm Pat the Lad, said he, the eejit that chatted up the witch that lived in the glen between Dog Big and Dog Little, and your story about me is as true as you'll get, and if any man says I'm a liar, I'll give him a puck in the jaw with my hurley-stick.

A big red-haired man took the floor. Introducing Larry the Red, said he, the man that slept in the witch's house, and overheard the conversation of the cats, and got the pot of gold, and found the flower at the bottom of his garden, and cured the princess, and became the richest man in the district; and every word of what you said about my derring-do is true.

Two men rose as one. One was a noble-looking fellow, the other a beetle-browed giant of a man, and one of them said, Earl Minor, at your service! My friend here, the Black Rogue, that I killed in GlenSpell. I hereby verify your narrative. God save the King!

Up came two other brave-looking men, and the younger of them said, I'm the boy that went beneath the waves, and saw the mermaid's boudoir, and you have told my story as it happened; and my companion here, the leader of the Black Knights of the Baltic, who killed the mermaid, will back me up regarding the details of the battle.

Another woman got to her feet. I'm Sally Gardens, said she, the girl that carried the dead man on her back, and brought the two boys back to life, and the way you described me and all that I did is as true as I'm standing here.

A droopy-looking being roused himself, and put up his hand. And I'm John the Fog, said he, and I can't speak for what Miss Gardens here got up to in the graveyard, or where she got her pots of gold, for that matter, but I can tell you she fairly put my nose out of joint when she turned me down, after her making me promise I'd marry her, and it just goes to show you that you can't believe a word a girl tells you these days, and if you ask me —

John the Fog was about to go on, but the lady of the house put her gold whistle to her lips and silenced him with a blast.

ZOETROPE

Everyone was silent for a moment. Then the three men who had not spoken rose gravely and majestically to their feet. Jack, indeed, had been impressed by them as he told his stories each night, for their figures seemed to emanate a noble aura. Eventually, the eldest said: My companions Oscar and Oisín here have been saying that it's been a long time since they heard a linked narrative as exquisitely crafted as that we have been privileged to hear these past seven nights. Most storytellers these days are contented with a one-night stand. Finn McCool never stinted his praise where praise was due; nor did he ever fail to award an appropriate prize. Here is a purse of gold for the storyteller; it will make him a rich man for the rest of his days. And storyteller, said he – looking at Jack the Lad – when you shuffle off this mortal coil, and the story of your life has reached its end, you will be welcome in my stronghold in the Otherworld; for I am Finn McCool.

Jack took the purse gratefully and humbly, and was finally about to make his departure when the Lady of the House spoke up.

— I have resided in this house, said she, for more than ten and threescore years, hoping against hope for news of the man I loved, the Knight-at-arms, but not a word did I hear until I heard his story from this storyteller's lips. Now I know his whereabouts for sure, and being in possession of the means to free him from his spell, I will leave this house, never to return. She bowed to Finn McCool, and said, And if it please you, sir, tomorrow eve the Knight-at-arms and I will join you in your stronghold in the Otherworld; for our time has come round at last in the Great Wheel of Life.

Jack the Lad heard no more. He fell into a deep sleep, and when he awoke, the house was empty. The morning sun shone through the uncurtained windows. The lady, and the doorman, and all the gorgeous furniture had vanished, as if they'd never been; and he never saw them again in his life. But the purse of gold was still in his hand and he went home a rich man.

His father and mother were overjoyed to see him, and they asked for an account of his adventures, but Jack the Lad was smart enough to keep his mouth shut. In the due course of time, his parents died. Jack married a squire's daughter, and built a magnificent residence. He had gold enough for the rest of his life, and he left behind a family of sons and daughters. Jack is now in the Otherworld with Finn, where they pass the time contentedly telling each other tales. And some of Jack the Lad's descendants make a living around the Lough shore to this day.

So my father came to the end of his story. When he'd been in the process of summoning up his dramatis personae to corroborate Jack the Lad's stories, and as their presences were registered on my inward eye, it seemed to me that this verbal sleight of hand was not far removed from that of the flicker-books he would make for his young children by drawing a series of stick figures on the edges of the recto pages of a cheap jotter, and riffling them like a deck of cards to produce a jerky illusion of move-ment: this was before we had become aware of the commercially produced flicker-books, and it seemed to us that my father was some class of a magician. Yet we did not pause to think how mere articulated sound could produce vestigial outlines of people in our mind, who would be fleshed out more and more as the story progressed, the more we imagined what they were supposed to look like, and who resided in the chambers of our memories long after the story had been told. For the illusion of the flicker-book is made possible by the optical phenomena known as persistence of vision and the *phi* phenomenon. The first of these causes the brain to retain images cast upon the retina of the eye for a fraction of a second beyond their disap-pearance from the field of vision, and is therefore a type of involuntary memory; while the latter creates apparent move-ment between images when they succeed each other rapidly, by linking up the memories, like a stick drawn across the iron railings of a fence to produce a musical blur, or a piece of cardboard stuck between the spokes of a bicycle wheel.

These memorable properties of the brain are the basis of the more sophisticated cousins of the flicker-book: the phenakistoscope (from the Greek for 'to cheat') is a disc with figures upon it arranged radially, representing a moving object in successive positions; in the zoetrope ('wheel of life') the figures, on the inside of a revolving cylinder, are glimpsed through slits in its circumference; the Praxinoscope ('action') deploys mirrors; all are spun rapidly to produce a dynamic impression, and are hence the forerunners of all motion pictures. Of these, the zoetrope, patented in 1834 – though no doubt similar devices have existed for centuries – is the most familiar, and cardboard self-assembly zoetrope kits may be readily purchased in specialist toy-shops. The kit contains strips of paper depicting various actions, which you glue together to form reels to place in the slitted cylinder, which revolves on a pin stuck into a piece of dowelling rod. These moving pictures are rudimentary: one reel might show a leaping dolphin, another a man riding a bicycle, another a frog standing on its head and juggling a ball between its hind legs. Yet they never cease to entertain and amaze; for they appear to move in the realm of paradox.

In 1877 Eadweard Muybridge, financed by a Californian millionaire who had laid a wager that all four of a horse's hooves must leave the ground at one point, set up a battery of twelve cameras along a Sacramento racecourse, with wires stretched across the track to trip the shutters: as the horse strode down the course, its hooves tripped each shutter individually to expose a successive photograph of the gallop. The developed film proved the millionaire's point. When Muybridge later mounted these images on a rotating disc and projected them on a screen through a magic lantern, they produced a 'moving picture' of the horse at full gallop, as it had actually occurred in life. This experiment moved some viewers, using arguments rehearsed by Zeno of Elea in the fifth century BC, to postulate that the horse only appeared to gallop in life; and that all motion was illusion.

None of Zeno's writings has survived: all that we know are fragments of his thought as represented by other authors, whether as paraphrases or quotations of his arguments, or what are alleged to be his arguments. Nevertheless, Bertrand Russell was of the opinion that 'Zeno's arguments, in some form, have afforded grounds for almost all the theories of space and time and infinity which have been constructed from his day to our own.' Zeno, it is known, was a disciple of Parmenides, who maintained that reality is one, immutable, and unchanging; and Zeno, according to Plato's testimony, propounded a series of arguments designed to show the absurdity of the views of those who poked fun at Parmenides. The chief of these arguments are Zeno's four paradoxes of motion, known respectively as the Dichotomy, the Paradox of Achilles and the Tortoise, the Arrow Paradox, and the Paradox of the Stadium. We have neither space nor time to examine them in any detail, but let us briefly outline the Arrow Paradox, as it is the most germane to the illusion of cinematography. Philoponus represents Zeno's argument as follows: Everything that occupies a space equal to itself is either at rest or in motion; but it is impossible for anything to be in motion when it occupies a space equal to itself, and it is therefore at rest. The arrow, therefore, at every instant of the time during which it is in motion occupies a space equal to itself and so is at rest; but if it is at rest at all the instants of this time, which are infinite in number, it will be at rest during the whole time. But it was supposed to be in motion: and our conclusion is therefore that the moving arrow is at rest.

More succinctly, Epiphanius records that Zeno argues thus: What moves, moves either in the place in which it is, or in the place in which it is not; and it does not move either in the place in which it is or the place in which it is not; therefore nothing moves.

In like manner, it is clear that a galloping horse is static at any given instant of its photographed career. The French philosopher Henri Bergson, who was a cousin-in-law to Marcel Proust, confronted this problem in the early part of this century, by stating that the mind takes snapshots of the passing reality, and strings them together; so that the mechanism of our ordinary knowledge is of a cinematographical kind.

Seen in this light, narrative, which includes biography, is possible only because we make factitious links between one instant and the next: blinks of the eyelid, adumbrated by the ghosts of things already swallowed by the void. It can be said of Henri Bergson, that he was born in Paris on 18th October 1859 (the feast day of St Luke, patron of, among others, doctors and painters) to a Polish Jewish father and an Irish mother, and was equally competent in French and English from an early age; that his lectures at the Collège de France in the early years of the twentieth century were so popular that they were attended by philosophers, scientists, men of letters, priests, students, rabbis, and fashionable ladies, who would send their grooms to keep seats for them; that his voice was remarkably sonorous and musical, the words 'slipping out as if on silk'; that he might have become a Catholic were it not for the growth of anti-Semitism, which led him to declare himself among the persecuted; and that he died on 3rd January 1941 (the feast day of St Geneviève, patroness of Paris) in occupied Paris, from pneumonia contracted after standing for many hours in line to be registered as a Jew. So we can blur these details together in the memory, and produce an adequate Photofit identity; but another selection of characteristics might make a different and as plausible a picture.

In like manner, we know that King George V of England collected stamps, particularly those of the British Empire, many of which were authorized by his own image, thus placing him in a uniquely privileged position in philately; but a biography of him based only on the George V who appears in the *Stanley Gibbons' Postage Stamp Catalogue* might be considered by some historians to be inadequate; yet George, I believe, liked nothing more than to retire to his study to pore over his stamp collection with a magnifying glass, and, for all we know, this royal self-indulgence might have far outweighed the more apparent trappings of his majesty. For on stamps the immense Empire was miniaturized and made tangible; and millions of his subjects were enabled to behold him, ensconced agelessly amid scenes of pomp and native circumstance. On the stamps of India appeared the Rameswaram

Temple, Madras; the Golden Temple, Amritsar; the Jain Temple, Calcutta; the Taj Mahal, Agra; and the Dominion Columns and the Secretariat, commemorating the inauguration of New Delhi. On those of St Helena, the Government House, and the Wharf. On those of Nigeria, illustrations of Cocoa, a Tin Dredger, the Timber Industry, a Fishing Village, Fulani Cattle, and the Habe Minaret. On those of the Cayman Islands, a Cat Boat, Booby Birds, Hawksbill Turtles, Conch Shells and Coconut Palms, and a map of the Cayman Islands.

Taken together, these images make up one portrait of King George V; for me, they form the greater part of my knowledge of him, at this point in time. And I can state with some certainty that the first image of George that ever flashed into my consciousness appeared on a postage stamp, though exactly when this was, I cannot tell; but I might have been about ten or eleven, and the year therefore 1958 or 1959, when my father, who was a postman, brought home a postcard bearing a Georgian stamp which had mysteriously turned up in a batch of letters he was sorting. I had inherited from him an interest in science fiction, and this event seemed to suggest to us that some kind of time-slip had occurred within the premises of the General Post Office. I can still see the stamp in my mind's eye – it was the ½d green issue of 1912, on which George has not yet fully developed the imperial beard with which we associate him, though he does sport the impressive moustache. But scrutinize it as I might, I can't make out the postmark, and the message is illegibly blurred. I am sure I used to have this postcard in my stamp collection; but I have no idea of its present whereabouts, nor do I know if it exists at all.

Perhaps the Archangel Gabriel, 'Heaven's golden-winged herald', had a hand in all of this; for he is the patron saint of postal services, and of philatelists. These are extensions of his patronage of the telecommunications industry, which was formally declared by Pope Pius XII in his Apostolic Letter of 12th January 1951: workers in that industry, he said, 'transmit words to people far away very quickly, allow people to speak to each other over long distances, send messages through the æthereal waves, and bring before the eye images of things and events, making them present even though they occurred afar off'; and later, by further extension, Gabriel was also made patron of the signals regiments of Italy, France and Colombia; of the diplomatic services of Spain and Argentina, and specifically of Argentinian ambassadors.

As I contemplate this Archangel of the mail, I think of the secular Annunciations of Jan Vermeer: the pregnant *Woman in Blue Reading a Letter*, for example; or *Girl Reading a Letter at an Open Window*, whose face reflected in the window-glass looks like a ghost. These recipients' eyes are intently downcast, their lips slightly parted as if silently shaping the words conceived in another time and place. It is generally thought that the model for *Woman in Blue* was Vermeer's wife, Catharina Bolnes, and that the picture was painted some time around 1663. On 3rd July 1666, Tanneke Everpoel (thought to have been the model for *The Milkmaid*) testified to a notary in Delft that in 1663 Catharina's brother, Willem Bolnes, had pulled a knife and tried to wound his mother, Maria Thins, 'also that Bolnes committed similar violence from time to time against the daughter of Maria

Thins, the wife of Johannes Vermeer, threatening to beat her on divers occasions with a stick, notwithstanding the fact that she was pregnant to the last degree'. Vermeer's *The Art of Painting* is thought to have been painted in 1666: we note again the swollen bap of the artist's brush hand supported by the maulstick, a hand that looks as if it has been broken and is holding the brush in an act of calm defiance.

On 24th May 1921, Marcel Proust had been seized by a terrifying giddiness on the stairs of 44 rue Hamelin; he swayed and paused, then pressed on. When he reached the exhibition of Dutch painting at the Jeu de Paume, Jean-Louis Vaudoyer had to take his arm to guide his tottering steps towards Vermeer's *View of Delft*. In *A La Recherche du Temps Perdu*, the writer Bergotte dies after seeing this painting. Proust survived. He felt briefly well enough to have his photograph taken immediately afterwards. Pigeon-chested, head thrown back, his appearance recalls how he and Henri Bergson, 'like two black nightbirds', had debated insomnia and the use of sleeping-drugs during the negotiations for the Blumenthal Prize, on whose committee they served, in September 1920. They were such experts on their malady that more than one observer thought 'that insomnia seemed almost a blessing'. The conversation was dazzling. They spoke of Hypnos, son of Night and twin-brother of Death; of the ominous whirr and clank of the dawn tram-car; of the efficacy of amber, 'wherein are buryed flies and spiders, finding there both a Death, and a Tombe, preserving them better from corruption than a Royall Monument'; of Dympna, patron saint of sleepwalkers; of laudanum and veronal; of stars visible only on the darkest nights; of telescopes and microscopes; of Vermeer's *A Girl Asleep*; of John Keats's 'drowsy numbness'; of hemlock and of Socrates; of nightingales, and horses passing in the night; of the metamorphoses of dreams; of Xanadu and Kubla Khan; of Hermes, and his sleep-inducing wand; of snake-root and valerian, measured in apothecaries' scruples, pennyweights and drachms; of atomic structures of the brain; of fears that they might cease to be; of the glimmerings before full dawn; of the cinematographic reels of memory; of the cabbalistic implications of the alphabet; and of the stories they had told each other over seven nights. Proust died from acute bronchitis on 18th November 1922, the feast day of St Odo of Cluny, patron of music. His last word was 'Mother'.

It was a sleepless night in the Bay of Biscay, and the Captain and his sailors were seated around the fire. Suddenly one of the sailors said, Tell us a story, Captain. And the Captain began, It was a sleepless night in the Bay of Biscay, and the Captain and his sailors were seated around the fire. Suddenly one of the sailors said, Tell us a story, Captain. And the Captain said, My name is Captain Jarniewicz; my friend here, Captain Both. Before we embark on our narratives, let us sing you a duet, a song we picked up when first we met each other in the port of Belfast. It goes as follows:

> *One evening in September*
> *In the middle of July*
> *It was raining very heavily*

And the streets were very dry
I jumped on board a tramcar
Bound for New South Wales
But before we'd gone a hundred miles
The boat ran off the rails
I fell in love with an Irish girl
She sang me an Irish dance
She lived in Ballyhackamore
Just a few miles out of France
His father was a bin-man
He worked on the Bangor Boat
He used to steal the coal-brick
To feed McGinty's Goat
The goat took sick on Saturday
And died the night before
And that's the end of my story
So I'll tell you lies no more.

SOURCES

As will be clear from the list of sources which follows, *Fishing for Amber* is as much about reading as it is about writing. All of the books mentioned afforded some inspiration to the writing of my own book: sometimes a mere turn of phrase, or a snippet of information; sometimes significant trains of thought; sometimes whole stories. Most of these have been revised to a greater or lesser extent, depending on the context. However, some acknowledgements should be made. My versions of Giraldus Cambrensis (pp. 26–7 & 204–5) are indebted to John O'Meara's translation (*The History and Topography of Ireland*, Penguin Books, 1982). The instructions on how to cut a quill on p. 47 are more or less *verbatim* from Donald Jackson, *The Story of Writing* (Cassell, 1981). The Dutch poet and translator Peter Nijmeijer provided me with the gist of the four Dutch words for 'horizon' on pp. 187–9, though he is not responsible for my elaboration of their possible meanings. I owe much of the story of van Meegeren's career (pp. 303–18) to Lord Kilbracken (Nelson, 1967). Much of the infomation regarding plant attributes has been paraphrased from

Mrs M. Grieve's wonderful encyclopaedia, *A Modern Herbal* (Jonathan Cape, London, 1973 and 1994). The particulars of Vermeer's domestic circumstances on pp. 320 and 348–9 were gleaned from John Móntias's exemplary study, *Vermeer and his Milieu: a Web of Social History* (Princeton University Press, 1989). The illustrations accompanying each chapter are reproduced by permission of Larousse from their 1927 edition of the *Petit Larousse Illustré Dictionnaire*. Last, but not least, is my wife Deirdre, without whose inspiration the book would not have been written.

Alpers, Svetlana, *The Art of Describing: Dutch Art in the Seventeenth Century*, University of Chicago Press, 1983.

An Craoibhín (Douglas Hyde), *Sgeulaidhe Fíor na Seachtmhaine*, Oifig an tSoláthair, Dublin, 1947.

Antoni van Leeuwenhoek 1632–1723 (edited by L. C. Palm and H. A. M. Snelders), Editions Rodopi, Amsterdam, 1982.

Arasse, Daniel, *Vermeer: Faith in Painting*, Princeton University Press, 1994.

Aubrey, John, *Miscellanies upon Various Subjects*, Reeves and Turner, London, 1890.

Bachrach, Fred G. H., *Turner's Holland*, Hacker Arts Books, New York, 1983.

Baedeker Netherlands, Automobile Association, 1996.

Bailey, Martin, *Vermeer*, Phaidon, London, 1995.

Barbree, J. and Caidin, M. A., *Journey Through Time: Exploring the Universe with the Hubble Telescope*, Penguin, 1995

Baring-Gould, Revd S., *The Lives of the Saints*, John Grant, Edinburgh, 1914.

Bergson, Henri, 'The Cinematographic View of Becoming' in Wesley C. Salmon (ed.), *Zeno's Paradoxes*, The Bobbs-Merrill Co. Inc., Indianapolis and New York, 1970.

Bergström, Ingvar, *Dutch Still-life Painting in the Seventeenth Century*, Hacker Art Books, New York, 1983.

Blankert, Albert, *Vermeer of Delft*, Phaidon, Oxford, 1970.

Borges, Luis, *Other Inquisitions* (translated by Ruth L. C. Simms), University of Texas Press, 1964.

——, *The Aleph and Other Stories* (edited and translated by Thomas di Giovanni, in collaboration with the author), Jonathan Cape, London, 1971.

Bracegirdle, Brian (ed.), *Beads of Glass: Leeuwenhoek and the early microscope: Catalogue of an Exhibition in the Museum Boerhaave and in the Science Museum*, London, 1983.

Branch, Edward, *Tea and Coffee*, Hutchinson, London, 1972.

Brennan, Walter L. and Mary G., *Crossing the Circle at the Holy Wells of Ireland*, University of Virginia, 1995.

Brooke, Iris, *Dress and Undress: the Restoration and the Eighteenth Century*, Methuen, London, 1958.

Brown, Christopher, *Carel Fabritius*, Phaidon, Oxford, 1981.

——, *Scenes of Everyday Life: Dutch Genre Painting of the Seventeenth Century*, Faber, London, 1984.

Browning, Gareth C., *The Book of Wild Flowers and the Story of their Names*, W. & R. Chambers, London and Edinburgh, 1927.

Butler's Lives of Patron Saints (edited, with additional material, by Michael Walsh), Burns and Oates, London, 1987.

Butler's Lives of the Saints (edited, revised, and supplemented by Herbert Thurston and Donald Attwater), Burns and Oates, London, 1956.

Chambers's Miscellany of Useful and Entertaining Tracts, Vols V, VI, IX, X, XVII, XVIII, W. & R. Chambers. Edinburgh, 1845, 1846, 1847.

Clark, Kenneth, *Looking at Pictures*, John Murray, London, 1960.

Clark, W. J., *International Language Past, Present and Future*, J. M. Dent, London, 1907.

Clay, Reginald S. and Court, Thomas H., *The History of the Microscope*, Longwood Press, Boston, 1978.

Coremans, P. B., *Van Meegeren's Faked Vermeers and de Hooghs*, Cassell, London, 1949.

Dam, Raymond van, *Saints and their Miracles in Late Antique Gaul*, Princeton University Press, 1993.

De Amicis, Edmondo, *Holland and its People*, Putnam's Sons, New York, 1881.

Dictionary of American Biography (edited by Dumas Malone), Charles Scribner's Sons, New York, 1932.

Dictionary of National Biography (edited by Sidney Lee), Smith, Elder, and Co., London, 1900.

Dictionary of Scientific Biography (edited by Charles Coulson), Charles D. Scribner's Sons, New York, 1981.

Disraeli, Isaac, *A Second Series of Curiosities of Literature*, John Murray, London, 1823.

——, *Curiosities of Literature*, Frederick Warne & Co, London, 1881.

Dobell, Clifford, *Antony van Leeuwenhoek and his 'Little Animals'*, John Bale, Sons, and Danielsson Ltd, London, 1932.

Drake, Stillman, *Galileo at Work: his Scientific Biography*, University of Chicago Press, 1978.

Dunhill, Alfred H., *The Gentle Art of Smoking*, Max Reinhardt, London, 1954.

Edwards, George Wharton, *Holland of Today*, Penn Publishing Co., Philadelphia, 1919.

Encyclopaedia of Religion and Ethics (edited by James Hastings and T. T. Clark), Edinburgh, 1909.

Farr, Carol, *The Book of Kells: its Function and its Audience*, The British Library and the University of Toronto Press, 1997.

Flemish–Netherlands Foundation, *The Low Countries: Arts and Society in Flanders and the Netherlands: a Yearbook: 1995–96*, Stichting Ons Erfdeel, Rekkem, 1996.

Ford, Brian J., *Single Lens: the Story of the Simple Microscope*, Heinemann, London, 1985.

Franits, Wayne, *Paragons of Virtue: Women and Domesticity in Seventeenth Century Dutch Art*, Cambridge University Press, 1993.

Gayley, Charles Mills, *The Classic Myths in English Literature and in Art*, Ginn & Co., Boston, 1911.

Genders, Roy, *The Rose: a Complete Handbook*, Robert Hale, London, 1965.

Gerald of Wales, *The History and Topography of Ireland* (translated and with an introduction by John J. O'Meara), Penguin, 1982.

Geyl, Pieter, *The Netherlands in the Seventeenth Century*, Ernest Benn, London, 1961.

Gibson, John, *Chips from the Earth's Crust: Short Studies in Natural Science*, T. Nelson & Sons, London, 1887.

Goldscheider, Ludwig, *Jan Vermeer*, Phaidon Press, London, 1958.

Gowing, Lawrence, *Vermeer*, Faber, London, 1952.

Grieve, M., *A Modern Herbal*, Jonathan Cape, London, 1931.

Grimaldi, David A., *Amber: Window to the Past*, Harry N. Abrams, in association with the American Museum of Natural History, 1996.

Grünbaum, Adolf, *Modern Science and Zeno's Paradoxes*, George Allen & Unwin Ltd, London, 1968.

Guéard, Albert Léon, *A Short History of the International Language Movement*, T. Fisher Unwin, London, 1932.

Handbook for Travellers on the Continent, John Murray, London, 1858.

Hanna, Thomas, *The Bergsonian Heritage*, Columbia University Press, 1962.

Hare, Augustus J. C., *Sketches in Holland and Scandinavia*, Elder & Co., London, 1885.

Herbert, Zbigniew, *Still Life with a Bridle*, Jonathan Cape, London, 1993.

Herodotus, *The Histories*, Everyman's Library, London, 1997.

Hertel, Christiane, *Vermeer: Reception and Interpretation*, Cambridge University Press, New York, 1996.

Horton, Edward, *The Illustrated History of the Submarine*, Sidgwick & Jackson, London, 1974.

Jackson, Donald, *The Story of Writing*, Cassell, London, 1981.

Jan Steen: Painter and Storyteller (edited by Guido M. C. Jansen), National Gallery of Art, Washington, and the Rijksmuseum, Amsterdam, 1996.

Janton, Pierre, *Esperanto: Language, Literature and Community*, State University of New York, Albany, 1993.

Joyce, P. W., *Old Celtic Romances*, Talbot Press, Dublin, 1961.

Kahr, Madlyn Miller, *Dutch Painting in the Seventeenth Century*, Harper Collins, New York, 1993.

Keats, John, *The Complete Works* (edited by H. Buxton Forman), Gowers & Gray, Glasgow, 1901.

Keightley, Thomas, *The Mythology of Ancient Greece and Italy*, Whittaker, Treacher, and Co., London, 1831.

Kerényi, Carl, *The Gods of the Greeks*, Penguin, 1958.

Kilbracken, Lord, *Van Meegeren*, Nelson, London, 1967.

Kirrschenbaum, Baruch D., *The Religious and Historical Paintings of Jan Steen*, Phaidon, Oxford, 1977.

Kolakowski, Leszek, *Bergson*, Oxford University Press, 1985.

Langer, Herbert, *The Thirty Years' War*, Hippocrene Books, New York, 1980.

Laufer, Berthold, Hambly, Wilfred, and Linto, Ralph, *Tobacco and its Use in Africa*, Field Museum of Natural History, Chicago, 1930.

Lee, H. D. P., *Zeno of Elea: a text, with translation and notes*, Adolf M. Hakkert, Amsterdam, 1967.

Livingstone, A. D. and Helen, *Edible Plants and Animals*, Facts on File, Inc., New York, 1993.

Logan, Patrick, *The Holy Wells of Ireland*, Colin Smythe Ltd, Buckinghamshire, 1980.

Lucas, E. V., *A Wanderer in Holland*, Methuen & Co., London, 1905.

MacCulloch, J. A., *Medieval Faith and Fable*, George G. Harrap & Co., London, 1932.

Mackay, Charles, *Extraordinary Popular Delusions and the Madness of Crowds*, Office of the National Illustrated Library, London, 1852.

Masters of Seventeenth Century Dutch Genre Painting, Philadelphia Museum of Art, 1984.

Meldrum, David S., *Holland and the Hollanders*, Mead & Co., New York, 1898.

Miall, L. C., *The Early Naturalists: their Lives and Work*, Macmillan & Co., London, 1912.

Montias, John Michael, *Vermeer and his Milieu: a Web of Social History*, Princeton University Press, 1989.

New Catholic Encyclopaedia, McGraw-Hill, New York, 1966.

Norris, Ruth and Frank, *Scottish Healing Wells*, Athea Press, Bedfordshire, n.d.

North, Michael, *Art and Commerce in the Dutch Golden Age*, Yale University Press, New Haven and London, 1997.

Ordnance Survey Memoirs of Ireland, Vol. 19 (edited by Angélique Day and Patrick McWilliams), Institute of Irish Studies, Queen's University Belfast, 1993.

Ó Ríordáin, Seán, *Eireaball Spideoige*, Sáirséal agus Dill, Baile Átha Cliath, 1952.

O'Sullivan, Sean, *The Folklore of Ireland,* Batsford Ltd, London, 1974.

Ovid, *Metamorphoses* (literally translated into English prose by Henry T. Riley), George Bell & Sons, London, 1893.

—— (with an English translation by Frank Justus Miller), Harvard University Press, 1916.

—— (the Arthur Golding translation, edited by John Frederick Nims), Macmillan, New York, 1965.

Painter, George D., *Marcel Proust: A Biography*, Chatto & Windus, London, 1989.

Pliny, *Natural History*, Harvard University Press, 1962

Plummer, Charles (ed.), *Vitae Sanctorum Hiberniae*, Oxford University Press, 1910.

——, *Bethada Náem nÉrenn: Lives of Irish Saints*, Oxford University Press, 1922.

Proust, Marcel, *Remembrance of Things Past* (translated by C. K. Scott Moncrieff and Terence Gilmartin; and by Andreas Mayor), Chatto & Windus, London, 1981.

Rean, Louis, *Iconographie de l'Art Chrétien*, Presses Universitairies de France, Paris, 1959.

Rice, Patty C., *Amber: the Golden Gem of the Ages*, the Kosciuszka Foundation, Inc., New York, 1980.

Ridpath, Alan, *Star Tales*, Lutterworth Press, Cambridge, 1998.

Rosebury, Theodor, *Life on Man*, Secker & Warburg, London, 1969.

Rudgley, Richard, *The Alchemy of Culture: Intoxicants in Society*, British Museum Press, London, 1993.

——, *The Encyclopaedia of Psychoactive Substances*, Little, Brown & Co., London, 1998.

Ruestow, Edward G., 'Piety and the Defence of the Natural Order: Swammerdam on Generation', in *Religion, Science and Worldview* (edited by Margaret J. Oster and Lawrence Farber), Cambridge University Press, 1985.

Rükl, A., *The Encyclopaedia of Stars and Planets*, Ivy Leaf Press, London, 1991.

Schama, Simon, *The Embarrassment of Riches: an Interpretation of Dutch Culture in the Golden Age*, Collins, London, 1987.

Schierbeek, A., *Measuring the Invisible World: the Life and Works of Antoni van Leeuwenhoek FRS*, Abelard-Schuman, London and New York, 1959.

Seyffert, Oskar, *A Dictionary of Classical Antiquities* (revised and edited, with additions, by Henry Nettleship and J.E. Sandys), Macmillan, New York, 1902.

Shaw, Eva, *Divining the Future*, Facts on File, Inc., New York, 1995.

Smith, W.S., *Gossip About Lough Neagh*, Mayne & Boyd, Belfast, 1885.

Smoke Rings and Roundelays (edited by W. Partington), John Castle, London, 1924.

Snow, Edward A., *A Study of Vermeer*, University of California Press, London, 1979.

Sutton, Peter C., *Pieter de Hooch*, Phaidon, Oxford, 1980.

Thompson, C. J. S., *Mysteries and Secrets of Magic*, John Lane, London, 1927.

Turner, George L'Estrange, *Essays on the History of the Microscope*, John Lane, London, 1980.

Vat, Dan van der, *Stealth at Sea: the History of the Submarine*, Weidenfeld & Nicolson, London, 1994.

Verne, Jules, *20,000 Leagues under the Sea*, Collins, Glasgow, 1970.

Vickery, Roy, *A Dictionary of Plant-lore*, Oxford University Press, 1995.

Viller, Marcel, *Dictionnaire de Spiritualité*, Gabriel Beauchesnes et ses fils, Paris, 1936.

Ward, R. H., *A Drugtaker's Notes*, Gollancz, London, 1957.

Wheelock, Arthur K. Jnr, *Jan Vermeer*, Thames & Hudson, London, 1981.

Wheelock, Arthur K. Jnr, *Perspective, Optics, and Delft Artists around 1650*, Garland Publishing, Inc., New York and London, 1977.

Wigglesworth, Sir Vincent B., *Insects and the Life of Man*, Chapman & Hall, London, 1976.

Wilkins, Right Revd John, *Mathematical and Philosophical Works*, Frank Cass & Co. Ltd, London, 1970.

Wilson, Catherine, *The Invisible World: Early Modern Philosophy and the Invention of the Microscope*, Princeton University Press, 1995.

Zumthor, Paul, *Daily Life in Rembrandt's Holland*, Weidenfeld & Nicolson, London, 1962.